Zoë Foster Blake enjoys writing her biography because she can write things like, 'The literary world was shocked when Foster Blake was controversially awarded the Man Booker prize for the third time', despite the fact that this is patently untrue.

Things that *are* true include a decade of journalism writing for titles such as *Cosmopolitan*, *Harper's BAZAAR* and *Sunday Style*, as well as being the founder of all-natural Australian skin care line, Go-To.

Zoë has written four novels, *Air Kisses*, *Playing the Field*, *The Younger Man* and *The Wrong Girl*; a dating and relationship book, *Textbook Romance*, written in conjunction with Hamish Blake; and *Amazinger Face*, a collection of her best beauty tips and tricks.

She lives in Springfield with her husband, Homer, and her three children, Maggie, Lisa and Bart.

BOOKS BY ZOË FOSTER BLAKE

Air Kisses

Playing the Field

The Younger Man

Textbook Romance
(with Hamish Blake)

Amazinger Face

The Wrong Girl

Zoë
FOSTER
BLAKE

Air Kisses

PENGUIN BOOKS

PENGUIN BOOKS

UK | USA | Canada | Ireland | Australia
India | New Zealand | South Africa | China

Penguin Books is part of the Penguin Random House group of companies
whose addresses can be found at global.penguinrandomhouse.com.

First published by Penguin Random House Australia Pty Ltd, 2008
This edition published by Penguin Random House Australia Pty Ltd, 2017

1 3 5 7 9 10 8 6 4 2

Cover design by Allison Colpoys © Penguin Random House Australia Pty Ltd
Author photograph by Michelle Tran
Typeset in Fairfield by Post Pre-Press Group, Brisbane, Queensland
Colour separation by Splitting Image Colour Studio, Clayton, Victoria
Printed and bound in Australia by Griffin Press, an accredited ISO AS/NZS 14001
Environmental Management Systems printer.

National Library of Australia
Cataloguing-in-Publication data:

Foster Blake, Zoë, author.
Air kisses / Zoë Foster Blake.
9780143784920 (paperback)
Subjects: Romance fiction.

penguin.com.au

*Dedicated to the original Penguin, Dad,
whose writing is a biodynamic hothouse tomato
to my tinned and peeled, and who generously gave
me his skill, assistance, support and love.*

1.

The perfect headshot

> For a flawless look in photographs, make sure your foundation doesn't contain SPF. The chemicals in the sunscreen reflect the flash, making your face look washed-out and not at all pretty.

Ding.

The receptionist's name bounced into the top position of my inbox.

To: Hannah@gloss.com
From: Kate@gloss.com
Subject: Your headshot
Hannah, they're ready for you upstairs.
Have fun! ☺

I took a deep breath. It was go time.

I grabbed my phone and pondered taking some lip gloss. Noooo, what would I need that for? There would be people to do my hair and makeup there. Wonderful, talented people who had mastered the exact smoky-eyed, illuminated-cheekbone look I wanted.

As I bounded up the stairs to our in-house photo studio, I was giddy with excitement. What would they *do*? How would they morph me from slovenly desk girl to glorious beauty minx? I smiled, thinking of all the possibilities. Most likely I would be presented with several different 'looks' – fresh pink lips and rosy cheeks, or sultry night vixen; hair up, hair down; seated or delicately perched on a stool – and then I would sit with the art director and select the most flattering and beautiful photos. *Everyone* knows that a beauty editor's headshot has to be a masterpiece of shiny, bouncy hair, lacquered lips, twinkling eyes, and well-blended eye shadow so that the readers believe that the woman instructing them on bronzer application actually knows how to apply bronzer, because just *look* how delicately tanned and pretty she is up there in the top right-hand corner.

I knocked lightly on the door and, getting no response, pushed it open. It took less than thirty seconds for me to surmise that there would be no time for friendly banter.

As my shots had been tacked onto the end of a huge fashion shoot, it had reached that delightful stage of the day when everyone involved has 'I was supposed to have pissed off home two hours ago' burned into their irises. Two fashion juniors were in the corner, perspiring slightly after having won a fierce battle against a mountain of unruly, tangled coat-hangers, which they were now attempting to jam onto a rack already frothing with beautiful clothes. Which they then wheeled out of the room. I looked at my drab grey dress, which did nothing for my skin tone and had an empire-line seam that flattened my boobs. Oh, and look, there's my frayed black bra peeking out over the bust line. Brilliant.

I gulped and walked over to where the makeup artist had all of her utensils laid out. She appeared to be busy sorting out living arrangements with her boyfriend.

'You *said* he would be off our lounge LAST week. What are we? A shelter for drug-fucked losers?! For fuck's SAKE, I want him OUT! *TODAY!*'

While she would probably be a lot of fun to sit with as she held pointed implements near my eyeballs, I felt I should let her finish chatting.

I turned around to face a young girl sitting on the lounge reading a magazine. I looked at her with raised eyebrows and 'Sooo, what should I do now?' eyes. She looked at me, shrugged, and went back to her reading.

Finally, the makeup artist got off the phone.

'Sorry, I had to deal with that.' She wasn't sorry.

She came over to me, frowning and looking at my face. She pulled back some of my fringe and scanned what was on offer.

'Oh, you've already got makeup on.' (Hour-old lip gloss.) 'So you're already made up, yeah?' (Bare-faced.) 'And you're a beauty writer?' (Editor.) 'So you're probably an expert at applying makeup anyway, right?' (Rubbish.) 'So you could just finish it off yourself, probably, couldn't you?' (Absolutely not.)

She nodded and scrunched up her nose as though we were agreeing on these questions.

'Cool. Well, I'm out of here then. Don't worry, you look fine,' she yelled out as she started packing up her stuff. Three minutes later, she was gone.

I couldn't believe it. No makeup. No hair. No clothes. I was fucked.

I was trying to at least smooth down my hair when a small man in tight black jeans and a white T-shirt exploded through the door. His hair was curling from underneath a black fedora and his eyes darted around the room. He had a camera in one hand and a Black-Berry in the other, and he looked far more interested in the latter.

'We ready to roll or what?' he said in a loud cockney accent.

He was not going to be the encouraging type. I started to fret. But no more than, say, a deer being chased by a large spotted cat.

'Uh, ready . . . I guess,' I said.

'Over you go, then. Ain't got all night, 'ave we?'

I looked at the blank white 'set'. No props, no chair, *and where was the wind machine*? Everyone knows you need a wind machine! I walked over and stood awkwardly on the spot marked with tape. I put one hand on my hip. I took it off. I folded my arms. I unfolded them. I had no idea what to do, and I never would. It didn't matter how often I was photographed, in the face of a lens I suddenly became less exciting than bark. I just froze up.

'Just smile like you're happy to be 'ere,' the photographer said lazily, as he focused his lens.

I smiled.

'Like you're happy, not terrified, luv.'

Easy for him to say, he wasn't the one sans makeup with a monstrous camera pointed at him.

I took a deep breath and smiled again. He snapped a few shots.

'Head down.'

I put it down.

'Not that far down.'

I raised it.

'No one wants to see a double chin, do they?'

I raised it even higher.

'Chin down, not head, just chin. Okay, now, look at me, but not *at* me.'

I moved my head ever so slightly to face him, concentrating intently on which way my head, eyes and chin were each facing.

'Jesus, smile, darlin'. *Smile!*'

Cue fake smile.

'Teef? You got any?'

I flashed my teeth, trying to think happy thoughts.

He took maybe ten more shots and then put down his camera.

He was probably just checking the settings.

'You done good, luv. Nice work. Now, Amber, where's my fuckin' loight-a? I need a dart and I need to be at the pub and I need both now.'

Ohshitno. Please no. We were done? That was it? *That* was my moment? As I watched Pete Doherty pack up his camera while the girl from the lounge searched for his lighter, I realised with horror that we were indeed done.

If I never saw those photos, it'd be too soon.

The following morning, Kate popped around to my office and dropped the proof sheet onto my desk. And oh, what proof it was. My décolletage-length brown wavy hair was parted unflatteringly in the centre, my normally quite olive skin appeared pale, the fine lines under my eyes were pronounced and my dark-brown eyes seemed dull and dead. Fish-like. The shots were extra ordinary. Note the gap.

'They're nice, Hannah!'

'They're awful, Kate.'

'No they're not. Don't be silly. It's probably just that you look better in the flesh.' Even Kate – adorable, always-sweet-and-complimentary Kate – was struggling to wheel out her usual hyperbole.

'Well, *I* think they're nice.' She smiled and frolicked away.

I looked at my shots again. They were gross. I would have to sweet-talk Antonia, *Gloss*'s retoucher, into performing some magic. I knew she liked Body Shop stuff; maybe I would make her a little bribe hamper. I needed shine and colour on my lips! Warmth in my skin! Eyes that sparkled! Blush that gently hugged my cheekbones!

I sighed loudly. Like a guy with a bladder full of beer and a tree in his sights, the photo going into *Gloss* was unstoppable: you gotta have a headshot, and this was mine. I tried to think about it philosophically. In a way, it was symbolic: I was always going to be the girl with unblended foundation, a wobbly trail of liquid eyeliner, and a cluster of anti-frizz balm sitting nonchalantly behind her left ear. In fact, the more I thought about it, it was an absolute farce that I was advising women on how to look perfect.

But somehow, *somehow*, I had managed to hoodwink everyone into thinking I had a clue about this beauty thing.

Until now, anyway.

2.

Ultra-confident and sucky

> Be sure to always keep a spare cosmetics kit in your desk at work for emergencies. Blotting papers, a pinkish lip colour that can double as crème blush, a sample size of a fragrance you love, a foundation stick that also masquerades as concealer, black kohl and a comb for teasing your hair should be your starting point.

I looked at the pigsty in front of me. It was as though a teenage girl had unloaded the contents of her bathroom vanity onto her father's work desk: nail polishes mingled with overseas magazines; shampoo and conditioner with expense forms. It wasn't that I was a filthy girl; it was just that the sheer volume of 'things' coming in to my area every day was too much for me to handle. I *could* clean it, but my desk would only be stacked with a whole new mountain of mess within twenty-four hours, so why bother.

My phone beeped.

Han, can u please bring me some plum lipstick tonite? Hv hot 40s dress that NEEDS plum lips. Thx, luv u xx

I only have 768 plum lipsticks here. To begin frivolously handing them out could start a precedent I couldn't possibly maintain. I'm sorry.

u can bring me 5 for that ☺

If possible, my best friend Isabelle, aka Iz, loved my new job as the beauty editor of *Gloss* more than I did. The perks, after all, were multiple and obvious. For both of us. I was sent bags and bags of product every single day. And because *Gloss* was one of the country's bestselling magazines it wasn't the no-frills kind of gear either. Sharing it with Iz made me feel like some form of Beauty Claus, handing out makeup, fragrance and skincare as though it were candy.

But it wasn't all Jesus juice and cupcakes. I had a whole new art – beauty writing – to learn, and a whole new breed of women to befriend. Like any new job, the hours were all-consuming and mildly soul-destroying, but I took solace in the fact that a new job would only be new for so long, and soon enough you'd be able to slacken off because no one would care which ring tone you had, or that you did your makeup at your desk in the morning. Iz, who loved the idea of life imitating art, was labouring under the illusion that magazine jobs were an exact replica of *The Devil Wears Prada*, but the reality was not nearly as horrendous. That's not to say I wasn't 'enjoying' the unique brand of self-confidence building that comes from constantly being out-dressed and outwitted at *Gloss*. But, like I said, I was still new, and things were bound to get better over time.

My last job had been as a slave-slash-PA to a beast of a man who highlighted his hair and thought monogamy was a type of board game. He was the kind of man who told people how wealthy and brilliant he was (he was neither) as a valid form of conversational currency. The kind of man who called young women 'baby' and openly looked them up and down. The kind of man who wore white dress shoes. That his wife was an executive with the Beckert Group, *Gloss*'s publisher, and had suggested I apply for this job had been enough of a pay-off, though. Without her I'd still be filing his shonky tax receipts.

Iz was my rock of normalcy in my flashy new world, and she had warned me not to turn into 'one of those magazine bitches.' I guessed that deep down she was worried I would become all refined and snobby, leaving her and her (our) rip-off Chloé bags for dead. She needn't have worried. We'd been friends since we were fifteen years old, and I wasn't about to give her up for some blunt-fringed, chain-smoking nutjob. And besides, it was her non-refined side, her innocence and her insatiable curiosity that I loved most about her.

It wasn't like I was killing it with my sophistication anyway. The girl whose job I had taken, Michelle, had left before any handover could take place, and Karen, the editor of the magazine, openly admitted that I'd got the job because, in a field that failed to inspire, my quirky CV, the recommendation from my ex-boss's wife, and the fact I was an ultra-confident, enthusiastic, sucky freak had got me over the line. Karen knew I was out of my depth, and so had enlisted Jacinta, the *Gloss* features editor, to look after me in my first few weeks.

Jacinta Trevelli, aka Jay, was my best friend so far at *Gloss*. She'd been lovely from day one, although I'd given it a week or two before deciding to be her friend. I knew not to make best friends with anyone on the first day as they would definitely turn out to be mental. But Jay was far from mental. She was unreal. All lips and hair, she was half Italian and, in certain outfits, could pass as Monica Bellucci. She was *Gloss* personified. One of those girls who couldn't possibly have any other job than one on a women's magazine. One of those girls who inspires you to spend more money on your wardrobe. One of those girls you see at the gym who makes you think: why is she at the gym? She doesn't need to be at the gym. She could be making better use of her time. Like starring in a Snoop Dogg video clip.

Jay waltzed over to my desk and stopped to peer at the new line of lip glosses that had just come in from Dior. Today she was wearing a slinky olive-green dress – it looked *very* Gucci and probably was – of the calibre I would save for special occasions. Her skin was flawless. She had shampoo-advertisement hair, and one of those svelte figures that allowed me to use the word 'svelte' for the first time in my life. I always felt like a schoolkid next to her.

'So, what are you up to tonight, New Girl?'

Jay loved to ram home the torture of being the new kid.

'Just meeting up with Iz; got a birthday dinner on.'

'That pretend boyfriend of yours back yet?'

I seethed for a second. Jesse was still away for work and wouldn't be able to make it. He really was the invisible boyfriend. It was both embarrassing and boring having to make excuses about his whereabouts all the time, not to mention fronting up to everything from weddings to fat Uncle Bart's sixtieth solo.

I still missed him when he went away – after two years and four months together you'd have thought I'd be used to it. But his job as a news presenter meant he was often on location, and I had to deal with it.

I gave a grim smile and shook my head.

'Nope. Not till next week.'

'That must get boring, him always being away . . .' Her focus was still on the glosses, as she twisted the wands out to inspect the colours. She suddenly snapped to attention. 'Anyway, have fun tonight, darling. I'm off to a real-estate awards night – don't get too jealous – so I'd better haul arse. Kisses!'

With that she pranced back to her desk, and I was left with the scent of her Chanel Chance and roughly four minutes to redo my makeup before leaving.

3.

I know how Jessica Simpson feels now

Fake a rosy, dewy flush by using a crème blush instead of a powder. Unlike powder, crème sits on top of your skin, giving a fresh sheen. Apply to the fleshy part of your cheeks and gently dab it upwards and backwards. So fresh! So fast! So pretty!

'Another coffee?' The waitress hovered over my table, jamming a pen into a bun she'd made of her long hair. She was wearing lashings of black mascara, tight black jeans, a tight black T-shirt, black trainers, and would've weighed about the same as a grasshopper. She raised her eyebrows impatiently.

Why not? I wasn't in a rush. It was Saturday morning and the only thing I had planned was a manicure and pedicure at Lovely Luck Nail at two. With Jesse away and Iz always working, having recently set up her own catering company, I was getting used to luxurious, lazy weekends to myself. Plus, I had only made my way through a quarter of the papers. I had been intently reading the *Times*' beauty pages, trying to figure out how their beauty editor managed to write about exfoliation and make it sound enthralling. It was an art, I realised. I spooned in another mouthful of my gluten/fun-free muesli and began flicking through the gossip pages, where I was abruptly faced with a huge picture of a smiling Jesse, with an inset image of a pretty brunette.

What the —?

My heartbeat quickened as I read the headline of the quarter-page article.

News anchor falls for gorgeous weather co-host

Channel 3's resident ladies' man, Jesse Carey, is clearly enjoying the station's addition of the exotic Lisa Sutherland, with the pair said to be absolutely smitten with each other. One co-worker said of the two, 'They can't keep away from each other,' while our sources saw the photogenic pair cuddling up at last week's Care for Cancer ball, before making a quick exit as soon as the formalities were over.

These sentences had the right letters and syntax, but made no sense at all. I was shaking and felt overwhelmingly alert, in the same way I imagined you would just before you were hit by a car.

'Here we go – skim latte.' Grasshopper placed the coffee down right on top of Jesse's face and spun away.

I didn't know what to do except to read the article again and look at the photo of Jesse, all preppy private school with his blond wavy hair, blue eyes and broad chest – only it wasn't him but a complete stranger, because surely none of this was really about him. Surely they had the wrong guy. Surely it was all some big mistake.

After a few minutes, my conviction that they had made an enormous error made way for the revolting possibility that, in fact, they had exactly the right guy – only he was supposed to be *my* guy.

I closed the paper and focused on not being sick. I suddenly felt ill. Just-eaten-a-warm-oyster-milkshake ill. Rage and hurt and embarrassment and completely irrational thoughts flashed through my head. Like, who would see it? My new workmates?

Ladies' man?

Smitten?

Can't keep away from each other?

I reopened the paper and stared at his face, unable to process it. And what did 'exotic' mean anyway?

I grabbed my phone and called him.

'Hi, you've reached Jesse. You know what to do.' Beep.

I hung up.

Dialled again.

Same thing.

Why was his fucking phone off? I took a deep breath and dialled again. This time I'd leave a message. But what the hell was I going to say? I hung up, realising I had no idea.

I dialled Iz instead to blow off some steam. It rang out, and as she didn't have voicemail I couldn't even leave a distraught message.

I belted out a text:

Call me NOW please and look at gossip pages of Times.

I dialled Jesse again and, holding back tears so as not to give myself away, very slowly said, 'Hi, it's me. I need to speak to you. Call me urgently please.'

I didn't want him to know he was in deep shit or he might never call. He was rubbish in confrontational situations. Hang on: why was I making allowances for him? For all I knew he'd been sleeping with some weather wench.

I wanted answers. Time to text.

Is Lisa Sutherland someone I should know about?

Sending . . . sending . . . sent. I immediately wondered if I'd now given him ammunition to lie with. He wouldn't dare. He was my boyfriend. I deserved a goddamn answer. A truthful one. Jesus, where had this all come from? I'd thought we were happy; in love; that everything was going well – although I never *could* understand why I wasn't invited to things like that ball. He just said they were work functions, and that as I had so many of my own work functions now he didn't want to put me through more.

Struggling to compose myself under the weight of all that was racing through my mind, I got a twenty-dollar note out, left it on the table, gathered my things and the offending paper, and left in a hurry. Outside it had started to rain. Of course it had. I ducked for cover and thought about what I should do next. My phone buzzed.

What are u talking about? I can't talk right now. Will call soon.

I called him straightaway but his phone rang out. What the *hell* was he playing at? My rage was building by the second. I called again – no answer. Three times – nothing. Huddling under a flimsy awning, I texted him with such anger and speed that I kept punching in the wrong letters; I cursed as I retyped.

Your little love affair made the papers. I deserve a fucking phone call.

Nothing.

I walked down the street, calling Iz. Dammit, why was no one answering their phone, today of all days? I had almost made it home – and was consumed by what I would say to Jesse when I finally got to him – when my phone beeped.

I've just seen papers. It's complete bullshit, Han. No idea where it's come from. Lisa's just a workmate, nothing going on. I'm sorry you're upset, understand why of course, but it's nothing to worry about.

Can't call cos we're in crisis meeting about being sued, but will call asap. X

His text threw me. What exactly do you write back to something so dismissive? *Okay, honey, I believe you – can't wait to see you next week! xxx* Not likely. A text was the easy way out. He was a coward. I needed him to defend himself in person, or at least over the phone.

Oh, well, okay, I guess everything's fine then, cos you say so. Are you for real?! Be a man and at least defend yourself over the phone.

I told you, I'll call when I can. Settle down.

Oh no he didn't. He did not just patronise me when *he* was the one who had been busted cheating. Mumbling a brand of swear words usually reserved for angry pirates, I pumped out a few replies, but none of them nailed the exact sentiment I was trying to express, which was along the lines of: *Gosh, you've really annoyed me! I am quite upset with you and wish you many hours of torture in a Chinese prison and a string of nasty STIs also.*

Midway through composing The Text, my phone rang.

It was Iz. Finally.

'What's going on?'

'Have you seen the papers?'

'No, not yet. What's happened?'

As usual when talking to Iz, I exaggerated a little for dramatic effect.

'There's a huge story on Jesse in the gossip section saying that he's having an affair with the weather girl!'

'He's what? What do you mean he's having an affair? Jesse

doesn't have affairs . . . Jesse can't be in the gossip section. Han, this is mad; I don't understand!'

'And he's denying it, but in such an arsehole of a way that I'm starting to think *it might even be true*.'

'Oh Han . . . this is just awful. Is there proof? Like a photo of them together? Do you think that it might just be total rubbish, like when they say Lindsay Lohan is pregnant but really she's just eaten pasta?'

'There's no photo – but several eyewitness accounts. And you know these things don't just come from nothing. And he does always work back, and travel for business, and she would too, so it's not like it's far-fetched to think he could be, be . . . cheating . . .'

The tears came on without warning and with great ferocity. As I sobbed into the phone, Iz comforted me with 'there there' and 'Han, you just let it all out,' until finally I calmed down to sniffs and eye-wiping.

'I guess you're right, Iz. I should get some better proof before I take this as gospel. But how? It's not like I can call this Lisa girl and ask if she's been sleeping with Jesse, is it?'

'Hmmm. Well, I guess you'll have to rely on Jesse to tell you the truth. Which I'm sure he will, and, you know, you're fierce at body language so I'm sure you'll be able to tell if he's lying.'

'Fierce' was Iz's new favourite word, and she used it to describe everything from a new bra she'd bought to the weather. Last month everything was 'magic'.

'That's all fine and good, but he's away for another three days. How am I meant to see where his eyes are looking over the bloody phone?'

Iz was the right person to ask – she was the chief detective of love gone foul after having overstayed her time in a self-destructive relationship with an absolute arse of a man called Finbar. He hadn't so much as cheated on Iz as brought her into his harem of women.

'Okay, when he calls you do the psychologist's trick and be silent so he does all the talking. Works a treat: they get all awkward and over-talk, and that's when you'll catch him out. If there's anything to catch him out on. People always feel they have to fill any gap in conversation. Oh, and if he ridicules it all, and defends himself excessively without being prompted, that's a bad sign too. All bad liars do that. They usually even protect the tart they've been cheating with, too, can you believe it? And if he starts making final comments, using you being pissed off as a sign that you two may as well give up altogether? *Very bad sign.*'

Realising how serious and morbid what she'd just said was, she backtracked. 'But I don't think you'll get any of those, darling. Seriously, I mean, this is *Jesse* we're talking about! He adores you! I'm sure it's just stupid gossip.'

The idea of staying alert to all of those things exhausted me in advance, but I promised to play silent on the phone when Jesse called, and to phone Iz straight after so she could dissect his words. I consoled myself by confirming I now knew how Jessica Simpson must feel when she read gossip about *her* relationships.

Not two minutes later, the phone rang. It was him. I stared at his name flashing on my screen and proceeded to start crying all over again. I couldn't answer in this state – no way. I'd be useless at playing policewoman. He'd just play Doctor Soothe and make everything okay, and my only chance to catch him out would be gone. I let it go to message bank, finger poised on the voicemail button for the second the little envelope to come up. Beep beep.

'Hannah, why aren't you answering your phone? You're clearly all worked up over this silly article. I know you're upset and it's not a very nice thing to see, but I haven't done anything wrong and I'd at least like the chance to tell you that in person before you write me off. Lisa's just a friend. Nothing more. And yes, we go to work functions together, but there's nothing seedy about going somewhere with workmates so I've never felt I needed to mention her.' (Sigh.) 'Look, call me back, okay?'

So he HAD been hanging out with her! *Dirty little tramp.* My mind hit the red zone. Maybe the gossip dragon *was* right! Maybe he *was* cheating with gorgeous, flirty Lisa Sutherland! I felt my breath quicken.

I had no idea what I would say, but I dialled his number.

'Hello?'

That he answered like that when my name would've come up irritated me immediately.

'It's me.'

'Oh, hey, Hannah. Did you get my message?'

'Yep.'

'Well, I don't have much else to say really.'

I bit my lip so as not to explode and ruin my psych-out effect. He was *already* being an arsehole.

'Are you there, Han?'

'Yes.'

'Well, aren't you going to say something? I mean, I feel like I'm pretty unfairly under attack here.'

Shhh, Hannah, shhh.

'And, you know, put yourself in my shoes for a second – how would you feel being accused of this and not having a chance to defend yourself?'

'This is your chance.'

'All I need to say is that it's crap, and that if Lisa and I go to a function as workmates, why should we be crucified? If she were a fat old man, this wouldn't be happening. It's a joke.'

He was being defensive. He was defending her. My heart was beating furiously with the realisation that there was a real chance the papers weren't lying. I had to say something.

'Why would this just come from nowhere? What does the paper have to gain from making up a story on a couple of over-hairsprayed news muppets?'

'Oh, gee thanks, Han. Great to see you're taking some gossip writer's word over mine. Talk about guilty until proven innocent.'

Hold back, hold back, *hold back.*

'I mean, really, is this what our relationship comes down to? Me defending myself against a fucking gossip columnist? Honestly, I thought we were stronger than this, that my word would mean something, but no, seems you'd rather believe the tabloids. But, you know, if that's all it takes to spell doom, well then, maybe we really are doomed, Hannah.'

There it was. The slimy cop-out. I couldn't believe it, this was textbook stuff – he had done everything Iz had predicted!

'Are you for *real*? You're busted cheating and *that's* your out?'

'I'm not taking any out, Hannah, because, as I keep stressing, *there is nothing going on between Lisa and me.*'

'Could've fuckin' fooled me, Romeo.'

'Is that necessary? Look, maybe we should wait until I'm home to talk about this. You're angry and being unreasonable and this conversation isn't getting us anywhere.'

'Great idea. And with Lisa up there with you, I'm sure you two can nut out a brilliant exit speech for when you decide to tell me that you've been thinking, hey, know what, maybe it's better we don't see each other and —'

'Oh, for God's sake. I don't need to listen to this.'

'Yeah, well, neither do I. Or read about it either, for that matter. I mean, Jesus, how do you think I felt when —'

'We'll talk Thursday. Goodbye, Hannah.'

Click.

I blinked a couple of times. I couldn't breathe, let alone comprehend what had just happened. I had a furious urge to call him back and demand he explain himself, but I knew Jesse. He wouldn't answer. He preferred to let me steam off my anger when we fought, while he carried on with his lunch/surf trip/toenail-clipping in non-emotional-man bliss.

I sat on a stranger's brick wall and openly cried. It was a quiet street, but a procession of half-naked Italian male models could've walked past and I wouldn't have had the strength or inclination to hide the fact I was in emotional ruins. After ten minutes, when I had finally got home and the tears had eased to loud sniffing, my phone beeped.

I am sorry about the story in the paper, Han, but I've said all I can, and after seeing how little trust you have in me, and with all that's going on with work, I think I – we – need some space. I'm sorry to do it by text but you're impossible to speak to right now. I can't say when but I'll be in touch.

Had I just been dumped by text?

I could've sworn I'd just been dumped by text.

I reread it and realised that, yes, I had been dumped by text by a man. A man who had possibly been cheating on me. Today *had* to be some sick, twisted joke.

'I need some space.' I'll give you space, fuckface. 'Space' was just boy-speak for 'we're finished' and I knew it. How stupid did he think I was, exactly? I wasn't going to wait around for him to think, 'Hmmm, maybe I'll get back with Hannah today. No, wait, I've got that golf tournament. Maybe tomorrow . . .' Suddenly, a thought flashed through my head. It was, I guessed, the same brand of thought that popped into people's heads when they were about to be eaten by a grizzly bear and the brain chucks it in and starts misfiring. It was a calm thought, one that cooed that I'd be fine, I'd be totally fine; people break up all the time, right? *I'd be fine.*

Plus, he had probably, no, *definitely* been cheating on me, and if he was cheating on me, then I was better off without him anyway.

Prick! *Cheating prick!*

Was he a cheating prick? I was so confused.

I called Izzy. After three rings, I was screaming into the phone, 'Answer, for fuck's sake. Just this one time, *answer*!'

She picked up.

'Iz . . . Iz . . . he . . . he . . . we . . . dumped by . . . by . . . text. It's *over!*'

'Hannah, what happened? Ohmigod, Han!'

'I . . . he . . . he . . . Jesse . . . you were right about psychology. He ch-ch-cheated on me!'

'I'm coming over. You're in no state to be alone.'

I heard Izzy coming down my street before she appeared at my door. Her car wasn't noisy, but her dragging muffler was. Her car was always dented or dinged or derelict. She barely noticed. Two minutes later she was inside. Her white-blonde backcombed ponytail gave new meaning to the term 'bedhead', her green-brown eyes were locked into place with layers of black eyeliner and she was wearing a skimpy coral-coloured slip-dress that would be appropriate in, say, Miami, and ugg boots that would be suitable in, ooh, Siberia. This was one of her post-work outfits, based on comfort rather than style.

'Oh, honey, I am *so* sorry . . .'

She held me and allowed me to just cry all over her bare, tanned shoulder.

'I just can't believe he could be so cold,' I said.

'Let it all out, darling. I'm here now.'

With Iz holding me, rubbing my back, a strange peace washed over me. The situation clearly hadn't sunk in.

Iz made us some chamomile tea and then listened as I raved about Jesse for two hours. As what came out of my mouth was largely rhetorical, Iz's job was just to mm-hmm and nod.

'And, you know, he's just so *selfish*, Iz. This whole thing was because of him. I didn't do anything wrong! And yet, *I'm* being dumped in one hundred and sixty characters or less! Oh, *I hate him*. Good luck to that Lisa skank, I say. She can have him.'

Cue more tears.

Iz didn't know it that afternoon, but as she sat with me I was silently awarding her an A in Best Friend Break-Up Management. (She *would've* got an A+, but the criteria for that included producing Jesse, the two of them admitting it was all a big joke and then hugging me before suggesting we all go for ice-cream.) She was genuinely soothing, and didn't suddenly morph into a marine biologist generously highlighting the fact that there were plenty more finned, gilled animals in the sea. She just listened and nodded and found positivity where there wasn't very much.

By 7 p.m., I was exhausted. Now that I'd verbally vomited up those first raw feelings, I kind of wanted to be alone so I could be overly dramatic and carry on like a bit of a loser. Wail a bit, slap pillows in anger and rip photos: that sort of caper.

'Now, are you sure you don't want me to stay over?' Iz stood at the door, eyebrows raised, keys jangling in her hand. If her nail polish had been any more chipped, she could have skipped the remover altogether.

'I think I just need to be alone. But thank you, my love.' We hugged and finally I broke away, fresh tears in my eyes.

'Love you, girl. Call me anytime – my phone is on and in my hand for you. Promise. We'll talk tomorrow, okay?'

As she drove out of my driveway, I cried and cried and cried until it got to the point where I couldn't help but watch myself cry in my built-in wardrobe's mirrored door as I lay on my bed, because it was so theatrical.

And so, alone and miserable and with nothing to do but fall into a restless slumber, I pulled back the covers and went to sleep, fully clothed.

When I woke up on Sunday, I had to think about why I felt so odd. Within seconds it hit me: Jesse had turned into an alien and I had been relocated to hell, albeit sans the flames and small, malevolent devils running around with pitchforks. I grabbed my phone from the bedside table: no missed calls, and two awkward texts from well-meaning friends about the papers. But nothing from Jesse. He hadn't contacted me. After all this time, I meant that little to him.

I figured a funny movie would be a good distraction, and that Iz would be brilliant company. I dialled her number, praying she would answer.

Bingo. 'How are you today? Have you heard from him?'

Tears sprang immediately. 'No . . . Iz, he hasn't even texted.' My voice cracked on 'texted'.

'Oh darling . . . I'm so sorry. Poor sweetie . . . And my *God*, what a king of an arsehole! How can he just drop you into this situation, and not even check how you are? I tell you what, I've half a mind to call him myse—'

'Don't give him the satisfaction, Iz,' I sobbed. 'I'll be okay. Can you come round? Can we watch some movies? It's shit weather anyway . . .'

'Oh, Han . . . I would love to. But I have that Jewish wedding at three, remember? Mr Goldberg and his homosexual poodles? I'm so sorry – you know I will be there the *second* I am done, right? And if he calls or texts, call me immediately.'

'Pfft. Unlikely. Probably having a long brunch with *Lisa.*' As I said the words, my gut coiled over itself in pain.

I schlepped down to the shops, wearing the same oversized tracksuit pants and stained hoodie I'd had on since noon yesterday. I was one stinky bitch. I did not care.

When I got home, chocolate, popcorn, trash magazines and ice-cream in one hand, DVDs in the other, I sat down with everything within arm's reach, committing myself to a Freshly Broken-Up Stereotype fit for any chick-flick montage.

To laugh I watched *Anchorman* and *Starsky and Hutch*. Next, feeling brave, I watched *The Break-Up*. I sobbed and closed my eyes in agreement ('It's like she's *me*') when Jennifer Aniston had her heart broken, cheering internally when Vince Vaughn was miserable without her. Stupid men. When will they *learn*?

Hang on.

What exactly had made him miserable? It was that she was getting on with her life. Showing him that she didn't care. Didn't need him. Being busy. Extremely well-dressed. Slim. Tanned. She could date other men, look fabulous even when nude, and didn't even *think* about the foolish man who had let her go.

I sat up with a start. It was a revelation. *This was what I needed to do.* I made a pact with myself that this had to be a bleach-clean break. Jesse had said, 'I need space.' Well, he was gonna get it. After all, who was he to dictate when and how our relationship was severed and when it could resume? He'd *cheated* on me!

How could Jesse realise *how much* he missed me if he didn't *miss* me? Even with Lisa Slutface to fill the void temporarily, he would have to be a bit tortured that I wasn't begging for reconciliation. I would need to ensure that I stayed strong and fabulous and untouchable, and as far away from weak and hopeless and pathetic as possible. I was suddenly very glad I hadn't called or texted him, even though I had come extremely close. Phew.

It had, of course, killed me that he hadn't contacted me yet, but I had a plan now, and so even if he did contact me, I wouldn't respond. It was a magnificent plan. It was empowering. I felt the best I had since seeing that piece in the paper.

I considered texting Jesse to prove how strong and awesome I was and to kick-start my Totally Brilliant Plan. I would write something devoid of emotion, and totally businesslike, such as:

Please drop over all of my things as soon as you return home.

This would prove that I was already shutting off emotionally, and thus held the upper hand. Then I wouldn't have to play the carefully calculated, just-had-to-pick-up-my-DVDs-while-looking-amazing game. But I decided against it. He might not reply, and then I would be *really* tormented. Bored of masterminding – how did Bond villains do it as a profession? – I put my phone on silent and shoved it deep inside my underpants drawer. Staring at its dark screen was killing me; it was as though it were quietly laughing at me and, quite frankly, I was tired of its derision. I lit some candles, put on the mournful strains of Billie Holiday, and peeled off my clothes to shower.

As I massaged conditioner into my hair, my mind went into overdrive. Maybe he really did mean he needed space and I was blowing this all out of proportion. I *had* been known to crowd him sometimes . . . Maybe he'd get home after a few days with no contact from me, and that would be all he needed. Maybe I was making a terrible mistake by cutting him off! Maybe our relationship would be stronger than ever after this fight! And make-up sex was wonderful, remember?!

Or maybe, in his mind, it was actually already over. He *had* been seeing Lisa on the side, and I was foolish to assign any hope to this situation. I was exhausted. Conflicting thoughts whirred and spun wildly through a head that throbbed with confusion, and I resorted to leaning my forehead against the shower wall, releasing fresh tears that mingled with the hot water flowing down my face. Stuff it; I was going to sleep, Iz would understand.

At roughly 3.56 a.m. I sat up sharply in bed. That was it! *Gloss* magazine would be my saviour. It would keep me aggressively busy because I would hurl myself into it so much that I wouldn't even notice I was single and hurt and sad and working like a fool to crush the quiet riot in my head that said I wanted Jesse back, needed Jesse back.

After hours of angsting about it, I had brilliantly devised a way to combine my two schools of thought: the hardcore no-contact element would provide the foundation for the getting-my-relationship-back element. Jesse would realise how much he missed me, become near-suicidal and beg to have me back by way of Spanish guitar and midnight serenades at my window. It was genius.

The first and most crucial part of my plan was that I was going to courier all of his things – DVDs, Abercrombie & Fitch hoodie, thongs, Phoenix and Foo Fighters CDs – to his work. It would be a pleasant surprise for when he got back to his desk, I thought. And quite the message about where I stood on this whole 'space' bullshit, too.

Feeling satisfied with The Plan and my new rules and regulations, I lay back down and went straight to sleep.

4.

Project Mansion

Need to disguise an unexpected crying session? A few eye drops, some creamy concealer patted in under the eye and a white-based eyeliner on the inner-rim of your eye will cover your tracks, while slathering on a bright lip gloss will deviously distract.

As with each morning since starting at *Gloss*, I found looking 'magazine glamorous' to be a mammoth, intricate task requiring much thought and skill.

It would come to me in the shower, I decided.

It didn't come to me in the shower.

I realised I would need food to think. But after lying in bed for almost an hour, I now had no time for such luxuries. *Think.*

Aha! Black-and-white A-line dress. Perfect: pretty but not too pretty. I yanked it out of my drawer. There was an oil stain on the dress. From that stupid housewarming. That I went to with Jesse . . . I sighed heavily and tried not to get stuck in 'that' headspace again.

I pulled out my lovely newish blue skirt. There. Easy. But what to wear on top . . .

I grabbed a pink top that was a replica of a designer top that a magazine girl would probably wear. Good one.

Shit. It was torn under the arm. How the hell had I done that? I mean, really, you pay $25, you expect quality.

Okaaay, what about . . . the . . . peachy vintage dress! Yes! Cute, safe, perfect. Shit. Damn shit. The slip I needed to wear underneath it was at Iz's.

Oooh, *hello.* I gently pulled out my magnificent pink strappy shoes from my shoe rack. Why on Earth didn't I wear these any more? Such alluring little beasts. Right, shoes sorted. Now I would work backwards.

I looked around my wardrobe. What the hell did I used to wear with these? I figured it would have to be something simple; they were the shoe equivalent of a spider on a white bedroom wall.

I remembered my black wool wrap-dress. God, it was so offensively dull. The shoes *were* phenomenal, though. I checked the time. I was running so, so late. Dull dress it was going to have to be. I figured I could employ a cunning use of hair, makeup and jewellery to state my sophistication.

I slapped on my foundation, then stopped. Was lilac eye shadow appropriate or was it too matchy-matchy with the shoes? The *Gloss* girls might snigger into their lattes about my awful makeup. I decided to stick to liner, bronzer and a pinky-beige lip gloss. Timeless and polished. Perfect.

My hair had already hijacked twenty-five minutes post-shower, and while it wasn't too bad, I went over it with my straightening iron once more. I got some sticky-outy fried bits for my effort. Great. I applied some more smoothing balm. No good. Now my hair was sticky-outy and greasy-looking. I swore a few more times as I brushed it, then gave up. Why was this happening? We had a 9 a.m. production meeting and I did not want to be late. Especially if the girls had seen the piece in the paper – they would be expecting me to look like hell and be tardy. I was not about to give them the satisfaction.

At work, I quickly applied some watermelon gloss and brushed on some more bronzer before I was called into the meeting. Conveniently, I was able to use the mirrored wall to the right of my desk. That I had a huge mirrored wall, beckoning me every day, whispering for me to apply more foundation or fix my hair, or just check myself out when I was bored was still a novelty. Karen had given one to the fashion girls as well in an effort to remind us that as we were the public faces of *Gloss*, since we attended the most functions, we should always be especially aware of how we looked. I was quietly pleased that, while I felt like shit, I had managed to look surprisingly polished. Take five, watermelon gloss and bronzer; you've done your work today.

Obscene mirrored walls were just the start of our violently chic office space. There were wooden beams and polished concrete floors, floating steps up to the advertising department, plasma screens, leopard-print beanbags, Philippe Starck chairs and a long glass bench covered with newspapers, fruit and bottled water that was the common area. It looked exactly how a magazine office should look. In fact, it looked a little *too much* like it should look, like the designer had referred to a Hollywood movie starring Eva Mendes or Kate Hudson for the template. But I was growing to love it in all of its magaziney perfection.

A little envelope lit up the face of my phone and my heart lurched. I prayed it would be from Jesse. No such luck. Just a sweet 'thinking of you' one from Iz.

Tears pounced, bored of their artificial hiding place. I sat still. I focused on breathing, slow and steady. I was not going to cry at work. I was keeping it together. Keeping it together. Keeping it together. As long as no one asked if I was okay, I'd be okay. All of a sudden, I was attacked by mass of black hair and Chanel Chance.

'Haaaannnnah,' hair and perfume said, with enthusiastic

intonation and the kind of flashing, smiling black eyes that belonged in a contact-lens campaign.

'Hi, Jacinta,' I said, smiling weakly.

She took one look at me and made that sad face that was the last thing a person who was two gulps from crying needed. I inhaled. I knew this would be coming today, now I just had to be strong and not cry. There would be *no goddamn crying*.

'Oh honey . . . oh Hannah.' She bent down and wrapped her arms around me. 'I saw that nasty piece in the paper. Those arseholes will rot in hell, don't you worry . . .'

I was anxious that no one else see me upset, and half-nudged her away so that I could get myself together for the meeting. I was too new to be having relationship-drama tears at work.

'So, did you speak to him about it?'

'Mm-hmmm.' I looked up to stop the tears coming. 'It ended rather badly. He kind of dumped me over text.'

'He didn't! I can't *believe* this! Why are you here? Go home! I'll tell everyone you're sick.'

'No, no, home was doing my head in. I'll be fine. I just need to keep busy, you know?'

'Well, all right then. But if you need to go, just go. That *filthy* excuse for a man. I'm not going to ask if you're handling it okay, but I will just say that you are totally, totally allowed to be sad, and if you need to chat, I'm here. Let's go for lunch, in fact. Oh shit, I can't – I have an advertiser lunch . . .'

'It's fine, Jay. I'll be fine. Besides, I've had all weekend to cry.' I suddenly remembered my plan, and a jolt of strength surged through me. I really would be fine. I'd be better than fine, in fact. I'd be un-fucking-believable, right? *Right?* I knew I had to believe my own hype or I'd crumble.

Jay's eyes were filled with genuine concern. 'Really?'

'Really.' I checked the time, anxious to get off the topic. 'Hey, is this meeting on?'

'Think we're just waiting on Karen to arrive. But mark my words, he'll regret this more than anything in his life; they always do.' She sighed and shook her head in the way that only a woman who has suffered the same fate can.

I always panicked a little at the idea of a whole-office meeting, but add the fact that everyone would know that my boyfriend – *ex-boyfriend* – had been cheating on me and it became unspeakably scary. Keeping my head down, I took a seat against the back wall and exchanged some platitudes with one of the art girls whose name I couldn't remember. She was an exotic-looking brunette and was wearing more eye shadow than was legal at such an hour.

In the interest of distraction I began stealthily checking out what everyone else was wearing. This was a Big Mistake. The Glossettes looked *unbelievable*, like they'd fallen off the layout board. There were lots of beautiful dresses and designer jeans and cleverly cinching belts and high-waisted skirts and exquisite new-season shoes. I looked down at my dull black dress and wondered what the *Gloss* girls thought about their new beauty editor. Total fraud, probably. My dreariness flashed like Vegas lights next to a collective of girls whose butts would fall off if they were any hipper. Plus, everyone's hair was perfect. Every single one of them. I touched my own and vowed *never* to put in less than 100 per cent effort again.

After a minute or two of loud chatter, everyone quietened. I caught one of the fashion girls watching me and whispering to another fashion girl, then they both looked at me with pity. The gesture was not intended to be seen by me, and when they saw that I'd noticed, the awkwardness was palpable. I badly wanted not to be in this meeting. Jay was right; maybe I should've stayed home.

I refocused on Karen, who was going through the production schedule for everything that was going in the upcoming issue. She was wearing a simple blue shift-dress, excellent ankle boots, and I noticed she had dyed a stripe of her black hair dark purple over the weekend. Because she was beautiful and slight and confident she could get away with any look. Her only jewellery was a simple eternity band (she thought big rings were crass) on her wedding finger, and her makeup consisted of nothing but a slash of alarming red lipstick. On her olive skin it worked beautifully. She was cool, clever and really knew her stuff, having been in magazines (in several countries) for a good fifteen years.

I liked her. She wasn't the devil, she didn't wear Prada, and I knew I would learn a lot from her. I had already discussed my pages for this issue with Karen, but I knew she'd put me through my paces in front of everyone.

'Hannah – wow, look at those shoes – just run through your pages quickly for subs and art, please.'

'Um, okay, so first we have a feature called "Never get a spot again," which is three pages —'

'And the art for that one?'

'I was thinking a few backstage shots of models with really clear skin?'

'Sounds good. What's this lipstick shoot?'

'Um, that's one we've bought from a photographer in New York, and it's all about red lipstick, and there are three girls of different colours wearing the right lipstick for their skin tone.'

'Good. And the hair story?'

'Um, that's a cut-and-carry hairstyle piece. I've already got all of the celebrity shots ready to go for art to lay out into, um, long or short or curly —'

'Perfect, it's time I tried a new cut . . .'

Everyone laughed; Karen changed her hair almost weekly. 'And Beauty Beat, anything of interest there?'

'Just the regular five pages, and one is a full-page shot of pink makeup, nail polishes, glosses and blush, and, um, I thought maybe we could shoot them with little sweets and candies?'

'Gorgeous. I think I saw one like that in *Elle*, so make sure it's not too similar, okay? All sounds great, Hannah. Okay, Bianca, where are you at with your pages?'

Too Much Eye Shadow spoke up. 'Um, sorry to interrupt, but is the Soppy Couple Story' – this was actually how it was described on the schedule – 'going to need us to shoot the couples?'

'No. I think we'll use drawings this month. Yes, Annabelle, we're going to shoot them, you nutter. Bianca?'

Annabelle grinned bashfully and wrote on her schedule.

Tess, the baby-faced fashion junior, put her hand up. Today she was wearing a bright-yellow scarf as a headband, a white vintage dress, wild roman sandals that stopped just below her knees, and twenty nails' worth of chipped black polish. She looked fabulous.

'With the denim shoot, is that sponsored or are we all right to use a variety of labels?'

'*Great scarf*, Tess. All you need are some cat-eye sunglasses and a red convertible! I love it! Okay, denim. I need to chat to Laura about that. Kate, can you schedule a meeting for this morning? No biscuits, as per Laura's orders. Oh, did you all know our advertising manager, Laura, is pregnant? Have I just ruined her news? Probably. Oops. That's two ad girls in the last month gone the way of the baby. I'll have to sell my own pages soon. Don't drink the water upstairs, girls . . .'

We laughed because she was funny and she was nice and the way she spoke was interesting and we were glad that, unlike so many of the other magazines in the industry, we didn't have an editor who terrorised us and belittled us and made us want to leave the industry entirely and become belly dancers.

Twenty-three minutes later and Karen was done. Back at my desk, I answered a few emails and then got stuck into writing a story about glycolic acid and why it was so brilliant for acne. But after a few paragraphs I got stuck. Not only was my brain not on task – it was back on Saturday morning again – but I actually had no idea what I was writing about. I leaned my head on my hands and sighed. I wasn't sure what had made me think this was going to be a fun/easy/achievable job for a monkey from an advertising company because it clearly wasn't.

To take my mind off that now-familiar sick feeling of missing Jesse, I decided to start calling in products with glycolic acid. Perhaps reading the press releases and learning about their celebrity fans would give me the inspiration to finish the story. I opened up my Beauty Contacts document. There were no less than 456 Beauty Contacts listed, and each was liable to swap jobs, brands or agencies within the next week, just to further confuse me. They were a transitory bunch, beauty PRs.

I had worked out that this was a huge part of my job, knowing which PR company or person looked after which beauty brand. *But how was I supposed to remember them all*? Just then an email from our advertising manager, Laura, popped up in my inbox, reminding me that our new presentation to advertisers would be 'live' from next week, and could I please have a five-minute spiel on what the *Gloss* reader loves about our beauty pages ready for her by this afternoon to slot into the PowerPoint presentation.

A huge wave of Fraud Complex washed over me. I felt entirely out of my depth. I had only worked here for a few weeks. How could I be expected to speak convincingly about my manifesto?

My phone rang.

'You know, now would be the perfect time for Project Mansion, Hannah,' the voice at the other end purred. Iz preferred to start a phone call by leaping straight into conversation.

I laughed. Project Mansion had started when we were fifteen. We hated the small country school we went to and bonded over a mutual desire to leave it, and all of the germs that occupied it, as soon as we could. Of course, we would be extraordinarily wealthy within months of making said move: Iz as an internationally renowned chef with her own Oprah Winfrey-style TV show, and me as a world-class actress, which was what I was positive I would be back then. This wealth, naturally, would enable us to buy mansions in every city we fancied. Hence the name.

Even though life hadn't *quite* panned out the way we had imagined, we were still young, and somewhere underneath the schoolgirl frivolity a real plan to move overseas together sat quietly, knitting jumpers and sipping tea, just waiting for us to be ready.

'Oh, come *ON*!' Iz squealed and clapped her hands. 'Admit I'm right. Neither of us is tied down; we're young and unattached . . .' She paused. 'I don't mean to be insensitive about Jesse. I just mean sometimes, you know, a break-up can be a great time for a fresh start and stuff . . . and these times when you're free and in your twenties are precious, you know? And . . . and . . . well, maybe *Gloss* could find you a job on one of their overseas mags?'

'But I just started here!'

'Well, we wouldn't go *straightaway* . . .'

I thought for a second. 'New York?'

'Too cold at this time of the year. How about Amsterdam? We could live with Dec until we find our feet and our first million euro!' Her voice smacked of genuine excitement; this was a plan that actually seemed feasible to her.

Declan was Iz's older brother. He was an events manager at

one of those hyper-modern, groovy companies housed in a terrifyingly hip office that made the rest of the street look like a medieval camping ground.

I'd always had a bit of a crush on Dec. He had simultaneously formed the foundation of my teenage insecurities and my sucrose-laden daydreams. He was something of a god at school – not only was he Very, Very Good-Looking, all tall and toned without being bulky, with perennially tanned skin from surfing, chestnut hair and warm, brown eyes, he was the first to get his licence, the first to lose his virginity, and the first to be suspended for smoking dope on the back seat of the school bus. All the key ingredients to rule the school.

I remembered sleeping over at Iz's as a teenager and wearing a push-up bra under my pyjamas, even to bed, just because he might see my teeny mounds masquerading as breasts during the run from the bathroom to the bedroom, or at the breakfast table, and that, obviously, was unthinkable. He used to make me blush simply by asking me how I was doing, and I would trip up steps when he waved at me in the quad at lunch, and on the occasions Iz and I rode home with him after school I imagined how it might feel to be his Real-Life girlfriend.

I'd never go near him now, of course. Partly because it would be *completely* weird: he had taken the shape of a (kind of) brother over the past nine or so years – and had lived overseas for near all of that time – but also because he had possibly the most stunning other half that had ever mutated from a single DNA cell – Pia.

Pia was a Colombian girl who was a model-slash-photographer. Of course. Whenever they came to visit I ravenously consumed what she wore, and attempted to style-bite her once she'd gone, with varying degrees of failure. Pia had an impeccable, internationally travelled glamour about her, and could blend things like Dec's waistcoat with denim shorts and stacked heels and a cascade of plastic necklaces and look impossibly perfect. Kind of like Ashley Olsen meets Helena Christensen. I was just Hannah. None of her creative fashion splicing worked on me; I just ended up looking like Lily Allen wearing Mick Jagger's wardrobe.

Pia and Dec lived an idyllic life in Holland, with other cool, equally genetically impressive wunderkinds. Last I heard Dec and Pia had bought a houseboat and remodelled it to look like *2001: A Space Odyssey*, and *Wallpaper** had photographed it.

'I guess Holland could be nice . . .'

'What about Tokyo?'

'You're crazy and I love you, but can we maybe talk about this tonight? I'm drowning in work.'

'Of course. But we *will* be talking about this again, miss.'

'Hey. Project Mansion is no pipe dream. We'll do it.'

5.

The face-cream mafia

> The best way to find out if a lip colour will really suit you is to test it on your index fingertip, not the side of your wrist; this is the closest possible match to your lips. Tell your friends: they're probably doing it wrong, too.

Without a doubt, the most thrilling part of my job was the frenzied stream of products from cosmetic companies. I had to keep remembering that they were sending them to the magazine, and not me as a person, because it was very easy to get swept up in a spell of megalomania when you were constantly being sent Tiffany's necklaces, perfumes, entire makeup collections from Giorgio Armani, and invites to the hottest restaurants.

'Gosh, balls,' I said to myself, blinking in amazement at this morning's loot.

I carefully opened parcels and bags from Lisa K, Estée Lauder, Clover, Lancôme and Voluptuous cosmetics. It was like Christmas. But the last thing I wanted was to appear greedy, so I simply sorted them into order of which month they would go into the shops – to be reviewed later in thematic order – and put some in my subtle 'Take Home' pile to try that weekend. There was even a full makeup collection from Blush, which I was *100 per cent allowed to have.* The note even said, 'Please try these before you write about them as they are just heaven. We can send more for photography.' I knew how much that stuff cost. A lot. It was what *celebrities* used. I tucked the box into the Take Home pile. I knew what Iz and I would be doing tonight.

'Michelle was like that at first, too,' Jacinta said, laughing, her voice coming from nowhere.

I jumped a mile, feeling like a thief. I *hated* that my desk faced the wall and my back was to the door. Anyone could sneak up on me. Plus, I was pretty sure it was bad feng shui.

'But you get over it, trust me. Soon every lip gloss starts to look the same, and even a Chanel palette won't make you bat an eyelid. But knock yourself out. It's all yours to use and abuse, baby. Have you got a system sorted yet?'

'Yep, well, for now anyway: I put potentials in those boxes according to month' – I pointed to a set of mammoth pink tubs – 'and anything else in that crate' – I pointed to a mammoth green tub – 'which I get the interns to unpack into the beauty cupboard every few days.'

'Nicely done! Can tell you've worked in admin. Michelle had no boxes, no strategy – it was always a mess. Used to drive Karen insane when the publisher would come for a "surprise visit". You look nice. Where are you off to?'

'My first big function.' I grinned nervously. I had my first big beauty launch today, which meant I was finally going to meet all the other beauty editors for the first time, and begin refining the art of professional chitchat.

'I'm surprised you haven't already been going to five a day. Don't make that face, I'm serious! That's normal for beauty girls!'

I really hoped she was exaggerating.

'Where is it?'

'I think it's called Vine?'

'Ooh, yum. The food there is so good. Now, any word from Jesse?'

My heart sank at his name. It had been a week, and still he had made no contact. I thought that when he'd seen all of his belongings messily packed and waiting on his desk I would've at least been granted a venomous text about how childish I was, but instead I was tortured with a thunderous, heartbreaking silence. He was either really angry with me – but that made no sense, because HE was the one who had urinated in the garden that was our relationship – or he was just having too good a time with that vacuous wench to recall he once loved a girl called Hannah. Either way, it was killing me softly. *Any* contact would've been good contact at this stage, even if only for me to inflict some torture back on to *him* by not replying.

'No . . . but that's okay,' I said, breathing out. 'It proves that I was right about it being a break-up. He can go to hell for all I care. Hopefully he's already there.'

Jacinta saw through my bravado, but decided not to press it.

'Hey, can I grab a few things from the goo room? Just some body wash and stuff?'

'Of course!' Grateful for the change of topic, I grabbed my keys and opened the door to the beauty cupboard, or 'goo room', as the Glossettes referred to it.

Cue clouds parting, sun streaming through and some form of triumphant classical arrangement. For me, it was a simultaneously terrifying and beautiful sight. Because while normal people simply saw shelves and shelves of beauty products, all I saw was a neon sign saying, 'See all this stuff? You now have no excuse to look terrible. *Ever*.' Oh, it was a sight to behold, though.

Once we had picked out some body wash and shampoo for Jay, she left me to it, calling behind her, 'Have fuuuun at the function!'

Why did she say it in that singsong voice? Would the other beauty editors be mean to the new girl? Would they be nasty, catty, cliquey girls who would make me feel left out and make me work for their friendship? I didn't know if I was up to it. Everything was still so new and weird.

She popped her head back in. 'Oh, a tip: make sure you find the PR and whoever else is from the brand before you start mingling with your new friends. Karen hates mag girls who just talk among themselves at functions, and she'll find out, so *always* introduce yourself to the hosts straightaway. They'll just love you, honey. Especially after Michelle, who was completely jaded, God love her.' She blew me a kiss and was gone.

I made my brain store Jay's information somewhere easy to retrieve, like near primal requirements (food, sleep, lip balm) so that I wouldn't forget.

I figured I should unpack my green box into the goo room, as we had no workie that week and it desperately needed doing. Searching for the hair-removal section, I paused a moment to take it all in, which I realised I hadn't really allowed myself to do since starting. There were shelves and shelves and shelves of hair products, gleaming and colourful, waiting to improve the condition of, or add volume and thickness to, or deposit minute amounts of colour into people's hair; there were hair dryers, rollers, curling tongs and ceramic irons crouching in a corner, their cords snaking out gently as if coaxing me, Garden of Eden-style, into doing something, *anything*, with my floppy, dull brown hair.

There was a constellation of exotic, exquisite and blatantly practical lotions for arms, stomachs, thighs, boobs and legs. A hairy, untanned, cellulite-ridden leg with dry heels and rough cuticles wouldn't last sixty seconds in here.

There were sleek, sophisticated face creams with names that

were difficult to pronounce sporting seemingly unbelievable claims. These were the kinds of products that would command three-digit price tags and a talent for understanding words like '*nuit*' and '*yeux*'. They looked at me threateningly, as if daring me to smile and expose some fine lines.

I was scared of them. It was obvious that these guys were the mafia of the beauty cupboard. They made me feel, think, believe I was older and wrinklier than I should be, and that I needed them, had to use them, or I would lose my looks, appeal, friends and probably my home too, judging by their menacing demeanour.

There were pink, plum and port-tinted blushes waving gaily from a shallow box, looking infinitely more jovial and frisky than the sleek gold and metallic bronzers that merely glanced in my direction and then got back to being all sexy and J-Lo-ish.

My smile was at full capacity. This room was a dream. I made a mental note to sneak Iz in here one day. She would lose it.

I peered into the mammoth box labelled 'Lips'. It was a brutal understatement: lipsticks and lip glosses and lip liners and lip balms and lip plumpers and lip salves were all crowded into the deep carton, where they tussled and jumbled with each other aggressively in all their various forms and packaging and levels of prestige. The YSL lipsticks, looking glamorous and expensive in their gold boxes, were starkly contrasted by the cheap, pharmacy-brand lip liners, who had settled for a plastic lid and a sticky-tape seal and a life that held no promise of department-store placement. I promised to love them all equally.

And then there was the mega-box: 'Eyes'.

This beast held three internal boxes: one for eye shadows and eye-shadow palettes and eye crèmes; one for eyeliners; and one just for mascaras. One particularly lurid shade of turquoise eye-dust had managed to spread itself throughout all three boxes, the shelf the box rested on, the carpet underneath it, and had in all probability sprinkled its way onto the desk of whichever magazine staff member sat on the floor below us.

Talk about 'kid' and 'candy store'. Coming from being a PA to this was on a par with having worked in a suburban Gloria Jean's, then scoring a job as a barista in St Mark's Square, Venice.

Feeling drunk on power, I reached in to the lip menagerie and grabbed a tube of M.A.C lip gloss. It was a lovely peachy-coral colour. Perfect. I put it in my pocket, half-feeling as though I were shoplifting, half-feeling like the luckiest woman in the world.

Life wasn't all bad, I thought.

When I arrived at Vine there was a gaggle of colourfully dressed, loud women standing around holding champagne flutes and flashing 100-watt, brilliantly white, probably bleached smiles. It looked a bit like an affluent bride's hens' night.

I walked over to the group, clutching my handbag as though it were saving me from falling off a small cliff.

'Hi, I'm Liz!' said a short woman with wide-open eyes who was wearing all black, save for some enormous red lips. She went straight in for a guerrilla air kiss, and as I wasn't expecting this, she copped a mouthful of my nose. Awkward didn't quite cover it.

Brushing my hair nervously behind my ear and laughing uncomfortably, I managed to say, 'Hi, Liz, I'm Hannah, from *Gloss* . . .'

'OHHHH! Welcome! How lovely that you could come. We've all been *dying* to meet you. Phoebe, Hannah's here. Hannah from *Gloss*; Michelle's replacement. We just loved Michelle. She's so cool, so fresh, so gorgeous! And how great that you got this job! What an *amazing* job. We love *Gloss*. Such a *gorgeous* magazine. I love your shoes, aren't they fab?! They're just heaven. *So* nice to have you here. Grab some bubbles; relax, darling, it's Friday! Now, you *must* meet Francis; he's a makeup artist who's here from the Big Apple, where he was backstage at all the shows, and he's just divine. He's available for interview till Tuesday so we must lock in a time. Phoebe's just chatting but she'll be over in a se— Carly! HI! How lovely that you could make it! Don't you look *gorgeous*!'

And Cyclone Liz departed. I must've been visibly shaken because an older woman wearing a lovely sari-type dress and beautiful ruby-drop earrings came over to me.

'Don't worry, you'll get used to them, their bizarre intonations *and* their compliment overload.'

I laughed nervously, momentarily remembering the rule about not making best friends on the first day.

'I'm Kath. I work at *Polished*.'

'I'm Hannah – the new beauty editor at *Gloss*.'

'Well, welcome to the mad world of beauty, darling.' She extended her hand dramatically. 'You'll love it. We all do, which is why half these silly cows have been in the industry for a hundred years, me included.'

With that, she smiled, tipped her champagne flute toward me and walked over to another older-looking woman wearing the wildest, loudest flamingo-pink skirt I'd ever seen. It was awesome.

A perky blonde manifested from thin air beside me. She was sporting a huge weathergirl-style blow-dry, a navy-blue dress and incredibly high caramel-coloured heels. I couldn't help noticing she had an engagement ring with a diamond the size of a chickpea. She noticed that I noticed and looked quietly smug.

'Soooo, how do you like beauty?' she asked excitedly, as though I were her husband and she had just redecorated the lounge room. Not waiting for a response, she continued, 'Aren't new jobs just *crazy*? I mean, they're just so weird, don't you agree?' Her eyebrows were so far up they were in danger of relocating to her hairline.

'Um, I'm really enjoying it. It's been fun,' I said quietly, slightly frightened by her big teeth and big hair and big questions.

'So, where did you go to school?'

Did people really still ask that?

'Um, I'm a country girl originally. I grew up in a little town called St Neely, about three hours south of here.'

'Ooh! I'm from the country too!' she shrieked.

I couldn't quite understand her rapture. Sensing this, she explained. 'City girls are bitches,' she said matter-of-factly. 'They're *everywhere* in magazines. But country girls? We're *nice*.'

I was shocked at her judgement based on whether I was a twisted city sister, who apparently roamed unfettered in this industry, or a 'sweet' country girl. She needed to meet some of the girls I'd gone to school with. Suddenly, Perky took on a more serious tone. She looked at me, flicked her hair behind one shoulder and furrowed her brow. Then she placed her hand on my arm and said, 'I just wanted to say I saw the article in the papers and I think what she wrote was just terrible. How long were you together?'

Her facial expression looked as though it were modelled on an illustration from a book on how to fake body language. She was doing everything to look genuinely concerned, but unfortunately her eyes were screaming, GOSSIP, GOSSIP! I NEED IT! FEED IT TO ME! FEED IT TO ME *NOW*!

I managed to utter, 'Um . . . two years . . .' How would she have even known I was Jesse's girlfriend?

'Oh, sweetie. That's *so* awful. And to have it written about for everyone to read. I saw him at a function yesterday, actually. You should probably know that he *was* there with Lisa Sutherland – she's a friend of a friend – but it was on a table of Channel 3 people, so that's totally kosher. And they weren't acting like a couple. I swear it. Anyway, I'm here if you need to chat. Oh, what a *silly*! I didn't even introduce myself. I'm Jill. I'm at *Fame* magazine. If there are no place cards at the table, sit next to me, okay?'

With one final patronising gaze, she spun around and stalked off to chat to a platinum blonde who knocked her head back to finish off her champagne before whisking a new one off a waiter's passing tray. The bomb Jill had just dropped suddenly asserted itself somewhere near the top of my throat. Jesse and Lisa Sutherland. Jesse and Lisa Sutherland. Gorgeous, flirty Lisa Sutherland and my Jesse sitting together at charity lunches, toasting their new love in between silent auctions. But that can't be. *He's supposed to be asking me to take him back any day now.*

I wanted to run.

I didn't belong here.

I wanted my old life back.

I wanted my old job and my boyfriend and my life to be easy.

I felt a flush travel up the back of my neck and was a little bit shocked because it implied that, physiologically, I was close to tears. I stood there, still clutching my bag and looking around, trying to maintain composure. Please, someone rescue me from here. Anyone.

Suddenly the volume of some hyper-hip music was turned up and all the beauty editors' voices quietened down. Liz and Phoebe and Francis, who was looking understated in gold cowboy boots, a snakeskin waistcoat and a lot of bronzer, had taken to the stage.

'Francis, fresh from New York fashion week, is now going to talk us through Fire's new spring collection.'

A PowerPoint presentation came up and Francis highlighted a trend called 'Mascufemme', which to me looked to be about making young, pretty models look as frightening as possible. They all had angry, thick brows painted on, no blush, and nude, dead-looking lips. After what seemed like an hour, and a million slides of backstage models wearing very theatrical makeup, Francis bowed, and Liz announced we would now eat.

We were all place-card seated at three long tables, and I was very pleased to find that I was between two sweet young girls who seemed as reticent as I'd become since being bamboozled. They were beauty assistants, I discovered. The wine flowed, and the first course – duck and pureed orange on buckwheat pancakes – was served. One girl on my table, a blue-eyed blonde with a pixie haircut, was talking loudly about her fashion editor's habit of thieving clothes from shoots. She downed her wine as though it were water and clearly loved the attention. I simply sat and watched. I was aware that first impressions counted, but I was too deflated to care. I felt sick. Maybe it was the duck. Or maybe it was the creature who felt it was appropriate to discuss my ex-boyfriend and his new girlfriend at a work function during our first conversation.

At 2.52 p.m. I headed back to the office. I waited until at least three others left before making my move. It was amazing how the chain reaction worked – it took the noise of just one chair scraping backwards to get these girls out the door.

Once back in the Beckert compound, I decided that a coffee would make me feel happy again. It might also make me a shaking, excitable psycho who couldn't fall asleep till 1 a.m., but I was willing to take that risk. I ordered my latte from the espresso bar across the road, and noticed the barista staring at me as he frothed my milk.

'You have beautiful eyes,' he said.

I frowned. 'What?'. I replied in an irritable tone.

He smiled. 'I *said* that you have beautiful eyes.'

'Oh . . . thank you,' I replied, blushing.

'Do you work around here?'

'I do.'

'Well then, hopefully I'll see you and your pretty eyes again sometime soon.'

'Well, I'm not going to leave them at home, now, am I?' I said without thinking.

He recoiled slightly.

As I walked back to work, taking a sip through the plastic lid's hole thingy and retreating from the heat of the liquid and the pain my now-burned tongue was experiencing, it dawned on me: I had absolutely no idea how to flirt. I hadn't even realised I was being flirted upon. *I didn't even know how to use the word 'flirted' correctly in a sentence.*

6.

But mostly, you will look like shit

Not sure where to apply that illuminator of yours? Dab it onto the 'boomerang' of your brow and cheekbone, taking it from the mid-brow bone and curving it down around to the highest point of your cheekbone. This will emphasise your bones and give your face a delightful, luminous appearance.

What a selfish arsehole. Leaving me in the rain n no cab. And he's supposed to be a yoga teacher! I'm so pissed!!

Can you not go on any more dates with hippies, please. You're always wrong star sign or not Buddhist enough for them anyway. Maybe switch to strippers? ;)

Ur right. Strippers it is. Dec flies in tonight – we r having few ppl over – come if u can?? Xxx

I had forgotten Dec was flying in from Amsterdam today. There was some big music event he was putting on, so he was staying with Iz for a week or two. I felt a teeny shiver of butterflies. I think it was more my body performing a memory response from the heady days of high-school crushes rather than a genuine shiver of nerves, but it always happened when I heard his name. I was so used to it I barely noticed it now. I was excited to see him; it was always nice to have Dec around – he substantially inflated our cool factor just by being in the same hemisphere. I was sure it would lift Iz's spirits too, although she never let a guy faze her for long. It usually took Iz around twenty-four hours to get over a guy if he gave her a) the shits, b) too much attention, or c) a marriage proposal.

I wondered, though, if this latest guy of Iz's might have slipped quietly under her skin, because she'd decided last night, after we'd agreed that Project Mansion could wait another year until I was more established in magazines and she'd paid off all of her credit cards and loans, that she might like to stop being single and have a 'real-life' relationship.

I'd have to remind her that she always had the most fun with the inappropriate ones. The ones who throw rocks at her windows at 4 a.m. The ones who take her to Disco Bowl-a-rama on the first date. The ones who want to have sex in public places.

I put the final touches to my minimal, 'un-made-up' makeup. I was aware that after work I would only be going over to Iz's, but if Dec was going to be there, I had to, of course, look pretty. Just to show him how much I'd grown up, and how well I could blend my foundation now. I dabbed some Benefit Hollywood Glo onto my cheekbones, which I loved because it made me radiate as though I'd never seen the sun, alcohol or a cigarette in my life. It was my newest discovery and current beauty love, which wasn't saying too much as I had taken to falling in love with at *least* one new product every day. Last time I had worn it I received several compliments from other beauty editors, which was kind of a big deal as they weren't easily impressed. That said, I had noticed that beauty functions were the praise equivalent of a war zone. Compliments came shooting in from everywhere, flattery flew from all angles, and just when I thought I wasn't looking my best – bang – a sniper was there saying they loved my shoes.

And people said magazine girls were nasty. Tsk tsk.

Of course, I wasn't sure yet if all the flattery was genuine, but everyone else did always look quite excellent. Naturally, I was at least four train stops from looking as put-together as the other beauty eds, but I was learning more each day about how to dress in a world where we permanently looked like we were off to a birthday party.

It had been almost a whole month since Jesse had asked for space and I still had not heard from him. As two weeks had been my self-imposed deadline, he was now officially dumped. Even if he wanted to get back together, I was so disgusted at the way he had just slipped off into oblivion that I would reject him on the spot. And probably throw a large piece of office equipment at him, too.

Ultimately, all of this rage had worked in my favour. At work, I was feeling the best I had in weeks. I even knew how to use the colour printer now. I'd become very close to Jay and had taken to going out with her after work on a fairly regular basis.

Karen was happy with my work, or at least she said she was. I was putting in 400 per cent so as to make sure she neither regretted her decision to hire me, nor fired me. I read *Harper's* and *Allure* and *Glamour* and *Elle* and *Cosmo*'s beauty pages in a manner usually reserved for the pious; and they gave me some amazing ideas. Like the shoot I'd just done with twenty mascaras entwined in electrical cord under the heading 'Electrifying Lashes', and my feature on the danger of DIY peels, which featured a shot of a girl peeling back a mask with hazard signs all over it. Karen had liked that. Me good employee.

My next feature was about cleaning out your makeup bag, and the art director and I were going to shoot a mess of smashed-up, filthy cosmetics as the opening visual. It was going to look wicked. The month after was our party issue, and next week I had booked two top models to wear my makeup looks, which would be done by Justin Havlen, the hottest makeup artist around at the moment. One of the models, Paola, had just been on the cover of UK *Vogue*, so I was thrilled she'd said yes to *Gloss*. Of course, she'd only said yes because she was dating the photographer, Lloyd Montagne, who I was also lucky enough to land. It was an audacious shoot, but Melina, *Gloss*'s fashion director, said she would come along and help out, and thank baby Jesus' cradle for that, as I was starting to flip *out* with nerves.

Of course, to get all of this done on top of 678 launches a week, I was overcompensating with fourteen-hour days. My whiteboard, which I affectionately called Ron, was so swamped in details for each day's functions and meetings that he looked as though he were displaying a mad scientist's equation-solving scribble. But Ron was always a pigsty. As he showed five weeks at once, and the space for each day was tiny, he was covered with abstract scrawl like *9 a.m., Dove @ doppio*, or *6.30–8.00 p.m., Art Gall, Elizabeth Arden*, all of which ran into each other, or was written in shorthand so that it made no sense to anyone in the office trying to figure out where the office phantom was when Karen needed to see her five minutes ago.

But it wasn't like I wanted to sit at home and reflect on the fact I had been completely abandoned by the man who I'd thought might father my children. I wanted to be busy, needed to be busy.

An email suddenly popped up from the PR for Flaunt makeup, snapping me back to the present. There was an attachment. I opened it. And was greeted with a quicktime of an obese man stripping.

'*Hannah!* You're a sicko!'

Jay had crept up behind me without me noticing.

I clicked the window closed and flushed a deep shade of crimson. 'I didn't know that was going to come up! A PR sent it. Can you believe it? You'd think twice about sending that to a close friend let alone a client you barely know. Jesus.'

'Some PRs are freaks, aren't they? One invited me to her wedding, and I'd only met her three times.'

I shook my head in bewilderment. I didn't believe in science fiction, but I was starting to believe that some of the public relations girls were actually aliens. They were so . . . strange.

One had left thirteen messages in one day asking when her new self-tanner would appear in *Gloss*. One had emailed me a detailed account of a fight she'd had with her boyfriend and how miserable she was. And then there was the one who'd sent our porcine stripper friend.

At least the odd ones made an impact, I suppose. There were just *so many of them*, all trying to lock me down for coffees or launches or brand overviews or interviews with obscure facialists from Iceland called Gjorg. And too much of anything is always scary, as Joan Rivers' face kindly demonstrates.

'But there's no use complaining, Hannah. We have to be nice to them, even if they're freaks. Now, are you ready?'

'For what?'

'That big hair awards thing we all have to go to tonight. Karen said we're leaving at six . . . which is, uh, three minutes from now.'

Panic gripped me. I did not know about any big hair awards thing, and, as I had no functions or meetings today, I had elected to wear my no-effort outfit: man-style tweed pants, a black vest and a baker-boy cap. *I looked like a boy.* Oh, and there were *flats* on my feet. I didn't care what those osteopath people said, I loved heels, adored heels, wore heels every day because they made me feel confident. Except this day. Nice one.

A swipe of mascara, some blush, a spritz of fragrance and a dab of gloss later, I was cramming into a taxi with Karen, Jacinta and

Eliza, on our way to the big hair awards thing being held in a derelict – and thus achingly hip – warehouse.

As we walked down a lit-up pathway covered in floral arrangements, I felt an urgent prod in my back. It was a Jacinta finger-jab.

'Keep walking,' she said through her lips. 'I've just seen Jesse, but keep walking and he won't see yo—'

'Hannah! *Hannah!* Hi!' Jesse jogged over to where we were standing. My heartbeat thundered and I flushed with the embarrassment and shock and utter surprise of it all. I quickly tried to think of some of my Hardcore Man Rules. Of course, just when I actually had a real-life situation to engage them, they had slunk off to the part of my brain that handles Year Four maths equations and second-verse national anthem lyrics. I turned for support, but Jacinta had traipsed upstairs with the others. Thanks, Jay.

I licked my lips and tried to make sense of things. I couldn't believe he was standing right in front of me. After weeks of thinking about him incessantly, now he was actually here *in front of me.* He was wearing a black suit and an open-collared black shirt. His eyes were shining, his hair was cut short, and he looked healthy, happy, *hot*.

'Um, hi,' I muttered, looking down, hating that he had popped up today when I'd dropped the vanity ball. Especially as I'd had such a tight grip lately. Since having an ex-boyfriend floating around the same town, I had become one of those girls who always 'puts on her face'. Because obviously when you see your ex, you're supposed to look so stunning that they remember what they're missing. But mostly when you see them, you will look like shit.

'So,' – deep breath – 'how are you, Han? Are you . . . are you doing okay? I mean, you look great, you look awesome, what I meant was – how's the new job?' he said, stumbling over his words as though they were jagged rocks and he was barefoot.

I looked wistfully, desperately to my stroppy fellow employees and boss waiting for me at the top of the stairs, and mumbled that I had to go. I wasn't equipped for this situation; I had to abandon ship. It was sinking anyway, so what would it matter. I belted up the stairs, got my name ticked off the list by a gorgeous girl who couldn't have been older than fourteen, and tried to stop my body from shaking. I looked around to see if he was in the room. The cocktail of adrenalin, shock, embarrassment and upset inside me refused to calm.

'Honey, are you okay? I left because I thought you two might want to be alone, I wasn't abandoning you . . .'

'I know, Jay, it's cool. I'm just a little rattled, that's all. That's the first time I've seen him, since, you know . . .' I trailed off, knowing tears would surely follow if I kept going.

She squeezed my hand and promised she wouldn't leave my side again. The lump in my throat snuck up another few centimetres.

Suddenly, from deep in the haze of loud, laughing, tipsy people, I saw Jill heading towards me with nosy questions and thinly veiled gossip-hunger. I leapt behind Karen to hide, and tried to focus on Jacinta's calm, soothing words. I couldn't help skimming the room for Jesse as I listened. I didn't trust my composure at this point. It had a distasteful habit of skipping off at the exact moment I needed it.

As my mind spun, Jacinta kept on. 'Hannah, you look cute, you do. *He* even said you look great. So what if you're wearing flats? I think you look adorable.'

After three oily canapés and eighteen minutes of torturous chatter with happy people whose ex-boyfriends were not at the same party, I backdoored it. I quickly snuck down the stairs and out onto the pavement. I was aware that the consequence of my premature exit might be that Karen scratched my eyeballs out, but I didn't care. As I walked at lightning pace to the cab rank (flat shoes can be good in some ways, I *guess)*, relieved that I could now cry in solitude, I saw a couple walking in front of me.

I bet they nick the first cab, I thought. Screw that.

I walked faster. When I looked up again, I stopped dead.

It was them.

Jesse and Lisa Sutherland.

She looked stunning. Of course she fucking did – she was a weather girl, for God's sake. She was wearing a long black-and-white dress with her long black hair loosely curled just so, and she had one of those stupid tiny clutch purses. How can anyone seriously fit everything in there? My mobile wouldn't get a start. Keys would be a struggle. A lone tampon *might* just fit. Only elegant, grown-up women could master the clutch. More reason to hate her.

It was a scene I'd thought about so many times, and I had dreamt about what I'd say to them, and how sharp and cutting my remarks would be, and yet now it was right in front of me I couldn't believe it was really happening. Were they holding hands? I peered as hard as I could and evaluated that no, they were not. I watched as he opened the cab door for her and she stepped in. Oh *please*, that would have to be the first time he'd ever done that in his whole life. As I watched him follow her into the cab, I realised I'd seen more than enough. I swivelled around and walked towards the wharf. I sat on the edge of the wall, overlooking the water, and cried. A little envelope lit up my mobile.

It was *him*.

Nice to see you tonight, Han. x

I became very angry. Was he sending that as he cuddled fucking Lisa fucking Sutherland?! I HATED HIM. I HATED THEM BOTH AND WISHED THEM DEATH BY FALLING PIANO.

I *wished* I could just delete the message, but I couldn't stop rereading it. Every cell in my body wanted me to write back and tell him to get fucked and rot in hell, but I made myself wait fifteen minutes.

It worked. Within ten minutes my urge to text had gone. It dawned on me that I was exhausted of being strong all the time. Why couldn't I be normal and get drunk and go completely psycho and wait on his steps at night so that I could throw things at him and cry and then initiate break-up sex?

I replied to Jacinta's frantic series of where-are-you texts, stood up, and then walked slowly to the road. I got a cab straightaway, one that was driven by a man who knew better than to talk to a girl who was sniffling and wiping her eyes.

It was still early. Maybe I would go over to Iz's. She would flip my mood pretty quick; she always did. Plus, I was dying to tell her I'd seen them together – it served as proof to me, proof that I wasn't mad, and that I hadn't overreacted about Jesse and his 'break'.

As I walked up the stairs to Iz's apartment I heard the boisterous mish-mash of tipsy voices, Bill Withers and the barbecue sizzling. Shit. *That's* right – Dec was here, and, judging by the sounds of it, so were 800 other wine-fuelled strangers. Awesome.

I stopped. Was I going to be able to cope with this kind of scene? I heard a loud burst of laughter. *Yes!* This was exactly what I needed. Not to be a self-indulgent sook, but to snap out of it and have a laugh and a glass of wine. Or seven.

I took out my new-season Bobbi Brown palette and touched up my under-eye concealer, my blush, slicked on some gloss and applied some liner around my eyes to make the whole area look deliberately undone. I looked down at my outfit. This would be the last time I ever wore flats or frumpy clothes outside my front door again.

I took a deep breath, pushed the visual of Jesse and Lisa out of my head, and slowly opened the door.

It was at that exact second that Dec happened to be walking past the front door, balancing five wine glasses and a bottle of Peroni on a tray.

'Well, hi, *hi*, little Hannah!' Dec offered a 2000-watt smile, put his load down on the hallway dresser and came over to give me a kiss. He smelled like vetiver and cedar, and if it were possible, he was even better looking than the last time I'd seen him. He was deeply tanned and was wearing jeans and a loose, buttoned T-shirt and his feet were sheathed in brown leather sandals. His hair was closely shaven, and that, along with his five o'clock shadow, made him look like he should be starring in his own TV show. A show about a hot guy . . . who's . . . erm, hot. I blushed.

'Hey, Declan. I like your hair. Or lack thereof. You look all, you know, Europeany.'

'Thanks, Han – you're looking well. How are things?'

Before I could answer, Iz galloped into the hallway and ran over to give me a kiss.

'How are you, honey? So glad you came. Hey, Dec, Josh is struggling with the fish – would you go and help the poor little man before he ruins all my Atlantic salmon?'

Dec walked away and I watched him go, taking in his muscled back and how his jeans sat on his bum.

'Honeyyyy, look at you. You've still got a crush on him.' Iz squealed and jabbed me in the arm, before pulling me through to an empty lounge room. I was relieved to note everyone was out on the deck or in the kitchen.

'I haven't! He just looks . . . good.'

'I've always said you two should get it on. Now's your chance, baby. He and Pia are kaput.'

'Really? Ohhhh . . . They were so good together. Why did they break up?' Despite my adoration for Dec, he and Pia were my version of the fairytale couple. If they couldn't make it, no one could. It was like when Jennifer and Brad split. Was there *any* hope?

'Just before he left Amsterdam. It was all very amicable from what he tells me. She needed to move to London for work, and he didn't want to. He seems fine, actually. She's fine with it; he's fine with it. Arty people: they're all liberal and free-loving; they don't do psycho break-ups like the rest of us.'

I was beyond impressed. What a guy. So emotionally progressive.

'Speaking of which, I bumped into Jesse at this stupid event I had to go to.' I felt the tears prickle behind my eyes. 'Then I saw him and Lisa Sutherland leaving together. I was walking behind them, and they got into a cab.' I tipped my head back and took a deep breath, fanning my face at the same time.

'Oh darling. Okay, it doesn't necessarily mean anything . . . but, well, it *might* . . . Oooh, I don't know how you restrained yourself. If that had been me behind them, I would've been pulling her hair and spitting on his face before they'd even had a chance to hail a goddamn cab!' She shivered. '*God,* I'm so *angry* for you right now!'

At that moment, Dec walked into the room, holding a plate of cheese and a glass of chilled white wine for me. I thanked him and took a long sip. Sensing he had interrupted something, he raised his eyebrows and looked from me to Iz. 'Well, the salmon's cruising along fine, so . . .'

'Thank you, Dec darling. You know, I'm just gonna go and quickly check it all the same.' She shot me an 'Are you okay?' look before walking out. I smiled and closed my eyes to signal yes.

Dec leaned against the sofa and put down the cheese plate. 'So, how's the new job? Iz says you're loving it?'

'It's really good,' I said, perching on the arm of one of Iz's deranged old armchairs. 'It's so flash there; I feel like a bit of a fraud, to be honest. The mag girls are all so polished and sharp. I still feel like a little girl from the country.'

'*What?* Look at you! You've got great style. And you're extremely sharp. Don't let their façade of togetherness get to you. Inside, everyone feels a little bit out of place. That's why they overcompensate with their expensive shoes and their attitude.'

'Hmmm, I guess. I've got good at faking it, in any case.'

'Faking what?'

'Looking like I belong. I'm still the girl who spills food on herself every day.'

'And I'm sure that's precisely why they all love you. That's why *we* love you.'

I blushed. I wish I had an off button for that.

'It's pretty full-on,' I continued. 'Especially regarding what you wear, which, as I'm in beauty, not fashion, kind of spins me out.'

'Tough crowd. Sounds like you need a BA in Costume Design. But as long as you're enjoying it for now, Han. We all know you're destined for bigger and better adventures.'

'We do?'

'Of course. I see you maybe on TV one day. Have you thought about moving overseas? Or is that a no-go because of Jesse's job?'

What? Why hadn't Iz told him? 'Actually, Dec, we split a few weeks ago.'

'Oh, Hannah, that's awful . . . I've just been through the same thing. Not nice at all.' He looked down and scuffed his foot on the table leg.

'Really? With Pia?' I feigned surprise, although even I wasn't buying it. But Dec wasn't looking at my face; he was still looking at his feet, the way people do when they are really sad about something. Like losing their gorgeous model girlfriend.

'Dec, I'm so sorry.'

He looked up and exhaled. 'No, it's for the best. You never find yourself fully while you're in a relationship, don't you think? Unless, well, unless the other person has already found themself.'

I nodded in a deep way, with my eyes squinted so I looked intelligent. Truth was I had no idea what he meant. I hadn't found anything post-break-up, except that my body was much more tolerant to drinking than I'd ever suspected it could be.

'So, have you been having fun since you've been single, Han? I'm sure the men have been filling up your various inboxes with fervour?'

I blushed. Again. What was *wrong* with me?

'No, no, gosh. Not at all.'

Not the *greatest* response.

'I mean, sure, Iz and I have been having fun, but nothing serious.'

Just at that moment, Iz scooted out of the kitchen to yell 'Dinner's up', before racing back to a hissing wok and a crowded kitchen. A crowd I had no intention of mingling with until I'd inhaled this glass of Semillon.

One glass turned into two, which turned into three and then four, and before long I was telling outrageous stories of wicked magazine women, much to the amusement of Dec and Iz's largely alternative friendship circle.

'And then, at the next function, she said, "Can you believe they only gave us Tiffany's!" Like she was expecting Cartier or something!' The table collapsed into laughter at my tale of petulance and greed. I hoped no one there knew anyone in beauty, or I was as good as dead.

Iz stood up and started clearing the plates. 'Well, guys. Now is the part where I kick all the drunks out. Which makes . . . oooh, all of you, I'd say.'

'You included,' piped up a blonde girl wearing a muted gold bikini under her grey marl hooded mini-dress as a kind of showing-but-not-showing gesture. Clearly she was not off to the beach, nor had she been there earlier, but I liked it. It was very representational of the group – slightly avant-garde, slightly bohemian, and terrifyingly cool. *Noted and appreciated, noted and appreciated.*

I began helping Iz clear the plates, and tried to hold three wine glasses using only one hand. Of course, one fell and smashed. Eight people screamed out 'Taxi!'

'Hannah, leave it, you'll cut yourself. Dec! Can you bring out the dustbroom and shovel? Dustpan and . . . broom?'

'Dustpan and shovel?' I offered, as I bent down to pick up the broken pieces of glass.

'Whatever it is! Can you please bring it and —'

'Ow, *fuck*!'

I looked down at my finger. Blood was gushing out at a volume that my intoxicated eyes couldn't quite comprehend. I felt a surge of faintness wash through veins that were already struggling with the weight of several litres of alcohol.

'Oh Han! You silly! I not you told to . . . I mean . . . I told you not to!'

We both burst into giggles at her word jumbling, and I blinked a few times to get focus and properly assess the situation.

'It's not funny, quick, go to the bathroo—'

'Show me, Hannah.' Dec appeared from nowhere.

I flipped over my now red index finger.

'Quick, give me that.' He held a napkin firmly over the cut. 'And we'll just hold that there for now. Okay, now follow me, and I'll bandage it properly.'

I stumbled after him, wondering why my finger was stinging so much all of a sudden. He tripped up a step and I laughed out loud, bending over to catch my breath.

'Hannah!' He was smiling despite his 'serious' tone. 'Cut it out – you've cut yourself pretty badly and you need to behave while I fix it.'

'Yes, sir.' I made the zipper motion over my mouth and followed him into the bathroom, which was glowing with the light of haphazardly placed candles, and the scent of frangipani and coconut. It was kind of romantic, even with Iz's washing basket overflowing in the corner.

Dec had to close the door in order for us both to fit, and then he proceeded to run cold water over my bloodied digit.

'Duzzenhurt, you know.'

'It will tomorrow, when the booze wears off.'

'Oh. Well, I'll deal with that then. Maaan . . . wonder what time it is? I should go.'

'You can go just as soon as I've put on some disinfectant and a bandage, I promise.'

I looked at Dec's toned brown arm as he blotted my cut. He was a beautiful man, there were no two ways about it. Or three ways, even. God, I still had the biggest crush, even though I was clearly past the age you should be using the word crush, let alone admit to having one.

I sighed.

'Everything okay? You're not going to faint on me, are you?'

'No, no, just, no. I'm fine.' I looked up at him and smiled, not realising how close his face was to mine. He was completely focused on wrapping my finger, murmuring as he went.

'That should do it.'

I was still looking at his face when he turned. He looked at me. I looked at him. It reminded me of how a first kiss usually went.

Sobriety bolted through me and my eyes locked on to his. I couldn't look away; I didn't *want* to look away.

And then he kissed me softly, softly on the lips, as delicate and chivalrous as I'd always expected him to be. My entire body tingled and I started to kiss back into him, to open my mouth to signal that I was totally, incredibly fine with this, and gosh, maybe we should push the envelope a little seeing as though we were already —

'Someone in there?' A fist banged loudly on the door.

We pulled apart and my hand flew to my mouth, which was pulsing with the memory of what had just occurred.

'Yep. One second, just putting on a bandage, hang on a second . . .' Dec pulled open the door and put out his hand to allow me to go first.

'Thanks, Dec. Man – I'm *busting*. Hand all right, Hannah?'

'All fine!' I said brightly with a big smile. I walked out into the hallway in a daze. What had just happened there? Had I started that? *Surely not.*

As I neared the kitchen, Dec grabbed my hand gently. 'I hope this isn't going to hurt through the night. It should be okay, but you might want some painkillers in the morning.' He stopped and looked squarely into my eyes. 'Hannah, I'm so sorry. I don't know what got into me. I'm so sorry . . .' His eyes were wide with concern. 'Are you okay?'

'Totally.' I smiled, feigning absolute control and calm. 'It's so fine. Our little secret.'

His look didn't change; I had expected relief.

'Okay, yeah, probably a good idea.' He nodded, but was still frowning.

'Well, it's late and I can already feel my hangover creeping in – I think I'll go.'

'You need a cab?'

'Yes, please.'

'I'll call one now.'

But I didn't want a cab, and I didn't want to go home. I wanted to lay down on the sofa with Dec, wrapped up in his arms, and let him kiss me like that again and again . . .

He turned and walked into the lounge room, allowing me a small precious moment to reflect on what had just happened before Iz bowled into the hallway.

'Oh! There you are!' Her eyes went to my hand. 'You're all bandaged up. Good. He's a good boy that Declan.'

I blushed but she didn't see it. Now would be the time to tell her. The *only* time. After this, she would feel like I'd kept something from her, and she'd get the shits.

'Do you need a cab?'

'Dec's calling me one now.'

'Ever the gentleman. I'm telling you, girl, you should make your move.'

I cleared my throat. That's what liars did, Mum always said, they cleared their throats in a subconscious effort to release the lie. 'You're crazy, my little Iz. Hey, thanks for dinner, it was just what I needed. The cut, too – I was dying to try out the sliced-skin look.'

She laughed. 'You're always welcome here. Now, let's get your bag and I'll walk you out the front.'

As we walked to the front door, I considered telling her that I had to say goodbye to Dec, but that would've been way too obvious.

Our little secret it was, then.

7.

Boozy the Clown

> Heading out for a party? The easiest way to ensure your makeup lasts is to use a makeup primer under your foundation. It contains silicon, which gives your makeup something to hold on to, and stops your skin from 'eating' your foundation.

'But we need to make it look as though it's editorial. Do you know what I mean?'

'Yes, Marley, we did it for Crunch gym-wear, remember?'

'Good, cool, nice one. Hey, is Hannah around?'

'Not sure, she might be in the goo room.'

'What do you think of her?'

'I love her. Why?'

'But isn't she like, boring?'

'You're such a bitch. She's gorgeous and cute and has become a very good friend while you've been away. Be nice.'

'I'm always nice.'

'No you're not; you're a bitch. A rotten advertising bitch, single-handedly proving why stereotypes exist.'

'I resent that.'

'You know it's true.'

'All right, but does she have to come tonight? You'll have to babysit her all night and you'll be boring.'

'I will not. It's *you* who'll be hard work.'

'All right, shit, I'll be nice! Be ready at six. And can you wear your hair up? I love it up.'

'Jesus, anything else? Should I buy a new top at lunch? Pop into Prada, maybe?'

Still facing my computer, I turned my head a very surreptitious nineteen degrees to watch Marley leave. She was wearing possibly the best-fitting jeans I'd ever seen, lush brown boots that went past her knees to romantically cuddle her child-like thighs, layers of white and grey singlets, and a cool cropped black jacket that radiated a price in the high three digits or low four. Her hair was a shade of rich-woman caramel. Her arse was a video-clip arse. It was perfectly round and high and smugly suggested that she worked out with a handsome young personal trainer to maintain it.

I knew she was close to Jay, but *why* mystified me. Jay was so warm and affectionate, while Marley strutted around the joint as though her last name were Beckert. She was on the *Gloss* advertising team. She was a demonic saleswoman, and earned triple the salary of us editorial kids, a fact her wardrobe reflected: she was always extraordinarily well-dressed.

She was an account manager now, but there was talk she was soon going to be made advertising director of *Gloss*, aka 'top dog'. Which meant I would have to deal with her. A lot. I was constantly being pulled into meetings to discuss events and sponsorships with Karen and Laura, the current ad director. Thing was, Laura was pregnant, and her pregnancy brain was becoming a major issue. She had recently presented us with a proposal for doing a sponsorship deal with a lawnmower company.

Despite the fact I found Marley to be a complete bitch, I desperately wanted her to like me. I tried to figure out why, and it took about three seconds: she's pretty and dresses immaculately.

Obviously, she appealed to my inner caveman. Or magpie. Whichever it was that liked shiny, pretty things.

As Jacinta tapped away nonchalantly on her keyboard, I wondered if she knew I'd heard her exchange with Gnarly Marley. I was too lame to ask her in person so I sent an email – yes, to someone sitting five metres away – and asked if she was sure it would be cool if I came tonight, because I could easily not, it'd be no problem at all.

'Don't be silly, Atkins,' she yelled out. 'We'll have fun; Carter Communications know how to throw a good party. Too much money, that lot.'

'Okay, cool,' I said, *dying* to ask if it was okay with Marley, because from what I could ascertain, my simple jeans, top and heels combo was going to make the whole crew look unfashionable and repulsive.

Then with a ding, a name dropped into my inbox: a group email from Marley.

To: (undisclosed recipient)
From: Marley@gloss.com
Subject: Eating's cheating. Sort of.
Let's get sushi before the party. Want to line my stomach with more than slithers of duck on a skewer tonight. We leave at 6. Meet in foyer. X

I was stunned. *She included me*. This was monumental. I decided to swallow my insecurities and accept her Fendi coat-hanger of kindness tonight at the party. After all, it's easy to be confident and friendly when you're drunk.

And I'd know. It's no fiction that when you're single you go out drinking more. Around 400 per cent more. In fact, if I was honest, part of the reason I'd been okay about the whole Jesse thing was because I was drinking four nights out of seven.

Tonight's party was the perfect example. It was on a Wednesday night, and it was for a cable TV show none of us had to write about. Regardless, a group of mag fillies were off to consume exotic cocktails and deep-fried canapés like we hadn't just done it on Monday night and wouldn't follow it up with a similar imprint on Friday night.

The thing about working in magazines – well, in lifestyle or fashion magazines – is that there are *way* too many functions. We weren't celebrities, but as we made the party look good with our bright colours and shiny hair, we got invited to most things.

And because with invites comes pressure to look good, my wardrobe was taking an absolute hiding. I no longer had a line between 'work clothes' and 'going out' clothes.

My shopping expeditions had become not dissimilar to working out long division:

'All right, so, if I buy this dress, I can wear it to afternoon tea or breakfasty beauty launches, but I won't be able to wear it to that posh fragrance cocktail party because I'll look like I'm off to a baby shower. No good. Put it back. Oooh, but this *Stepford Wives* blouse will make the crossover beautifully. Sextastic with a pencil skirt. *Reeowr* – you clever little minx. Oops, hang on! Get a load of those puppies! Toooo much cleavage. Terrible if I suddenly get pulled in to make a presentation with the advertising team. Okay. Ooh, *this* dress looks good. *Pretty* . . . What a delicious Salma Hayek-esque shade of red. Innocuous enough in the breast department to see me through a fine-dining lunch, but still slinky enough for Friday-night drinks without making me look like I went home and got all tarted up. Perfect. *Excellent* work, Hannah. Take five . . .'

And this was only when I was *buying* the threads. Once I had them safely home, I was expected to:

a) coordinate them with shoes, non-visible undie-lines, the right bra, belt, necklace or earrings
b) consider all of the functions they must cater to on that particular day
c) take into account the weather (exclude all suede materials, or add a jacket or cardigan, which will inevitably not match and thus render the rest of the outfit unfit)
d) factor in any long periods of standing around, and question if five-inch heels would be appropriate (hint: no)
e) think of all of these things at 7.12 a.m. on a weekday morning, while feeling dusty from the previous evening's champagne-soaked function.

It was utterly exhausting.

My alarm screamed into my skull the morning after the Carter function, and it took thirty-five minutes of snooze-buttoning for me to finally shift from my cotton cocoon. I saw roughly fifteen packets of chewing gum on the floor, and remembered that they'd had bowls of them at the party last night, and that I'd thought it would be hilarious and entertaining to thieve them really obviously for what I'm sure was a fascinated audience.

Idiot.

When I finally got to work, wearing an outfit even Stevie Wonder would've rejected, Jay caught me as I walked into the office, echoing similar requests for hospitalisation, or at least greasy food. Immediately, if not sooner.

'Oh Han. What went wrong?'

'No idea. Maybe it was not eating dinner?' I was pretty sure it was. That and the cheap wine.

'Shall we go to that diner on Thomas Street and get breakfast?'

'Oh, that'd be *perfect.*'

I turned around with Jay and went straight back downstairs. I had no meetings or launches that morning, so what did it matter?

We waited silently in the diner for our egg-and-bacon rolls, both deeply entrenched in self-sympathy mode. Jay had her sunglasses on inside, which spoke volumes.

Once I got to my desk, filled with grease and caffeine and feeling vaguely more human, it dawned on me that I had a function in the afternoon that I would not be able to get out of, even though the idea of making small talk was on a par with a large angry horse kicking me in the stomach.

Jesus, what was that *fricken* smell?

It was unbearable. It wasn't one of my regular beauty-office smells; they're usually quite lovely and reminiscent of clean hair. This was more like . . . like . . . off food, or a bunch of rotting flowers. I had to find the scent, which meant attacking all the bags, boxes and parcels that surrounded my chair like a cosmetic moat. This was a good move, I decided. Being physically busy would, hopefully, use enough brain power to stop me from thinking about how revolting I felt.

I started with the pretty bags first, and the brands I liked best. The ugly boxes that required scissors and caused cuticle damage could wait until last. Served them right for ignoring the power of pink tissue-paper.

A new colour collection for NARS. A new variant of Bumble and Bumble hair powder. Bo's new first-signs-of-ageing face cream. A new M.A.C lipstick range. A new self-tanner from Clinique. A skin-brightening range from Show Off. A fruit-infused Decleor body oil. Revlon's latest lip-gloss assembly. Maybelline's new crème bronzer/blush hybrid. A fresh, flirty new fragrance from Marc Jacobs.

I tried to imagine how this could become routine for *anyone*. Jay said she no longer got excited by the things that hit her desk, but I didn't believe her. How could you not be thrilled when every day was Christmas? Plus, sometimes we got gifts with the product – as if the luxury of trying the product months before everyone else wasn't enough of a treat. In my stash I had already scored an underwear set, a key-ring, a desk mirror, some chocolates, and a voucher for a session with a personal trainer.

Last week I had even been sent a *list of possible gifts* from Sheen, a haircare company that had recently sent us Tom Ford sunglasses to go with their new 'solar protect' range. One of the questions was:

Which would you prefer to receive with a product

(circle your preferences)

- Gift vouchers
- Trips
- Food items
- Gadgetry (i.e. iPod)
- Flowers
- Jewellery/accessories
- Clothing

I couldn't take it seriously. It felt like it was some form of prank and that if I actually answered the question, my response would be met with shrieks of laughter and then forwarded with great speed and fury. I'd ended up writing, 'I am grateful for anything you choose to send as a gift.'

And I was.

The last box I opened was from a small natural-cosmetics company who were only stocked in one state, in one store, had no online shop, and who constantly called and emailed me wondering why I wouldn't put them into *Gloss*. Straightaway I knew the rank stench was coming from this bag. Had they sent me dead vermin in their rage? It wouldn't surprise me. As I delicately peered into the box,

I saw the culprits – a small collection of tropical fruit gone very, very bad. As in, 'be sixteen, get drunk, steal the mayor's car and drive it into the police station' bad. The fruit was covered in a film of mould and had spread slime throughout the entire box.

This was not a friendly smell to my already volatile stomach. I dry-retched, packed up the box and bolted out of the office to the industrial bins near the lifts, into which I slammed the box. Who knew beauty could be so ugly?

Two coffees, an enormous salty-sweet stir-fry for lunch and roughly 0.9 per cent of the work I had planned for today completed, and it was 5.30 p.m. Which meant it was time to head off to the Torture Function. Woooonderful.

In my numb state I lost some of my nerves about the beauty ed clique. I decided to email Yasmin, the beauty editor at *Foxy* magazine – another women's glossy owned by Beckert – to see if she wanted to share a cab with me. I chose Yasmin as she was even newer than me to beauty. I liked that. She had come from an online magazine I'd never heard of, which I also liked because it was clearly underground and edgy, just like her.

Yasmin was half-Japanese, with an ironic mullet and beautiful deep pools of black liquid for eyes. She liked skull motifs, had a penchant for the word 'fuck', and looked as though she might date a tattooist called Slayer. Although her 'uniqueness' was obviously frowned upon in Beauty Land, she did her best to play the part of 'pretty girl'.

When I got to the foyer, wearing more makeup than I'd normally wear in an entire week in an effort to look 'alive', Yasmin wasn't there yet.

I took a seat, musing that being in our foyer was like being inside an iPhone. I'd never seen so much black. Everything from the floor to the desk, chairs, coffee table and lounges were gleaming with just-been-polished blackness. Even the front-desk girl's hair was jet black.

But the foyer was lively for all its parallels to a Bond villain's underground lair. A constant stream of amazingly dressed women passed through to the lifts, and there was a small, always busy espresso cart in the corner, hissing and steaming with fresh coffee for The Addicted.

After a minute, Fiona Rogers stepped out of a lift and walked towards the exit. She was the beauty editor on *21 Magazine*, and I had failed to really bond with her yet.

'But did you see his face when she said that,' Fiona said loudly to the girl she was with. 'Un. Be. Lievable.' Dramatic pause. 'I loved every second!' They dissolved into laughter, applying gloss as they walked out. Fiona gave me a sideways glance and, after a second, kept walking.

Well, that was a bit bitchy. She must know who I am by now. She must. We'd been to loads of the same functions. Maybe she genuinely hadn't recognised me . . .

My thoughts were interrupted by Yasmin screaming out of the lift and apologising for being late. She was wearing a black leather pencil skirt, black strappy heels and a silky peach singlet, but because she had the height and frame of a Ukrainian supermodel, what was a very simple outfit looked incredibly beautiful on her.

'Hannah, I'm *so* sorry; my editor had me by the balls in a meeting and then I couldn't find my heels but I'd actually taken them to get re-heeled at lunch, so I had to fucking borrow some from the fashion girls and they weren't there and —'

'Yasmin, Yasmin, it's cool. You're not even late.' I smiled at her and stood up. We hailed a cab and she told me about the rest of her shitty day. I was grateful not to have to talk, still numbed by my hangover and fatigue.

Arriving at the venue, all ready to learn about a new unisex razor, we had to walk up five flights of stairs because the lift had broken. When we finally got inside, the bar was packed, but was lacking the only thing that was of interest to me right then: food. Okay, there were oysters, but everyone knows they don't count.

I grabbed a glass of mineral water and sidled up to Yasmin. She was talking heatedly with Fiona – how come they were already friends? – and another girl about the latest *Big Brother* housemates. I smiled at them without showing teeth (too much effort), nodded occasionally and drank my water.

'Oh come *on*. As if she didn't give him a hand job under that doona! Please! Ray Charles could have seen that!' Fiona said adamantly.

'She didn't, I'm telling you. Big Brother said to confess or get out, and she still swore she didn't do it,' the other girl retorted with equal conviction.

'That's just ratings bullshit. As if they'd kick off the big-titty blonde. She's the show's ticket to getting male viewers,' Fiona guffawed.

'Are you serious?' Yasmin cried. 'Men don't like *her*! They'd probably like to fuck her, sure, but she'd never get a hello at the family roast. All men prefer brunettes deep down.'

'Is that true, do you think?' said a male voice behind me, and in my sleepy, stupid daze I flinched about ten centimetres.

I turned my head, with my hand on my heart, took a deep breath in, and said, 'You scared the *absolute* shit out of me,' to whoever it was that had spoken.

I then realised that the person who owned the voice was Jude Law. Or his antipodean twin, maybe. He was gorgeous. All olive skin and slim-fitting grey suit, with sexy stubble the same dark-blond shade as his tousled-but-completely-styled hair. And he had beautiful green eyes. He was the reason they made posters for teenagers' bedrooms.

And he was smiling at *me*.

'Sorry for scaring you, it's just that I've been dying to talk to you since you arrived. My name's Gabe. It's Hannah, right?'

'Yeah . . . it is,' I said, shocked by the fact he knew my name.

'I'm not a stalker, sweetheart. You're wearing a name badge.'

I looked down, and there was the large white plastic rectangle with 'Hannah' emblazoned in bright red.

'Oh,' I said sheepishly. 'I'm not really with it today.'

'You went to the party last night too, then?'

Something about the way he spoke was overly familiar, like we'd been friends for years. It should've been creepy, but it was actually quite nice. I felt instantly comfortable around him.

'I did,' I said, shaking my head. 'Feeling pretty wrecked from it, truth be known.' I laughed a nervous little laugh so he wouldn't think I was a total trashbag, raving about how smashed I had been last night.

'I missed it, but I heard it was a circus – everyone filled to their wigs with cheap wine and carrying on like a bunch of frogs in a sock.'

'Yeah, that's a pretty good description.'

'So, the reason I wanted to speak with you, sweet Hannah' – I blushed – 'is that you're flaunting possibly the best haircut this city has ever seen.'

Wow. That was a pretty amazing compliment coming from a guy – Jesse barely noticed when I chopped off ten centimetres, and this guy was assessing my haircut on our first meeting? He needed to be my future husband.

'Thanks, Gabe, that's really nice of you to say.'

'Who cut it?'

Wow, he *was* keen to make a good first impression!

'Okay, I promise I'm not bragging, but it was Gisele Bündchen's hairdresser. He was in town last week, launching his new hair-care range, and I was one of three who scored a haircut.'

'She's a little mannish, I find,' he said. 'Great tits and legs, but her face is a little masculine, don't you think? I mean, she's *divine*, of course, but she's not *pretty*, you know?'

Did he just say 'great tits and legs'?

'Anyway, it's an amazing cut – best in here by a Golden Gate Bridge. Yasmin has good hair too, but yours is better.'

Okay, now I was confused. He knew Yasmin?

He sipped on his straw, furiously stirring his drink with the muddling stick, and asked, 'So how's *Gloss* going for you?'

Confusion squared. How did he *know* all of this stuff? In my state, I was unable to keep up the spritely façade required when you're pretending you know who someone is, when you really, really don't.

'I'm . . . I'm really sorry, Gabe, but we haven't met before, have we?'

'No, but that's because I've been overseas. But I've managed to catch up fairly fast over a few of these heinous cocktails.'

Seeing the look of utter confusion in my eyes, he stopped.

'Sorry, allow me to do a proper introduction.' He put his drink down, stiffened his collar, and cleared his throat. 'I'm the beauty girl at *Phillip* magazine. Well, grooming editor is my official title, but grooming to me implies small spoilt dogs, so I'd rather just be called beauty editor and be done with it.'

Two billion light-bulbs switched on simultaneously in my head. One of them flashed, 'He's gay.' Another, 'He's in the industry.' And another simply went with, 'You are a *fool*.'

It all made sense! The sharp banter, the fashion-forward suit, the obsession with my hair . . . No straight man would ask who cut my hair, or speak openly about a woman's mammaries in such a vulgar manner.

God, I needed some sleep; my brain wasn't even able to distinguish a happy camper in a sea of straighties.

'Hannah, I already know that I like you and we're going to be fabulous friends, so I feel entirely at ease telling you that you should probably head home once you've handed over your card and kissed whoever's arse it is you're here to kiss.'

'How so?'

'Your face: it's beautiful, but it's weary. You need a hot bath and a good back rub.'

'Are you suggesting I look like shit, Gabe?' I asked with a twinkle in my eye.

'Not at all, but come *on*, darling, we're beauty fascists! We know we're supposed to look superb every single day! Don't waste a crack in the veneer at a dive like this.'

He was far too 'on' for me. All I could do was laugh and reach into my bag for a card.

'Oooh, what an excellent card! Whore-lipstick red, how gloriously appropriate for the beauty girl of *Gloss*! I *love* it!'

I took his – it was thin, shiny, black, and had only the word 'Phillip' on one side, and on the other the initials GHF, one phone number and an email address. All lower case, all in silver, and all uber-cool.

'Try not to be blinded by how hip I am, sweetheart. Now, get out of here and go get some beauty sleep. You need it.'

I laughed. 'You struggle with honesty and assertiveness, don't you?' I said, picking up my bag and doing up my jacket.

'Very much. But one thing I'm good at is modesty. I'm probably the best at modesty. If there were an award for it, it'd be mine.'

I laughed as we air-kissed on the cheek, and I deftly manoeuvred out of the room to the stairs, a cab, and the bed I'd been fantasising about all day.

8.

Sperm-brows

Style and set those wild little face-caterpillars by spraying hairspray onto your brow brush and combing them into shape. Alternatively, if you have dark, full brows, lightly sweep some brown mascara through them. Or just buy a really good brow gel.

Since starting at *Gloss*, I'd begun to view women as blobs with hair and makeup rather than the more socially prevalent term 'human beings'. I didn't *mean* to mentally divide women into sophisticated blush blenders and amateur blush blenders, but since it was all I read about, wrote about and thought about, I couldn't seem to find the off switch. It was one of the beauty editor side-effects.

Yasmin and I were on our way to a skincare launch in the city's Botanic Gardens, when a woman walked past us. I gasped.

'What's up with you?' asked Yasmin, without taking her eyes off her mobile phone, which she had been neurotically prodding the entire journey.

'Did you not see her eyebrows?' I asked in disbelief.

'Sperm-brows. Awful.' Yasmin was always coming up with cool sayings.

'Hmm. I want to help women like that, you know?' I said, with absolute sincerity.

Yasmin sniggered. She found my naivety, sincerity and most of all my Susceptibility to Gullibility (STG) enormously amusing.

It was at one of my first beauty launches, not long after the fateful Fire lunch, where Jill's arseholey and unnecessary discussion of Jesse and Lisa Sutherland had spoilt my appetite, that I had displayed classic symptoms of STG. It was a foundation launch, held in the back area of a brand-new bar, the kind that has a one-word name and elaborate chandeliers and staff who believe they are too good-looking to serve you a drink, let alone clean up the mess you create when you spill it on the *white lounges.* (Whoever puts white lounges in a room where red drinks are served and the intoxicated roam unfettered deserves to have them ruined.)

The PR team had been hard at work preparing the room, plastering it with seductive, creative visuals for this exciting new foundation. Before the first canapé had time to wiggle down my gullet, the call-to-action on the posters had me.

Are you sick of your foundation falling off by lunchtime?

You bet I am!

Wouldn't you like it to last all day?

Is it even *possible?*

Well, we've got you covered: our new base stays for twelve hours.

I have cash: I will buy your magical potion immediately.

Next came the PowerPoint presentation, complete with beaming quotes from women who had already had the great privilege of trying this foundation, followed by info graphs, charts, statistics, and even footage of leading makeup artists from recent Hollywood movies talking about how radical it was, and how superjazzed they were that a product like this had *finally* been invented.

After this circus of persuasion, it was all I could do not to take the PR by the collar, shake her and demand she hand it over. I was giddy with anticipation and wondered how soon I might be able to try this exquisite commodity. As it happened, despite the fact that the product wasn't on sale (or 'on counter', as we say in the biz) for another three months, the lucky, lucky people in that room would be *allowed to take some home today*. And that included *me*.

I wasn't sure how it happened, but, without my permission, my hands joined and separated quickly several times. I *actually clapped* at the idea of getting this foundation. To take home. To wear. Months and months before anyone else in the country. That last point was by far the most pertinent for me, and was probably one of the primary reasons I loved being a beauty editor so much: *I have stuff before anyone else does.*

Yasmin denied she felt this way, but I saw her. I saw her with her limited-edition Chanel palettes and La Prairie illuminators, flashing them around as though they were Olympic medals at a closing ceremony. But me, I was fresh off the beauty boat, and I was light years away from cynical. The moment I walked into a boardroom/café/elaborately decorated garden tent, I unwittingly fell to my knees before the religion of face wash. Or eyeliner or teeth whiteners, depending on what was being offered in between mini fruit-salads and scrambled egg concoctions fit only for people who think capers count as an actual food.

Of course, during a function I played it ice-cool, so the other beauty editors didn't start referring to me as The Suck.

'It's the cheek crème the Olsen twins swear by,' the PR would gush.

Shrug.

'It contains a blend of the two rarest – and most expensive – types of zucchini extract known to man.'

Roll eyes.

'It's been clinically proven to take away *every single* dimple of cellulite.'

Pfft.

'It will take ten years off your face in one application.'

Snort.

Of course, internally I'd be all oohs and aaahs, and praising modern science, but I was a fickle beast. The next week I'd be oohing over another product with similar zeal. However, I figured disloyalty was part of the job. I had to stay impartial. I mean, imagine if I only used the first products that ever impressed me? Completely unprofessional. Besides, it invariably gave me currency at dinner parties: women *always* wanted to know about the latest new beauty products, and I *always* knew what they were. It was a beautiful dance.

'Hiiii, Hannah!'

I had just, *just* stepped into the ye olde-style tea-gardens café and the PR had already zeroed in.

'Oh, hey, Olivia!' I smiled and air-kissed her, careful not to mess up either of our gloss jobs.

'I *love* coral on you – you look amazing,' she gushed.

'Speak for yourself,' I said, commenting on her beautiful, obviously expensive frock, which, with its busy colours and high floral quotient, *should* have looked atrocious, but actually looked amazing.

'Sooo, how's everything?' she asked.

As I answered that things were good, but busy – the standard response – her thickly glossed smile didn't waver. But her eyes slid down to my chin.

To them.

The twins that had sprung up that morning like tiny volcanoes, waiting to erupt and ruin my complexion for a good five days.

Olivia obviously realised she'd been caught staring, and so jumped in and awkwardly started her own version of how busy things were. But she couldn't help it: *everyone stares at a beauty editor with a blemish*, no matter how small.

I'd come to realise that as a beauty editor, you are not, by law, allowed to carry a flaw. There was an unspoken expectation that because you had every form of prevention, correction or concealment at your disposal, you had to look perennially flawless.

In addition, because you had elected to spend your working days advising/lecturing the public on how to avoid acne/cellulite/greasy hair/bad eyebrows/chipped nails/yellowed teeth/fake-tan lines, in theory you couldn't ever sport any of those things. You had to live and breathe your gig. Your job shouldn't define you, but in the beauty-editor game it absolutely, utterly, have-you-ever-seen-a-badly-dressed-fashion-editor did.

This had come as a bit of a shock to me, as pre-*Gloss* I rarely wore foundation, let alone concealer, which I was now expected to know how to master in the same way a model masters her kilojoules. I found that I'd actually come to adore this part of the job – I loved playing dress-up each morning with all of my 'toys' – but simultaneously it was very tiring. It bred vanity, induced insecurity, and paved the way for obsessive paranoia and way too much compact-mirror-glancing and surreptitious concealer-dabbing.

Friends had noticed. Well, some of them. When Gabe and I had gone for schmucktails – as he called them when I had suggested we go to a bar where there were lots of handsome, suit-clad men – he'd commented that I had reapplied gloss to my lips no less than four times in the one-hour sitting.

'You've become a touch-up tart,' he said dismissively as he sipped his gin fizz.

'What does that mean?'

'You're one of those painful beauty girls who touches up her makeup a thousand goddamn times whenever she's further than a metre from the mirror that sits on her desk in place of her computer monitor.'

'Gabe, I am *so* not a touch-up tart! Um, maybe the fact there are good-looking men everywhere has something to do with it?'

'Forget it, honey. They all think you're with me. You're not getting any let's-catch-up phone numbers tonight.'

'You're *such* a bitch.'

'*Totally.* Do you love it?' He'd said this in the style Paris Hilton so often did, and it always made me laugh, even when he was being nasty.

But today I was definitely being a touch-up tart. Just a very stealthy one.

On days when I had big unhappy pimples, I prayed that the function would be in a dark, moody bar. Of course, thanks to Murphy, that rotten prankster, and his foul laws, they would always be in rooms entirely themed in white, or in a science lab with cruel fluorescent lighting or a courtyard flooded with natural light.

Today was a prime example. In this sky-lit palace there'd be no missing the twins.

Yasmin had stopped outside to take a phone call so I walked through to the function solo. A handful of beauty girls, all anti-pants and pro-frock, were scattered throughout. I wasn't friendly enough with any of them to make conversation. I saw Fiona pouring herself some coffee. I decided to *make her like me.*

I walked over to her. She was wearing a black cinched-waist dress, black pumps, and some exhilarating red lipstick. She looked very chic. As always.

'Hi, Fiona!' I said with gaiety, like we were old friends.

'Oh, hey,' she said. And went back to her coffee preparation.

No. Had she really just done that?

'So, uh, how's your day been so far?' God. Was I trying to pick her up? I should've just asked what a pretty girl like her was doing at a launch like this.

She shrugged her shoulders, concentrating on her sugar-spooning. She said nothing, but she didn't need to. Her indifference screamed.

'Oh-kaay,' I said quietly to myself, wondering what to do next. 'Well, um, I'd better go take a seat.' She was diabolical. I needed to abort. Where was Yasmin?!

I watched as Fiona took a long sip from her cup, completely entranced, before turning away. That was it. I was done with her.

'Sorry, I'm no one's friend until I've had some coffee.'

Facing the room, I closed my eyes and smiled with relief. So she *wasn't* a total cow. I turned back to her and, feeling extremely congenial all of a sudden, decided I needed a coffee too. Being not-psychotic together could be the glue that would bond us. I tried to do my best 'Oh, me too' face.

'Know what you mean. I've already had one, but another won't hurt.' There was a pregnant pause. She'd missed her cue. Time for me to prompt. 'So . . . um . . . do you think they'll be launching that new serum today? I saw an amazing write-up of it in *WWD Friday* last month.'

'Imagine so. Have you tried that three-in-one cleanser of theirs?' She spoke vaguely; she was still totally engrossed in her coffee, holding it up to her face, taking desperate, scalding little sips every ten seconds or so.

'Mm-hmm, it's actually really nice. The exfoliating beads are really tiny and soft, you know, so you can use it every day. I never usually believe it when they say that, but —'

She half laughed. 'Do you still try everything you're given? I love it. Adorable.'

I wasn't sure whether she was mocking me, so I shrugged and laughed with my mouth closed.

'You'll get over it,' she said knowingly. 'Trust me, I've been in the industry for a thousand years, and soon you'll stick to the brands you know work. No matter which celebrity or bloody dermatologist swears by it.'

'Mmmm.' But I couldn't allow myself to agree, no matter how much I wanted her to like me. I knew that for as long as my skin could cop it, I would try every last product that arrived clad in tissue paper in my office.

Suddenly a dark figure landed beside me, furiously clanging coffee cups and pots with the kind of wild abandon coffee addicts think nothing of. Yasmin had finally come in. 'Hey, Fi. Hannah, can you pass the skim? And then can we sit down? These shoes are fucking murder.'

All three of us took care to balance the weight of our handbags with our precariously balanced cups and saucers as we sat down on a large white-leather ottoman. All very, very dangerous for our attire and their furniture.

As we sat sipping, and Yasmin detailed the drama of her photo shoot last night – 'The model was so fucking hung over, no amount of coffee or makeup could do anything, so we sent the stupid bitch home and used the work-experience girl, can you believe it?!' – I watched Fiona out of the corner of my eye, fascinated. Her makeup was *absolutely* flawless. So was her skin. And her hair; there wasn't a single hair out of place. And no roots either; just a head of perfect, shiny, Gwyneth Paltrow-like blondeness. Fiona's hard work was admirable, but there was something a little bit creepy about it, too. Like she was a Real-Life Doll who seduced people's boyfriends and then killed innocent civilians en route to her murdering said boyfriends after dark.

Still, it was impressive. I finger-stroked my running-late, semi-blow-dried waves and vowed to put more effort into my appearance. Again. I seemed to make that promise every second day.

'Hannah, where did you work before *Gloss*?' Fiona cocked her head to one side and squinted her eyes as though she already didn't believe my answer.

'Um, Colourblock Advertising.'

'And what made you want to be a beauty editor?'

Was this a job interview?

'Um, well, I guess, you know, I studied journalism at university, and I kind of always wanted to work in magazines, and, well, actually, I kind of fell into it, to be honest. I don't know that I did want to become one.' It was the truth. I'd never wanted to be a beauty editor because I'd never even known they existed.

Fiona frowned. 'Really? Isn't that *interesting*.'

'I didn't even know what beauty editors were. Sounds like a bloody made-up job if you ask me,' Yasmin piped up.

I laughed. 'I know. Who'd believe we get paid to eat canapés and test lip gloss!'

'Well, it's a bit more than *that*,' Fiona said, her voice tinged with righteousness.

'She's right,' said Yasmin with an earnest look, pursing her lips and nodding. 'We test mascara too.' Yasmin grinned at me and took another gulp of her coffee.

Olivia, the PR, had walked onto a small white platform and was nodding manically at a tech guy sitting to the side of the stage with a laptop. He snapped into action and a giant welcome sign lit up the screen behind her. She switched her microphone on to begin, and looked around to see if we'd noticed and would eventually shut up.

'Good morning, ladies. Thank you so much for your time today, we appreciate how busy you all are, so we're really delighted you could all make it.' She was smiling, but her hands were shaking. 'As you may have guessed, today we're here for a very special reason, and what will be a very important launch for us this year, so we hope you'll all love it so much you'll feel inspired to include it in your pages!'

'She should be more passive-aggressive about us giving it editorial,' smirked Fiona.

I laughed along with her, because that's what you do when there's a clear ringleader: you laugh at their jokes.

'A first-to-market product, the new Rewind serum uses papain, an extract from papaya that works as an enzyme on the skin to dislodge dead skin cells and let the fresh new ones shine through, and is the natural alternative to Alpha Hydroxy Acids (AHAs), which can be too harsh for some people's skin . . .'

'Oh, come *on*, as if we've never heard of papain.' Fiona rolled her eyes.

'Shut up, Miss Know It All. I've never heard of it,' Yasmin hissed.

'. . . and of course, our patented antioxidant elixir, which contains eight of the most potent antioxidants available in skincare today, which where possible are cold-pressed for greater effectiveness.'

Sold.

I'll take two.

'I want to wear it *now*,' said Yasmin, clenching her fingers in a gimme-gimme motion. 'Love their shit. Fuckin' love it. Their eye cream with the cooling stuff in it? Best eye cream ever.'

'Rewind is pretty good actually,' agreed Fiona. 'One of the few brands who actually deliver half the promises they churn out.'

'I could never have afforded it in the real world,' I said.

'Honey, we'd all be using Nivea if we weren't beauty editors!' said Fiona, and we all laughed – but me a little more than the others, because she was finally, finally being nice to me.

'Hey, I used Neutrogena then, and I still use it now,' said a defiant Yasmin, who was watching the testers being sent around with a hawk-eyed glare.

Olivia's spiel was coming to a close, and her relief was palpable. Her PowerPoint had gone flawlessly, and all her video clips had worked like a dream, and we were hungrily rubbing her goo onto the backs of our hands, doing the *rub rub sniff, rub rub sniff* thing we always did with any skincare product, be they cleansers, scrubs or crèmes. 'So there are some samples being passed around for you all to try, and of course you'll get some to take home, so please, enjoy, and thank you again for coming.'

I looked to the ringleader for a snide remark or observation, but Fiona was too busy rubbing and sniffing. Even the jaded could still be moved with an impressive product it seemed.

9.

It's just an irony

> Make the boys melt by smelling like a dream, sans reapplication. The trick? Apply perfume to all the 'bendy' parts of your body: neck, elbows, knees and wrists. Your body heat and movement will distribute your fragrance evenly all night.

Later that day I was typing furiously to get my 'Six Steps to Smoky Eyes' article finished and filed before five. I had got all the tips from an interview with an M.A.C makeup artist, but was having difficulty turning her creative talk into succinct, reader-friendly tips.

It was funny, because during the interview, when she used phrases like, 'And then with a mid-sized blending brush gradually build the charcoal shadow over the lid like a thunderstorm gently brewing,' I nodded and a-*ha*-ed as though I had *finally* found someone who spoke my language. But hours later, listening to my tape recorder and staring at a blank document, it came off sounding as though we had both been happily clicking away in Swahili. My phone beeped and I welcomed the distraction. It was Iz.

Is 2nt a legs and heels night or a jeans and boobs nt?

You mean you're not going to make the most of your loan and wear The Top?

OMG, I totally 4got I still had ur top! So sorry! Can I wear again? pls??

Of course! It's boobs and jeans for me. See you sooooon x

Love u long time xxx Iz

Immediately after this textversation, my concentration clocked off. Because, it being a Friday, and me being single, I was going out. Yes. It was definitely a night for jeans and boobs, I confirmed to myself. Everyone knows that Saturday night is wardrobe-effort night, not Friday. All *I* had to do, thanks to being a mag hag, was switch tops and increase my eye makeup by around 300 per cent. Perfect.

We were meeting for a drink at 6.30 p.m. at a bar in the city called Frisk. I arrived at 6.32, Iz at 6.53.

'Sorry, honey – I've had an absolute bastard of a day,' she said as she kissed me and dumped her coat on the floor.

I held out the white wine I had bought her and told her she looked sexy. Which she did: she had her blonde hair blow-dried and all flicky, and wore black skinny-leg jeans with my new black top, which pushed her already ample bosom up to her chin. I could already sense men staring at her, mentally sketching plans to weasel their way into our conversation before anyone else had the chance.

'So, how was your day?' she asked with a sigh and a relieved sip of her wine.

I explained to her about the whole Fiona thing, careful not to make Fiona sound too evil, for fear of Iz getting a bad first impression and hating her forever.

'Well, she sounds mental to me,' she said decidedly. 'Why waste time letting someone like that into your inner circle?'

As if I had one in the beauty world.

'But you're making friends, aren't you?' she asked. 'That Jasmine girl sounds cool.'

'Yasmin.'

'Yasmin. She's nice, right? Decent enough to spend time with at all those functions, anyway.'

'Yeah, she's unreal. But, I dunno, Iz. It's just a weird world. They're not, you know, normal. Not like you and me.'

'Oh yeah, we're totally normal.' She exploded into laughter.

'Whatever. I guess it will just take time.'

'Look,' Iz rearranged herself on her seat, signalling that she was about to make a Wise Comment, 'unless or *until* someone proves they're an outright bitch, I reckon just be nice.'

Iz said this as though up until this point I had been deliberately spilling red wine on them or sleeping with their boyfriends.

'Kill them with kindness and all that. Rise above. But watch that Felicity.'

'Fiona.'

'Fiona, whatever – two-facey. She sounds shonky. Ooh! Speaking of shonks, I met a *guy*! And I didn't tell you because I knew you wouldn't mind, but he's coming here with some friends for a drink. Is that okay? Don't worry, if they're losers, we'll brush them off and go to another bar. But he's hot. So hot. A model! He's in that base-jumping Pepsi ad! Can you believe it?!'

Male models were obviously Iz's new flavour. After having had her fill in Suit City, helping herself to finance lads and stockbroker boys at will, then passing through Hippie-ville, she seemed to have moved on to Young Studs. If only I had such confidence. I couldn't imagine myself with one guy right now, let alone a whole stable.

As if reading my mind, Iz answered the question I hadn't asked.

'Oh Han, I don't know that I want to go chasing Mr Right – cash, looks, age, experience and brains. *Whatever.* Too much ego and too much baggage for me. I want someone fun. Someone who will make me laugh, not bolt off with his sexetary.'

We sipped our wine in agreement.

Iz's swift movement between men didn't mean she was easy, even though women who didn't know her and who were threatened by her confidence liked to label her so. She was just enjoying every opportunity single life afforded an attractive, secure young woman. She had done her five-year fiercely loyal relationship; now she wanted to play. And it wasn't like these guys were all bedding her – she was excruciatingly slow to give up the candy. I truly admired her. I could never be so bold, or manage so many personalities in such quick succession.

As it so often did, one glass turned into one bottle and one cheeky cigarette turned into four. Then the catwalk kids arrived.

One wore a trucker's cap and a T-shirt that said 'I Only Fuck Models'.

One wore a short mohawk, a snarl and layers of attitude.

One wore a winter scarf, thongs and tight red skinny-leg jeans.

And the other one, well, within a minute or two he was wearing Iz.

She winked at me, and nodded towards the guy in the trucker cap. Who saw her do it. Which was apparently all the encouragement a shy boy like him needed.

'So.' He paused to look me up and down. 'You're pretty hot,' he said, as he took up a stool next to me. I noticed that he was *absolutely beautiful*. The type of guy you don't date because you can't trust your friends around him. Deep-blue eyes, olive skin, dizzyingly perfect smile and sexy man-cheekbones. He looked like he'd stepped out of one of those Dolce & Gabbana ads where dozens of sexy young boys just writhe around on the floor in their underpants. Judging by his overwhelming bashfulness, I was pretty sure he'd tell me he had just come back from Milan, where he'd done precisely that.

He sat folded-armed, eye-balling me as though I were a new Ferrari, and although he had wanted a Lamborghini he'd be prepared to settle.

'A lot of girls who look good from afar are no good up close. I'll need a better look.' He raised his eyebrows and then *he actually tipped his cap back to get a better look.*

He was a walking, talking caricature.

'Your T-shirt means I'm out of the question anyway,' I said, openly flirting.

He cocked his head to an angle, I guessed in an attempt at being cute.

'Don't worry about that, babe. It's just an irony.'

I choked on my wine before laughing out loud. Having absolutely no clue as to his gaffe, he nodded, smiling a smug, no-teeth-showing smile, as though he had successfully broken the ice with his genius.

'I think you might cut the grade, missy,' he said. 'You're a cutie. So, what will we drink now that we're friends? How about some one-two-three-floor tequilorrr!' He said the last part loudly so his friends could hear, and together they all repeated it and laughed. I felt like I had accidentally crashed a college party. I looked at Iz and raised my eyebrows.

Two tequilas, two wines and two clubs later, my enjoyment and Trucker's adoration had escalated to a dangerously high level. I was now *wearing* a certain person's trucker cap. A siren wailed faintly in the back of my mind: I was meant to be tough on men from now on! Play hardball. Make them work. Keep the upper hand at all times.

Keep an air of detached cool. I had rules and regulations about this stuff, which *I was supposed to be following*. Was I so weak that the first guy to show me a twinkle of interest made me forget all of them?

I looked over at Trucker dancing and laughing. He caught my eye and blew me a kiss, before galloping over.

'You gonna give that back?' he asked, motioning to the cap on my head while smiling, clearly not caring either way.

'Nope.' I smiled and sipped my drink.

Bah, so what? I thought. *Time to have a little fun*. I was sure Jesse was out there doing the same. Or worse. I shivered at the image.

'Well then, guess I'll be needing to go home to get me another one.'

I decided he needed a chaperone.

'But what are you *feeling*? I mean, where are we *going*? What is the path we're on? Emotionally? You know hair is a reflection of your state of mind, don't you? It needs to progress as you do. Don't make me explain that to you again, not you of all people; I mean, darling, that's your goddamn job! If you don't know that, well then, we're all screwed, know what I mean?!'

With that, Johnson Tyler, Hairdresser of the Year two years running, dissolved into scary high-pitched laughter. He was the best hairdresser in the city (country, world, galaxy, universe) and his PR had given me six months' worth of free haircuts, in return for him being the hair guru in my beauty pages. This made things hard when super-celebrity hair royalty swooped into town, but as Johnson's cuts were so extraordinary, it was worth the sacrifice.

Johnson was a tiny Hispanic 'hair artist' who had more presence than an irritated lion in a small room. He had cut and styled everyone from Goldie Hawn to Cindy Crawford, and until he had fallen in love with a young photographer, Julie – yes, a woman – who lived here in Sydney, he had lived in Manhattan. He liked to remind me of that fact roughly ten times per haircut.

The thing about Johnson was that he carried on like Señor Gay of Gay Street, Gay Town, when in fact he was entirely heterosexual. He was just a little bit camp. In the same way the Antarctic is a little bit cold.

On his insistence, I gave some serious thought as to how I was feeling. I was feeling the best I had since being dumped. Life was starting to come together. That or I had finally mastered the art of repression. 'Um, I guess I'm feeling okay? Kind of, um . . . cruisy?'

'Darling. Cruisy is not a state of mind, it's a kind of day we have when the sun shines and the Veuve flows and there is no fucking work to be done! Are you screwing anyone yet? It's time you were over that ex of yours. So boring for me. Waste of time. Life is too short to slobber and sob over past fucks.'

'Well, I mean, there's this . . . but it's . . . no. I mean, we've hung out a few times, but he's silly, it doesn't mean anything . . .'

'Ohmigod! We have *action*! Frank, FRANK! Turn that off! Did you hear that – the little one is getting laid!'

Johnson was screaming across the salon – and several customers – to his assistant, Frank. Frank winked at me and went back to his blow-drying.

'Johnson, please. You're embarrassing me!'

'Oh, stop it. What are you, a grandma? Okay! Enough chit. Now you be quiet.'

With that, he put his iPod on and started cutting. As Johnson snipped and razored my hair, I wondered what exactly it was that Trucker, male model extraordinaire, was to me. He was definitely an A-class rebound. He was undeniably replacement therapy. He was also doing a cracking job of administering ego enhancement and distraction treatment.

Yasmin was thrilled for me, and had even had a dalliance with one of his model friends, Jimbo, during a post-party party at Iz's place.

Jacinta had taken to calling me Issues.com, claiming the short amount of time since the break-up was irrelevant, but Trucker's prowess in the sack and his hot shirtless Nike campaign were not.

Post-haircut, with a new fringe and looking like someone way cooler than the person I really was (Johnson had surmised my emotional state to be 'butterfly hotness'), I schlepped back to the office. It was already 6 p.m., but I had some stories that needed to be done, and I figured that, with a full day of functions tomorrow, it would be best to get ahead tonight. I'd thought when I started that I was working long hours, but I'd since realised that beauty editors don't ever do normal hours. We have the same deadlines as everyone else, but only half the time in the office, so it wasn't unusual for me to be at work at 7.30 a.m. and to leave at 8 p.m.

When I walked into the *Gloss* office, I was disappointed to see Eliza, Karen's crazy deputy, at the photocopier. Her blonde mane was freshly blow-dried and excessively voluminous. From behind she looked like a kind of hyper-cheerleader, with her tiny frame, leather bomber jacket and tight jeans. She was pressing buttons aggressively and pulling out paper trays before slamming them shut again, swearing and hissing loudly. I tried to sneak past, but she saw me.

'Hannah! What the fuck does this mean? Check the cartridge positioning, tray four?'

I had no idea. None. I was even worse with antagonistic office machinery than I was with psychotic superiors.

'Do you want me to take a look?' I said, hoping she'd say no and shoo me away. She had a reputation for being very scary once every four weeks.

'Yes, fix it, please, Hannah. I need to print out finals.' And with that she whooshed back into her lair.

I put my bag down and slowly started tinkering with trays and touch screens, trying to understand why this sadistic machine was trying to get me verbally clocked.

When my phone rang, I let it ring out. When it rang again, I did the same. I preferred to focus on the copier, and thus preserve my life. When the shrill tone sounded for the third time, Eliza opened her door and screamed, 'Hannah, would you please answer *that fucking phone*.'

She startled me so much I actually jumped. I hadn't felt this scared and tiptoey around someone since school. It would be funny tomorrow, but right now it was frightening.

I checked the phone. It was Trucker. Shit.

'Hannah speaking.'

'*Hola!* Sexy *señorita*, what's the G-O? I love your phone voice, you sound foxariffic. I've had the *worst* day; my agent was being a total toss, trying to get me to do some lame-ass supermarket show, and I'm like, "Uh, *Phil*, I think we both know I don't do shopping centres." Loser. Anyway, flash forward, who cares: what time am I seeing you tonight?'

'Oh, um, can I maybe call you back?'

'Why? Your husband there? Tell him I said hi, and that tonight you're all mine.'

'No, I mean —'

'The party starts at nine, so we'll meet Kyle and Shaun at the Duke for a drink at eight. Can you wear those jeans that show off your arse? Hot. *Damn*, you look fine in those. You should wear them every friggin' day.'

'Hannah! Is that copier fixed? I'm pressing print right now.'

'Look, I've gotta go. I'm not sure if I can come tonight, but I'll text you.'

'What? *Like hell.* I'll hunt you down and carry you out like a caveman.'

'I'll call you. I've gotta go, bye.'

He spoke like a teen in a Seven-Up ad. And I hated the way he informed me of plans, instead of asking me if I wanted to go. It was way too relationshipy.

Ten minutes later and the copier was still not fixed. I had magenta ink all over my hands and the Hormonal Ogre with her cursor on the print icon was about to lose it.

'Um, I'm really sorry, but I can't seem to figure it out – maybe you can print it out on Level Ten? We're connected to their colour printer.'

'How? Can you do it?'

Why, I'd be happy to, I thought. Doing things for you is an *absolute pleasure*.

After I had printed out what she needed, and fetched it for her, Eliza raved with insincere gratitude, saying I was 'the absolute best'. I noticed a packet of M&Ms and a bag of crisps on her desk. All we needed now were tears and we'd have the PMS trifecta.

Exhaling in an attempt to expel her energy from me, I settled in at my desk to type about my favourite new beauty trend – enchanting emerald eyes – and set about testing blue and green waterproof eyeliners on my wrist.

I liked to do the testing by product group, and then, if I had time, by price range. Karen loved the whole spend-versus-splurge thing, and so I always included both cheap and luxe items in my pages. Readers needed something to aspire to (cue Chanel, Dior, La Mer, La Prairie), but they also needed to be able to afford some of it too (cue Maybelline, CoverGirl, Revlon). It was only too easy for me to remember how expensive beauty products were when I was being sent them for free every day.

After an hour, I was hungry, covered in a rainbow of eyeliner, agitated and in need of a drink. Maybe I would meet Trucker and his Next Top Model crew after all. His ego injections were far too hard to resist.

10.

One of those bastard men

Fake the bedroom minx look: apply black liner along your upper lash lines and inside your eyes' inner-rims before going to sleep. By morning it will have settled in beautifully. Just maybe don't do this too often. It's not so good for your peepers.

Iz seemed to think I was severely mistreating Trucker. I was on the phone to her at the same time as laying out a full-page shot of stills for the next issue. The photographer was outside smoking, and the art director had nicked off to get a coffee, so I was the only one left to style it. This actually suited me fine; the control freak in me liked my products displayed exactly the way I imagined it in my head, and today's shot was one I'd entertained mentally for some time.

'So, let me get this straight: you invite him back to yours, light candles, sip on Baileys, get jiggy, then you kick him out?'

'Well, that's putting it a bit harshly.' I took the lid off the blender I had called in for the shot, and started to place my goodies inside. The theme was tropical beauty, and I had gathered a selection of wild orange lipsticks, yellow nail polishes, red lip glosses, pink cheek gels and green eye shadows, and was organising them just so in the glass blender.

'Honey – that's exactly what you're doing! Can you imagine if a guy did that to you? Or me? We would have a conniption! We would despise him. Poor little boy. He's fallen for you, you know. Kyle told me.'

Dammit! There were too many products. I hated it when that happened. Each had been chosen specifically and each deserved to be in the shot. I *hated* deciding which ones would miss out.

'He has *not*; he just loves the chase. And anyway, I've told him I've just come out of a long-term relationship and that I'm not looking for anything. It's not like he doesn't know how it is.'

I scrapped one polish and a large pink blush, and the rest all fitted. Next, I filled the gaps with small coloured ice cubes in the shape of palm trees. I folded my left arm across my ribs and stood back to admire my handiwork. It was genius. God, I loved this part of the job.

'*How it is*?! Listen to yourself! You're a man! You have become one of those bastard men *Gloss* warns girls about.'

Secretly, I had to agree. I was finding it a little curious that I could have a gorgeous man adore me and not want anything more than a casual hook-up. Which in turn seemed to be making him keener. Bizarre. Last weekend I had read a book I'd found on the *Gloss* bookshelf called *Men Prefer Bitches*. It was all about how if you don't show you're keen, and just get on with your super-fun, super-excellent single life, men won't be able to get enough of you. Problem was, this book was founded on the premise that woman *wanted the man to eventually commit*. And that was the last thing I wanted. Well, from Trucker, anyway. Although it fitted well with my plan to completely avoid Jesse, and thus make him miss me terribly. That he hadn't exactly been breaking my door down was something I tried to push from my mind.

I *was* being kind of mean to Trucker, if I thought about it. But I was aware something inside me was changing. I had become less, well, me. The sweet, do-anything-for-a-guy girl had been shut down. I desperately hoped Jesse hadn't scarred me so that I'd be doomed to live a bitter, anti-love existence, like Sam on *Sex and the City*, except with a scummy apartment and twenty-seven cats.

I decided my tough exterior was proof I needed some single time, some 'me time'. Just like all those articles in *Gloss* said. But I'd be fine. It was a time thing. Everything would be apples.

Plus, I had bigger things to think about. Like an interstate trip with Marley.

We'd been sent to attend a series of meetings with beauty clients. Marley had come because she'd recently taken over Laura's position (baby boy; Mitchell; eight pounds), but Karen had to cancel at the last minute, so it was just the two of us, flying, getting cabs and checking-in together. It would be forced work-bonding, basically. Just minus the squalid strip clubs and sweaty lap dances slimy businessmen opt for in such situations.

'Want to get some dinner? Or are you feeling room-servicey?'

This was the only non-work-related thing Marley had said since arriving at lunchtime.

'Sure, why not? Dinner sounds great.'

Marley, a different person after having showered and slipped on some beautiful leather sandals and a white shift-dress, suggested a small restaurant in Chinatown, where, after a few wines and some MSG-drenched Chinese, we became loose-lipped. Some of us more than others.

'So, what's happening with you and that B-grade TV-star ex of yours?' she asked, as I sat with a scrunched forehead, investing enormous amounts of energy into reading a very blurry dessert menu.

'Oh, nothing. We're completely over.' I answered a little too quickly.

'You're lying,' she said, studying me as I coolly took a sip of wine.

'No, I'm not. I'm over him. Seriously.'

'Has he been contacting you?'

'Um, no – I mean, once or twice, but . . . no.'

'Got a new girl, has he?' Evidently, tact was not Marley's strong point.

'Um, well, I'm not sure, but the rumour is he has, yeah.'

'She pretty?'

'Mm-hmm. Weather girl. Huge boobs. Great hair. Perfect skin.'

'I knew that. I was just testing to see if you did. She's okay; you're cuter. Plus, she has terrible dress sense.'

'What do you mean, "if I *did*". What, it's gospel now? That they're a couple?' I was starting to talk faster and could feel a surge of anger.

'Well, no, but this isn't about them,' she said with complete calm. 'It's always very telling how people react to news about their ex having a new lover.' She had a mischievous glint in her eye, and she circled the bottom of her wine glass with one dark plum-painted nail.

'Marley, did it occur to you that maybe, you know, the *delivery* of your information could be what makes people crack the shits?' I folded my arms and glared at her. I must've been drunk, as I was suddenly not scared of her at all.

'Don't get upset, I'm just trying to make you see you're not over him. You can freak out if you want to, but this will all help in the long run. Because knowing they're not thinking about you is the best way to move on from thinking about them.' She sipped her wine and stared at me. 'Trust me. I know.'

This was the most insightful thing I'd ever heard Marley say. She usually just ran her mouth or made jokes. I was too shocked to respond.

Realising she had let her emotional fortress down, she immediately sat up straight and requested the bill. 'Let's get out of this dump, shall we? I need a ciggy.'

Apparently the conversation was over. And now I had an empty hotel room and a head full of Jesse and Lisa fucking Sutherland. Brilliant.

But as I fell into bed, drunk and lethargic, I felt sadness, not anger. That had to be progress.

The next morning, after a horror meeting with a bulldog of a marketing manager ('We just feel that *Gloss* and Hot Catwalk makeup are perfect synergy' – their makeup is so tacky that even the work-experience girls won't take it – 'and yet for some reason your pages don't seem to reflect our relationship' – we have less rapport than France and the US) we dragged our sorry, hung-over arses onto a plane and back into the office.

Once back at *Gloss*, I sat down at my desk and braced myself for an onslaught of appointments, functions and emails.

But fun stuff first.

I opened my non-work emails. There was one from Trucker with an outrageous photo of him from a Japanese catalogue he'd just shot, wearing a fluoro-pink poncho and looking quite serious about the idea of potential rain, saying he missed me; one from Mum saying they were now in Peru and that I would love it there; and then one from a reader.

The subject was innocuous enough. I really hoped it wasn't going to be a nasty left-field attack. I was too fragile today to deal with a rant from a righteous reader, telling me how awful I was at my job.

To: Hannah@gloss.com

From: Joseandpaul@gmail.com

Subject: Your story

I am writing in regards to the piece in your latest issue of *Gloss* on makeup for coloured skin.

The girl you used for coloured skin was latte at most. She could have used the white girl's makeup with ease.
I am described as ebony. It's hard enough for me to find makeup that shows on my skin, without being insulted by a photo of a caramel girl as the poster girl for black skin.
Can I suggest you put a little more work into your articles rather than using the prettiest shots?
Regards,
Jose Frey

I read it a few times, my heart racing. I felt awful. She had made me feel as though I'd personally offended the entire non-Caucasian population. My hung-over head was pounding like a jackhammer, and sounded like it might implode at any second. I was *definitely* too fragile for such an e-attack.

Jay came over to ask some questions about the story I'd pitched on candy-coloured makeup being huge. If I didn't give her a picture reference for my makeup trends, she thought it never really existed.

She saw my face and asked what had happened.

'Oh Jay! This, this reader, she just laid into me! About the fact I used a bad example of a dark-skinned girl in my "Base for Every Face" feature last month.'

'And?'

'And what?'

'That's what's got you so upset?'

'Yes, because she's right! I *was* being racist. It was wrong of me to discount the really dark women out there.'

'Oh my God, honey, you've lost it.' Jay was looking at me in dismissive disbelief. 'Just write back and say maybe she'd like to supply a shot of herself for next time.'

'I'll have to tell Karen, of course.'

'Tell her what? Some loser with too much time on her hands had a sook about one of your pics? Just reply with a sucky apology and she'll be fine. There are too many freaks in this world to worry about all of them, Hannah.'

She ruffled my hair and walked off.

She was right. I wrote a four-paragraph apology to Jose, then texted Trucker to say that yes, I would like to see that movie with him tonight.

I'd had enough of women today.

'But how funny was the part when she stacked the bike right into his car?'

'Crazy.'

'I loved that guy, that main actor guy, he's the bomb! So funny, man. Yeeeow! Soooo good. Love him.' Trucker smacked his hands on the steering wheel in appreciation.

We were on our way home from a cheap-arse Tuesday-night movie. Models never have money, and so even though the film was half-price, I still had to pay for us both. So much for my rules about making men woo and impress you.

His childish enthusiasm, which I usually liked, was grating on me. I was irritable and wanted to go to bed, so holding a conversation with a five-year-old was proving hard work.

'Your house or mine, baby?'

'Um, maybe not . . . I've got an eight o'clock meeting.'

'Cool, well, I can drive you to it. Easy.'

'No, no, I think I just need to get a good night's sleep.'

'I promise I won't annoy you. I'll be a good boy.' He winked at me lasciviously.

Everything he was doing was normal, but tonight I just wanted to punch him.

'I just want to sleep alone, okay?' I snapped.

He looked at me with a frown, and didn't say anything till he pulled into my driveway.

'Okay, what is your problem?'

'Nothing.'

'Bullshit. Tell me.'

'I'm just tired, and I've got a big week.'

'Well, that didn't stop you last week.'

'Okay, you want to know what my problem is? I'll tell you. I always told you I wasn't looking for a relationship, and now it's like, like . . .' I was lost for words. My nastiness was shocking even to me.

'Um, we're not, like, in a relationship.'

'But you, you always want to stay over, and you invited me to meet your mum and dad . . . And I just thought that was —'

He looked at me with a scowl. 'Get over yourself, Hannah. I just think you're a cool chick and that my parents would think so too.'

I put my tail between my legs. 'Okay, I understand.'

'And you know what, you so don't put in as much as me anyway. I always call you, and text you, and you never, ever contact me, except when you're drunk or toey, or I happen to see you because you're with Kyle and Izzy.'

Ouch.

'I'm not going to argue with that, because you're right. And I'm sorry. You've been so excellent and —'

'Save it, Hannah. Write it in your bloody magazine. I don't want to hear it. I've gotta roll.' He stared ahead, waiting for me to get out.

'I'm sorry.' I didn't know what else to say. 'Goodbye' seemed a bit callous, and anything else seemed futile considering the mood he was in. That I'd put him in.

Walking upstairs, I wondered why I felt so low. I figured it was because what he'd said was right. I never contacted him. I *was* a shithead. I didn't deserve someone as sweet as him.

I texted him three kisses as a kind of goodbye. No response.

Over the next few days, Trucker did not contact me at all, even when I texted him to see how he was, which is the very best way to screw with someone who has hurt you. It was a disturbing reality check about how painful no contact can be, whether you're the dumper or the dumpee. It wasn't like I needed him to reply, or beg to stay friends, but I did think he was being a bit severe. And because he had always been in the palm of my inbox, it was a violent transition.

As it happened, Iz and Kyle were going through a nasty patch just as Trucker and I finished up. This was of great concern to me, because I knew how much she liked him. Even though he was three years younger than her. Even though he worked at a bar when he wasn't modelling German software or Tahitian spring water or organic bloody pet food. Even though he thought showing four centimetres of his brand-name underpants over his jeans was unreal.

They'd had a fight because he'd told her he'd come over to her place after he finished up at a bar, but he still hadn't arrived by the time she left for work at 7 a.m. And he hadn't called or texted to let her know what had happened. She'd tried calling, but he hadn't picked up, which made her very, very anxious. And, by 11 a.m., very, very angry.

When he'd finally called her, at 4 p.m., she had been so irate he could barely get a word in. Turned out he'd ended up going out with his mates and they'd taken some pills and ended up at a day club, and he'd left his phone at work and didn't know her number off by heart.

As *she'd* thought he was dead in a gutter, and was now embarrassed for thinking that, she told him to get fucked and hung up. He called back, told her she was overreacting and carrying on like his mum. She hung up. She called back, told him he was a juvenile and she needed a 'real' man. He hung up. And so on.

We had heard that Kyle and Trucker and the whole catalogue-collective were going around telling everyone we were bitches, old hags, hos, whatever they managed to spit out in a drunken rant at someone's party. I was definitely offended, and thought about texting Trucker to tell him what a little arsehole he was being, but Iz was not only offended, she was hurt. Deeply.

'Han, why would he do something like that? I mean, I get why Trucker would . . .'

I laughed. 'Thanks.'

'You know what I mean. Is Kyle really that much of a child? Dissing me to everyone? Seriously. How dare he?'

I felt so bad for Iz. Kyle was being a little gremlin. I felt like tracking him down and giving it to him, but that would hardly make him race up to Iz with foliage and apologies. If only I hadn't ended things so badly with Trucker, we could've masterminded The Great Romantic Comeback.

I decided the hurt had to end. Iz had to tell Kyle how she was feeling – after all, she wasn't into communication starvation like I was. If she was upset, it was in her nature to simply call a guy and tell him her feelings.

'Why not call him, Iz? Get it all out?'

So she did. And gave it to him. But then she accidentally cried. And he came over. And apologised. And promised never to fight again. And they 'made up'. All night.

I couldn't help but miss Trucker a little when I saw Kyle and Iz all happy and together again the following weekend. Or, rather, my ego missed him. But I knew finishing it had been the right thing to do. Even if I had felt a little lonely for the last few weeks. And all that loneliness made me think of Jesse, because I still had reserve loneliness left over from him.

I wondered if he and Lisa were choosing engagement rings yet.

11.

Send/Receive, Send/Receive

Too busy to get your roots done? Try one of the ten-minute touch-up products. Or apply a colour refresher. Or switch your part. Or do a teased quiff and ponytail. Or just don't dye your hair.

For the first time since starting at *Gloss*, things had slowed down. My usual crazy stream had stemmed to a paltry trickle. All at once, the cosmetic companies eased up on PR activities, which meant no functions. And no busy. Just as I craved frantic, extreme busyness as a substitute for Trucker, who'd distracted me from thoughts of Jesse, the universe stripped me of it. Being stuck at my desk all day – rare, near unheard of – meant I got lots of work done. And could leave at 6 p.m. Which was great. Except that *I hated it.*

I missed my regular routine. I was used to, say, a natural skincare launch at 8.30 a.m., complete with soy smoothies, bio-dynamic eggs, a yoga class and free iridology consultations, followed by a 12.30 lunch with a PR to talk about their new tanning range, then a 2.30 two-hour boardroom meeting with Karen and Marley, and, to finish, a 6 p.m. cocktail function in a hotel lobby with every hairdresser in the metropolitan district. It was loopy but, just like the strange rash I'd contracted from a cheap dry-body oil a few weeks back, I was used to it now.

Not having stuff on made me all clingy and strange. I forwarded stupid clips from YouTube, changed my Facebook profile picture incessantly and wrote inconsequential ramblings on Iz's wall; I Googlestalked Bailey Thomas, my high-school sweetheart, but mostly I found myself hitting the Send/Receive button above my email inbox.

It wasn't just me. Yasmin was cranking out the emails too. We both had work to do, but we were bored. *So bored*. We were used to fragmented office time, screaming out of hallways and impatiently jabbing lift buttons, redoing our makeup four times a day, stomping in contempt when a taxi failed to stop for us.

Ding.

To: Hannah@gloss.com

From: Louisa@frenzypr.com

Subject: Free offer from Dr Kalward

Hi Hannah,

Dr Kalward, one of the country's top cosmetic surgeons, would like to extend to you the offer of one free Botox session. He believes the best way to be able to write about the procedure is to experience it. Of course, he is happy to give extensive quotes for your ensuing piece.

The offer is only available until the end of the month, so get in fast!

Lx

I touched my forehead. Was it so frowny that they thought I needed Botox? I grabbed my mirror and peered at my skin, making faces to accentuate the lines. Surely I wasn't at the Botox stage yet? I looked at my face again, pulling my skin back to test for elasticity. Seemed fine to me. But was I silly to knock them back? After all, I knew how expensive Botox was.

I shook my head, tsk-tsking. I wasn't going to be sucked into an expensive obsession out of insecurity caused by a PR desperate for a story. I was shocked at how vulnerable I had become. If someone had offered me Botox a few months back, I would've burst out laughing.

Out of nowhere I suddenly wished I had Dec's email. Not to use it, necessarily, but just to have it. In fact, scrap that – I wished he had *mine*, so he could send me a quick-fire shot of his elegant humour and cheekiness. He had a way of making me see the forest for the trees, or rather the forehead for the frowns. I smiled, thinking of his kiss a few months back. Why had he done that? And why then? He had probably just been drunk. Or *maybe* he was not as perfect as I painted him to be; maybe he was a sleazy little octopus who loved nothing more than locking nubile nymphs in candlelit bathrooms under the guise of 'helping'.

I shuddered at the thought. No, that wasn't Dec. I knew he wasn't like that. He was the Nice Guy. He was definitely the Nice Guy, I was just over-thinking the situation. I sent a text to Iz to break the train of thought.

Drink tonight? Please say yes. I'll bring you some new makeup?

Ha! Bring it! Can do Randys @ 630 x

Finally, I had something I could look forward to. I didn't love the Randy Panther, which was smack bang in the city's hobo-chic ghetto, but I would've drunk from a puddle to have a plan that night.

By the time I arrived at the Randy Panther, which should've been renamed the Drowned Kitty for the evening, I was in a foul mood: it was raining, there had been no cabs and I'd had to walk three blocks in uncomfortable – and now ruined – suede heels. My hair was flat and greasy-looking and I was sure my mascara had run. I stomped to the bathroom to quickly fix myself up.

Walking out of the bathroom, I looked up to see Jesse. *Fuck!* What was Mr Boat Shoes doing in a grotty bar like the Panther? I panicked: my top was clinging to my stomach in a most unflattering fashion, and my quickly-tied-back hair, now happily having made the transition from soaking to frizzy, was about as chic as the brown stained carpet under my feet. And why, *why* had I not reapplied my bronzer and blush in the bathroom? This was all just *awesome*. Thank you, Universe.

I wondered if I could quickly duck behind the group of loud artistic types to my right. No dice. Jesse saw me, and his face immediately broke into a big grin. My expression was more like that of a teenager busted shoplifting. He came over and went to kiss me on the cheek, but I pulled away so he kind of grazed my chin instead.

'Hannah! How are you? I've been meaning to call —'

Jesus! It was all so awkward.

'Don't, Jesse. Just don't.' My voice shook a little bit, but I tried to remain strong. I was *supposed* to be acting agonisingly indifferent. I was irritated that I was having such a stupid reaction to him, when in all my revenge daydreams I was ice-cool when faced with his blue eyes and blond, floppy mop.

He dropped his eyes and took a deep breath before looking at me again.

'I'm so sorry that things turned out this way . . .'

'*Don't.*' I could feel tears rising.

'So!' he said in falsetto. 'How is the job?' Sensing I was about to bolt, he was trying to normalise the situation by babbling.

'Oh, you know, it's okay . . . keeps me busy.' Insert fake smile.

'So, I've, ah, I've been pretty flat out, you know, travelling and stuff for work . . . just got back from overseas, actually.'

'Really? How nice.' Clearly he was gagging for me to ask about his job, but I was not going to give him the satisfaction of showing I was interested at all, even though every hair follicle and pore on my person was screaming, 'How's your new girlfriend *Lisa*? Are you happy with *Lisa*? Is *Lisa* good in bed? Does *Lisa* cook French toast as well I do? Can she reverse park as well as I can? Does *Lisa's* breath smell when she wakes up in bed next to you in the morning, or is she just one ongoing, flowery-smelling fairy princess who you would never, ever cheat on?

I could suddenly hear, feel, *smell* the hurt and rage bubbling within me. I needed to get far away from him. *Now.*

'So, are you seeing anyone?'

He came out with it just like that. As if he were asking if I had seen the new Pixar movie.

What the hell are you supposed to say when your ex asks you that? 'Yes' would make me sound as though I had moved on, and although that *could* work by making him jealous, it was a big risk to take if he was at all interested in trying again . . . while 'no' made me sound like a loser who couldn't get a date. I knew the fundamentals, at least: always ensure the ex-boyfriend thinks you are having far more sex than he is.

'Actually, I've been doing a bit of multi-dating.'

Ohmigod. What did I just *say*? I had *no* idea where that had come from.

Jesse's eyebrows shot up. Fast.

'Multi-dating?'

Can't back down now. 'Sure. Everyone's doing it. And, you know, as long as you don't sleep with any of them, it's totally kosher.' I nodded for extra sincerity and authority.

Jesse's eyebrows still hadn't come down.

I cleared my throat.

There was an excruciatingly loud silence.

I needed to leave. Terrible things were streaming out of my mouth without my permission.

'Uh, well, I should go.' I smiled with my lips closed and eyebrows up and swivelled away quickly.

Yes! I secretly cheered, at least I had salvaged the farewell. It was crucial to end any conversation first, so you appeared busier than him. Hopefully, Jesse would now be wondering if I was here with a guy. Or five. *As long as he didn't see Iz.*

Just as I had spied a table in the far corner where I could hide and wait for Iz, I looked up to see her walking through the door. Thank *God*.

'HE'S HERE,' I said through clenched teeth, as soon as she was in hearing distance. 'I just spoke to him. I need you to find out who he's here with, except I'm meant to be here with a harem of young sexy men, so be subtle for chrissakes.'

'Slow down, honey, *who* is here? Trucker? I thought Kyle said he'd moved to Milan for work?' She took off her jacket and placed it on the back of the chair, then tousled her wet hair.

'JESSE. *Jesse* is here. I need you to see if he's with Lisa Sutherland. *Now*. Please?'

'Oooooh,' she said, drawing it out to show she now understood perfectly. She started looking around furtively before stalking away.

Three excruciating minutes and 67 million possible-outcome thoughts later, and she was back.

'He's not with her,' she said, settling into her chair.

'Oh thank God.' My heart soared.

'But he is with another bird . . . butdon'tworry, I didn't see any body contact and she literally looks as though she might be seventeen years old.'

My heart sank. Swear words swirled around my head. Jesus. Didn't take him long to move on, jumping from one pretty thing to another as though he were some form of hyperactive-mating tree frog.

'Honey, that she's seventeen is *good*. It means she's just a toy.'

'He's disgusting. I hate him.' I folded my arms and glared in his general direction.

'Do you want to go?' Iz could see how pissed off I was.

'Can we? Sorry, Iz. I'm not really in the mood . . .'

Sitting in the taxi, I fell completely mute. Once again it felt like Jesse had won. And what did it matter if I'd said I was multi-dating? It didn't, since he was the one actually doing it.

12.

The Bitchy and Scratchy Show

Fake tan on your fingernails? Get some whitening toothpaste and an old toothbrush and scrub those digits. Fake tan on your sheets? Stick to dark-blue or chocolate linen.

'I always harboured a desire to be one of those girls who sashays in and out of buildings and elegantly hails cabs, all the while looking glamorous and composed and New Yorky,' I said wistfully, as Gabe swiped some of the fruit from the top of my muesli. We were having a quick pre-work breakfast at Doppio, and, as always, Gabe had under-ordered because he was on a diet. He then, as always, thieved half of mine.

'You have a way to go yet, darling. I've seen you: you claw your way out of the back seat like a Michael Jackson *Thriller* extra exiting a grave. It's not right, sweetie: you're flashing areas of the thigh no one needs to see. Honestly.'

'I *do not*.'

'Darling – oh look, you've spilled some food on your top for something different – you know you do. It's simple: keep the stilts snapped shut. That way you can't flash any of the nasty stuff.'

I told him I would try, and the topic was closed. He was very fixed on improving my decorum – he called it Mission Elegant

Bitch. He thought my small-town idiosyncrasies were vulgar, and needed desperate, urgent chic-ifying. 'In fact,' he would say, 'and this is something I'll probably sell as a thesis one day to finance a beach house, I'm pretty convinced that one's elegance is directly proportionate to how much time one spends with a stylish gay man. Obviously, this means you should up your time spent with me. A lot. Now, don't dwell on the astounding complexity of that philosophy; just know that it's pretty much, totally, 100 per cent, probably, a fact.'

He liked to bait me by saying my becoming an Elegant Bitch would be the clincher to Jesse's decision that he couldn't live without me. Even though Gabe made it no secret he thought I should move on and find a man with 'more money, more style and less inclination toward loose weather tarts'.

I listened to him because he was tough on me, whereas Iz wasn't. She sympathised; Gabe chastised. And also because he was so stylish and commanding and knew all the fashion people. Even though this morning's pirate-style frilly blouse was a bit hard to take.

'For fuck's *sake*, can someone gag and bind those silly cows?' Gabe swivelled his head to look at two squealy, giggly women standing near the barista.

'Oh shit, it's Jill —'

'It is, too. Bloody creature. She's so wrong. And look at that bag – honey, if you're gonna buy the fake Chanel, at least get it in a colour Karl Lagerfeld wouldn't be embarrassed to be in the same galaxy as. Honestly, I don't know how you lot meet your deadlines, you must be so flat out lapping up saucers of milk and sharpening your claws.'

'It's not like that, Gabe. I just don't get a good vibe from Jill, is all.'

'Oh, stop the cover-up. You're rubbish at it. I know exactly what beauty editors are like: it's the bitchy and scratchy show behind all that lip gloss and hairspray.' He leaned over and stole a sip of my latte, because he had already had two of his own and knew he couldn't have three during one sitting, because that would be uncouth.

Gabe wasn't alone in thinking that of beauty editors; everyone asked me if the girls were catty and cliquey. It stemmed from that universal belief that the bowels of any women's glossy were rife with the kind of petulant backstabbing that would make a Vegas showgirl blush.

'I disagree, actually. For every blunt-fringed, black-clad fashion editor stomping on a trembling intern's foot, there is a beauty editor with big bouncy curls and a floral frock singing about sunshine and flowers and handing out cupcakes.'

He laughed. 'That's a stereotype and you know it – fashion editors don't *all* have blunt fringes.'

When I got to my desk an abnormal number of courier bags and parcels awaited me. They were lined up and piled neatly, but still entirely overwhelming. I had completely forgotten I'd done my beauty call-in yesterday afternoon.

The monthly beauty call-in was a major event for me. It was what I did after planning my beauty pages, when I had decided (or made up) what the trends were for that month.

Yesterday I had asked for comfort crèmes, face washes to clear up spots, tuberose-based fragrances, sea-salt sprays, coral-coloured lipsticks and some blushes. I had put all of my requests into a group email to every brand's PR. They then started sending in samples at the speed of lightning.

I needed to set aside a full day to test and sort through all the suggestions, and put aside those I wanted to photograph and write about. Things like price, how the product would come up on the page, and whether an eyeliner was the perfect shade of aqua (as per the latest Miu Miu ready-to-wear) were crucial. I always had to double or triple edit the list before I hit send. If I didn't ask for the right things, it would be too late to ask for more, because my shoot day closely followed my call-in.

On top of that, I had to factor in all of the really big cosmetic launches for the on-sale period of each issue of *Gloss*. This was always confusing because we worked three months ahead, and by the time the mag was on sale, the products for that month were old news to me. But missing them meant I could potentially get into lots of trouble indeed.

Last month I had completely forgotten to mention the new Karen Jones mascara. It was their biggest launch for the year, as well, they were the first company to market mascara with a special silicon comb-wand thingy, *and* they had booked all of their advertising for said mascara in said issue. I got slammed by Marley, the psychotic media-agency girl Lindsay, and, in the nicest, as-inoffensive-as-possible way, the PR girl, Jane.

'We were really disappointed to see that Flexilash didn't receive any mentions in the current issue, especially considering how important a launch this was for us,' said Jane in a scary passive-aggressive email. Lesson well and truly learned: Fleixlash to receive many adoring words and a large, beautiful picture in the next issue.

I took off my heels, slipped on the ballet slippers I kept under my desk for schlepping around the office, and started opening the boxes, wondering if anyone had understood what on Earth I had meant when I'd requested 'non-bronzer, slightly shimmery peach and apricot shades of powder – not crème – blush'.

13.

The barefoot fugitive

Crusty, dry feet will turn off even the creepiest foot fetishist. Use a pumice stone or a pedi-paddle on heels and rough spots on dry feet, wash, then apply a thick moisturing balm. Put on some cotton socks and hit the hay. Twenty-four hours later, do the same. Repeat seven times. Enjoy soft feet.

I had sworn off dates and flirting and men in general. I was now all about me: getting myself together and focusing on being happy. My newfound mantra had come from a book called *He Ain't Thinking 'Bout* You, *Suga'*, which encouraged women to stop placing so much emphasis on men and relationships.

And, as always happens, the minute you stop looking . . .

Dan was one of those guys who when he walked into a party, roughly four hours after everyone else, women turned to their single friends and hissed: 'Dibs! Right, who else do I have to tell?'

Well, that's how I felt, anyway, when he walked into Yasmin's house-warming party.

Dan just radiated . . . *something*. Insouciance blended with a dash of confidence, most likely. But he wasn't overcompensating the way super-hot or super-wealthy dudes do. He was well-dressed, in unbranded jeans and a dark T-shirt, and he reminded me of that actor from *The Motorcycle Diaries*. He had fluffy long hair, which was endearing in a fashion-ignorant way.

Dan must not have sensed how predatory I was feeling, because he kept smiling in my direction. I decided to strike. Breaking several of my hardcore-bitch rules en route:

I *sauntered over to him.* (Violation of Rule No. 34)

I *initiated the conversation.* (Violation of Rule No. 56)

'So. You're that famous guy, huh?' It was a line Jacinta had put into her latest 'How to Find a Good Guy' article. I'd been dying to try it. The fact that I had my Boozy the Clown shoes on helped. Right now I was the funniest, sauciest girl in the world; irresistable pick-up lines fell from my mouth with ease and perfect timing.

'Um . . . I don't think so. But I can be, if it helps?'

Perfect.

'No, no, being common is nothing to be ashamed of. I'm Hannah, by the way. Totally common Hannah.'

He smiled. 'Dan. But you can call me Famous Guy.'

'Accent, huh? That's not very common.' As I rearranged my hands, I nicked the tip of my glass. Wine splashed all over my top.

Dan tried not to smile as he watched me frantically blot it.

'So, now that I've proved that I'm definitely common . . .'

'I'm from LA,' he said, pouring more wine into my glass.

'So you're trying to be famous?'

'Nah, who needs fame when you're already a multi-millionaire?'

Oh, he was good. I laughed and sipped my drink.

After an hour of flirty getting-to-know-you talk, I discovered that Dan was a property developer-slash-real-estate agent-slash-crazy entrepreneur who was about to become obscenely rich. He worked with his brother selling ridiculously expensive property for people with too much money and not enough time; he'd then reinvest their money into commercial developments that would make the clients far more money, because even though they didn't actually need the extra cash, they enjoyed having it all the same. I also learnt that Dan never finished high school, that he hated bananas because their consistency reminded him of snot, and that he wanted desperately to own a python. I found all of this fascinating, especially as I'd been known to eat up to three bananas a day. But eventually I grew bored of the usual platitudes and began speaking with *lascivious intonation.* (Violation of Rule No. 98)

According to Iz, who swore she saw the whole shonky honeytrap assembled, and who tried in vain to hold back snorts of laughter as she retold the story the next day, I *winked at him* before going to *get him a drink.* (Violation of Rule Nos. 23 and 45)

But it worked. We moved to the sofa and kept talking while the party wound down around us. I have no idea what about, but he was very funny and clever and knew lots of things about lots of things. I suspect I was terribly engaging and witty too, as he seemed to enjoy himself. Or else he was drunk.

In any case, when he stood up and asked if he could walk me home, I happily accepted.

On the street I took off my shoes, which I *never* did, but they were new and absolutely killing me.

'I never do this, I swear. I have never been the tramp with her shoes off at the end of the night.'

'Actions speak louder than —' I threw a shoe at him.

Once we reached my door, I turned and smiled at him. '*So* . . . this is where it gets awkwa—'

He swooped in and kissed me.

We stood there and kissed. We fell against the wall. I gripped the back of his head, and then he moved his hands up under my dress to squeeze my bum. My brain was screaming 'TAKE HIM UPSTAIRS,' but, immediately after, my conscience piped up with, '*No!* You mustn't! You've just met him!' I felt daring, as though I was being offered an opportunity that would only come along every so often, where I could be wild and crazy and throw caution to the midnight breeze, and *live*, just for a few wild hours. Then I thought of my rules. Nuts.

'What happens now?' Dan mumbled, as he kissed my chest and I arched my back to let him.

'You say goodbye and I go upstairs . . .' I said slowly, reluctantly.

'Alone?'

'Yesss, alone . . .' I hated what was coming out of my mouth. I so, so wanted him to come upstairs. It had to be a clean break or I would never go.

'OkayI'mgoingnow!'

I broke free of his grip, turned my key in the lock and jumped through the door of my apartment-block foyer. I turned to face Dan before closing it. His hair was everywhere and his face was flushed. His eyes were disbelieving.

'You cheeky little monkey,' he said with a smile, straightening up his jeans. 'I'll get you, don't you worry.' He started walking backwards.

'We'll see . . .' I replied, smiling, as I closed the door.

I looked at my reflection in the lift. My hair and makeup would frighten the elderly and my smile suggested marijuana use. I glanced at my phone. Ah yes, the very respectable time of 4.34 a.m. Thank God it was Sunday.

Once in my bedroom, I removed my makeup with the facial wipes I kept in my bedside drawer for late, lazy nights, and fell into bed, the goofy, gooey smile refusing to leave my face. I hadn't felt a glow like this for a long time. There was a quiet, urgent voice bubbling away in the back of my head, whispering caution about getting hurt again, but I chose to ignore it.

At around 11 a.m. Iz came around and we cooked up bacon

and eggs and laughed at how ill the other looked. She was wearing a frilly summer dress over jeans, with ballet slippers, a scarf, large hoops and sunglasses on her head. None of it matched.

'You look like shit.'

'You look *worse*. Thought you beauty editors told us not to go to bed wearing slap.'

'I took it off! This is just . . . leftovers.'

She laughed and I sighed dramatically. I felt like hell.

'So, do you think Dan will call?'

I hoped so. I'd already checked my phone three times. 'Not sure. I'm pretty sure I gave him my number, but who knows? And anyway, he could be a total flake.'

'Doubt it. He spent all night with you. And you didn't sleep with him. He'll call,' she said knowingly.

'Well, we'll see. Joowanna see a movie?'

She looked at me for a second before answering. 'I'm supposed to work on a new menu, but yeah. Screw it. Let's go.'

Once we got into the movie, a silly romantic comedy, Iz promptly fell asleep, while I ate my body weight in cold salty popcorn. When we walked out, Iz went into the bathroom and I checked my phone. Two missed calls from a private number. I listened to the voicemail.

It was *him*. Dan had called, asking to see me that night.

I hung up with a whopping big grin. There was a small envelope still on my phone; I checked my inbox. There was a text from a number that I didn't recognise.

Girl with no shoes reported on Carlot St at approx. 4 a.m. Please call back if you have any details about this barefooted fugitive.

Oh, he was funny. And cute. And *wanted to see me tonight*. Iz had come back from the loo looking one drip of morphine off comatose.

I grabbed her hands and squealed, 'He called, he called, and he wants to see me tonight!'

She immediately came to life. 'Oooooh! Honey! Look at you! You're all excited!'

'But I can't see him tonight – no way, that's too keen. You know my rules: three days till tickets to the second show are available.'

'Oh for God's sake, Han. Cut it out. Be human for once and see the poor guy. Didn't you say he was going back to LA soon? To sell Donald Trump's beach house or whatever? Live a little!'

'How do you expect men to value your time if you drop everything to see them at a few hours' notice? You might as well have a flashing neon sign saying: "I have no life."'

'Right. And which plans, exactly, would you be dropping for him?'

I sighed, exasperated. 'Not the point. It's about making them wait for you, pine for you, get excited about seeing you again.'

'You're insane. You sound like a Fifties housewife. See the boy or miss out on what could have been excellent. Regret what you do, not what you don't – isn't that what you used to say?'

'I've changed, baby.'

'For the worse. I know Jesse screwed you over, but that doesn't mean every guy is out to hurt you. Text him and say yes.'

'God, *someone* needs some sleep.'

'I won't argue with that. But my point still stands.'

As we drove home, I struggled with what to do. Seeing him tonight really would be going against all my rules. But then, I'd already broken most of them last night . . .

'All right. I'll *go*,' I said, leaning my head back on the passenger seat and sighing dramatically.

'Course you will. Good girl,' Iz said with a smug smile.

Now I just had to text him. And it had to be good.

I have heard of this creature. She drinks too much and does inappropriate things with boys she does not even know. She must be locked up immediately.

I hit send and waited nervously. What if he didn't respond? Twenty minutes went by. Nothing. I took it out on Iz. 'See, this is why I've sworn off men. They are torture. They do my head i—'

The magical two beeps chimed in.

I will send squad car five at nineteen hundred hours to collect her. Try your best to keep her sedated till then, as it is very very very important we capture her tonight. VERY. Very.

He was winning. I melted more and more each time I reread his text. How could I possibly rebuff? He was practically telling me he wanted to father my children.

Refer to said alcohol consumption: if she were any more sedated, she would be comatose. Make sure officers wear full uniform. In one size too small.

I wasn't anxious as I got ready – the *one* upside to a hangover is the numbing of nerves – and when seven hit, Dan called to say he was outside. I was impressed with his punctuality. I was impressed with everything he did. Kisses especially . . .

I strutted outside like I did this kind of thing all the time. I was dressed in what Iz deemed to be a no-fail date outfit: jeans that made me look skinny (as opposed to my skinny jeans, which made me look fat), saucy tan heels that made my coral toenails look like yummy little lollies, and a white singlet filled with chicken fillets and a push-up bra, which would serve to remind him that I was the proprietor of mammary glands.

He looked me up and down from his driver's seat. The car was a Hertz hire car, a dull white family sedan. 'Service car, babe. Ferrari's getting some work.' He winked and nodded sleazily.

I laughed.

'You look fresh, so fresh!' he said with zest.

I liked him even more. 'Fresh' is one of the highest compliments you can offer a woman. I jumped in, and he kissed me on the cheek. Then on the mouth. I giggled like a schoolgirl. He looked hot, in that same devil-may-care, I-didn't-put-in-any-effort way. He was wearing a blue grandpa-style top, checked golf pants and fruity pink-and-yellow Adidas trainers, which he caught me gawking at.

He had style. His *own* style. Jesse always wore the same thing: jeans and a polo shirt.

After a few ridiculous exchanges about the monster with no shoes escaping once more to terrorise the neighbourhood, we arrived at a posh pub near the house Dan was staying in. Once inside, he took charge, ordering two glasses of a lovely red wine, salami-swamped antipasto and some salt-and-pepper squid.

'And what if I were vegetarian?' God, I was being so *flirty.*

'Ah, but you're not, because I saw you eating that sausage sandwich earlier this morning. At roughly 2 a.m., if memory serves.'

He remembered me hoeing into a late-night booze meal. This could be love.

'You've got me there.'

'You say this with surprise? Hannah, you're not giving me enough credit.'

Who was this man? He was too good, too smooth. I wondered how many dates he must have been on, and how many women he must have bedded with these very same moves. It was probably in the hundreds. But, right then, I didn't care. And so I flirted, and he flirted, and we were both clever and quick-witted, despite our hangovers, and it was dreamy.

'So, why are you here again? Not that I wasn't completely listening last night, of course . . .'

'I'm looking at a development down on the river that's about to be built. A lot of people back home are keen to invest here, because it's a growth area and the tax is a joke for foreigners, and also because the girls here are supposed to be really loose.'

'They are, are they?' I smiled cheekily, internally amused that I could quite possibly be about to prove his joke to be correct.

'The shoeless, sausage-sandwich-eating ones are supposed to be the loosest.'

I giggled and blushed. I'd never been with a guy who was so flirtatious, funny and sexy all at once. I was used to the three being exclusive.

After he told me a story about a malevolent squirrel, an overweight neighbour and his front doormat, which had me crying with laughter, I decided to buck all of the rules. I wanted to see him every day for the rest of his time here.

Which, at the end of the date, after a delicious goodnight kiss that involved wandering hands and gentle moans, I found out was only 11.3 days.

Thank God Iz had made me go out tonight.

14.

If you expect sex, you won't get it

Can't master dark-coloured polish? The rules: nails filed short and neat. Cuticles pushed back. Stop the polish three millimetres above the cuticle to avoid an uneven, sloppy finish. No coffee before attempting application.

'Because he is sexy. And leaving the country forever. And because I have decided to stop being so prim and dull, and start being the girl everyone expects you to be if you're single and you work for *Gloss* magazine.'

Iz looked at me with a surprised smile. Then she cocked her head and grinned. 'No explainers or disclaimers required, baby. I am beyond stoked that you have a fully fledged holiday fling going on. In your own hometown. And that you've stopped those silly rules, too.'

I wasn't sure why I had worried about what Iz would think. Maybe I was now so used to the idea of being tough on guys that I was anxious Iz would think that it had all been a façade, and the real me, the weak girl who fell for boys after one walk home and a date, had fallen so hard she had bruises.

'I've gotta be at work in ten minutes, but I'm *very* happy for you, and I don't want to even have the discussion about whether you should sleep with him tonight, because there is only one answer and it starts and ends with YES.'

An hour later I was heavily glossed and smoky-eyed and sitting across from Dan at a café frequented by people who liked to wear black and talk loudly about films and galleries. We were here because next door was an art-house cinema and we were off to a movie Dan had been dying to see. Which was about an Amazonian tribe and an ancient cursed canoe. Apparently.

As I sat across from him, wondering if he used product in his hair or if it just naturally went like that, and what our children might look like, I realised that Dan was everything Jesse was not. He spoke with fervour about worldly things, was well-travelled, liked to cook, and was a brilliant surfer. He was an 'active' guy, whereas Jesse was a 'papers and coffee' guy. And, as any women's glossy magazine will tell you, such a contrast to one's ex is like kerosene to a freshly heartbroken girl's flame.

Dan ate his mussel linguine, twirling it like a pro, as he talked about his impending snowboarding trip to Osaka. I started to speculate on whether I would in fact sleep with him later that night. The thought made me very nervous. He seemed so confident, so sure of himself. What if I were no good? Or he was too good? Or he expected a head job? The more I thought about it, the more terrified I became. The solution was simple: I would have to get raucously drunk. I gulped down the remainder of my red wine.

Iz had been concerned nothing would happen because I had performed not one but *two* fateful acts of sexpectation: getting a Brazilian wax and cleaning my room. I knew the immutable law that if you expect sex, you won't get it. Whereas if your room is a pigsty and you are wearing your nastiest, oldest undies, you'll get lucky for sure.

I had to stop thinking about it; it was too much pressure. I was even biting my nails, which, as a beauty editor, was a very bad thing indeed. Especially as I was wearing red polish. You can always tell when a woman is getting some: she'll have red nails. I was a case in point: the day after meeting Dan I applied a fire-engine red polish to my fingernails and *I never wore red.* Pink was as dark as I got. But now, since meeting Dan, I wanted red this and red that. Red lips, red dresses, red shoes. It was bizarre.

I stood out with my red talons – every other beauty editor wore OPI's Bubble Bath. 'It is easy to apply and maintain,' I'd written in *Gloss* a few issues back, 'and can be done at your desk three minutes before you race out the door!'

'Hannah? Are you listening?'

'Hmm? Oh, yes. Sorry. What were you saying?'

'Never mind. Hey, I like your dress. Your style is very LA, you know. Cool LA,' he corrected himself. 'West Hollywood LA. Not Beverly Kills LA.'

'Um . . . thanks. Don't they all wear velour tracksuits there?'

'Not in my hood. It's a velour-free zone. And you're colourful, I like that you wear colour.'

I looked down. I was wearing a red-and-white polka-dot shirt-dress, and black peep-toe patent pumps. It was another no-fail outfit: sexy but pretty, the kind that was perfect for a midweek after-work date, because it was great for daytime functions but held its own at a restaurant, too. With an extra button undone, of course. Hussy. I smiled coyly and took another enormous gulp of wine. I needed liquid courage. Lots of liquid courage. I realised, looking at his olive skin and watching him animatedly tell a story about the house he was staying in, that I didn't want to see a movie. I wanted to talk and kiss in his car.

'Do you want to skip the movie and go get a cocktail up the road?'

I smiled in shock; it was as though he'd read my mind. Shit balls. What else had he seen while he was poking around in there? I got all nervous about sex again. But then, if we were going for cocktails, my get-drunk plan would work beautifully.

'Are you sure? I know how much you want to see the movie . . .'

'Bah, let's go get high on sugared-up rum and lime. I'll get the bill.'

'Thank you, Dan. That'd be nice.' I grinned like a fool. He smiled back and his dimples pricked his cheeks in the way that had made me think of his face all day during work.

'I'll be right back.' I grabbed my bag from the back of my chair and headed to the bathroom, trying to walk in a sexy way. I touched up my concealer and gloss and added some more crème blush to disguise the fact I'd been up since 6.30 a.m. My phone beeped as I was applying it. I checked the message. It was from Dan.

I want to take your dress off, Minnie Mouse.

Sexpectation nothin'. I was *very* glad I'd had that wax.

15.

Perfect-breasted imps

Enhance those tatas by applying a line of shimmer or illuminator to your cleavage, following your bra-line along each breast. This will create the illusion that you have a fuller cup than you actually do. Or, that you have a great surgeon.

Fiona took a deep breath. She was sitting in the back seat of a taxi with Yasmin, telling A Story. I was sitting in the front and so had to keep stretching my neck back to listen.

Yasmin had become quite close to Fiona lately, and Fiona now accompanied us to functions most of the time. I'd got over being scared of her, but I was still shy around her, because, well, she was still kind of indifferent to my existence.

But Fiona was a terrific, dominating storyteller. My role was simply to listen and offer terrifically encouraging eyebrow movements. She relayed stories with wild gesticulation and deliberate pauses and dramatic hair flicks. She wore her singledom like some form of glorious evening gown, and was always dating lots of inappropriate men. She had such a number of boy tales she had to give all her men nicknames so we could keep track of them. These were attributed according to appearance (Bad-Hair Boy), stand-out traits/incidents (Tongue Guy/Married Man) or job (Vet).

'So, like, Tight Shirt and I are sitting on the couch, and I'm completely sober, because I'm on antibiotics for my ear infection, and all of a sudden he starts kissing me.'

'Is Tight Shirt "Gappy Teeth"?' Yasmin asked, texting furiously as usual, but still listening in.

'No, Gappy Teeth had left the party – remember, he had tried to kiss me goodbye while he was holding Midriff Girl's hand? Tight Shirt is the unemployed guy with the Diet Coke body and the stubble.'

'That's right, sorry. Keep going.'

'So, we're kissing and he's gorgeous, right, but all these thoughts race through my mind: "I haven't waxed; I haven't fake-tanned; what if someone walks in —"'

'Ohmigod. I smell threesome,' Yasmin said.

For beauty girls, taxis were the arena for the most salacious talk, as though we were in some form of secrecy bubble and the person driving were deaf or invisible.

I kept nodding encouragingly at Fiona as she described her dramatic brush with a sexual sandwich, but my mind wandered. Today's function was bound to thieve at least two hours, and when I was going to finish writing my very-due beauty feature – 'The Lazy Girl's Guide to Glowing Skin' – I had no idea. With precious few days till Dan left, I was not at all interested in staying back at work. Plus, this evening we were going to a new Spanish tapas place that was supposed to be brilliant. Suddenly I was beside myself with excitement. And not about the chorizo.

My buzz lasted around twelve seconds.

'So, Hannah, I saw your ex yesterday,' said Fiona casually, as if she were commenting on the state of the traffic. Seems I was to be included in the taxi talk today, after all.

'Mm-hmm,' I said, feigning a nonchalance that *I* thought was convincing.

'He was with one of the Taylor sisters. Not sure which, all three are so tall and gorgeous and insipid,' Fi continued, throwing out more worms.

I was refusing to bite, but Yasmin was ready for a nibble: 'Aren't they those lingerie-model sisters?'

'Don't know if they all are; I think the youngest one is just bikinis actually. We shot her last month for our denim issue. She ordered a platter of raw vegetables then proceeded to drink four coffees and smoke a deck of Marlboro lights instead,' Fiona said with relish. We all *loved* to hear about what the models ate, or didn't, on a shoot.

'Well, that's flattering to you, isn't it, Han? I mean, think of Jennifer post-Brad: if you were gonna get dumped for anyone, you'd want it to be Angelina, right? Or a bikini model, in this case.' Yasmin was trying to salvage the situation. Poorly.

I was aware both girls were waiting for my reaction. But I didn't quite know what to do.

'Anyway, Fi, what makes you think they're dating? Maybe they're just doing a TV show together. Or plotting a new route for NASA to get to Mars.' Yasmin was now trying to diffuse things with a paltry attempt at humour.

'I didn't say they're dating, I just said I *saw* them together.'

Yasmin exhaled dramatically. 'Actually, and Han, baby, you know I'm on your side, we all are . . . But, Phoebe, my fashion editor, said word is they *are* dating. We shot the girl last week and apparently she spent the whole time she was getting her makeup done talking about Jesse.'

My heart sank.

'I'm sorry, but Phoebe's so full of shit.' Was Fiona now trying to play Switzerland? These girls were switching from good cop to bad with such speed that I was getting confused about who to hate more.

'Yeah, okay, usually she is, but why would she make this up?'

'Yeah, well, maybe you should stop now anyway. I'm sure Hannah doesn't want to hear any more . . .' Fiona had noticed the conversation had become a little too heavy, and, despite her having triggered it, was now trying to backpedal.

And all the while, I couldn't say a thing.

'No, shut up, Fi. I know Hannah better than you, and she knows I'm not doing this to hurt her, I'm doing it to help her. Han, I'm only telling you this so that you don't hear it from someone else. And so you can feel safe knowing he is still clearly going through his compulsory sleep-around-with-every-dumb-pretty-slut-available phase, which he'll inevitably get over.'

That was enough for me. 'Driver, can you pull over please?'

I needed to get out. I needed to be away from these creatures, these bitches who pretended they were doing the right thing by me, when really my life was just another arrow in their gossip bow.

'*Yasmin!*' Fi was desperately trying to hold on to her slipping halo. 'Hannah, honey, stay in the car. It's finished now.'

'I'm fine. I'd just rather walk.'

'Excuse me, holy fuckin' one, but it was you who brought this whole thing up,' exploded Yasmin. '*Hannah.* I'm not trying to fuck with you. You know that. I only say this because I'm trying to protect you. It's what decent friends do.'

We pulled up to a red light. I grabbed my bag and opened the door.

'Yeah, well, strange version of friendship you've got,' I said, and slammed the door.

In a matter of minutes I had changed from excitable honeymooner to an angry, angry person. I had not needed that information. It surprised me how upset I was, because I was so consumed with Dan, but I was pissed at the news Jesse was with yet another perfect-breasted imp.

But I'd be fine. I was fine, fine, fine, fucking fine. Stomp, stomp, stomp, search for invite to check address, stomp, stomp, go in door, wipe tears, take deep breath, smile, see PR, kiss on the cheek, overcompensate with cheerfulness and sound like on speed, relax, remember comments in cab, seethe, seethe, sip, smile, shudder, feel lump in throat rising, excuse self, walk to toilet, slam door, sit, sigh, sniff, sob, shake head at self, sniff, sigh, slump.

I needed to pull myself together. I couldn't just walk out and run, this was work. I looked up to the roof to stop the tears dribbling down. It was a nice one, all Art Deco style. I took some more deep breaths and tried to think happy thoughts. Like how Dan had lecherously tongue-kissed me this morning at breakfast in front of a whole café full of people. And how I would be seeing him in mere hours' time. But it wasn't like I could tell him about all of this; it was about my ex, for God's sake, and Dan wouldn't care anyway, he'd probably never had a bad break-up in his life. Ah, Dan, Dan, the miracle man . . .

Pfft, I suddenly thought. Who *cared* what Jesse was doing? I had Dan, and he meant far more to me than any vapid bikini model could ever mean to that germ.

I went over to the basin and started to reapply my makeup, which was all smudged and blotchy. By the time I'd finished putting eye drops into my red, puffy eyes I was feeling a lot better. I had overreacted a little, I guess.

I triumphantly walked back into the restaurant, sporting a smile that could bluff even Iz. As I turned the corner, past an immaculately placed array of candles, I was ambushed by a flurry of hair and eyes.

'Oh, you're here!' Fi exhaled in relief.

'Guys, I'm *fine*; I am truly fine. I'm good. Don't look at me like that; I am okay, really.'

'H, I'm – we're – so sorry we were such arseholes,' Yasmin said, in a tone I'd never heard from her.

'Okay, well, I just think maybe – maybe – I don't need to know that he's dating other girls.'

'Totally understand. No more.' Fi crossed her heart with her finger.

'*Stop staring at me* – you're making me uncomfortable. I'm fine!'

Truth was I was nowhere near fine, but I was going to fake it till I felt it. I was getting good at that.

16.

Don't you go getting all serious

On a date and worried you've got the breath of an ox? The best way to check is by discreetly licking your wrist, allowing it to dry, and then sniffing it. If you smell nothing, or a faint 'breath' smell, you're fine. But if it's tangy, or spicy, or plain nasty, you need to stop talking and start walking. Towards some mints or gum, that is.

'Can you *believe* she was behind the whole thing? You brunette bitches sure do pull some nasty-ass tricks out of your devil's weave.'

Dan was whispering into my left ear as we watched the plotline of *Black Dahlia* unfurl at an outdoor cinema. We were lying side by side under a clear, twinkling night sky, our glasses of champagne precariously lodged between dip containers at our feet, and our legs and arms wrapped around each other, the way lovers entwine even though they're fiercely uncomfortable.

'Don't hate us because we're pretty and clever and murderous,' I whispered back.

'Oh, I don't hate you for it, sugar,' he said, in a sleazy mobster voice, and started kissing my neck in a way that was appreciated by me, but probably not by the hundred or so people lying on the grass around us.

'Stop it . . . DAN! *Stop it!* You're being inappropriate . . . Dan, I said . . . I said . . .' But his kisses made me melt. I took a deep breath in an attempt to keep control of where my mind and body were heading. He was always throwing curveballs, catching me off guard with a cheeky bum grab there, or a full-out neck lick here.

'Let's go, baby,' he said in his new favourite accent. 'Youw house, my house, the goddamn moon for all I care.'

'We can't just walk out mid-film; we're lying on the grass . . . in front of lots of people who probably don't want us moving about and cleaning up plates and rugs and —'

'So we'll leave it. I don't want any of this stuff – do you? It's all going in the bin anyway. Who cares about an old rug? Come on, sweet'art, waddya say? Let's you and me live a little, huh?'

'We can't —'

'Can't is the town next to Cannes and nothin' more. Stop your fussin' and let's go already.'

I couldn't help laughing at his accent, and, taking that as a yes, he jumped up, grabbed my hand and darted to the left of the amphitheatre. I was stumbling behind him, whisper-screaming, 'We can't just do this, Dan! That's littering! And I, I left my bottle-opener!'

We reached the gate and kept running, him tugging my hand, me laughing and trying to catch my breath.

'You're insane!' I said, once we were far enough away.

He leaned against a street pole and pulled me in for a kiss. After we'd finished, he said, 'That makes *you* a sucker, then, doesn't it? Falling for the mentally unfit?'

I went to slap him but he ducked and belted off for his car, whooping and hollering like a schoolboy. Every now and then he'd leap onto a fence or wall and look back at me with a freakish Jim Carrey-like expression on his face. I had to stop and bend over I was laughing so much. I couldn't remember the last time I'd had so much fun with a guy.

When I finally reached the car, where he was propped against it smoking a fake cigar, looking me up and down like I were a hooker for sale, I crossed my arms and smiled.

'You're quite the piece of work, aren't you, Daniel?'

'That I am, Miss Atkins, that I am. And for the low, low price of a dollar ninety-free I can be all yours . . .'

My smile faded as I realised that, even if I wanted him to be, he wouldn't be mine, because he was leaving in a few days.

'Miss Atkins, what's wrang? I've seen happier faces on death row.'

'Nothing, nothing, I'm fine.' I offered a weak smile and walked over to the passenger door.

He came over, swooped me up and sat me on the bonnet, so that I was looking directly into his eyes. I wondered if I had garlic breath from the hummus.

'Don't you go getting all serious on me now, Han. You know the rule: serious people have to eat dirt.'

'I'm not. Promise.' I kissed him to prove it. But, truth be told, I was. Of course I was. How could this man, the first man I'd actually felt something for since Jesse, be leaving! It was unfair and I hated it. I'd been on Iz's back about Project Mansion in the vain hope we could move to LA, or at least somewhere near there to be closer to Dan, but as her business and her relationship with Kyle were both going along so swimmingly she wasn't so keen any more. Dammit.

'What did we say about this?' he said, brows raised.

'That this was only an' – he chorused in – '*entrée*; we've still got main and dessert to go.' This was how we were getting around the ugly idea of him going back to LA. We were treating these two weeks as merely the start of a great meal.

Whether he was stringing me along with this line, I couldn't be sure. It frustrated me that he never took off his jester's hat. More worrying still was that I was looking at a relationship that was utterly

Geographically Impossible. And I knew that a high GI relationship never, ever worked.

My feelings were too intense for a 'fling'. This wasn't my rebound; poor, sweet Trucker held that foul honour. I cursed myself for breaking all my rules at the start of this thing. This was what Iż didn't understand: my rules existed for precisely this reason! You played hardball at first so you could figure out if they were worth your affections, so you *didn't* become their emotional puppet, they *couldn't* pull the heartstrings when they felt like it, and, most fricken importantly, you *didn't – get – hurt!*

Which was bound to happen. Because, if I was honest with myself – painfully, brutally honest – I was pretty sure I was falling for Dan. Only he was still perfectly balanced, and holding all the cards.

17.

I signed up for sitting at a desk and trying on lip gloss

Shed a kilo from your shoulder by minimising your handbag makeup. All you really need is a foundation stick that doubles as a concealer, blush, lip gloss or lipstick, black kohl and bobby pins. And a mirror. Guess work is never, ever a good idea. Ever.

Today was going to be vile, I could feel it in my nose.

I screamed into the Beckert foyer ten minutes late for the Monday morning production meeting. I was late because Dan was leaving this morning, and so he'd stayed over, and we hadn't got to sleep till late, and then I'd pressed snooze a record six times. I was awful when I was late. I got cranky, and slammed things, and swore about everything, because when I was all rushed and really needed everything to work for me (clothes, cabs, cash) nothing did.

I was feeling very gloomy about Dan leaving. I tried not to think of the possibility that he would now be my benchmark for guys. Surely there were no boys as sharp and sexy as he in this city. I resolved that, as per my rules, I wouldn't contact him first; he could contact me, and I would take my cue from that. I was damned if I would be the lovesick loser left behind.

My ludicrous walking pace meant my coffee was frothing dangerously as I stepped into the lift. I began my usual intense scrutiny of the floor-numbers lighting up. At the seventh floor, I looked down to see that my coffee had started dribbling like a teething toddler onto my muted-mint frock. Then, in some sick choreography, my handbag handle slid . . . clicked . . . then snapped. There was a thud, and then there were lip glosses and coins and eyeshadow brushes and crusty cardboard nail files and empty chewing-gum packets and tampons, *of course* tampons, everywhere.

I scurried awkwardly to collect the hairy bobby pins and a half-eaten muesli bar that were wedged between the Italian loafers of two Important Men. I was jamming everything back into my bag with one hand, while holding my coffee with another. No one offered to hold it, or help.

When we finally reached the eighteenth floor, staggering while trying to carry everything – including a bag that was now on death row – I lost it and started swearing to myself. It was all too stereotypical cheesy Magazine Job Movie starring someone way too gorgeous and together for it ever to be very believable. If I were in that film, I'd be the mail girl.

Once I got to my desk, I dumped everything on it and started wiping my dress using a tissue dunked into my drinking water. I had my cranky pants on, and ooh-wee did they fit snugly.

Once settled, drinking what was left of my coffee, I turned my PC on. Immediately my Outlook chirped at me cheerfully about a 10 a.m. presentation with Annick Taylor, an upmarket makeup-artistry brand that felt it entirely appropriate to charge 100-dollars-plus for foundation.

I swivelled my head with neck-crunching velocity to face the whiteboard. There was nothing written for today except an interview with a makeup artist who had apparently worked with Victoria Beckham. I couldn't wait to ask which fake tan Posh bathed in daily.

But there was no Annick Taylor presentation. Nor was there an appointment to hotwire a car, which sat right next to Presenting to a Boardroom Full of People on my scale of expertise.

I exhaled and dialled Marley.

'Marley, do I have to be at this Annick thing at ten?'

'Of course. Is there a problem?'

'Aside from the fact you know I've never done this before, and that I would rather drink my own vomit? No. Everything's fine.'

'Relaaaax, you'll only have to speak for five minutes. If that. And you're only speaking about your job, which I presume you know a little about?'

'Please don't make me do this.' Jay was signalling I had to get my arse into the production meeting. 'Oh, I've gotta go. See you at ten.'

'You'll be fine. And if you're not we'll laugh about it later. Kidding.' Click.

I put down the phone and turned my attention to Jay, who stood by my desk with a mischievous glint in her eye.

'How's my little lovebird?' she said, grinning. 'Still high on Dancaine? Has he proposed yet? Decided to move here for good?'

'No, no, no.' I blushed. 'Oh Jay, it sucks so bad. He's leaving this morning . . .'

'Ohhhh, honey, I'm sorry. God, that came around quick. How about we have dinner tomorrow night, and you can tell me how mind-blowing the sex was, and then we'll drink your blues away?'

'I think I have a launch, but definitely after?'

'Perfect. There's a new Japanese place I want to try in Barker Street.' She pirouetted and pranced back to her desk.

Kate walked past and did the neck-chopping thing to indicate the meeting was off. 'Karen's too busy with finals. It'll be later.'

Thank God.

Now I just had to work out how to impress a boardroom full of steely-eyed cosmetic people. It would be worse than a wisdom-tooth extraction, eating raw liver and nibbling my father's toenails all at once. You had to excel in these situations, to be memorable to the clients, and thus end up scoring the biggest piece of their budget. My hair was being very 'memorable'. I had lied to myself this morning that my hair wasn't oily. But now my lie had betrayed me, and, just like an old rock star about to go on *60 Minutes*, it wouldn't be styled. I teased it angrily then shoved it up into a quiff and ponytail. That would have to do.

I noticed that the coffee mark on my dress had barely shifted despite my scrubbing, and also that my red nail polish was chipped. What a picture of good grooming I was.

I sat down to write some speech cards, and felt a princess tear starting to well. Princess tears are those you know you shouldn't be shedding, because you're all grown up and you don't cry over insignificant, unchangeable or frustrating things any more. But I had a right to be petulant: I hadn't signed up for public speaking, I'd signed up for sitting at a desk and trying on lip gloss.

Ten o'clock came. I applied some gloss and walked to the Beckert boardroom. My gut was swarming with agitated moths. Butterflies could never be so wicked.

'Hi, Hannah from *Gloss*. Nice to meet you.'

'Hi, Hannah from *Gloss*. Nice to meet you.'

'Hi, Hannah from *Gloss*. Nice to meet you.'

Small talk before presentations? That I could do. Weather, outfits, striking accessories, upcoming holidays; I knew the score and sang it well.

As we sat down – the Annick people in their suits and sensible flats, and us in our trendy dresses and heels – I noticed a sheet of paper highlighting the running order of the day. This served as a tender reminder that there were twelve other beauty editors from Beckert who were way, *way* better at talking in front of a live audience than me, and that I was pretty much going to choke. I wondered how Fiona went in these things. And Yasmin – could Yasmin really not swear for a whole fifteen minutes?

'. . . And now it's over to our wonderful beauty editor, Hannah, who'll fill you in on what *Gloss*'s beauty pages are all about. Hannah?'

Oh shit. My mouth was so dry. My hands were shaking. Shit, shit, shit. I smiled and looked around the table.

'Um, thanks, Marley. Hi, everyone. I'm Hannah.' Insert lame wave. Cue polite chuckles.

'Um, well, as you know, *Gloss* has over fifteen pages of beauty every month, and they're just loaded with great products, because the *Gloss* reader only wants to know about great products. She can't get enough of beauty. It's like her daily hit of caffeine. And she loves Annick Taylor – that's exactly the kind of product she wants to read about. And see, you know, because they're such lovely products, and they shoot so well, and, you know . . .'

A lady with brown hair pulled back tight and frameless glasses suddenly interrupted. Her voice was faux-friendly and her smile stopped at her mouth.

'Hannah, we had our team do a quick tally before we came over here today, and it seems that we aren't getting nearly as much editorial as Blush or Carmen Jo cosmetics.'

Oh. My. God.

'Is there any reason why? I mean, is there anything more we can do to help you, Hannah?'

There was no correct answer. In fact, there was no answer at all as far as I was concerned. I looked to Marley for help. She opened her eyes wide, as if to say, *Go on, tell her, but do it in a way that will not jeopardise my ad spend.*

I cleared my throat.

'Um, well, there's no, you know, reason. I mean, it's probably just that those, uh, those particular stories, um, lent themselves, product-wise, to, um . . .'

'What Hannah is trying to say,' swooped in Marley, 'is that it's a very noisy market out there, and it's hard to please everyone, but Hannah does her best, and as long as she's kept abreast of all your launches . . . Hannah, is that ever a problem, is the PR always on top of everything?'

Ooh, she was good. Flipping it back onto them.

'She's great – oh, except last month I didn't actually receive your 24-hour Fresh Foundation until I had already shot my stills, but I understand that was an international issue . . .'

'Is that so? We weren't aware of that.' Glasses wrote something down.

Great. Now I'd got the poor PR fired. Jesus.

Time to grovel.

'Did you catch your bronzer in the current makeup feature?' I pushed the magazine open to a page featuring their SunKiss bronzer. Thank *God* I'd featured it. Glasses perused the page then turned it. Tough crowd.

'Mm, it came up really well, looks great, such a fine texture, really nice stuff, staff are raving about it, It's just lovely . . .' I waffled on with what I hoped passed as conviction.

'Going forward, Hannah is going to be doing some amazing things in the next issue. In fact, there's an eye-makeup master class that you guys will simply *love* . . .'

As Marley tried to smooth the whole situation over, I attempted to relax. That had been full on. There was no way I could've prepared for that. Glasses was basically questioning my editorial right to choose the products I wanted to feature.

Suddenly, Marley threw back to me so I could continue my spiel. My mind was blank. I had completely forgotten what I did for a job.

'Hannah, why don't you tell us all about your role in relation to the reader?'

Jesus, now Marley was feeding me my lines.

'I guess you could say I'm a kind of big sister to the reader. Or her best friend. But, like, a best friend with the most awesome cabinet full of cosmetics you've ever seen. And so I talk her through what's the best, and why she should buy it. And she listens to me, because I am trying and testing everything there is, so obviously I know what's worth buying. And also because I speak to her as you speak to your friends. Without all the flowery waffle you see in other beauty pages.'

Oh, dissing the opposition. Nice one.

'And, like the reader, I still get excited about beauty products, and want to be completely in the know about what's hot. Because that's her social currency. Knowing what's hot. Just like me. I guess you could just say I'm obsessed with booty! I mean beauty. Beauty. I'm obsessed with beauty.'

It was an out-of-body experience. I felt like a stand-up comedian after his jokes had fallen flat, that at any moment someone would start heckling about how I should go back to funny school. I hoped this presentational train wreck would at least mean I would never be asked to speak again.

'And, uh, what do you have coming up for next issue's beauty pages, Hannah?' Marley was now glaring at me.

'Well, as we're going into the colder months there'll be a big focus on skin, but also on hair and makeup, too. Because we've realised that when it's colder, girls are willing to experiment more with makeup. Maybe it's because they're all covered up and all that's left to project their image is their face.'

Now I was just making shit up.

The MD was checking his BlackBerry. The Women's Titles

Advertising Director, Pauline Erica, who I'd thus far avoided meeting, was wearing an expression that was both terrifying and terrified. She perversely kept nodding, I could only assume in agreement with how fired my arse was.

I have no idea. I have no idea. I have no idea. Despite what was coming out of my mouth, this was what I was saying: I have an absolute dearth of knowledge. Spend with another magazine, because at this rate I am more likely to be feeding pigeons in a park than writing intelligently about your products.

Marley finally realised that I was going to be as helpful as a poisonous jellyfish, and moved on to talk about tailored sponsorship opportunities. I fixed my hair and twiddled my thumbs and tried not to think about the appalling show I had just put on.

'Thanks so much for your time, and, please, enjoy your *Gloss* hampers. Especially the pink-lemonade cupcakes – they were baked fresh today.'

I could not get out of there fast enough. A few nods and lovely-to-meet-yous and I pulled a Backdoor Benny that I knew Marley would go off her nut over later. Right now, I didn't care. I went back to my desk, sat down, and told myself to take a few deep breaths to cleanse that awful memory from my mind forever.

A text message chimed. I hoped it was Dan saying that he'd decided not to go, and that we should probably head to Mexico together forever. It wasn't. I read Iz's text, deflated.

Dec n I cooking dinner 2nt, come round? food on @ 7.

Dec was back? *Dec was back!*

Dan's plane would be in the air by then, so at least I wouldn't be torturing myself wondering if he'd text. I'd just be rereading the ones he'd already sent.

18.

A two-week honeymoon with a total stranger

The rule of black-tie hair: if your dress is super-glamorous, go for a loose, gentle hairstyle (try some hot rollers). If your dress is low-key, balance it with a chic up-do (try a slick low bun). And please, no glitter.

When I arrived at Iz's at ten past seven I was feeling dangerously dependent on fun people to lift my mood, and was trying desperately not to feel nervous about seeing Dec for the first time since we'd kissed. The table wasn't set, the food was still in grocery bags, and Dec and Iz were drinking beers on the balcony. This was far from ideal. I was ravenous – ready to eat my own appendages – and a scene indicating I was hours away from being fed was not what I wanted to find. I tried not to be snarly.

'I see dinner is about to be served?' I said as I opened the sliding door to the balcony. Mission not to be snarly had failed, then.

'Oh shit, Han's in a food mood. Quick, Dec, offer your arm.'

'Hi, Han.' He smiled and my heart melted a little bit. He was a rude shade of health. His skin was tanned, his teeth freakishly white, his hair had grown a little and he had a freshly shaven face: he looked fragrance-advertisement incredible. There was a warmth in his eyes that I'd missed the last time I'd seen him. Maybe he was in love again? Or back with Pia?

He took me inside. 'You look amazing, Hannah. You been on holiday?'

I blushed and adjusted my hair. 'Um, nope. But thank you. So, Dec, what brings you back to these parts?'

'I've taken on a pretty huge telco client over here. They're about to do a stream of massive teen-consumer events, which means I'll be back and forth for a while, annoying my dear sister and crashing in her spare room to sleep among all of her derelict saucepans . . . Are you sure you're not on a detox or something? You're glowing.'

I blushed again and shook my head.

'Dec, cut it out, you're killing her. Now, Han, a beer? Some wine?'

Grateful for the distraction, I turned my attention to Iz. 'I'm cool for now, actually. Starving, though – can I steal some crackers or something? I'll find them —'

'I'll get you some, you stay here.'

Ah, Dec, ever the gentleman. I watched after him as he walked out of the room.

I wondered if Dec would've mentioned the kiss to Iz. I doubted it, but they *were* exceptionally close.

'Decka, can you please get onto that linguine you've been bragging about all day?' Iz yelled. 'Oh shit, what a pig! I didn't even ask: did you get to say bye to Dan in the end?'

'Who's Dan?' Dec asked as he came back in.

Whoa. Dec didn't miss a beat.

'Just a friend. I mean, this guy I . . .'

'Han just had an amazing two-week honeymoon with a total stranger. Best sex she's ever had. Isn't that right, Han?'

Okay, Dec definitely hadn't told Iz about us.

'IZ! Shut up! It wasn't like that! Dec, your sister is being inappropriate.'

'Oh, right, sorry: you and Dan played scrabble the whole time. Ha! Don't play nun with me, baby – you was gettin' it *onnn*.'

I wanted to maim her. Dec was looking at me with an unreadable expression. I decided to be mature and abort the situation entirely.

'Iz, you're a twit. Dec, excuse me while I go to the bathroom.'

I walked through the screen door into the kitchen, and Iz followed me.

'Iz, I don't want Dec to think about me doing those things!'

'Why not? As if he doesn't know you're doing them!'

'I just, it's just that, well, he's like a brother to me.'

'Oh, *really*? That why you still blush around him? After all these years? Do you honestly think I can't tell when you have a crush? Hannah. Please. Giz the Iz some credit.'

Right on cue, I blushed.

She smiled and shook her head. 'You're so obvious. Honestly . . .'

'Iz! Shut *up*!' My voice had an edge to it. She knew better than to keep going. Sadly, she also knew that when I snapped about silly things there was usually some truth behind them. *Whatever*. I had always been awkward around Dec; why was she making a big deal out of it now? I was relieved I'd never told her about Dec; the way she was carrying on now was already too much to handle.

I wondered if Dec had thought of me at all since our drunken bathroom kiss. I decided that he might have for a few intoxicated moments, but then he would have forgotten about it pretty much straightaway. We had been drunk, and even though he'd definitely made the first move, it was nothing I should think too much about. And anyway, I had fresh, delicious memories of Dan to be focusing on. An electric flutter floated through my body at the memory of our final session together that morning.

'Okay, okay, I'll stop.' Iz put her hands up in surrender.

'*Thank* you. I'll go to the loo then help you set up the table.'

It wasn't until I was in the hallway that I heard her say, 'And I'll have a little fish to see if Dec was all tortured about the idea of you and Dan just now.'

A stab of irrational rage pierced me: why would she do that? I could kill her! Dec wouldn't care, and even if he did care, so what? Dan was a completely different species; you couldn't even compare the two! Dec was the handsome, sensible, settle-down, see-you-at-the-altar type, whereas Dan was the fun, sexy, wild, spontaneous, let's-do-it-on-the-loungeroom-rug kind of guy that your friends were privately envious of and your family openly feared.

And right now, that suited me perfectly.

19.

Pumpkin-head and schnooky

Bad frizz and no product? Grab some hand cream, rub between your fingers and smooth down your crazy hair with it. Don't even have hand cream? Face cream? No? Use some goo from your little pot of lip balm. Don't have THAT? You almost deserve your frizz.

Next to obscenely famous people and general practitioners, I was convinced beauty editors were the busiest people on Earth.

Being a beauty writer himself, Gabe knew this, and yet he still gave me grief about it. He said I was a goody-goody, a beauty suck who did everything she was told and went to everything she was invited to, even when it was after hours.

But I was still enjoying all of my outings. Especially if an international makeup artist or hairdresser was in town and I scored freebies. That was tops. I'd recently, to my regular hairdresser Johnson's disgust, had my hair cut into a beautiful layered dream by the man who cut Scarlett Johansson's hair (Winner, Best Haircut of My Life). His assistant's blow-dry, however? Not so hot. It was way too high on top and flicky on the ends. I looked forty-five at least, and, at the function that followed, Yasmin kept saying, 'And now to Hannah with the weather.'

These days even my weekends were full of beauty stuff – I had spent all of last Saturday getting my hair ionically straightened at a small Japanese 'salon' in the depths of the fish-gutting district of Chinatown. My curls were gone; frizz was a thing of the past. I just had this amazingly straight, shiny hair. And it was flat. Stuck-to-my-head flat. The Japanese girl who owned the salon assured me that it would only be like that while it was setting, which took three whole days, during which I couldn't wet it, put it up, or even tuck it behind my pretty-big ears.

The first time I washed it I was scared that my hundreds of dollars would all be made worthless by the water, but as soon as I dried my hair, I could see there was no curl; no cowlick; no boof. Just straightness and a totally normal, non-flat texture.

I was overjoyed. I could swim whenever I wanted, not care about rain, always look groomed and not feel like Homeless Holly when my hair wouldn't play nice on the morning of an important launch. *This would change my life.*

Jay thought it was a total waste of a good Saturday's worth of shopping. She would, with her glossy Italian hair that had never needed to be introduced to a GHD.

Another recent job-related development was that I had put on weight. My tummy was chubby now, whereas before it had been flat, and my bum had jiggles where before there had been close-to-none. It was the new diet, although 'diet' was completely the wrong term.

Breakfast was coffee and toast. Mid-morning snacks were launch food – usually a muffin – lunch was merely a nice idea, or else completely over-the-top restaurant food, and dinner was sushi on the way home, porridge with banana at home, canapés and champagne at a function, or squid and wine with Iz at a bar.

I was doing my best to counter the gentle filling up of my jeans with Bikram yoga classes with Jay at dawn, a pre-work walk a few times a week, and saying 'No' to chocolate-dipped strawberries, pastries and cupcakes four times a day. But I had become used to my new life and its side-dish of weight-gain. I still preferred busy over desolate. 'Busy' filled the void of 'empty' perfectly.

But the thing that consumed me most, and that had me feeling most tender, was Dan's lack of contact. He had texted a lot – mostly filth – for the first week, and then we'd shared a few epic emails and some Facebook-wall banter, and there had even been a phone call or two, but now it was three weeks since he'd gone, and contact had petered out to a couple of texts a week. And whenever I texted him first, I always felt like I was interrupting him doing something, as his responses were either rushed or missing his old spark. This was precisely why I never texted first: you lost all of your emotional power.

It seemed that as quickly as I had won one round in the game of happy and loved-up Monopoly, I was now owing $40K and on my way to jail. I mentally kicked myself for having thought he would be as adoring via broadband or phone. He was a live-in-the-moment guy, a guy who had to have something directly in front of him (preferably sporting impressive cleavage) to pay it any attention.

In my more Zen moments I tried just to be grateful for the time I'd had with him, but it pissed me off that I had given myself to him so openly – no easy feat for a girl who had just put the last brick in place in her enormous self-preservation fortress – and then, mere weeks later, I represented nothing more than an envelope flashing on in his phone that was apparently too hard to find the time or energy to respond to. Arsehole.

I knew that on some level I was having a kind of emotional regression back to when Jesse and I had split, like all of those abandonment-type feelings had been quietly hiding in my sock drawer until the time was right to hit again.

Sitting at my lounge-room window, smoking (a nod to Forties' screen sirens, who looked fabulous even when they were feeling murderous, and drank scotch and smoked thin cigarettes and made aggressive phone calls to jilting lovers on clunky black phones), I wondered what would become of me if guys kept toying with my head like this. Was I going to be able to feel 'normal' about a guy again anytime soon? Iz had it down pat – she and Kyle were so in love. Which made it a bit hard, seeing them clambering all over each other all the time, and calling each other things like 'Schnooky' and 'Pumpkin-head'. They were even considering living together.

I wondered if I'd get to a point where there would be no weirdness, no freaking out if a guy tried to get close to me or showed signs of retreat. I started to feel angry at Jesse for making me the sort of person who viewed a boyfriend as a threat rather than a pleasure.

That word: boyfriend. It sounded so foreign. I had completely avoided the word, and in fact the entire notion, for almost six months. Trucker barely scraped a mention, and if he did he was a 'bit of fun', or a 'friend', while Dan was only ever referred to as a 'fling'. Dec was, well . . . Dec was different altogether. It was impossible to repress the guerilla thoughts of him that snuck into my conscious mind every so often, but I had grown used to quickly sweeping them away.

I felt ill at the thought of a new boyfriend. When I tried to imagine getting used to a new person's habits, or meeting a whole new family, or going on trips with just one person for two whole weeks, my mind just kind of scrunched up and changed the topic.

Oh well.

In the movies the emotionally bruised loser always found love again. Here's hoping someone was filming.

20.

Best call in some sunscreen

Stay-put lipstick is a great idea, but unless your lips are in good condition first, nothing will stay. Use a face cloth and warm water and gently rub your lips to exfoliate them. Then apply balm. Then apply your magical stay-put lipstick.

'I'm actually surprised at how good it is.'

'Me too, they're usually so bad at anything to do with lips. Or base: that matte foundation they did was unforgivable.'

'I've been wearing the stuff ever since the launch.'

Fiona, Yasmin and I were on our way back to Beckert from Bio Spa, where, in an intimate group of eight, we'd been given herbal tea and fresh fruit while being told about a new salon foot-spa range based on sea algae. We had also received a deluxe pedicure and polish. I hadn't known about the pedicure part of the launch and so had worn closed-toe shoes. This meant that my lovely soft feet were currently sheathed in Bio Spa's complimentary flimsy foam cut-out thongs, so as not to ruin the polish resting on my toes. They might as well have been made of tissue paper: they were impossible to walk in, not that I could even entertain the idea of walking into the Beckert foyer with them on. With my luck, I just knew Karen would walk out of the lift at that exact second.

As we were nearing the office in our taxi, I was becoming

increasingly agitated about what I would do. I had needed the pedi because I had a black-tie function tomorrow night and needed to wear strappy shoes, but because I hadn't brought my own polish, I couldn't retouch it (after inevitably botching it).

'Han – have you tried it yet?' Yasmin asked.

'Sorry, tried what?' I was in the front seat, as usual, audibly and physically removed from the conversation.

'Gleam's new long-last gloss. The double-ended one with the balm top-coat we got last week.'

'Yes! *How good is it?* I love the Barely Buff shade.'

'Me too!' Yasmin said. 'It has just become my new Perfect Nude.'

'Whooooa, big call.' I'd forgotten that Fi was the Perfect Nude police. Perfect Nude was the highest compliment a lip product could be given. It had to be just pink enough, just taupe enough and just sheer enough to make the lips look juicy and lush yet deceivingly natural.

Fi had coined the term in honour of Jennifer Lopez's always perfect perennially nude lips. No one knew which exact product Jennifer wore (more than likely it would be a makeup artist's motley concoction of liner, lipstick and three glosses) but we were on an ongoing mission to find it, or one that gave the same results.

It wasn't just the beauty editors who were obsessed; so many of my reader emails revolved around the Perfect Nude gloss. Where could they buy it? How much was it? How should they apply it? What should they eat for breakfast after having applied it? And so on. My answers varied, but I usually suggested Revlon's Super-Lustrous in Nude Lustre, or M.A.C's C-thru lipglass, or NARS Lip Gloss in Orgasm.

'I thought it would do that revolting crusty-corners thing the long-lasts always do, but it stayed moist.'

'Fi! You said *moist*!' Yas squealed with disgust.

'Well, it's the appropriate word. Even if it does remind me of Japanese businessmen buying panties from vending machines.'

'*FI!*' We collapsed into a frenzied dialogue about how off the word 'moist' was.

'It's as bad as "member",' I said.

'Or "fingered",' Fi offered.

'No way. Panties is worse than moist. I mean, what woman calls her undies "panties"? It's so porn,' Yasmin exclaimed.

The girls carried on and my mind went back to my toes. Oh, screw it; I'd have to wear these absurd flip-flops upstairs. I'd just hide between the other girls. Luckily the traffic was taking a while, a good thing as every minute of polish dryness counted.

My phone beeped.

If I was to be in Hawaii next week and invited you to be in Hawaii next week, would we both be in Hawaii next week?

The hairs on the back of my neck stood up. My heart stopped temporarily. It was Dan. Dan, who I'd thought had forgotten my number. Dan, who I had actively tried to expel from my mind. Dan, who was now inviting me to Hawaii?

'Is he for real?' I whispered in disbelief.

'Who is it, what's happened, is it Jesse?' Fiona was awful at pretending she wasn't nosy.

'No, no, it's Dan. LA boy . . . He's asked me to go to Hawaii next week.'

'Oh my God! You HAVE TO GO!!!' Yasmin was squealing again. I turned to face her; she was clasping her hands together and bouncing in her seat. She never did that.

'I agree. You should go. Enjoy crazy-good sex in a tropical climate while you can. Is he paying? He should be. You should go. Lord knows, I would.' Fi made the decision sound as simple as cereal over toast.

'But, I haven't, I mean, I can't, I'm shooting next week and we have that massive Garnier function and —'

'And you place a higher value on that stuff than a whirlwind trip you'll be telling your grandkids about one day? Get a grip, girl.'

Fi had some salient points, but I was still in shock and couldn't process anything.

My phone beeped again.

I'm booking your flights this afternoon. Best call in some sunscreen. It's hot in Waikiki, dollface.

My hands were shaking. I read the girls his latest text with my eyes shining and a grin cemented onto my face. He was very, very hard to be angry at. Impossible, even.

'You are SO going!' Fi was clapping her hands Yasmin-style now.

'I'll have to ask Karen . . . and, oh shit, Eliza . . . and, oh, I am sure she'll be *super*-thrilled about it, but, well, I guess . . . I guess if they say yes . . .'

More squealing from the back. I tried to act cool, but I couldn't wipe the smile off my face. I was going to see Dan. And I was going to ignore the part of my brain that was screaming he didn't deserve my company, and what was I teaching him about my self-respect by leaping onto a plane for a dirty holiday when he had been such a bastard for the last three weeks.

'Ohhhh, wish *I* was off to be sexed by a hotrod in Hawaii,' Yasmin said in a wistful voice as we got out of the cab.

'Yas, my darling, your time for wild island-sex will come,' Fi said, and linked arms with her. 'We just need to find you a man. And me too, while we're at it.'

As I got to my desk and dumped my sack of algae foot scrubs and lotions next to it, Kate looked at my feet in bewilderment.

'Whoa! What are *they*?'

I looked down and broke into maniacal laughter.

'Your job . . . honestly . . .' She shook her head and smiled.

I was so excited about the thought of Hawaii that I had completely forgotten about my stupid 'shoes'. And no one had noticed them in the foyer.

Funny how things just work out when you let go.

21.

It's, like, totally hot

> If you're not using a skin serum, you should be. Think of a serum as the tequila to your face cream's glass of wine: it's potent and very effective. Choose your serum according to your biggest skin concern, whether that's hydration, acne, pigmentation, ageing or had-too-much-to-drink-last-night-need-some-radiance-fast. Use morning and night. Enjoy better skin.

Part of my week from hell before Hawaii was an interview with an upcoming model-slash-TV-presenter, Cassie Eaton. She was a pretty little thing who had scored a gig on TV by virtue of dating a racecar driver. From there, she had moved on to various high-profile jobs, including heading a clothing campaign, being a mobile-phone spokesperson, and now she had become the face of Bare cosmetics.

This was a regular gig: interviewing people who knew a lot about only one thing. The 'thing' could be serious, like sun damage or pigmentation or antioxidants, or it could be more frivolous, like eye makeup or using hot rollers.

Interview subjects, I had quickly surmised, were hit and miss. Perversely, the hits were often those I had tried to get out of because I had no interest in learning – or writing about – DIY hair extensions, or else they were the ones I had written while on a death-defying deadline.

In the same way my happiest nights out were always the ones

where Iz had to physically drag me into the taxi, the people I didn't want to interview were usually the most fun. Like the interview I'd conducted with the eponymous founder of Ken Brent cosmetics two weeks back. (There are two kinds of men in the beauty industry: the suits-and-stats managing-director kind, and the kind who wear Hermes loafers and emcee 'Bingay' at boys-only bars on Tuesday nights. He was the former.) I was swamped in copy, feeling dusty from Gabe's birthday drinks the previous night, and had spilled yoghurt on my dress in two very conspicuous spots in the breast region. I had tried to cancel but the PR wasn't answering her mobile – a very clever tactic they use when they simply will not entertain the notion of you cancelling. If you can't get through to them and don't show up, you're a bastard. And no one wants to be a bastard.

So I trawled up to their suite, and smiled weakly as the usual platitudes prevailed. But then this fellow, Ken, entered. He would have been late forties or early fifties, and was dressed like he had been styled by *Esquire* magazine. He was very Richard Gere circa *Pretty Woman*, all charcoals and chocolates and leather and cashmere. When he spoke, he sounded like a Hugh Grant–Ben Kingsley hybrid. His presence filled the room so completely that even the plumbing couldn't have escaped his aura.

'Magnificent dress. Not many people can wear that tone. I bet you look excellent in green, too. Or aqua, do you ever wear aqua? It would set those eyes of yours alight.'

'Um, aqua? Um, sometimes, I guess . . .' I was a little taken aback.

'Even a light blue would do the trick. The tones in your iris would look incredible.'

'Oh, uh, cool.'

The more interesting he was, the less articulate I became.

The PR cleared her throat in a passive-aggressive way that implied we should begin the interview.

We sat down; he poured me some tea – 'Do you know why it's called Earl Grey? Not many do, it stems from a time when . . .' – and as we chatted he was so charming that my cheeks flushed. The thing was, what he said wasn't flirty, or sleazy, or creepy, just commanding and fascinating. He referred constantly to his wife and children (*the* most attractive thing a man can do, even though this obviously rules out any chance of an encounter), and he had the kind of sparkling eyes usually belonging to game-show hosts or beauty queens. He promoted his products with an air of irreverence that made me think I needed them more than they needed space on my pages. Then he brushed over their celebrity followers with a dismissive wave, as though they were lucky to have discovered them: 'David and Victoria love the pomegranate-and-fig shower gel, but we always seem to be out of stock when they come into the store.'

He was the kind of man who, for the first time in my life, made me wonder if I *could* be with an older – much older – man, when previously I'd always thought a double-decade age difference was in the same realm of creepiness as people who wear nappies as a form of sexual fetishism.

On the flipside, the interview subjects I *did* get excited about meeting too often let me down: they'd keep me waiting for an hour; or they'd grunt their way through our conversation, as though they'd been subjected to a giant personality extractor only minutes before meeting me; or they were just rude.

As I was excited about interviewing (or at least looking at) Cassie, I wondered if she would prove my theory true. I hoped not.

I arrived at the interview, late because of traffic, and stumbled into the Hilton's amazing honeymoon suite, gushing apologies to appease the stern-looking PR.

Cassie was sitting on the sofa in that relaxed-but-camera-ready position which beautiful famous people are trained to do. She was wearing a stunning beaded singlet, jeans, and heels that appeared to be held together with a thread of gold string. Her skin was luminous and her hair was so full and shiny that when she nodded her head her curls formed a small chorus line of confirmation, dancing up and down with her. She didn't get up to shake hands, she just sat there, smiling her famous, toothy smile.

Totally affected, I thought immediately, storing a description of her outfit that I could dissect with Gabe later.

'So, you must be busy at the moment?' I asked, sounding like every other schmuck who had interviewed her.

'Yeaaah.' She smiled and nodded. *Uh-oh.* She was a blocker. A one-word answerer. Not good.

I scrambled for my recorder and pen, trying to set it all up, and she didn't say a word. Silence. This made me overcompensate, and to disguise my fluster I started asking her standard starter questions.

'Are you enjoying your newfound rise to fame?'

'Yeaaah, it's been gooood,' she said, smiling and nodding.

She tucked her hair behind her left ear.

'You must be exhausted with all of your commitments at the moment?'

'Yeah, but it's been really goooood,' she said, smiling and nodding. Whoa, it was lucky I knew shorthand.

She now flicked her hair to the other side of her head dramatically with her left arm.

'So, I work for *Gloss*, as Jane might have told you, and I guess my readers will be most interested in what you —'

'Can I get another Diet Coke?' She looked to the PR. She had an attitude that was disproportionate to her level of fame. She looked back at me and gave me a closed-lip smile. She flicked her hair again. I was momentarily stunned. The PR scarpered off to get the drink.

'. . . Um, I guess, I guess they'd want to know which are your favourite Bare products? Let's go with maybe five?'

'I like the mascara.'

I waited.

She didn't say anything. She tucked her hair behind her ear. *Again*. I was almost able to set a clock to her ridiculous hair-fiddling.

'Okaaay, great! Which one do you like best?'

'Um . . . the black one? It's real good for night-time and stuff. Makes lashes *so hot*. Love it.' Her phone went off on the table. She leaned forward and checked the screen, not bothering to silence its shrill siren.

'Lashification?'

'Yeah, that one. Hot.'

I was feeding her the names of products she was being paid fistfuls of cash to promote. That wasn't right. I stared at her.

I cleared my throat and tried again.

'Okay, and what about foundation? Are you a matte girl or a sheer girl?'

'Um, I really like the liquid foundation.'

There were seven liquid foundations.

'Right. The liquid one . . .'

I was almost too scared to ask about lips. 'And lip gloss? Which one do you wear?'

She screwed her mouth to one side. She flicked her hair behind her shoulders. She glanced at the PR, who handed her a glass of brown liquid bobbing with ice cubes. Her eyes searched the room, then suddenly lit up. 'Shine and Last! It's awesome. I, like, totally wear it every day.'

One out of three wasn't bad. Except if you were a Bare employee paying her many dollars to flog your products. Or a journalist who had to make a story out of her quotes.

After another few awkward minutes, I could get nothing more out of her. Asking for her makeup tips and secrets baffled her; simple concepts like 'beauty blunders' mystified her; and her phone kept ringing just as I went to ask my questions.

'Okay then! I think that should do it,' I said, after her phone rang for the fourth time and she took the call: 'Babe, I won't be home for hours, can't you just feed Princess now before you go?'

The PR started gushing about how excited they were about their double-page ads in *Gloss*, subtly reminding me to be kind in both my copy and my post-interview anecdotes.

As I thanked Cassie, she was rifling through her bag for something and appeared not to hear me. It wasn't till I started walking to the door that she realised I was going and yelled out, 'Thank you so much!'

'My pleasure,' I said, turning to offer her a weak smile. She looked up at me with a smile that could melt a thousand icy poles, and said, 'It was *reeally* great to meet you, Alannah.'

I smiled (twelve icy poles, max). 'You too, Carrie. Bye for now.' Slam.

I kept smiling all the way back to the office, thinking about what a twit she was and how unfair it was that twits were paid so much even while being so twitty.

When I got back to my desk it suddenly occurred to me that I was off to a beachy climate in days. I needed to book in a spray tan for starters, and get a wax, and then I would need sunscreen and tinted moisturiser and some monoi oil and after-sun stuff and some super-hydrating moisturiser for the plane . . . But was it wrong to call it in from cosmetic companies when it was for personal use, not a story for *Gloss*? I needed a second opinion. I picked up the phone.

'Yasmin?'

'Yes, Miss Hawaii Tropic?'

'Do you ever, you know, call in something that you really like, but, like, not shoot it in the magazine, and just, you know, start using it?'

'Are you for real? Jesus, I call in stuff for myself all the time. You might decide you love it so much you want to write reams about it one day.'

'And the companies don't get pissed?'

'They wouldn't even know!'

'Oh, cool. That's a good way of looking at it.'

'It's not a way of looking at it, sunshine, it's legit. Now you go call in that Re-Nutriv.'

I got off the phone giggling. I felt much better about it.

I needed the stuff by Thursday because I was flying out Friday morning. And I was stupidly busy until then. The functions were laid on thick, and if I wanted time off, I had to meet my deadlines before I went. Late nights were a gross understatement. Decent amounts of sleep were a fantasy.

And, until a few days ago, so was seeing Dan again. I was still fighting a ferocious little internal battle about my decision to frolic off to meet a guy who had found it difficult to find time to email me only a week earlier.

What if we didn't get on like we had here? What if I got bored of him after a day? Or he got bored of me? Or we fought? Or I wasn't attracted to him any more?

Part of me was sulking in a corner, arms folded, hissing that Dan didn't deserve my company after the way he had been treating me. In the other corner it was all fluorescent banners with the slogans 'Live in the now!' and 'How many times in your life will you do this?!'

I confirmed resolutely that I was going to Hawaii. I consoled the part of me that was shy of being bitten again with the reassurance that at least I knew what to expect post-holiday. This time there'd be no expectations of mutual long-distance longing. Uh-uh. I was no fool. I knew how to play this game now. I'd enjoy my holiday for what it was, and that was it. Too easy.

22.

'He wait with roses'

Long flight? Use a hydrating mask (cloth or from a tube) the day you leave, apply rosehip oil and hydrating face cream during the flight, and use a hydrating mask when you arrive. Also, ask for an aisle seat – you should be drinking so much water you constantly need the bathroom.

Honolulu airport was slightly underwhelming. Especially at 11 p.m., when you've just flown a long way to hang out with a man who's nowhere to be seen, even though your flight was twenty minutes late.

I sat down outside near the taxi rank and contemplated what I should do if he didn't show. I tried calling his mobile, but it rang out. A mild feeling of panic twinkled through me. I suddenly wanted a cigarette very badly. I contemplated asking for one from a weathered old taxi driver who was leaning against his car nearby, but he saw me looking, and shuffled over with his crumpled Kools outstretched. I hoped all Hawaiians could mind-read; it'd make for a very easy holiday.

'You want one, pretty lady?'

'Really?'

'Of course. Face like yours have anything it desires.'

'Oh, thank you. I wouldn't normally, but . . . I'm a bit anxious. The guy who's picking me up . . .'

'If a man love a woman, he never late. He wait with roses.'

'Oh, he's not my boyfriend, we're just, he's . . . I'm just . . .'

'You don't need explain to me. But for happy life, whenever you fall in love with man, let him love you more than you love him. That the key to happy love, and good life.'

And with that he looked over my shoulder, nodded to a Japanese couple and helped them heave their suitcases into his car. He glanced over at me before he got in and nodded with a smile.

I sat there, inhaling a cigarette, and wondered if I had just met an angel. His words were almost too movie-like prophetic for me to take in, but I couldn't deny they struck a chord. All of my relationship rules, all that stuff about keeping your emotions in bubble wrap and making men work for you, to prove they're worthy of receiving even the first password to your heart, now looked to be merely a chintzy effort at explaining what a funny little Hawaiian taxi driver had known all along: that to be happy you needed to let go, and let your man adore you.

I smiled at the simplicity of it. I wasn't about to fool myself into thinking I was ready to be so graceful about matters of the heart just yet; I still had some work to do on myself and my somewhat, uh, tainted perception of men. And, as Dan's foul post-fling behaviour had shown me, I still needed to be on guard, to cocoon myself in my code of conduct so as not to wind up a disillusioned love-fool – forever disappointed, forever getting hurt. My current instinct about having any semblance of a relationship with Dan was roughly as strong as a wet paper bag, but I figured that as long as I knew this, I was allowed to enjoy the roller-coaster ride I'd signed up for by coming here. At least I now had a more emotionally intelligent blueprint to work from when I was ready to give unconditionally again. Whenever that might be.

Following on from my emotional epiphany, as though in some

form of bespoke symphony, a white stretch limousine pulled up and a driver in a suit stepped out. He was carrying a card that said 'Princess Atkins'. Dan's nickname for me. I almost choked on the smoke wafting out of my mouth.

I leapt up. 'Driver, I think that's me.'

'Miss Princess Atkins?'

'Um, ahem, yes.'

He smiled and came over to get my suitcase.

'Apologies for the delay, ma'am. Awful accident on the freeway.'

'Is Dan with you?'

'Mr Daniel is waiting for you at the destination. Please, allow me.'

And, as he opened the door, I wished the taxi driver were here to see this.

Around twenty minutes later we pulled into the 'destination' – the W hotel, just out of Waikiki. The driver handed me a swipe card and told me he'd send the bag up to my room. I raced straight into the lobby bathroom and touched up a face that needed an entirely fresh start, but wouldn't be given such a luxury. My heart was racing as I applied concealer to ferocious under-eye bags, cheek crème to flush my cheeks and a thick layer of gloss. That was as fresh as I was getting. I sprayed on some Michael Kors – Dan loved it and I wanted to cement my signature scent in his mind like the little perfume bandit I was.

As I knocked on a door bearing the number written on my swipe card, I was sure I could actually hear my heart pounding.

The door opened.

'Mish H, you rook amazhing.'

Dan opened the door with a rose in his mouth. I couldn't believe my eyes. My hand went to my chest and my mouth fell open in a very unladylike fashion. He made a show of spitting out the rose, swept me up and gave me a big kiss.

'*So good to see you again,* you beautiful little thing. How was your flight?'

'It was . . . I mean this whole thing is . . . The car, the rose, the room . . . Are you for *real*?'

'Being a gigolo, you learn how to work the ladies, if you know what I mean.' He winked and nodded lecherously. 'I pull this gear all the time. Last night I used a hot-air balloon and dancing polar bears.'

'You're mad. But so good . . . thank you so much. But I should warn you – if you're going to propose, I only accept pink diamonds. And no less than five carat.'

'But I thought you'd like copper and Swarovski crystals? I had no idea you were so shallow.'

My nerves melted the moment we started bantering. He was still Dan, and I was still me, and I still loved the way he carried on. Plus, the rose . . . Was that some bizarre little sign from the universe? I mean, after the taxi driver's call about roses . . .

I couldn't think that way. I was here to have fun, and be wild, and live *la vida loca* and all that Ricky Martin jazz. No strings meant no thinking long-term things. I was Sexy Magazine Girl, doing the kind of thing people expected her to be doing – drinking champagne in Jacuzzis at 4 a.m. and that sort of caper.

My phone crowed.

'Turn it off or your husband will use GPS to track you down.'

I giggled as I checked the message. It was Gabe.

Are you safe? Have you had sex yet? If not, why not? Did you not wax again? Silly girl. What have I told you about that? Enjoy your hot Hawaiian humpathon, beauty. Gxx

Bless him.

'Am I allowed to respond?'

'To your husband? No. Your kids? I guess. But only if they have a life-threatening disease.' He was speaking like he was the psychopath from a James Bond movie, while filling champagne glasses and arranging fruit and cheese on a platter.

'It's the plague.'

Deep sigh. 'I sup*pose*.'

God, he was excellent. I'd forgotten how fun he was, how much fun we had, and how much fun was possible with him. Of course, he *would* have to live on the other side of the world.

The next morning, after a night of extreme drinking, starting with a bottle of Moët in the room, then cocktails, shots and dancing downstairs at the W's club, including Dan having a dance-off with several well-known NFL players, and winning due to his extremely crowd-pleasing body-popping, I was woken up just before eight to the sound of the Beach Boys singing '*Let's go surfing . . .*' at a level that would be more appropriate at, say, an outdoor concert.

'Rise and shine, sweet Hannah. We've got waves to catch.'

'Are you . . . what? Why? Can't we do it later? My head . . .' I rolled over and covered my head with the pillow. Which Dan promptly thieved.

'Sleep when you're dead, baby! Right now it's time to get those dainty hooves of yours onto the pristine sands and two-foot dribblers of Waikiki.'

'Right now?' My hangover clouded my vision and my desire to be alive. A sequence of mind-blowing thumps pounded throughout every nanometre of my brain. My stomach was churning. I felt as though a fire-truckload of water might *just* satisfy my parched mouth.

'Oh darling . . .' He came and stroked my shoulder and I melted, happy that I had changed his mind.

Two slaps on the arm and then, 'Ten minutes ago. Your lesson with a super-awesome surfing legend is at eight-thirty. Come on, princess, time to roll.' With that, he ripped the sheets off the bed, forcing me to scramble for something, anything.

'All *right*. I'm *coming*.' I irritably pulled things out of my suitcase, looking for my bikini and some shorts. Of course, because I was hung over, all I could find were underpants and a collection of stupid paisley-print sarongs that I knew I wouldn't wear but had packed because you always pack sarongs when you're off on a beach holiday.

'You're adorable when you're angry. Especially when you take it out on harmless g-strings. Coffee?' He had already brewed a pot and was sipping some.

He was impossible to be angry at.

23.

Seasick

Prevent crunchy summer hair by applying a leave-in conditioner with UV filters before you head to the beach or pool. Comb your hair back into a low ponytail, and roll with the slick look. Your hair will thank you for it when it doesn't snap off post-swim.

'Paddle, paddle, PADDLE! Two hands, faster, faster, come on, put your back into it, come on, Han, go, GO, up, up, get up, jump, yes, YES, bend, bend . . . no . . . face the beach, the beach, not me, the bea—'

'I AM . . . ah, ahh, ahhhhh!'

I fell off the back of a canoe masquerading as a surfboard. *Again.* No matter how good a teacher Dan was, and how small and easy the waves at Waikiki were, I just kept falling off. And because I was so hung over, getting back on the board and paddling back to where he was had become a colossal task that I had to undertake every few minutes. My head thumped and my guts were churning slowly.

'Nice arse.'

'Shut up.'

'Seriously – I love the way your bikini rides up your bum every time you jump up on the board. I'd do you for a dollar, put it that way.'

'Daniel. I'm shocked. I cost at least double that, thank you.'

He brought our boards together, forming a bridge with his arms. The sun was shining in his eyes, and his hair was falling over his face in a way that takes stylists hours to achieve.

'Did you know this area was once full of dolphins? Back before this place was colonised by the . . .'

He was in his element. The surf was his second home, and he loved it with a passion that, ridiculously, made me a little jealous. He tried to teach me about the swell, the technique, the correct way to paddle; no surfing stone was left unturned. I was less than vaguely interested but nodded and smiled continuously until – whoa. I didn't feel so good. I felt really, really not good, in fact.

'Uh, Dan . . . I think I might be . . .'.

Just as my wave of nausea manifested into vomit, a wave of water came and knocked my board up, back and into me. This wasn't very helpful, as I was doing my best to be sick on the opposite side to where Dan was, only now there were no sides, just water and boards and vomit. All in one spectacularly mortifying moment, I found myself treading water, trying to hold on to my board, struggling not to take in any water as my body urgently expelled the remnants of the previous night's 264 alcoholic beverages.

It felt like I might die at any second: there were far too many input and output issues, not to mention the whole flotation thing. It shocked me to realise that in the moments when I was gulping air and not actually being sick I was still trying to look ladylike in front of Dan, holding my hair back and aiming my sick into an area I hoped he wasn't.

And then another wave came, bigger than the last one. I got smashed, tumbling around under the whitewash, my leg rope tugging my board and my leg with it.

Suddenly I felt arms around me, holding me up straight, and a hand pulling my hair back and telling me it was okay.

'Dan, please, away, get away, you'll get . . . swim away from here.'

I fought to get free, pulled my board back over to me and slumped onto it sideways, face down, breathing, just breathing.

'Han, honey, it's okay, it's okay, the set has finished, just relax . . . I've got you, it's okay.'

Even though I should have been feeling grateful to be alive, all I could summon up was indescribable embarrassment.

'Did you just get covered in my . . . my . . . you know?' I asked Dan, still breathing heavily and pushing my hair out of my face to wipe the inevitable tears that follow being sick.

'Kind of, but *everyone's* doing it. It's the new matching tattoo.'

I smiled and closed my eyes. I concentrated on breathing and being still.

'Can I go in now? I think I'm done.'

'Nah, come on, Han – few more waves, you'll be fine. You're doin' great! Seriously! Don't look at me like that.'

'Dan! Are you for real? I just want to go back to the goddamn beach!'

'Stop being so dramatic, you'll be fine.' His tone was suddenly dismissive and irritated.

I squinted at him, incredulous, but he had already gone and climbed back onto his board.

'I'm going back to shore. I've had enou—'

I broke off as I noticed he had put his feet at the back end of his board and was gripping the nose of mine with it. Then he started paddling swiftly towards the shore. He turned his head and smiled. 'Of course we're going in, beautiful. I'm just screwing with you.'

I nodded my head and smiled. My mouth tasted awful. I washed some saltwater into it in what was a very silly move. Now it tasted bad *and* I was exceptionally thirsty.

The rest of the day was spent under heavy sedation. A big

room-service breakfast, a nap, a movie, and then sushi on the beach at sunset. I felt almost human by bedtime.

The remainder of the week was not nearly so dramatic, or restful. We flew to Maui, we drove to the northern beaches, we shopped, we ate squid and ice cream, we swam, we went surfing again (sans hangover), and I noticed that on more than one occasion I was feeling dangerously similar to how I'd felt about Dan back when I first met him. Whenever these romantic, idyllic thoughts shuffled into my mind, I belted them with a large baseball bat emblazoned with the words, 'Remember What Happened Last Time, Stupid'. The big, fat reality check Dan had served me after we'd previously kissed goodbye was waiting for me at the end of this meal too, and to think otherwise was foolish.

Oh, but the heart is a formidable opponent for the head. The idea of flying home after a week of decadence, sexiness, fun, and, well, Dan-ness gave me a sick feeling. I could sense that, despite all instruction, my walls had begun to crumble again, to the point where I was initiating cuddles and kisses in public and leading him to the bedroom friskily, and accidentally starting sentences with the phrase 'Next time', even though there was absolutely no guarantee there would be such a thing, and it would be much, much more helpful to think there wasn't.

He said, 'You're not going home, you're coming back to LA with me,' so often that I actually, foolishly started considering it. Could I do it? Was it one of those life-changing decisions I would regret forever? Was I just caught up in the whole funnymoon aspect of the trip? I decided that if he asked me seriously, then I would think about it seriously. Rather, if he could remember me once I'd sashayed through customs, then I would think about it seriously.

'Gorgeous girl, are you ready to roll? We've got rockshrimp dynamite to eat.'

It was our last night together; I would fly out in mere hours. I was wearing clothes suitable for a plane ride – jeans, singlet and hoodie – so, on top of feeling incredibly clingy, I was hot, uncomfortable and irritated.

'I'm coming, I'm coming . . . my bag won't close . . . I can't . . . bastard won't . . .' The more I tugged at the zip, the less it moved and the more upset I became.

'Babe, settle – here, let me do it.'

'I'm fine, Dan, I'll get it . . . It's gotta close eventually . . . just don't understand why it won't . . . SHIT!'

I had completely pulled the zip away from the zipper. The bag was now broken. I stared at the zip in my hand and felt tears spring to my eyes. Irrational tears over a metal clasp.

'Han? You okay? Here, give me that, I'm sure we can get it back on there.'

As I sniffed back a tear, he tilted my face up to his. 'Han, baby, it's okay. We'll fix it, and if we don't, we'll tie it all up and bag it at the airport. It's cool, this stuff happens all the time . . . Don't cry, baby . . .' He took me into his arms and stroked my hair.

'I don't think I'm crying about the bag, Dan.'

'What's up then? Oh . . . I get it . . . I see. It's because you're flying economy class, isn't it?'

I laughed through my tears and wiped my eyes, trying to compose myself. 'I'll be fine. It's cool, really.' He always joked when he could sniff a waft of conversational seriousness, and I certainly wasn't about to be the sole soppy loser this time.

Neither of us spoke for a minute.

'I don't want you to go either, Han.' Genuineness suddenly reflected in Dan's eyes, his voice and his grip on me. 'I'm going to miss you so much. And all week I've been racking my brains as to what might happen after tonight, how soon I can come back to see you, or how I can get you to come and stay with me in LA . . . But all I could come up with is that I have to see you again. Soon. Tuesday, preferably. You're my little Vomiting Gidget.'

Utterly shocked at his honesty, I nervously laughed, but he kissed me by way of stopping me. We kissed with our eyes open, and it felt like my flight and the hotel room and the broken bag disappeared, and all that remained was us. Tears fell down my face and I broke the kiss to hug him closely again. How could I leave this? What would happen next? Would he pull the same bullshit move on me as last time? Should I bring it up? No. Words spoke far louder than actions – telling him he'd upset me wouldn't make him contact me more, it would only make him feel obligated to contact me more, which, in my mind, was even worse.

'C'mon, beautiful.' He pulled away and looked at me. 'No point wasting our last moments carrying on. Let's enjoy our night, pretend like it's our first. And when you get home, know I'll be thinking of your brown little kicker on a surfboard.'

The fact that he had slipped back into joke-mode signalled the 'deep stuff' was over. I took a deep breath. 'You're right. Let's tie this stupid bag up and go.'

'See? That's why I love you, babe, you don't sook out.'

He was searching for something in the kitchen drawer to tie around my bag, and spoke as though he was asking where the scissors were.

Only *he'd said he loved me.*

Could he mean it? Or was it just a phrase he bandied around? Lots of people did that. He probably didn't even realise what he was saying. But, even as I was talking myself out of believing it, I was inwardly frenzied at the idea that he might've meant it. Talk about throwing spanners.

'Hey, Dan? No goodbyes at the airport, okay? I hate them. We have to make out as though I'm just catching a bus to work or something.'

'Or going to the bathroom?'

'Exactly.'

'Can we make out for a bit first?'

'Guess so.'

'Then okay. Even though I'll be a mess when you go through those gates. Especially as you look so good in those jeans. I'll have to take Xanax tonight, you realise.'

'I'm gonna get drunk at the airport bar,' I said resolutely. 'Talk to the barman about how sad and lonely I am, make the pianist play me a Fleetwood Mac song.'

'Don't miss your flight, will you. I'd *hate* for that to happen and you'd have to stay another night. Or twelve.'

The idea of another night with him made me melt. But the reality was that I was heading home tonight. And might never see him again. And, ultimately, I had to try to forget about him as soon as possible. It was too much to bear.

24.

The test

> The key to applying bronzer: apply it in two massive number '3's down each side of the face, beginning at the middle of your forehead, almost in the hairline, sweeping down onto the cheekbone, and then finishing on the jaw line. Go over the figure 3s several times to build up your desired Bahama-ness.

I felt like death physically, but like soft whirls of fairy floss mentally. I had kept my word to Dan and inhaled three red wines while waiting for my flight the night before, on top of two at dinner, and now I was hung over, and stiff from a sleepless night next to an overweight man who'd invaded half my seat and snored like a banshee. All of that aside, there was the afterglow of Dan, which cloaked me cosily and made me smile dreamily even when my circumstances were more deserving of a grimace.

I'd chosen to compensate for feeling foul with a turbo-charged appearance. As soon as the flight landed, I'd raced home to shower and dress, blow-drying my hair, and choosing a hot white dress to wear with the ravishing new Miu Miu wedges I'd bought in Hawaii. I couldn't wait to show them off to Iz, but as she was doing a mega-conference, she was busy until late this evening, when I would probably be soundly asleep. I completed my look with loads of bronzer and pink gloss to offset my tan. Looking roughly 678 times better than I felt, I set off for the office.

'Hannah! You look *amazing*!'

Kate greeted me with a mile-wide smile and a hug. She was illegally chipper for 8.25 a.m. and as I was still pre-caffeine, I wanted to put her on slow motion, and maybe dim her brightness a bit, too. Thankfully, Jay and Marley were both at a day spa on the coast for a conference with a yoga-wear client, so I didn't have to speak too much at work. And, as I had no functions, I was free to go home as soon as I was done filing my story on how highlights in the right places can change the look of your face. It took me eight hours to write 350 words, but once they were done, I was off.

Part of me was annoyed I had no functions where I could show off my tan and my wedges and my tales, but I'd see the girls soon enough, and an outfit unseen was an outfit that was as good as brand-new, I consoled myself.

Hang on, what about Gabe? I called his mobile; it rang out. How unusual. A text chimed in seconds later.

In meeting, can't answer phone but can text – you home, yes? Tell me ALL. Did you get hitched in a white triangle bikini? Did you tell him he's a pig for never contacting you? Are you in love?

I smiled and shook my head.

None of the above, sadly, but I did vomit on him while surfing hung over – equally romantic, non?

That's my beauty, always elegant, classy, chic. Are you sad? Miss him?

Do but wish I didn't. Was pretty amazing week and he's criminally good-looking and fun and sexy – sigh – but don't worry, I'm staying a strong bitch like we said I would. STRONG. BITCH.

Good girl. He's v lucky to have had you for a whole week. I barely get an hour per month. Now you stay a strong bitch and don't be down when he doesn't call, because we ALREADY KNOW HE WON'T and so it doesn't faze us because we are hot and don't care and just enjoyed Hawaii sex week for what it was. You SURE you okay?

No, but will be soon, promise. You free next few nights for dinner? Debrief?

Of course, beauty, will email you later. Love you and glad you're home safe and no longer vomiting on people xx

Feeling jovial after Gabe's texts, I decided to splurge on a cab. I waited patiently in the queue, enjoying the looks my summer-girl get-up was attracting from men in suits who walked by. I couldn't stop smiling and lightly swaying in the warm evening breeze. I must've looked pleasantly intoxicated. In a way, I was.

'Hannah, is that you?'

I knew that voice.

I did not want to see the person with the papers to that voice.

I turned my head weakly and swallowed. Jesse stood behind me, smiling like a loon.

I took a deep breath in and smiled widely. Stuff it. I looked good, I felt strong; hit me with your best, punk.

'It *is* you! You've changed your hair! Wow. You look great . . . really tanned. Where've you been?'

'Hawaii.'

'I love Hawaii. I went there myself a few weeks back.' He paused, hoping I'd ask why.

A taxi pulled up to the curb. Thank *God.* I began walking towards it.

'Han.' Jesse was calling from behind me. 'Han, um, do . . . do you want to get some dinner, maybe?'

Pardon?

'I . . . I can't, Jesse, I'm sorry but . . . I've got plans . . .' And with that I closed the taxi door. I had no idea what had just come over me, but it smelled faintly like strength.

As we pulled onto the expressway, I finally calmed down enough to reflect on what had just happened. Jesse had asked me out. I wondered why I wasn't smiling. Here was Jesse, saying something I had dreamed of for months, and yet I didn't feel excited. I just felt kind of confused. And numb. And like I wanted to be back in Dan's arms.

I got home and paced around nervously. My overtired brain began to go ballistic. Why hadn't Dan called to see if I'd got home safely? Why was Jesse suddenly wanting to hang out? And why was there never any fucking FOOD IN HERE?!

A text came through with 'I Suck' attached as the name. Jesse.

Han, I know this is out of left field, but seeing you tonight just reminded me of so many things. I'd love to see you sometime soon, even if just for a coffee?

I couldn't believe his arrogance! After months of nothing he thought I'd drop everything for a date with him! I reread the text disbelievingly. And then I read it again. And again.

I opened a bottle of wine that, being worth over $50 and a gift, was not meant for a solo session of angry drinking, but it was all I had. I was totally confused. My ego was popping the cork of some Bollinger, nodding smugly and doing a victory dance, but my head was standing with its arms crossed, tapping its foot and saying, 'Oh *really*? You want to go back *there*? After all you've been through? Remind me, why did we bother with all of those rules and regulations? Have you forgotten all the hard work we've done? ARE YOU ON DRUGS?'

This event needed immediate workshopping. *I needed* Iz. I called her mobile; it was off. Desperate, I called her home phone, even though I knew there was little chance she would actually be there. After a few rings, a male voice answered the phone.

'Hello?'

'Oh, Kyle, hi, it's Hannah . . . um, I think I know the answer but Iz isn't there, is she?'

'Nope, she isn't, but this isn't Kyle . . .'

Oh God. Not *now.* I needed her to be stable right now! How could she have broken up with Kyle already?

'Well, whatever your name is, do you know when she'll be back? It's urgent.'

'Hannah, Hannah, it's Dec. Are you okay? What's wrong?'

Dec. Dec! Of course! 'Dec, I'm so sorry. I'd completely forgotten you were staying with Iz.'

'Hopefully not for too much longer, I'm two-thirds of the way to finding a place of my own.'

'But surely Iz doesn't mind?'

He laughed. 'I wouldn't do it to her, Han. Not as I'm moving back for good. There's no way we could stand living together full time.'

What? Dec was going to be around all the time? I'd been given way too much information for one fifteen-minute span. My head was going to implode any second.

I cleared my throat and tried to play it cool.

'Wow, welcome home! Why did you . . . ?'

'Well, I've just signed a pretty meaty contract with my well-paying telco friends, meaning they basically expect me to be on call twenty-four hours, not every few weeks . . . and, you know, it had always been on the cards, but Pia never really wanted to . . .'

'Oh. Well, I mean, it's great that you're back home if you always wanted to come back here.'

'Yeah, it just feels right, you know?'

'Well, Iz is, like, the best person in the whole world, so it will need to be somewhere pretty flash to convince you to move out,' I joked feebly. Was I already trying to dissuade him from moving out?

He laughed. 'You know, I don't actually mind living with my sis, even if her male supermodel is over and playing Xbox twenty-four-seven. Hey, how was your trip to Hawaii?'

He didn't even need to be in front of me and I was blushing like a fool.

'Um, yeah, yeah, it was nice . . . Ilearnedtosurf!' I exclaimed, making the conversation light and not about Dan, even though Iz would've told him everything.

'Noooo, little Han's gone all surfer chick! That's unreal! We'll have to go out for a wave sometime.'

An image of me looking walrus-like in a wetsuit with my hair all over my face flashed into my head. No. There would be no surfing with Dec.

'Uh, maybe not. I'm kind of really bad.'

'Then I'll teach you so you're kind of really good.'

I laughed flirtatiously before realising I was laughing flirtatiously. Hannah! *Focus!* You're not here to flirt with your best friend's older brother. Your ex-boyfriend wants a date and *you need to speak to Iz!*

'We'll see. Hey, if you see Iz can you ask her to call me urgently?'

'Sounds serious – let me guess, you need to borrow a dress and it's a matter of life and death?'

'Dec, don't be an arse. Just ask her to call me, please.'

'Okay, Gidget, will do.'

I laughed and hung up. I shook my head at how my day was panning out. When you are finally into one guy, five other guys will always crawl out of the woodwork to confuse things.

I dialled Iz's mobile again. This time she answered.

'Iz, hi! I'm so glad I got you: Jesse asked me on a *date*! I saw him at the taxi stand, and I looked really good, and then he texted me asking me to catch up, and I should be over the moon but I'm not, I'm really not, and I'm thinking that maybe that was the test, you know, from the universe, and that it proves I am over him, like, for good, because if I wasn't, I'd be totally frothing about it, but I'm not, and —'

'Han, honey, slow down. What happened? Jesse gave you a test?'

'No, nooo. He didn't give me a test, it was a test from the *univer*— Forget it, have you finished work?'

'Just now. Shall I come over? I want to hear Hawaii stories, too! Shall I bring wine?'

'Nope, I already have a bottle with our name on it.'

'So you don't feel anything for Jesse? Nothing? Not a *thing*?'

'Honestly, I don't!'

Iz looked at me in a way that implied she didn't really believe me. She took another sip of her wine and screwed her mouth over to one side, as if she were weighing up whether to let me be over Jesse or not.

'And what if he calls?'

'I'll say I'm busy.'

'Sends flowers?'

'Enjoy them, send a thank-you text and tell Dan so he gets jealous.'

'AHA! Dan! It's about Dan, of course it is. Han, do you think that maybe you're only feeling like this because you've still got the scent of Dan on you?'

'Well, no – I mean, yes, I am obviously still thinking about Dan because I just spent a week in the same bed as him, and, you know, I guess I like him, even though I shouldn't – I mean, he hasn't even fucking texted me yet!'

'Back to his old tricks.'

'But, see, I always thought that the minute Jesse asked for another chance, I would fall to bits and dump any guy I was with to see him. But I have no urge to go on a date with him. Seriously.'

'I think you do.'

'No, Iz, I'm telling you to your face, with no crossed fingers or toes, that I do not.'

'No, no, ssshh, I mean, I think you should go on a date with him. Just to know, once and for all. What if you never go, and then you later realise, when you're barefoot and pregnant to a plumber, that maybe Jesse was the man for you?'

I hated that she was right. I hated the idea of having to go on a date with him when I was feeling so strong. What if I melted? What if he got me again? I didn't want that. I wanted Dan.

'Okay, okay. Say I do go on the date, and I start to like him again, and then he hurts me? Then what, huh? Does that make the last eight months null and void? I couldn't bear going through all of that torture again, Iz . . . I just couldn't.'

I was starting to get a lump in my throat. I really needed some sleep; I was being far too emotional.

'Just think about it for now. He may never call.'

'Oh, thanks.'

'No, I didn't mean it like that, I just mean maybe we wait until he calls again till we do our heads in about it? And anyway, you should be riding the high of riding Dan for as long as possible. Tell me about how you nearly drowned again.'

As I opened my mouth to start, Iz's phone beeped loudly with a new text message. She checked it and started squealing.

'Kyle got the job. Kyle got THE JOB!'

'What job?'

She stopped texting back and stared at me. 'This is all too much for one day. How about we have dinner at mine tomorrow and I tell you everything then?'

'Everything what? I just want to know what Kyle's new job is? Is he the new face of Calvin Klein? What? You can tell me, I won't say anything.'

She kept looking at me. Then she let out a big sigh and put her phone down. She took a large sip of wine and started clasping her hands together in a fidgety way. The way she did when she was really nervous.

'Iz, what's going on?'

She was mute.

'Okay, now you're being weird. I'm scared. Speak soon or I will physically extract the words from you.'

Another sigh, then, 'Okay, well, Kyle went for this job a while back, to be on this TV show. It's kind of a model reality TV show, I guess, but with not as many hot tubs and no Tyra Banks. Anyway, it follows him and four other models – three girls, two guys – around the world for a year as they go for castings and do jobs and stuff. They wanted someone really loose and fun and young in the show, and they couldn't find anyone suitable in America or Europe so they did one mass casting here about a month back.'

'And he got the gig?'

'Yep. They just called him.'

'That's *incredible* news! Wow! So what's wrong with that?'

'That's the thing. They're basing them all in New York – they each get an apartment right in the meatpacking district —'

'Ooh, how cool! He can buy you lots of things!'

'Well, yeah, I guess, except that . . .' She was visibly squirming in her seat, shifting from side to side.

'What aren't you telling me?' I stared at Iz as she looked anywhere but at me. My conversational composure betrayed the suggestion of panic in my stomach.

'Oh Han . . . I'd really rather talk to you later . . .' She reached across the table and grabbed my hands. I pulled them away and folded them firmly against my chest.

'Iz, just tell me. Are you knocked up? Getting married? What?' What the hell was so bad that she couldn't tell me? And why was everything happening at once? Jesus, I left the country for a week, one week, and everything went insane.

'Okay, okay.' She took another deep breath and looked into my eyes with her head lowered. 'It's just that Kyle and I, we kind of said that if he got the job, we would go together. I would go with him to New York. Because you know I've always wanted to go there and try my luck, and my friend Veronica said she could get me a job at this really amazing new French restaurant, and it's just a really good opportunity, and . . .'

She kept talking, but I wasn't hearing her any more. She was just a silent, moving mouth. Everything around me faded into a kind of white mist, and I felt like I might be sick. She couldn't be moving to the other side of the world. Leaving me behind. Leaving me here all alone. We had a plan to go together. She couldn't be going with him. I must have misheard her. I'd simply misheard her. Kyle was going, not her. She wouldn't move overseas with some guy she'd only been with for a few months and leave me here. What about Project Mansion?

'You're moving to New York. Is that what you said? Did you say you were moving, with Kyle, to New York?' I needed to hear it again.

'Yes . . . I'm so sorry. I didn't want to tell you now.'

Before I could register it happening, tears began silently rolling down my cheeks. I couldn't look at Iz, but her sniffling told me she was also crying.

'Please don't cry. That's what I wanted to talk to you about, because I know you wanted to be closer to Dan, and it could all work out perfectly, don't you see?'

The same sense of overwhelming nausea I had felt the night Jesse broke up with me invaded every artery, limb and cell of my body.

'When do you go?' I wiped my nose with my sleeve, not caring how revolting it was.

'Kyle has to pretty much leave immediately, because they start filming in two weeks, and I told him I would be there for that. For his first day.'

'Two weeks? You're leaving in two fucking weeks?'

'Han, don't be mad —'

'Don't be mad? I'm not mad; why would I be mad? You've known this guy for five minutes and now you're going to live overseas with him, even though we've been planning it all our lives? Yeah, you know what? You're right: I am pretty fuckin' mad.' I was overtired and being emotionally psychotic, but I didn't care. I was feeling monstrous. And, knowing that, I knew Iz should leave before I said something spectacularly hurtful that I didn't mean. I stood up and took the empty wine bottle to the sink as a hint.

'Han, what are you doing? Can't we talk about this?'

'Iz, I'm sorry to be so dramatic, but no, no we can't. You were right. Now was not a good time to tell me.' I wiped my eyes and cleared my throat. 'I think I'm going to go to bed.' I stood with my arms folded near the bathroom, waiting for her to go.

She took one long, sad look at me before standing up and putting her bag on her shoulder. She reached the door with her back to me, but as she turned the handle she spun slowly around to look at me. 'Han, I'm so sorry . . .'

I walked into the bathroom and closed the door. I waited to hear the front door close behind her before allowing the tears to stream down my face, going over the conversation in my head, getting angrier and sadder and more worked up by the minute. My head and the ferocity of my emotions were spinning so quickly. I felt completely, utterly out of control.

Fully aware of, but revelling in, my irrational, melodramatic mindset, I asked an invisible audience if my life could possibly get any more heinous at this point.

25.

Beauty border-patrol

You can get all the needles you want in your face, but your sagging neck and wrinkled décolletage will give you away instantly. The point? Your face ends at your chest. Always apply your face cream down to your neck and chest (buying a cheap one for just this region is a good idea), or use a dedicated neck cream.

At work the next morning Jay was very happy to see me, which was nice. Kind of.

'Honey, how WAS it?! Jesus! You look like shit! You didn't sleep the entire seven days, did you? You stay here; I'll find you something in the goo room to make you pretty again. Surely it exists – the celebs can't look that good in airport pap-snaps without something cosmetic.'

She walked into the cupboard and started tinkering around in the skincare section. 'Hydrating? Mmmm . . . Neck cream? *Gross*, who uses this stuff? . . . Anti-ageing? No . . . Oh! Radiance-boosting éclat . . . That's what you need! Here, slap this on . . .' She came back to my desk and held it out proudly. 'Here we go, this will fix you. Han, have you been crying? Oh darling, it's okay . . . of course you miss him.'

'No, no. It's not that . . . I'm okay, Jay, really I am, but can we talk about it later?'

'All right . . . But I'm watching you.' She leaned down and

hugged me, and then walked back to her desk. She turned to blow me a kiss. 'It makes me happy that you're home.'

I laughed through my sniffs.

I took a sip of my tea and went back to my emails – all 456 of them – and tried to forget about Iz. I checked my phone again. She still hadn't texted. What was *with* her? Why should I text first? She was the one ruining Project Mansion and abandoning me. I still couldn't believe what the last twenty-four hours had thrown my way.

I checked my phone again. Nothing. Not from Dan and not from Iz. The cocktail of incredulousness, hurt and rage under my skin simmered with a little more heat.

My mood lifted a little as I started going through all the packages that had arrived during my tropical absence. There were so many enticing new goodies I wanted to play with that my take-home-to-try box was overflowing. I couldn't wait to test the three-step at-home facial for hydration and radiance. I needed it, as Jay had kindly pointed out. At least one nice thing had happened while I was away. That it was the introduction of liquorice into a masque was a little bit sad.

From behind me a voice made a very deliberate 'ahem' sound.

When I turned around, Eliza was there, with her trademark mane and signature tight jeans, hand placed deliberately on one delicate hip.

'Do we need to talk?'

Great. She was in Slytherin mode.

'Um . . . no? Do we?'

'You look like shit. What's with you?'

I took a breath. I didn't actually think I looked that bad, but apparently I was delusional. 'I'm sorry, Eliza. I've just had some bad news this morning, that's all.'

'Are you okay? More importantly, will you be okay? You know we're presenting to Silk Effect this afternoon, right? And you need to look good.'

Oh God. Oh God, not today. A presentation would tip me over.

'I'll be fine, I just . . . I'll get a blow-dry at lunch and redo my makeup,' I said perkily.

'Good idea. We need you to be fine; this is a big account. Oh, and can you clean out your inbox – it's pissing everyone off that your emails bounce.'

With that, she turned around and walked back to her office.

At that moment, Kate came over with a stack of finals that needed approval. It was all of the pages I'd done prior to Hawaii. Superb.

My inbox dinged.

To: Hannah@gloss.com; Marley@gloss.com
From: Jacinta@gloss.com
Subject: Home
I'll drive us all home today. Meet in foyer at 6. We need to hear about Hawaii. xx

I looked at my phone again: still nothing from Iz. Or Dan. Silly me for thinking so. Silly me for thinking he maybe, possibly, *might* have found twenty-five seconds to text and see if I got home okay. But no, he was so terribly busy that he simply couldn't. Maybe the phone wasn't working. I turned if off and back on again. Nothing. *Bastard.*

At four o'clock Eliza came around and raised her eyebrows. 'Ready?'

I took a deep breath and delivered the first line in my false-bravado script. 'Ready squared. Let's rock this boat.'

'Whatever. Come on.' As she stalked off shaking her head,

I scrambled to follow her, clutching notes and trying to remember my new plan for presentations: three points, no more. Who the *Gloss* reader is; why she reads my pages; what I give her. Easy. Easy. Easy. I know this stuff. *I know this stuff.*

There was little time for pleasantries with these guys. They were seated, smiling, and, after six hours of magazine people all saying roughly the same thing just with a different colour-scheme on PowerPoint, bored as hell.

Marley wore an amazing nude-coloured, high-neck frilled blouse and a tight, high-waisted black pencil skirt. Add perfect hair, makeup and new-season Marc Jacobs heels and you could have mistaken her for Jessica Alba on a press junket. She passed out our brand presentation folders and special *Gloss* pens and leather notebooks she'd had made. She was frighteningly good.

'So, as you know, *Gloss* has been through a redesign, and we're really happy with it. We've had such an incredible response . . .'

Marley and Eliza carried the suck-up flame for a few minutes, before passing the torch to me.

I cleared my throat and launched. I was having such a revolting day that nothing these people could throw at me could possibly make a dent, so bring it on. I was going in fighting.

'The *Gloss* reader operates on a dual platform of necessity and luxury. Necessity because she'll always have blackheads and the occasional spot and hairy legs' – they laughed – 'and luxury because, while she doesn't have a Dior bag, or Chanel heels, what she *does* have is the ability to buy into each of these luxury brands with some lipstick or perfume. In that respect, beauty provides her with access to a world she otherwise wouldn't be granted, a world where spending two-hundred-and-fifty dollars on highlights and fifty dollars on lip gloss is not only acceptable, it's encouraged. And that's where *Gloss* is happy to help out.'

I took a breath. I caught Marley looking at me, smiling.

'My job is simple. I am her beauty border patrol. I scan all of the products coming in to make sure she is only privy to the best, newest and hottest. Because she likes to know first. She likes to be the one at the dinner party talking about the new mascara or fragrance – it gives her status; it makes her feel powerful.'

It must have been a solid eight minutes before I was done, but Eliza and Marley didn't seem to mind. They finished off the rest of the presentation, chatting about our circulation and what was coming up for the next few months. The clients shook hands and asked for further information about the *Gloss* pyjama party (they had a range called Bedhead; Marley knew this and made it crystal clear what a perfect fit the event would be for them to sponsor . . . for the bargain price of $450 000), and then we were out, walking back to the office.

'What the fuck did you take before you went in there, and where do I get some?'

I smiled. 'I've no idea where that came from. I just think I was so sick of saying what I thought they wanted to hear that I just spoke about what I felt was true, as dicky as that sounds.'

'Well, you did good, honey.' Marley patted my shoulder. 'You deserve a drink tonight, that's for sure.'

She walked on. I allowed myself a moment to loll about in my victory, small and insignificant as it was in the scheme of my job, beauty and even magazines in general. It felt good to know that, for once, I was not only competent but impressive. Thank God for that. It was tiring always feeling like a fraud.

26.

Would you listen to the Italian

Here's why your salon blow-dry lasts: every strand of your hair is completely dry. To make your DIY blowie last, blast your hair with a cool shot when you're done. If after that your hair feels at all damp, dry it some more. Don't and you're up for frizz and oily roots way sooner than you should be.

'So, let me get this straight – you've just come home from shagging Dan, Dan, the Orgasm Man all week, and you run into Jesse?' Jay's voice was high with disbelief as she took in the coincidence of it all. I had decided not to tell them about Iz yet, instead focusing on the whole Jesse thing.

'Yeah, weird, huh?' I could tell the girls were disappointed that I wasn't able to give the story the animation it deserved.

Marley piped up. 'How good that you looked hot when you saw him, though.'

'Uh, yeah . . .'

'Do you think he figured out you'd been away with another guy?' asked Jacinta.

'Don't be dumb, Jay – how would he know that? He would've just thought she was away for work or something.'

'Well, smart-arse, considering she looked so hot and he now wants to date her again, his paranoia would've kicked up a notch, so it *does* make sense.'

'Um, guys? None of that really matters. I'm not interested in Jesse any more.'

'You're funny. So, what will you say when he calls? Or is he more of a texter?' Jay, being a hopeless romantic, was the most interested and excited I'd seen her. I was increasingly worried about her having a car accident, as she kept looking at me for reactions that matched her questions.

'What a fairytale. You wouldn't read about it, not even in *Gloss*. The ex breaks your heart, screws around, then realises he only wants you. Jesus. It makes me sick when I think about it.' Marley corrected herself after having temporarily forgotten romance was for wimps and losers.

'Guys, I don't want to date him. I've moved on. *Seriously*.'

'Are you on crack? You have to go. There is no option but to go. You are going.' Marley was getting bored.

'I agree. We've seen how he's tortured you. And how much it's hurt. And now you've won! This is your time to shine. *You must go on a date with him*. If only to make sure. Because, God, you've just come back from a week with Dan, so of course you're a little confused, but when your tan fades and Dan stops contacting you like he did last time – sorry, Han, but he did – you'll start thinking of Jesse again. You know you will.'

I was irritated that they thought they knew me better than I did. I was also annoyed at the comment about Dan. Probably because on some level I knew it was true.

I felt my phone vibrate in my bag, but couldn't reach it in time because my hands were full with my take-home-to-try box of makeup. Ha! It was probably Dan, proving them wrong. Or Iz, finally apologising.

'Okay, so say I go, and it stirs up a bunch of feelings I had finally got rid of? Life's complicated already without him tap-dancing back in to shake things up. I'm fine without him. And I'm staying fine without him.'

I checked my phone. There was a missed call from a number I didn't recognise. Which ruled out Iz. And it wasn't an international number, so it wasn't Dan.

'But what if this is the biggest mistake of your life? What if he's genuinely sorry and wants you back, and you meet for dinner and then fall in love again over a glass of wine? How can you live knowing that is a very real possibility?'

'All right, *all right*. Does that mean you'll get off my back?' I sighed and shook my head. It was easy for them to say all of this; they weren't the ones trudging around in head-screw swamp.

Before they had a chance to say anything more, I finished off the conversation. 'Right-o. Whatever. Thanks for the lift, Jay.' I struggled to rebalance my take-home box before getting out. I'd bet Jesse wouldn't call anyway. I hoped he wouldn't. Or that he would, but only so I could reject him. Shit, I was confused and irritable and hungry and dangerously close to losing the entire contents of the box; I needed to get inside and into bed.

I leaned the box precariously against the lift's mirror, and almost lost the lot unlocking the front door before urgently dumping it onto my kitchen bench, two seconds away from the whole bottom falling out. A text message chirped, breaking the first moment of quiet I'd had all day. I sighed and got my phone out. If this wasn't Iz or Dan . . .

Han, it's Dec. I called before but thought I'd text too, in case you're not feeling like chatting. I just wanted to see how you're doing. Iz told me you were upset after hearing her news and she's a bit scared to call, so thought I'd interfere and speak to you first? I'll try you again later. dx

So Dec was the unknown number. Of course he was – anything that might simplify the day would be too much to ask for. I put my phone on silent; I'd deal with responding later.

I stripped off, chucked on an old T-shirt and daggy undies and got under my covers. The light coming in under my blinds was so bright; there was no way I could sleep. I yanked open my bedside-table drawer to get my eye mask. I looked around furiously with no luck. Fuck! Where was it? Why was everything so fucking hard! It was in my suitcase. My suitcase that was out in the lounge room. Fuck it, fuck it, FUCK IT.

I burst into tears of exhaustion, exasperation and frustration. As Iz would say, this was one mega Come Apart. Oh, Iz . . .

And I still hadn't heard from Dan.

Fuck them. Fuck them all. Who needed them? Not me.

27.

Seven missed calls

Multi-task: use a pearly lip gloss not only on lips, but on brow and cheekbones as a highlighter. Use hair serum on your collarbone and shins to get a sheen. And use bronzer on your décolletage, eyelids and cheeks.

The next morning, after twelve hours of sleep, I woke up thoroughly confused. My body had crept around so that I was lying horizontally across my bed. All of my pillows were on the floor. My location baffled me, and the time of day – 6.30 a.m. – seemed impossible. I rubbed my eyes and noted that I felt refreshed and revolting at the same time. I'd had way too much sleep.

I reached for my phone.

I grabbed it after much heaving. Seven missed calls, six text messages. Shit.

Three calls from Jay, plus one from Dec, one from no number, one from Yasmin, and one from Marley.

The messages were mostly voicemail notifications, aside from one from Dec asking if I was okay, one from Marley telling me she was drunk and did I want to come to Lizard Lounge, and – behold – one from Dan.

No sweet cheeks on my pillows or squished in my hands. Fun this ain't. Come back. That's an order.

I smiled. There he was. Dan was back. God, one text was all it took and I was smitten again. I wrote back a silly response without even thinking. All of the wrongness that had just crept out of me bolted back in, slamming the door behind it.

You miiiiiss me, you wanna maaaarry me.

I knew from experience that getting a decent reply from him would be a miracle.

The last text was from 'I Suck', aka Jesse.

So good to see you. I really would love to take you to dinner sometime?

I had to call Iz . . . *Shit!* I couldn't. Damn her! Damn this fight. It was stupid. I suddenly realised how dumb it was to carry on like this: she was leaving soon; I should be making the most of the time I had left with her. She was clearly still pissed at me, though, if she'd had all this time to call and hadn't made a move. It occurred to me that maybe that was part of the reason she wasn't calling: she wasn't actually in the wrong. I felt awful, realising my attack on her was entirely selfish. She deserved so much better from her supposed best friend.

Maybe calling Dec would be the best way to go about fixing everything. He would tell me how to best approach her and how she was feeling.

I called his number without for a second considering the time of day. It rang out. I called again. Third ring in, a groggy Dec answered.

'She's alive.'

'Hi, Dec . . . Shit, did I wake you? Oh God, I'm so sorry; I didn't even check the time before I called. Go back to sleep, I'll call back later. So sorry, Dec.'

'No, no, I'm up.' He cleared his throat. 'So, how are you feeling?'

'Thousand times better than yesterday. Sorry I didn't get back to you earlier, but I was feeling monstrous. Wasn't coping at all. Probably would've hung up on you in tears, that kind of caper.'

He laughed; I loved his laugh. It was one of those infectious laughs that made me want to laugh along with him.

'So, will you speak to my sister today, do you think? I'm pretty sure she wants to hear from you. In fact, I *know* she desperately wants to hear from you. She's really upset . . .'

'I want to hear from her, too, Dec, but I guess, I mean, it's up to me, I've realised that now.'

'She's scared of you, Han. She knows how angry you are that she's going, and she feels like, well . . .'

'What?' If he said anything about me avoiding her, or running away from things that caused me pain, I was hanging up.

'She feels like you think she's making a mistake, I guess. The whole Kyle thing, and how fast it's all happening, and all those plans you two had to move over there . . . I guess she just feels like you think she's making the wrong decision. And you know how much your opinion means to her . . .'

'She really thinks that?' I was stunned. Here I was, thinking she was being venomous, and all she was worried about was my approval?

'But how? Why? . . . I didn't say anything to that effect . . . all I said was, well, I don't even remember to be honest, but I know I was pissed. But who wouldn't be if their best friend of forever had just told them they were leaving for New York?'

'And you can't see how she might interpret that as disapproval?'

'It's not disapproval, Dec, it's . . . I just feel like . . . you know, we were supposed to move overseas *together*, that had always been the plan, and now she's gone and decided to go without me. It's not disapproval, Dec. It's just sadness.' My voice broke on the last few words. I was embarrassed; I didn't want Dec to hear me cry. I sounded like a bad soapy star when I tried to talk and cry at the same time.

'Han, of course you're sad . . . it's okay to be sad, I'd be devastated if my best friend was heading off overseas to live, too.'

'All it will take is one phone call and you two will sort it out. She needs to explain her feelings, and you yours, and then you two can get on with enjoying the next two weeks. I told her she needs to forget about Kyle for now, and focus on getting her life sorted, so if you're worried he'll be clouding her timetable, you needn't; she's all yours. And she always will be, Han – we Morrisons always fly back home. I'm living proof.'

'Oh, you're a good brother, Dec. She's lucky to have you.' I sniffed and wiped my eyes. I felt lighter already.

'She's lucky to have you. She'll miss you like crazy, you know that.'

'Not as much as I'll miss her,' I couldn't resist. 'Anyway, thanks so much, Dec. And sorry to wake you. I'm such a nong.'

'Pleasure, Han. Always enjoy our chats. Hey, have you got some function at the wharf this morning?'

'Yeah, I think I have . . .'

'I might see you there – my mate Chris is making me chaperone him.'

I felt a flutter of nerves. Dec at a work function! I made a mental note to look outstanding today.

'Great. Then you can see how glam these early-morning functions *really* are.'

'Excellent. Don't be too cool to chat to me, now, will you?'

'Hardly, Dec.' I giggled. 'Bye!'

I put the phone on the bed and stared at the ceiling. I smiled. He was so right. This was just a silly misunderstanding. And I needed to fix it.

Jesse would have to take a backseat for now.

28.

Horse doors

> Your eye area is very delicate. It has few oil glands, meaning if you pull at it, it won't spring back. And you'll get wrinkles. The key is to be gentle. Tap your eye cream in. Dab your concealer on. Remove your eye makeup by pressing and holding the remover-soaked cotton pad over your eye, then carefully wiping it down off your eyelid and lashes. None of this rubbing business, please.

'Hi . . . is Isabelle around?'

The old guy placing napkins on the table stared at me as though I were some form of predatory insect.

'Why?'

'I'm family. I need to speak with her.' I wasn't in the mood for games. Plus, the coffees I was awkwardly nursing were incredibly hot.

Old Guy didn't care. He looked me up and down and, mumbling, walked through swinging doors to the kitchen, presumably to find some insect-killer.

I tried not to feel nervous. It was ridiculous to feel nervous. Iz was my best friend. It was all just a misunderstanding.

A minute later, she walked out wiping her hands on a tea towel. Her face was twisted in confusion, but when she saw me her face became neutral and she stopped dead.

She said something to Mr Sourface, and, after looking me up and down again – what was his problem? – he went back into the kitchen.

She walked over, still fiddling with the tea towel, and stopped just in front of me. She looked at the floor.

'Hi,' my voice croaked.

'Hi.' She remained staring at the floor.

'I, um, I just wanted to know if you had time for a coffee and a quick chat?'

She said nothing. Tough crowd.

'It's okay if you can't, of course, I understand if you're too busy.' Perhaps she couldn't look at me was because her eyes were going to shoot laser beams into mine, blinding me for life.

Suddenly she looked up. There were no laser beams, just tears. She sniffled and wiped her nose with her finger, looked straight at me and let the words hurtle from her mouth.

'Han, I'm so sorry. I was scared that you thought I was making the wrong decision and, you know, maybe deep down I thought you were right, because I don't want to leave my life, I love my life and I love you, but then part of me knows I have to do this, and make a go of it, and I may only get a chance like this once, and I don't want to be a bitter old woman who looks back and thinks "What if?", you know? And I so badly wish that you were coming too, and that it would all work somehow . . .'

'Oh, Iz!' I was crying now too, and laughing at how pathetic we both were. I dumped my bag on the floor and put the coffees on a white tablecloth (my old mate was going to have a seizure), and walked over to give her a big hug.

With that, she burst into full sobbing, pressing her face into my shoulder and hugging me tight.

'Iz, I'm not mad at you, I'm not. I love you and of course I support you. I was just so scared you wouldn't talk to me before you left, and then you'd be overseas and we'd never get a chance to patch it up, and then you'd get all famous and have your own cooking show, and I'd sit on my lounge, all alone and miserable and friendless, and watch you whip cake batter and cry at how stupid I was not to fix things before you left, and, oh, I couldn't bear it!' She laugh-cried with me at that, and we both sobbed and hugged, relieved that such a vile scenario would never eventuate.

Finally, we broke apart, both discreetly trying to fix our running eye makeup.

'I'm so, so glad you came, Han.'

'If Dec hadn't told me where you were today, I was totally going to stalk you tonight.'

'He mentioned you two had spoken. He's got a bit of a crush on you, you know,' she said as she wiped her eyes.

Excuse me? Pause, rewind, play again in slow motion: Dec has a crush on *me?* This was monumental. This was the first time Iz had ever mentioned Dec liking me and not the other way around. Trying not to be obvious about my delight at this lovely little conversational missile, I searched Iz's face for a clue as to whether this was an appropriate time to make more of this topic. It wasn't. Dammit.

'So you're not still angry with me?'

'Of course not, Iz. I mean, here you are telling me your big exciting news, and I am a total bitch . . .'

We both stopped and reflected on how wrong it had all gone.

Iz broke the silence. 'Phwoof. Well. What a couple of days! I'm still in shock, Han, it's all so, well, scary.'

'Is Kyle being good and supportive?' I hoped that hadn't come out wrong.

'Totally. He's organised all of my stuff to be moved, and my flights, and is just being awesome. Poor love is freaking out, but is just beside himself with excitement. He's already completely changed his MySpace to reflect the New Him.' She smiled like a proud mum.

I laughed. Trucker would've done exactly the same thing. Silly little monkeys.

'Good on him. You two are going to have a ball. Truly. And, you know, it's nice that you're going into this whole new world together.' In the back of my mind I was fretting in advance for the moment Kyle became hugely famous, and realised he could have, be or do anyone, and Iz was just the loyal, before-he-was-famous girlfriend who stayed at home and waited for him to get back from the Emmys after-parties. I'd seen enough gossip magazines to know what happened over there. But Iz could handle it. She wouldn't hang around to be treated like shit – I hoped.

Iz shook her whole body and jumped up and down a few times. 'Enough of the sad shit! Man, can you imagine the airport scene? There'll be Oscar-winning performances, you can bet on it. Now, Jesse?'

I shook my head slowly, breathing out. 'He texted again, asking me to meet up. Oh, Iz, I really don't want to. I'm just starting to feel fully over him, and he's come in and shaken everything up. It's so like him.'

She squinted her eyes and pursed her lips to one side, in the way she did when she was thinking really hard.

'I think you should go,' she said triumphantly. 'Just to know for sure. And, you know, if Dan is the one you really want to be with – even though that seems a bit unlikely considering his location – or if Jesse is the one you want, or if you don't want either of them, a date with Jesse will tell you instantly.'

Somehow, hearing it from my dearest friend held a million times more gravitas than all of Jacinta's and Marley's arguments combined.

'Do you not think it kind of goes against all my rules?' I asked, already knowing it did.

'Completely. Maybe you should torture him for a few weeks

before going, or be late to the date, or even cancel at the last minute, but do go eventually. Selfishly – it's about you, not him. He's just a prawn in your hand.'

'It's pawn, Iz, like in chess.' I took a deep breath and grabbed my bag. 'I guess you're right. It will be good closure. And I'll definitely be administering some torture first. I'll start by not replying to his text for a few days. In fact, I'm putting his number under "Don't Answer" right now.' I changed his contact details, grinning. 'So glad we had this talk. Maybe we could have dinner tonight?'

'Oooh, I'd love to, but Kyle and I are going to his parents' place for dinner.'

I felt a stab of jealousy. I faked a smile. 'Maybe tomorrow, then. I'll call you later.' I gave her a kiss on the cheek and walked out.

I checked my phone for the time. Holy shit. I was so late for my breakfast function. It was for a new men's skincare range by a dermatologist based in London. Apparently, celebs were all over it like white on rice. I was happy enough to go, as Gabe would be there. Not to mention Dec.

As I walked out into the sunshine, I saw a cab with a light on heading my way. I threw my coffee in the bin next to me and hailed furiously. Finally, things were starting to go my way. I jumped in, gave brisk directions and began reapplying my makeup frantically. I didn't want Dec to see me looking anything other than amazing in my natural habitat.

When I walked into the restaurant, which was gleaming in the morning sunshine, its glass walls reflecting the bay foreshore, I couldn't see Dec or Fi or Gabe or Yasmin anywhere. The only person I could see was Jill, and there was no chance I would be chatting to her. As I'd never met the PR before, I didn't know who to find, and so I sauntered over to make myself a cup of tea.

The beauty girls, whose chirpiness wasn't even diluted by the obscene time of day, surrounded me as I stirred my tea. I enjoyed the warmth of the sun on my back, the fragrance of tuberose gently scenting the room, and the delicious food being handed around by wait staff with cosmetically whitened smiles.

'Mmm. What's that you're drinking?' Fi had arrived and was peering over my shoulder.

'English breakfast. What's yours?' Her tea was a red colour and there were suspicious bits floating around in it.

'Some hippie tea they're handing around. Foul. Of course, you haven't got a Hindu's chance in heaven of getting an espresso round here. Even though it's the crack of dawn. Honestly.' She shook her head and took another sip, scrunching up her nose as she swallowed.

'How weird is it having men here?' She was referring to the five or so men who awkwardly mingled with the beauty pack. 'Ooh, he's cute.'

I followed her gaze to see Dec and, I presumed, Chris walking in.

'Dec!' I said happily.

'You know him?' Fi looked at me in amazement.

'He's my best friend's older brother. Lovely, lovely guy . . .'

'Are you blushing? You're blushing!'

This was becoming boring. 'No I'm not. Shut up. I'm just happy to see him.'

'Apparently you are,' she said slyly.

Yasmin appeared from nowhere, clanging with bracelets and charms.

'Any espresso?'

'Nope, just tea. Fiona's really enjoying it . . .'

But Fi had gone.

'Starving too – any good food? Please tell me there's bacon of some description . . . Oh, look: horse doors. *Finally*.' Yasmin was clearly famished, and had spied some miniature food on a tray coming our way.

A cute young guy with an urban mohawk presented us with a tray of salmon and cream cheese on mini brioche bagels. The smell alone made me want to vomit – I couldn't handle fish sandwiches in the morning, no matter how hungry I was. It was just wrong.

'Can I get you a drink, madam?' Mohawk's eyes twinkled as he looked at me, holding his silver tray out for Yasmin to attack and destroy.

'Um, what do you have?'

'The drinks menu is just there on that board . . . I highly recommend the pomegranate and rosehip tea.'

I decided on a fierce forest-berry cocktail – I liked the idea of menacing fruit.

'Certainly, madam, anything else? We have vegetarian options for breakfast. Shall I bring some to you?'

Again, his eyes twinkled as he spoke. Was he flirting? Bizarre.

'Um, yes please. That'd be great.'

'As you wish.'

He spun around dramatically and disappeared into the mass of people. I saw Fi's face bob up in the crowd, and was surprised to see it was next to Dec's. She was flicking her hair and smiling, and he was smiling back as they spoke.

Was she flirting with Dec? I watched her long enough to see her tuck her hair behind her ear eleven times in thirty seconds, and laugh hysterically at everything Dec said, and surmised that yes, she most certainly was flirting. When women play with their hair, show off their neck and laugh at nothing, they be hunting.

I felt a pang of jealousy. Why would she do that? Why would *he* do that, knowing I was here?

Gabe's voice cut in. 'Hannah, that mischievous young man with the stupid hair wants to ravish you.'

'Gabe! Look, everyone, his royal gayness has graced us with his presence.'

'Hey, Gabe.' Yasmin kissed him on the cheek, not stopping to finish her mouthful first. 'Who wants to ravish Han?'

'The waiter! Wants to pour honey all over her and lick it off, from the way he's carrying on!'

'Oh, I didn't notice. Hair was kind of cool, though.'

Gabe stared at me with one brow cocked. 'What's with you? You're all vagued out. Do you need to eat? Let's get you some food.'

'Okay . . .' I followed his lead to the kitchen area, where we liked to intercept the waiters as they left the food preparation area. I was confused. What was Fi's caper? Latching onto Dec like that, knowing I clearly thought he was . . . what? Where was I heading with this? I was confused at my jealousy and tried to shake it off.

'So, um, see that guy in the navy top?' I steered Gabe towards Dec's direction. 'That's Dec.'

'*The* Dec?' Gabe looked at me wide-eyed. I nodded, mouth closed. 'He's so Polo Ralph Lauren it's disturbing. Are you sure he's into girls? I could make him a very happy husband. What's Fiona doing draped all over him like a cheap throw on an expensive lounge?'

'Who knows. She spotted him the second he came in and beelined for him not long after.'

'Silly girl, she has no chance with you around, but it's entertaining to watch her try. Have you spoken to him yet?'

I shook my head.

'Why not . . . ? Oops! No matter, he's on his way over now!'

I saw Dec apologising to Fiona and making his way over to Gabe and me. I nervously fluffed my flat hair and quickly dabbed on some gloss I'd left in the external pocket of my handbag for these exact situations.

Gabe murmured from behind closed lips, 'You look good enough to dollop on ice-cream, beauty. Don't change a thing.'

'G'morning, Hannah. You look radiant, even in a sea of similarly well-dressed women.' Dec pecked me on the cheek while Gabe made fluttering, fainting motions behind him.

'Hi, Dec, this is my friend Gabe —'

'Pleasure to meet you.'

I was nervous in Dec's presence. It felt strange having him enter my world, and to have everyone checking him out so openly, Gabe included.

'So what brings you into the land of lipstick and lilac shadow, Dec?' Gabe asked. He was digging his index finger into my back so hard I wanted to elbow him violently in the ribs.

'Oh, well, I'm actually here with —'

'Good morning, everyone. If we could please ask you to take your seats, as the presentation is about to begin. Thank you!'

I sprang into nervous energy-fuelled action. 'Oh, gosh, well, um, Dec – Gabe, you and I are on the table near the podium, I checked earlier, I didn't see your name there, Dec, but we can help you find your seat?'

Secretly I was cursing that he wasn't on our table. At least I had Gabe. And really, as long as Dec was nowhere near Fiona's battering lashes, I didn't mind.

'I need a coffee before this things starts, nice to meet you, Dec.' Gabe scurried off, leaving the two of us alone.

I spotted Fi staring over at us from across the room. I had a memory-flash of how scary she had been when I'd first met her.

'Thank you so much for your help with Iz, Dec. You went above and beyond brotherly duty.'

'Oh Hannah.' He looked at me strangely. 'Might catch up with you after the speech, yeah?'

'Sure, of course. We can discuss your new skincare routine.'

Over at our table, Gabe wasted no time. 'Okay, so I never got to meet Dan, and you know I despise Jesse, but this creature is sent from God above, or Buddha. Why are you two not married with two-point-five genetically perfect offspring? You clearly both like each other, because you're both carrying on like silly little teenagers.'

I grinned as I took my seat, which was happily between Yasmin and Gabe (a statistical anomaly – like the Naughty Kids at school we were rarely seated together). 'I think someone else likes him more than I do . . .'

'Oh, he's heaven on a skewer. And I know what happens with these things. See, with Dec being the older brother of your best friend, by law you must have an intense, ongoing crush on him that is never realised until you're a young, beautiful woman; and by law he must never see you as anything more than a duplicate of his kid sister. Then he must have an epiphany and fall desperately, hopelessly in love with you.'

I giggled and shook my head. 'Gabe, no more espresso for you today.'

I felt my phone vibrate in my bag. I pulled it out and stole a glance at who the missed call was from.

It was 'Don't Answer'.

Incredible. How the hell did you go from cheating on your girlfriend with some TV skank, to completely carrying on as if your ex-girlfriend didn't exist, to electronically stalking her?

Yasmin's voice came in on my left. 'Are you even listening? Is that Dan texting you how much he misses your booty already? Tell me, sleazebag.'

'Um,' I cleared my throat, 'actually, it's Jesse.'

Her eyebrows dropped, her jaw slackened, and her eyes widened.

'NO! Fuck OFF! Why? What did he say? And why is he even texting you?'

I hoped the presentation was a while off. I had a lot to tell Yasmin and not a lot of time.

29.

No more peels for that woman

Get smart, not broke, at the salon with a little thing called hairline highlights. If you colour just the hair that sits on your scalp and frames your face, you get an instant lightening effect. It's almost as dramatic an effect as if you had a whole crown of highlights. But around six-million dollars cheaper.

'Eliza! Why didn't you ask me before you had the treatment? I could've told you that! It's way too strong for your skin!'

I was playing Beauty Know All to Eliza, who had paid nearly two-hundred dollars for a peel that had caused her to look like a burns victim. Of course, having never had a peel, I was as qualified to speak on the subject as a praying mantis, but I figured that since I had been lectured on the topic roughly 183 times, I was absolutely allowed to speak with some authority.

'Well, I don't know. My friend had one and her face looked good after, so I thought I'd do it.' She peered at her face in the wall mirror next to my desk. 'How much longer will I look like Freddy Krueger? I can't take much more of this.'

'You should be fine by Monday. Did they give you some after-care? Something to soothe the pain of the melting flesh falling off your face?'

'No.'

'I'll get you some. I'll just send this email, and then I'll put it on your desk.'

'Make it strong, please.'

'Will do.'

She took a last look at her face before sighing and walking back to her desk.

No more peels for that woman. I sent my email through to the PR for Giorgio Armani, asking for one of their red lipsticks to shoot – they were superb – and then threw myself into the cupboard looking for some products for Eliza.

I found her some high-tech soothing balm for sensitive or 'surgically inflamed' skin and took it around to her desk. I was running late for a function, as usual, and after grabbing my coat and bag, I bolted out of the office.

I frantically hailed a cab and started applying my makeup as we shot through the early-morning streets.

I looked at my outfit, wondering if I was dressed appropriately: I was off on a sailing day courtesy of Petal cosmetics, who had organised a big boat for all the beauty girls. I really didn't have time for a full day out of the office, but Eliza and Marley had made it clear I had to go.

What did you wear sailing, for God's sake? I'd gone for what I hoped was 'St Tropez chic': white pleated shorts, a navy-blue singlet and glorious muted-gold sandals I'd bought in Hawaii. I stopped to survey my look. It had to be pretty close to right, surely: I looked as though I was an extra in *Fantasy Island*.

I arrived, still applying bronzer as the cab pulled up – I'd become very good (or very used to) doing my makeup en route to functions – and saw a few beauty girls milling about looking perfectly seaworthy in kaftans and loose, floaty tops, bejewelled sandals and enormous sunglasses.

As I paid the driver, I tried not to think about the fact Dan hadn't replied to my text. I knew I was supposed to be prepared for the way he fell off the face of the Earth when I wasn't in his face, but this was mind-blowingly rude.

Yasmin was exiting her taxi at the exact same time I was. She was wearing a lurid-green Seventies playsuit with a big gold belt and gold sandals. She'd cut her hair and done something different with her makeup – liner on the inner-rim? New eyebrow-shaper? – and looked incredible.

'Hannah, those shoes: *unbelievable*. Baby, you look fucking edible.'

We hugged and she excitedly told me she'd slept with the guitarist of a well-known band last night. So *that* was why she looked so good.

Fiona arrived seconds before the boat pulled away, laughing at how pissed off everyone was at her.

I made Yasmin tell Fiona what she'd done last night.

'You did WHAT? Yasmin! You've got to get his number!'

'Fi, shut up. You don't rely on rock stars for a relationship; everyone knows that.'

'Maybe he'll ask you to tour and you'll end up singing backup,' I offered.

'Anyway, whatever. If he calls, he calls. Who cares?' Yasmin said resolutely.

'Especially not when the captain looks like *that*,' Fi said lasciviously.

I followed Fi's gaze to where a gorgeous guy in a white polo shirt and white shorts stood, welcoming all the girls aboard. He was exceptionally tanned and had amazing green eyes. He reminded me of Gabe a little bit, in that Jude Law kind of way.

'Can I have dibs?' Fi was visually undressing the captain and biting her lip in a style that I thought was a little much for 10 a.m. in the morning.

'Dibs away, baby,' I said, laughing.

'Morning, everyone!' Grace, the PR girl, was standing on a chair, waving her clipboard around. 'If we can all please take a seat, we'll get this show on the road!'

Cue waiters with champagne. As I always did, I looked at how many girls took a glass. It was about a 96 per cent hit rate. That was good enough for me. I took one and sipped it delicately. Might as well relax and enjoy myself.

'I fricken LOVE this song!' Yasmin screamed. She was playing air guitar and head-banging, managing to look quite good as she did. Fi was doing her 'sexy dancing' – which was what she did when she was drunk and was trying to show off to guys – slowly swaying from side to side, with both hands above her head.

I was sitting on another lounge, trying to understand how it could be 1 p.m., and a boatload of women could be this drunk. I decided to check my phone. Just as I pulled it out, it started ringing. 'Don't Answer' flashed up on the screen. Clearly I couldn't read, or I was way too drunk, because I did, in fact, answer.

'Yellow?'

'Hi! Han, it's me.'

'Me who, sorry?'

'Jesse?'

'Oh Jesse. Hiiii.'

'Are you drunk?'

'No! Maybe. Who's asking?'

'You are drunk! At lunchtime! What's the occasion?'

'Work thing. We're on a boat.'

'Well, I won't keep you, in fact I'm just happy you answered – Hannah the Elusive.'

'Pfft.'

'Is there a band on that boat? It's so loud.'

'Nope. Oh hang on, yes, there is, it's Justin Timberlake.'

'You're a nut. Look, I'm wondering if you're free Friday night? I've got tickets to Cirque du Soleil?'

'Um, I'm not sure. I'll have to get back to you if I'm busy . . . or not.'

'It's supposed to be amazing, and I know you really wanted to see it last time it was in town, so I just thought —'

'Ohmigodyoushouldseethislobster!'

'Oh, okay. Sounds like you're having a great time; enjoy your day. I'll call tomorrow?'

I closed my phone, threw it in my bag and made a beeline for the mega-lobster adorning the table. In my champagne-fuelled daze, I didn't realise I'd just spoken to the one person I was not supposed to. Whatever. Hungry. Must eat.

'Pretty impressive bottom-crawler, huh?' Captain Hot, as Fi had christened him, was standing next to me as I piled up my plate.

''*Mazing*. Look at those pincers – they could take out someone's eye if they were, you know, um, scuba diving or . . . forget it. Impressive crustacean.'

He laughed. 'I'm Matt.'

'And you drive the ship. I know. We notice things, you know.'

Matt laughed again. 'Why are you the only one eating? Or is that normal in the magazine world, no one eating?'

Someone had his confidence jacket on.

'Please, that's the fashion girls, not us. We eat like sumo wrestlers.' I looked around – everyone else was dancing, drinking, smoking or talking. 'Well, usually we do, anyway. They're just tanked. Who cares? More for us, right?'

'Correct. Do you need me to do that for you?'

I was having immense difficulty taking apart my lobster claw.

'Oh, would you mind? Thanks so much. Never was very good at this.'

I looked at him with my head on one side as he masterfully took the crab apart. He was very good.

'There you go, ma'am. Wanna go sit up on the top deck? It's amazing up there. Where the rich people sit. Leave the heathens down below, y'know?'

I laughed. 'As a heathen, I find that exceptionally offensive. But enticing, no less. Let us go up to this top deck you speak of.'

I took my plate, and a freshly filled glass of wine, and tried not to fall up or down the stairs as I awkwardly clambered up after Captain Hot.

'Okay, sold. The top deck wins.' It was amazing, the view of the water stretching for miles. At the opposite end a few of the beauty girls were smoking and sunning their legs, and at our end a beautiful sequence of day beds and a delicate white sun-cover formed an outdoor lounge room. We could see the incredible mansions that adorned the shores, and a pure blue sky.

'So, been a pirate for long?'

'About five years. Love it. Who wouldn't? You get to be outdoors, meet new and interesting people every day, and dissect crustaceans for beautiful girls. It's the best.'

In my drunken state I forgot to blush and carry on at his comment. Instead, I thought of how perfect he and Fi would be, and thought furiously about how I could draw her into our conversation without it seeming obvious.

'So, my friend Fiona, downstairs? She loves boats.'

As subtle as a truck.

'That's nice. Are you guys at the same magazine? Which one is it again?'

'*Gloss*. That's me; she's at *21*. But we're really close. Everyone assumes you'll be enemies because your mags are competitors, but that's rubbish. I mean, we see each other at functions every day – as if you're not going to be friends.'

'Oh, come now, don't try to tell me you're all tight. I can see the cliques.'

'Well, yeah, I mean, obviously I like some more than others, but we're all civil at least.'

'What about the girl with the white sunglasses and white dress? Little Miss Boat Candy. She in your top five?'

He was talking about Jill. How did he know?

'You mean Jill? Yeah, we're cool.' I took a long sip of my wine.

'Liar.' He smiled and looked straight into my eyes. 'I know her through a mate – she's torture. Someone like you wouldn't have a bar of someone like her.'

'Awfully judgemental, aren't we?'

He leaned over and shook my shoulder playfully and laughed. At that exact second Fi popped her head over the top of the stairs from below, with a huge grin and a glass of champagne. One look at us, and her smile transformed rapidly into an evil glare.

I immediately shook his hand free and stood up. 'Fi! This is her, this is the friend I was telling you about!' But before I could even finish, she had gone back down the stairs.

'Where'd she go?' Matt asked innocently.

I dumped my wine glass and shimmied up off the lounge. Shit, shit, shit. She'd seen us together and assumed I was hitting on her man. I bolted down the stairs and began pushing through girls dancing to the Scissor Sisters to find her. I looked down the galley just in time to see her disappear into the toilet.

I banged on the door.

'Fi! Fi, open up. That so wasn't what you thought it was – please open up. You're being silly. I had been talking you up to him. Nothing – absolutely nothing – was going on, honestly. Fi . . . please . . . open up.'

Silence.

'Fi? I know you like him, I would never grass-cut like that. I'm not even interested in him! Please, Fi . . .'

I sighed and went to the front deck, from where I could watch the toilet door. A minute later, she walked out and into the room where all our bags were. I leapt up and followed her.

'Fi?'

'I'm fine, fine, don'worry, I'm fine.' She swaggered as she leaned down to get her bag.

'You're so not. If you're pissed at me, can we at least talk about it?'

She turned to me and looked me in the eyes. Hers were red and glazed. She was really drunk.

'What, Jesse and Dan and Derek – no, Declan – not enough for you? You need another guy to be falling at your feet?'

I reeled. Where had that come from?

She turned back to her bag and started fishing around inside.

That was enough for me. I grabbed my bag and walked out. I wanted off this stupid boat. I needed to find Grace.

I found her speaking to Matt. Of course. Where was Fi now? Maybe she'd lose it at Grace, too.

'Um, excuse me, guys – sorry to interrupt, Grace – I actually need to urgently go to the office. Are we docking soon, or should I call a water taxi?'

'Oh, no proooblem! I'll call you one right now.' She was drunk too. Jesus.

As she called the water taxi, I stood awkwardly looking out at the water.

'Is your friend okay?'

Dammit. I didn't want him to speak to me.

'Yeah, she's cool.'

I turned to him and smiled a smile of defeat. 'She'll be fine.'

'Will you? You seem a bit shaken.'

'I'm totally fine'. Lying.

'It'll be five minutes, Hannah.' Grace had finished her phone call and her loud confirmation broke up the awkwardness. 'Now, tell me, have you had fun? Has this been a fun day? Because, I know, I know that you girls do heaps of cool things, and so I juz wanted to do something a bit differen', you know? I thought, what could be more nicer than a boat, you know?'

'It was such a lovely day, Grace. We've all had the best time, truly. You spoil us, you do.' I smiled sincerely. It *had* been an amazing day until Fiona had lost the plot.

'Oooh, good. Oh, don't forget your goodie bag! I got you guys the *best* present!' She clambered off her seat and bounded at breakneck speed down the boat's stairs. As if we deserved a gift after a day of lobster and Sauvignon Blanc.

As Grace gave me my present – a stunning Missoni beach towel – the taxi pulled up. I leapt aboard and urged the driver to go. Fiona's words swirled around my head. It was Wednesday now – we had no launches tomorrow or Friday, and I figured if we didn't patch things up by Monday, I'd speak with her then. She was way out of line. Wasn't she? Maybe she was on to something with her comments about me selfishly hoarding several men. After all, why was I still hanging on to Dan? He wasn't worth any more energy than what he was putting into me, which was currently in the minus region. Jesse, well, my fascination with Jesse was fuelled partly by curiosity, partly by ego, and partly by revenge. And as for Dec – well, that was nothing more than what it had always been, and, if I thought about it, actually none of her business.

30.

A little sprinkle of ego dust

Leave cowlicks to the cows: blow-dry your fringe down and across your forehead, in the opposite direction to how your cowlick falls. Do it several times, and keep the tension in the brush tight. Bobby-pin it. Undo pin and flip back over to its natural side just before you walk out the door.

Jesse is forbidden. Marry Dec. Move to LA with Mr Hawaii. Turn Lesbo. Run away with Captain Hot. Just don't go back to TV toss. Love you. Gxx

Can't go to LA; boobs not big enough.

True. Guess it's the life of a sea maiden for you, then. You'll look pretty covered in fish guts.

Gabe and I had just had a lovely dinner at Spice, a small Moroccan restaurant where you sat on the carpet and ate delicious little delicacies on tasting plates, and I was in a cab on the way home. I had, over a bottle of pinot, given him a full debrief on Hawaii, Iz leaving, Jesse's strange behaviour, and Fiona's form on the boat. It was unintentional therapy at its finest.

As usual, Gabe made his feelings about each situation glisteningly transparent. I liked his 'outsider' perspective, although him having met Dec was proving to be a slight distraction – Dec was now all he could talk about. His final take was: Dan was both inconceivably rude as well as geographically unavailable, and therefore needed to be flushed from my mind. Jesse was a schmuck with bad taste in women and had a long way to go before getting my clothes off again. Dec was perfect in every way and should be stalked with fervour. And Fiona was one twisted little sister who was not to be trusted.

When I got home there was an astonishing bunch of flowers waiting at my door. Masses of white lilies tangled with red and tangerine roses, and they were all nestled in a forest of green leaves.

My heart-rate tripled. Who were they from? Dan? Please be Dan.

I ripped open the card.

Too little too late and possibly too soon all at once. You deserve these and so much more. Hoping so much to see you tomorrow? Love, Jesse.

No. This couldn't be. It was too much. But then I started thinking about what it would be like if I said yes.

It suddenly dawned on me that this time tomorrow night I might be hanging out with Jesse. I felt a shiver of nerves run through me: what would we talk about? Would he bring up other girls? Would I bring up other guys? Would we even have anything to say to each other any more? I panicked. Could I really go through with it? Surely I was above pulling these kinds of tricks just for a little sprinkle of ego dust?

Naahhh.

I decided I could make tomorrow night The Hannah Show. Jesse's role would be to sit there and lap up how fabulous I was, and how exciting and busy my life was, and that I didn't need him at all. It seemed I had made my decision.

Now I just had to tell him I would be attending. Should I wait till tomorrow? Torture him a little? Yeaaah. He deserved it.

That night, as I attempted to reach the impossible goal of sleep, the fake tan I'd put on making my legs sticky and my whole body gently sweating, it wouldn't register that I was going on a date with *Jesse*. A month ago this had seemed like the impossible.

Gabe would *kill* me if he found out.

31.

When you go backwards, you fall over

Got silly little spikes on top of your head post-blow-dry? Get a tissue, spray it with hairspray and then run it smoothly from the top of your part, down the hair. Spike-free zone.

I walked out of the lift into my foyer the next evening, and I saw him standing at the glass door. *With flowers*. What was this about? I'd had flowers from Jesse once in our whole time together, for my birthday, and now two bunches in two days? Maybe he'd started working on a gardening show.

I took a deep breath, and walked out.

'You look breathtaking, Han.' His eyes quickly slid up and down me and rested intently on my eyes. I felt a ball rise in my throat. No, no, NO TEARS! The shock of him at my place again, the flowers, the nerves, the expectation; the build-up had burst inside me and was now pushing its way into every available crevice, doing its best to make me lose control. It was such a familiar, normal scene to me, seeing him here at my door, yet tonight it was tinged with incongruity and wrongness. Weird, so weird.

I bit my trembling lip and tried to lighten things up. 'Who gave you those?'

He laughed, and I exhaled slowly.

'They're for you.' He held out the flowers. I took them, staring at the lush blooms. These were expensive.

'You didn't have to . . . Thanks, Jesse.'

'Beautiful flowers for a beautiful girl.'

Oh, please. Was he for real? How many girls had he used that line on, I wondered? Lisa Sutherland would be exactly the kind of loser who would fall for it, too. Thinking of them together sent a spear of anger down my spine, and a sick feeling into my gut. No, no, I'm not thinking that tonight – it's all about me. He wants *me*. Not her, not them. *Me*.

'Shall we?' I said, raising my eyebrows, desperate for distractions and movement so the unsavoury thoughts would go.

'I thought we could go to Sculpture for something to eat first? It's right near the big top.'

'Sculpture? But no one can get in there . . . We won't get in, no way, not on a Friday, and not without booking three months ahead.'

'I booked.' He looked straight ahead as though he'd just said the most normal thing in the world.

Presumptuous. What if I'd said no to the date? He would've brought in one of the imps, I guessed. Still, I was impressed.

'Well, yeah, of course. I'd like to check it out.'

'Excellent. I'd hoped you hadn't already been taken there.' Oooh, well played. Wasn't someone as cool as a cucumber.

When we arrived at Sculpture, the waiter knew Jesse by his first name and gave us peach bellinis on the house. Okay, that was weird. Everything was going so smoothly I felt like I was in some kind of American college movie. That or the *Thriller* video clip. Cue werewolves.

I inhaled my drink. It was superb, and to gulp it was sacrilege, but I needed alcohol's sweet anaesthetising. As predicted, it took the edge off my nerves and diluted my analysing beautifully. I actually started enjoying myself. I flirted with the waiter to piss off Jesse. I made funny jokes and talked up my job incessantly. I didn't reveal a thing about why I'd been in Hawaii, who I'd dated or what I'd been up to outside of work, which Jesse was fishing for like a bear hunting for salmon: clumsily but calculatedly.

'So, I saw you quoted in the *Gazette* as *Gloss*'s Single Girl Expert – how does one earn such an illustrious title, Han?' He smiled as he spoke, but his intent flashed like a neon light.

'Oh, you know. I wrote a single-girl piece in the mag a few months back.' I took a sip of my wine and let him figure out his next attack.

'You're a regular Carrie Bradshaw, huh?'

'Yeah, just minus the Manolos and New York crib.'

'Would that make me Mr Big, then?'

I almost choked on my mash. The audacity! Big and Carrie were an ongoing, twisted love saga that ended triumphantly. Jesse had dumped me, was giving one date a shot, and thought *that* earned him the title of Big? Jesus – waiter, ease up on the drugs in this man's food . . .

'I'll take that as a no?' As though he realised his arrogance, his voice was softer, but his eyebrows were raised in semi-defiance.

I cleared my throat. 'Hey, we should get moving; the show will be about to start.' Remember to always end things first: conversations, phone calls, email banter, excruciating meals . . .

Jesse snapped to attention, asking for the bill, checking if I wanted anything else to drink or eat before I went, and sending his little waiter mate to get our coats. It was while all this was happening that I realised I was quite drunk. Which wasn't supposed to happen.

'Bathroom calls. Meet you at the door.' I pushed back my chair, dropped my clutch. I leaned down to get it, covering my chest where my gaping dress failed to and giggled as I came up. Jesse looked at me with sleepy eyes, one hand holding his chin, and smiled with his lips closed.

'You're adorable, Han.'

I blushed and walked quickly away, wondering how my arse looked in this dress. It *was* extremely clingy.

As I redid my entire face – concealer, liner, mascara, blush, gloss – and doused myself in Michael Kors, I thought of Dan and sighed. Jesse would never send a naughty text while I was in the bathroom. Jesse would do it via fax, the most risqué line would be 'I think you're very nice', and it would be signed, 'Yours sincerely'.

I stopped and stared at myself. What was I doing here? All of the excitement I had felt tonight was a soybean substitute for the enormous thrills Dan had given me. Jesse was just so . . . Jesse.

I walked back through the restaurant and met him at the door. He kissed me on the cheek and told me I smelled amazing. I faked a smile and thanked him for a lovely dinner. Funny how the most expensive food can taste ordinary if the company you're sharing it with doesn't do it for you.

The circus was perfect as it required no conversation. I just sat there taking it all in, loving the temporary distraction from who was sitting next to me.

As we drove home, my conversation gradually slowed until I was entirely mute. I was tired from a big week, my nervous energy had transformed into lethargy, and I was still drunkish. I tried to digest what had occurred that evening, as well as forecast what I would do when he pulled up at my place. I wondered if he'd try to kiss me . . .

I flipped down the sunshade to check my makeup, just like I'd done a million times before. Jesse laughed. I stopped, flipped it back and stared out the side window. I wished he had a new car – there were too many memories in this one.

'Well, here we are, Madam Atkins.'

I sat up straight and collected my bag from the floor, pushing my hair behind my ear as I did so. I was acutely aware of Jesse staring at me. 'Thanks so much for dinner and the circus, Jesse.'

'I miss you, Han.' He put on the park brake and turned off the ignition.

Oh shit. Here it comes.

I looked down at my bag and smoothed my dress over my legs nervously. Suddenly I was completely sober and very uncomfortable.

'I had such an excellent time with you tonight, I can't even tell you . . .'

I looked out of my passenger window and fiddled with my hair. It was so quiet I could hear his breath. It was slow and deep, but not calm.

'Han, I want to see you again. Can I see you again? Can we do this again?'

I put my knuckles over my mouth and looked at him. The tears came without warning. I kept my head down so my hair fell over my face in an attempt to conceal it from him. He seemed to take this show of vulnerability as his cue.

'Han? I know I've been an arsehole, and if I could turn back time I would in a flash, in an instant. I never meant to hurt you, and I know you're fine, better than fine in fact, you're amazing, but I can see you haven't forgiven me, and I understand that. But I know who I am now. And I know what I want. And Han, it's you. It's only you. You're all I think of. And I want to make it up to you. I want to show you how good we can be; I want to prove to you that I've changed and that I only want you . . .'

He put his hand on my leg and shifted closer to me. I didn't move.

After a minute, I felt confident I would be able to speak without losing it. 'Well, you know, that's pretty heavy . . . I mean . . . God, you know, it's just . . . I don't know what to say . . . ' My voice cracked and I stopped speaking.

'Say you'll give me a chance.'

I audibly sobbed at his pleading. I was experiencing a fairytale most foul: Getting What You Wished For when the expiry date for your desire had already passed. He was saying all the things I had dreamt of. Now that he was saying them, I wasn't sure they were what I wanted to hear after all. *What was wrong with me?*

I suddenly felt claustrophobic, like I was being suffocated by his emotional outpour. I needed to get out. 'I have to go, this is . . . this is all a bit too . . . I have to go.'

'Han, Han, I'm sorry. I'm being unfair; I shouldn't dump it all on you like this. I'm sorry, Han. Please don't go, we'll chat, sort it out, please don't leave like this . . .'

His eyes screamed what his words couldn't. He looked scared, desperate, like a lost little boy. It gave me strength.

My hand paused on the door handle. I turned to face him, front on. 'Try, just for a minute, to think of this from my perspective. You cheat on me' – he began to defend himself but I increased my volume to quieten him – 'YOU DUMP ME, you date thousands of other girls, you don't contact me for months, and then within the space of a week you move from saying you've been thinking of me to asking for another chance at a relationship that, to be honest, I've cleaned my hands of.'

He recoiled.

'You have *no idea* what it's been like for me. So don't waltz in here, with your fancy flowers and your empty promises, and think you can just change everything that's happened. Because that shit doesn't fly with me. Not now, not ever.'

I pulled on the door handle for my Daytime Emmy award-winning exit and nothing happened. I tugged at it again; still nothing.

Again and again, and then, '*Would you open the fucking door*?' I screamed, facing away from Jesse.

A click from him, and suddenly the door gave, and I was out, lunging into darkness and wondering who had taken over my body, and what she had just done.

I dumped my bag on the breakfast bar, kicked off my shoes, and then, after delicately lifting off my dress and placing it on the bed, grabbed my feral pyjama tee, and yanked it on aggressively. I pulled out my bedside drawer and got my cigarettes and lighter. I stomped back to the kitchen, poured a glass of red wine that I was pretty sure was off, and sat on the floor under my lounge-room window. I heard my phone beep but ignored it.

With my cigarettes, my lighter and my sobbing, I sat alone on the floor. I wondered if I'd meant what I'd said in the car.

Would Jesse accept that as the final word and drop the whole issue? I hoped so – it would make life a whole lot easier. But did I really want that? I wasn't sure. Because, on some foul karmic strata within, I knew that maybe that shit did fly with me. Why else would I still be crying two hours later?

32.

Men don't buy flowers and then give up

> You've got home hair-colour so bright it's hurting your eyes? Shampoo a few times using a medicated type of shampoo, such as an anti-dandruff solution, as these can help lighten the hair a shade or two. And maybe enlist the help of a friend/paid professional next time.

I told Iz all about the date the next morning, after a night of restless, shitty sleep.

'So, what happens next, Han? Do you think he'll keep trying?'

'Uh, I don't know. If I were him, I probably wouldn't. I said some pretty nasty things.'

She paused. 'And he gave you two bunches of flowers, you say?'

'Yep. I reckon three-hundred dollars a pop, too. Pity I left the second bunch in his car.'

'He's not gonna give up. Men don't buy flowers and then give up.'

'Oh, you think so?'

'Totally. Mark my words: he'll call by Tuesday.'

'We'll see. If he does, I'll deal with him then. Right now, he knows where I stand. I feel like I'm in the power position, and I'm cool, y'know? Like, I can deal with it as it is. I went on the date – like everyone said I should – and now I know how I feel about him.'

'Which is?'

'Not going back there.'

'Definitely?'

'I've come so far, why would I?'

''Kay, well, let's just see what he does. Now, are you coming over so I can offload my shittiest clothes on to you?'

'Absolutely. Be there in half-a. Ciaooooo.'

Two hours later, and the novelty of watching Iz pack had worn off. I was feeling tired and lazy, and was finding it very hard to pretend Iz wasn't leaving when she was packing right in front of me.

'She's not quite *au fait* with the idea of packing light, you see.'

'Mm-hmm, I can see that.'

Dec and I were sprawled across the living-room floor, half-watching Iz do a terrible job of packing her cooking gear into a series of large suitcases. I was wearing a very low-cut, tight-fitting T-shirt and had to keep pulling it up so Dec wouldn't catch an eyeful of boob. At the same time, I secretly hoped he would, not that he was the type to be turned on by something so tacky and explicit. There was no weirdness between us at all; we were back to having fun like the old days, although I couldn't help but dissect everything he said, combing each sentence for possible double-entendres or sneaky references to stolen bathroom kisses. There were none, as far as my beady little mind could ascertain. Which, admittedly, disappointed me a little, even though I knew it was better this way, and he clearly did too, otherwise he would've been a lot flirtier.

Iz was currently struggling with her expensive French pots and pans, which, not being designed to travel across the world in trunks, were proving to be quite the nightmare.

'Fit, fuck it!' She threw her strainer across the kitchen floor in frustration.

'Iz, don't forget your strainer! I think you'll really need your strainer. Every dish requires something to be strained, wouldn't you agree, Hannah?'

'Oh, definitely. Strained is the new black.'

'Right-o, you two. You know, if you were any kind of brother – nay, *man*, Declan – you would be helping me instead of lounging around like a big fat walrus.'

'Hey, I resent that. I've been working out.' Dec flexed his arm muscles and kissed them by way of proof.

'Gosh, Dec, you don't get those from peeling potatoes,' I said in faux admiration.

Iz rolled her eyes. 'I'm so far over this. Is it wine time yet?' She put one arm on her hip and the other on the bench.

'Not quite, but it is . . . STRAINER-APPRECIATION TIME!' Dec ducked the missile Iz threw at his head by hiding behind me, tugging my T-shirt down as he did so, creating the perfect target for Iz's projectile. It hit my collarbone.

'Ouch! Iz, you little bugger!' Whatever she had thrown hurt, and produced blood. Dec moved around to see, and Iz put her hand to her mouth and ran over.

'Oh, that was meant for Dec. Oh honey . . . let me get you a Band-Aid.' She kicked Dec on her way upstairs to the bathroom. '*Walrus boy!* Look what you did!'

Dec was trying so hard not to laugh as he apologised that I started laughing, clutching my neck as I did.

'Guess it's a good thing she's looking after this bloody incident; I'm clearly not to be trusted in those sorts of situations . . .'

I flushed bright red. Was this the part where he said it never should've happened and it was just a silly mistake?

He looked at me with a cheeky grin and then burst into laughter. 'Han, I'm so sorry . . .' (giggle) '. . . what kind of walrus am I that I let a woman get hit by something . . .' (giggle) '. . . instead of taking the blow . . . I'm . . .' (repressed laughter) '. . . so sorry. Honestly. Awful. Bad man.' He cleared his throat and clamped his lips together so as not to allow any more laughter to escape.

I was grateful for a potentially awkward moment being diffused, but a little disappointed nothing more was said about The Kiss. Somewhere deep down I wanted him to say something – anything – about it, flirty or dismissive, if to do nothing but act as confirmation that he had been thinking about it too, and I wasn't still caught up in schoolgirl-fantasy land.

'Here, let me see.' As he pulled down my T-shirt's collar past my shoulder and inspected my wound, I could feel his breath on my skin and smell his aftershave – Jean-Paul Gaultier, I'd know it anywhere – and it sent the tiniest of tingles down my back. The last time we were this close . . .

'They live up to their stereotypes, chefs do,' Dec said quickly, nervously. 'Always throwing things and . . .' As I looked up to smile at Dec's comment, he moved his head to look at me, and our faces smushed. I pulled away instantly, as if bitten. The hair on the back of my neck stood up. My heart thumped. Quick, normalise, normalise!

'You always try to take advantage of me when I'm injured, you creature.' I laughed a high-pitched, self-conscious laugh and brushed off my legs, which were covered in the fluff from Iz's shag-pile rug.

'Hey, I'm only human.' Dec stood up and put out his hand to help me up.

I blushed, quickly turning my head so Dec wouldn't see. Just at that second, Iz came galloping down the stairs with a bandage fit for a lost limb. 'Sorry, Han, it's all I've got. We'll just cut some off and tape it over . . . oh, it's already kind of stopped bleeding. Hmm. Well, there you go. Maybe ice would be good.'

'I'll get it.' Dec walked over to the freezer.

'Now, Han, what time do I need to be there tonight?'

I had planned Iz's farewell drinks that night at our local bar, The Royal. It had a little cocktail room off one side of the main bar that could fit twenty people comfortably. I had invited forty.

'Um, maybe seven-thirty? What are you wearing again?'

'That vintage dress I bought on eBay, remember?'

'Ah, yes. Very good, Iz. You will raise the temperature very much, young lady with the pots and pans. I'd rather you didn't leave, though, if it's all the same.'

She hugged me gingerly on the opposite side to my cut. 'I love you, Han-ban. I miss you in advance, you know that.' She held me at arm's length and looked me in the eyes.

'Yes, Izzi-wah, and me you.'

'Your ice, ma'am?' Dec held out a packet of peas.

'Dec, can't you see this is a special moment?' Iz shook her head and released me with a kiss on both cheeks.

'Thanks, Dec, but you can keep your frozen vegetables, I've got prettifying to do.'

I grabbed my bag off the sofa and checked my phone. One new message. From Dan. Dan?!

You'd better wear that little dress you can't wear panties with, Blondie.

I beg your pardon?

That was weird. Wear it where? And I wasn't blonde. Was he texting another girl and had accidentally sent it to me?

Was that meant for me?

Nothing. Until . . .

Han, baby! You got a mis-fired textoid, but it wasn't from me, it was from a friend using my phone. How are you, sugar? Miss me?

A friend. Using his phone. How stupid did he think I was? Urgh! I felt like such a schmuck. He probably had fifty girls on the go at the same time, and here I was thinking all his smooth moves had been pulled out just for me. I felt so incredibly stupid. He'd played me like a goddamn banjo. I felt rage circulate wildly throughout my body as I thought of how much time I'd invested thinking about him. He was an A-class sleazebag and now I had proof. I felt dirty rereading his text, knowing some girl out there had been expecting it, and had sent him an equally filthy one to solicit it. Fuck you, Dan.

Save it for Blondie.

I impulsively hit send before I realised it was too dull a response to have even bothered sending. It was definitely a 'Save as Draft' situation. Oh well. Whatever. It wasn't like I was going to be seeing him again anytime soon.

Beep, beep.

Don't be sore, sugar. It was just a mistake! Hope you're well, anyway. Take care x

Take care? He was *Take Caring* me?!

Everyone knew Take Care was the weak way out of a relationship, no matter how faint it might be. What could you write back to that? And that was the whole point – you weren't supposed to write back. He was playing relationship executioner. Finality and brutality disguised with the thin mask of a pleasant sign-off.

I hoped he'd drown teaching Blondie to surf. As I walked home, I fought thoughts of Dan. We had basically had a fricken honeymoon in Hawaii, and then, just like the first time round, nothing. It was like if I wasn't directly in his line of sight, I didn't exist. Sure, I wasn't exactly chasing him, but why should I? It was the man's job to chase, dammit. I was the one who had flown to meet him, after all. And now he was already cavorting with another girl . . .

I shook my head and took a deep breath in, exhaling slowly with my eyes closed. I resolved to push him from my mind for tonight. Tonight was all about Iz, not some pig on the other side of the world.

I began planning hair, makeup and shoes to distract myself.

Hair would be out and hot rollers would definitely be used for big sexy volume. Except that I was really bad at using them. I found it easier to just hold my big tourmaline barrel brush on my scalp with the hair twisted around it for a few seconds. Tourmaline, I'd recently learned, made blow-drying your hair much faster.

Makeup would be the new smoky eye and gel-liner combo I had learned from Natalie Portman's makeup artist last week, as long as I could remember how to do that clever shading thing on the centre of the eyelid. The technique was to apply a white pearly shade in a panel on the middle of the eyelid, and then do all the dark stuff on the outer V, which created a 3D-type effect. It looked sensational and I *needed* to master it. Tonight.

I figured I would definitely be dancing at some stage, and so my new, extraordinarily high, 'homage to Christian Louboutin' shoes would not be worn. It would be my dearly loved black peep-toes. They had seen me through many a 4 a.m. finish, and not once had they demanded to be taken off and held in one hand as I walked upstairs from the taxi. They were good friends of mine.

As I walked up my stairs, I checked my phone. Nothing from

Dan. No surprises there. Nothing from Jesse, either. What was I playing at here? Was I *trying* to sever all ties with every man who was vaguely interested in me? I turned my phone on and off. Maybe it was playing up. Nokia welcomed me brightly, then nothing. I waited ten more seconds . . . Nope. *Humpf*. I was going to look like a fox tonight and drink myself stupid and dance like a drunken aunty at a wedding, and try to forget Dan's awful text and Jesse's stupid words last night, and that the reason I was there was that my best friend was abandoning me.

33.

A w-e-t p-u-s-s-y

Make your legs look longer by NEVER wearing ankle-strap heels, applying oil instead of lotion so they reflect light, and running a subtle strip of sheen/illuminator/shimmer down the front of them, from your thighs to your feet. You Amazon, you!

When I arrived at The Royal I was delighted to see Dec and Iz already at the bar, drinks firmly planted in their hands. Iz saw me and waved me over. Iz looked amazing; she'd had a spray tan and a blow-dry and her makeup was very fresh and pretty. Dec looked all Aqcua Di Gio-esque, as always, and I was quietly delighted when I saw him do a double-take on my entrance. The night was off to a good start for the girl who desperately needed a big fat ego-caress.

'Han! Look who's got their puppies out tonight!' Iz looked at my chest and nodded approvingly. Not only had I worn *two* strapless bras, but I had made the most of every trick I had ever learned about using shimmering bronzer and illuminator on your bust-line. I struck a pose and winked. I felt *good.*

'Hannah! You look . . . stunning.' Dec poked his head over Iz's shoulder.

'Thanks, Dec.' I smiled at him and thought non-blush-inducing thoughts.

'Declan, are you going to introduce me?'

The most genetically flawless creature I had ever seen was standing next to Dec. She had to have been South American, or Spanish, or Italian, or something. She was tall, her eyes were almond-shaped, her skin the colour of dark wood, and I was pretty sure she wasn't wearing makeup. Her long brown hair had that shimmering-with-flecks-of-gold look that women pay hundreds of dollars to emulate, and it sat in a perfect, wispy centre part, framing her perfect face and perfect lips. I hated her instantly.

'Oh, sorry. Elle, this is Hannah. Hannah, Elle.'

It wasn't likely to be Geraldine, was it? She smiled triumphantly and held out a limp hand. I shook it. 'Nice to meet you, Elle.' She nodded and smiled. Who *was* she? And why was she here? I didn't know Dec was seeing someone.

I subtly pulled Iz to one side. '*Who's the supermodel?*'

'Who? Oh, Ellie. She's an old uni friend of Dec's.' Iz went back to chatting with one of her workmates, and I went back to surreptitiously watching how Elle and Dec interacted. She was stupidly beautiful. I tried to check out her whole outfit, but could only make out that she was wearing a muted-gold slip dress under which her breasts – sans bra – sat perfectly. Bitch.

She sounded like she was whining to Dec about something. A moment later he got up, and they both walked out to the balcony.

Meh. He'd get bored of her looks eventually.

Iz handed me my drink, and we got down to the serious business of drinking and talking. Neither of us could believe she would be leaving on Friday. We decided to put a ban on thinking about it for tonight.

Two full glasses of wine later, and the food finally came around. Only by now I was already too drunk to want any. What I really wanted was a cigarette. Only I didn't have any. And buying some meant bowing down to my 'non-existent' addiction, so I refused to do it. I sauntered out to the balcony in the hope of scavenging one, and took in the warm evening air. But just as I got outside, 'our' song – Groove Armada's 'Superstylin' came on. I ungraciously bolted inside to find Iz. She was in deep conversation with Gina, a fellow chef. 'Sorry, Gina – how are you, love your dress! – Iz, we gotta dance to this one.'

I dragged her onto the dance floor where we shook it wildly for a good half hour, posing and being silly and faux breakdancing in that way only drunk girls can carry off. Or at least they think they can.

'Drink?' Iz was out of breath as she asked.

'Yes, yes, a drink, a DRINK! Marvellous!' I grabbed her hand and we squeezed our way through the masses of bodies at the bar to a tiny no-service area.

Iz felt her bag vibrate and pulled her phone out. Her face lit up. 'Ohmigod, it's Kyle! Han, do you mind if I . . . ?'

'Course not! Take it, take it! Tell him I said hi.'

She turned and bull-charged her way through the crowd to the ladies'. Ah, love.

'What's a pretty girl like you doing all alone in a seedy joint like this?'

I turned to find out which vile man owned this vile comment only to see Dec standing behind me.

'Dec!' I slapped his chest. 'You *silly*. Wanna drink? Shall we have a SHOT?'

He raised his eyebrows. 'Oooooh, not a *shot*!' he said disbelievingly.

'Hey, grandpa, relax. I'll help you find your false teeth when you spew them up later.'

He laughed and shrugged as if to surrender, then said, 'Which will we have? Sambuca? Tequila?'

'Well, I learned about this new one the other day – actually, it's an old one, but I'm dumb and only just learned it, called the . . . called the . . . oh, I can't say it, it's too inappropriate.'

'What is it? You can't leave me hanging like that.'

'Okay, I'll spell it. And I wouldn't bother even bringing it up if it wasn't really good. Okay, w – e – t, new word, p – u – s – s –'

'A wet pussy? Oh Han, you prude. We were doing them in college ten years ago.'

'So, doesn't mean I want to scream out, *"I want a wet pussy!"*' I clapped my hand over my mouth. Two guys to my left were looking at me with interest.

Dec was laughing loudly, slapping his knee in an attempt to recover.

'Oh, you're adorable. God, you make me laugh.' He shook his head, smiling, watching me trying to shrink in embarrassment. 'How *is* it that you're single, dear Han?'

'Sometimes a lady doesn't want the company of gentlemen.'

'Or is it just that the right gentleman hasn't presented himself?' He raised one eyebrow. This was the kind of conversation I'd dreamed of enjoying with him, and now I was too pissed to savour it, or give it the finesse it deserved.

'Maybe. But I'm not looking so it doesn't matter. Who'd be in a relationship anyway? I love being single. Relationships are too fricken hard.'

'Well, yeah . . . unless it's the right one.'

Even in my boozy haze I was embarrassed when he said that. It was all getting too heavy.

'Right-o, Gandhi,' I said with a new intonation, to imply that line of questioning was now over, 'order my . . . whatever already. Hey, where's your friend, Elle? Does she want one too?'

'She left.'

'Oh. Everything okay?'

'Yeah, yeah. She's hard work, that's all.'

I smiled smugly to myself. Serves you right, Miss I Don't Need a Bra.

Six minutes later and I was feeling my whole world spinning. Shots were a great idea until you drank them.

Dec kept asking if I was okay, and I kept saying yes, but I was kilometres from okay.

'I'll just get some fresh air, and I'll be . . . be totally fine. Seriously.'

'I'll come. It's my fault you're like this.'

'Pfft! I wanted the pussies, remember? My fault!' I smiled as normally as I could, put my clutch under my arm and pushed him back. 'I'll . . . be . . . fine. Seriously.'

'Han . . .' He grabbed my hand, and I felt a tingle.

I slowly unlocked my hand to put my finger over what I thought was his mouth, but was actually his nose. 'Shuuush.'

I turned and pushed my way through the dance floor. The music was too loud, the people were pushing back too hard; I had to get out. I reached the balcony, only to find it fuller than inside. Bugger. No good. Toilets. Toilets would be better. I started to walk in their direction but happened to look up to spot a massive queue snaking out the toilet door. Shit. I went straight to the stairs and walked down, out onto the street. The fresh air immediately made me feel better. I looked around for somewhere to sit, and, seeing nothing, perched daintily on the ledge of the wall, between the pub door and the café next door.

I tried to steady myself and just *breathe*. People were coming in and out of the pub constantly, but I didn't bother looking to see who they were. Who cared? What I wanted was a bucket. Or a cigarette. Or a bed. Or a de-alcoholiser. The lights of the passing cars were too bright, and the signage on the shoe shop across the street was so blurred I couldn't read it.

''Scuse me,' I managed to say to a person holding a cigarette, talking on the phone. It was a tall man, from what I could make out.

Nothing.

''SCUSE ME. Joo have anutha wunnathem?'

'Um, I'm on the phone here?' And tall man walked away, bitching about me into his mobile.

I sighed and put my head in my hands. Not so good. Best to face the way I was travelling. My feet hurt. I looked at them. I would take off my shoes, I decided. Just for a minute, one little minute. That's all. I slowly slid my feet out. The bright-pink polish on my toes contrasted harshly with the dark cement below. Seeing that jolted me into remembering how I despised girls who took their shoes off when they were drunk and sloppy and, most pertinently, in public. Sighing and humphing, I slowly, painstakingly, put them back on.

Safely shod and believing I was no longer at risk of looking like a hobo, despite the fact I was essentially sitting in a gutter, I got back to my task of remaining upright, and making sure my surroundings did too. They were being very naughty, sliding around and making me feel like I was on a bad circus ride.

'Hannah? Hannah, is that you?'

Another tallish man was on my left, with some men and women of varying heights.

Hang on. I knew *this* tall man's voice.

I looked to the left and saw precisely who I didn't want to see: Jesse.

He immediately kneeled next to me and put his arm around me. 'Jesus, what's happened? Have you been drugged? Where are your friends?'

'You alwaysshowup when I leasted expected it, don't I? I mean, you.' I pointed my finger at him, waving it.

'Han, are you okay? You sound very drunk.'

'Noooo, Jesse, silly, I'm fiiiiiine. I'm jus'gettin' some air.' I smiled to show him I was fine.

'Like hell you are. Where are your friends? Did they leave you out here in this state?'

On cue, Dec walked out of the pub, frantically looking in both directions.

'Hannah! I've been looking all over for you! Are you okay . . . ?'

He tapered off when he saw Jesse.

'Wet pussy! Bahahahahhahahahaaaaaa . . .' My head fell down into my lap without me realising.

'Are you supposed to be one of Hannah's friends?' Jesse stood up; there was anger in his words.

'Declan, and yes, I am one of Hannah's friends —'

'Some bloody friend. Anything could've happened to her out here while you enjoyed your night.' Jesse was really angry now.

I lifted my head to add my two cents' worth: 'He's Iz's sister . . .'

'Look, I completely see where you're coming from, but she told me she was going to the balcony fifteen minutes ago. When she wasn't there, I searched the toilets and then came straight down here.' Dec's voice was calm but firm.

'Whatever, *mate*, I suggest you go back up. I'll take it from here.'

'Excuse me? Hannah, do you even know this guy?'

'It's the ex-boyfriend,' I whispered loudly. Now even the bus stop I was using as a focal point had decided to betray me and start a psychedelic dance, too.

'Oh, Dan, is it? Well . . .'

'Dan? Who the hell is Dan?' Jesse's voice was bordering on hysterical now.

'Noooooo, it's JESSE . . .' I said.

'Oh, Jesse. Right.' Dec sounded mildly embarrassed. 'Well, Hannah, if you're sure you want to go with him . . .'

'Go where?' My head snapped up. 'Youse guys are crazy, I'm fiiiine. I want to see Iz. Where is Iz? I was going to make a speech.' I stood up too fast and fell toward Jesse.

'Hannah, I'm taking you home.' Jesse took my arm and picked up my purse from the ground. 'It's fine, mate, I'm just going to take her home, that's all,' he said by way of explanation to Dec.

Silence and then finally, 'Okay. Han, I'll tell Iz you're safe. It'll take twenty minutes just to find her up there . . .' Dec's voice was small.

'Jesse, I don'wanna go home. Jus' need some more fresh air and I'll be goodtogo.' As if confirming just how good to go I was, I stumbled as I took my first step to go back into the pub.

'Han, I think Jesse's right. You need to go home, darling.'

Jesse stiffened and took an even firmer grip on my arm. 'C'mon, Han, this way.'

With that, we were walking. I looked behind me to Dec, who stood with his hands in his pockets watching us leave.

'I love Iz, tell Iz I love Iz . . .' I yelled to him as I was guided away.

34.

I'll take you home first thing in the morning

The quickest way to revive your manicure or pedicure? Use a high-shine topcoat and re-apply it every second day. It will double the length of time your polish stays nice.

'I'm going to make you a cup of tea. You just sit there and drink that water for now, okay?'

'Yes, sir.' I was sitting on Jesse's lounge, dressed in one of his T-shirts, two strapless bras and my knickers, with a blanket over me. I wasn't sure how I had come to be in said position. A colossal glass of water sat on the coffee table in front of me. It was too overwhelming to even pick it up. I was exhausted at just the idea of it.

'If you feel like you're going to be sick, the tub is to your right, remember?'

'Mm-hmm.' I closed my eyes for a second, just to relax. The black hole behind my eyes spun, so I opened them immediately. When would this disgusting ride end?

'Where's my phone?' I felt around the blanket.

'It's here. Don't worry, your little mate Dick knows you're safe, he'll tell Izzie.'

'It's DEC, as in DECLAN, and he's Iz's sister, remember? Lived overseas. I mean brother. Her brother. He was jus' tryin' to help. He was good boy to look for me.'

'Yeah, little too late if something had happened to you, Han. It was just a good thing I came past.'

Was it? I think I'd rather Dec had found me first.

I looked around Jesse's apartment. Nothing had changed, except for a beautiful big fish tank.

'Nice fish,' I said. 'Tank,' I finished. As I couldn't actually make out any fish, I felt it was more accurate for me to just comment on their home.

'Oh, thanks. Amazing, aren't they? They're so beautiful to watch. Everyone's mesmerised by them.'

I bet they were. Bet he'd brought Lisa back to his apartment with the lure of seeing his 'amazing fish'.

'Here we go.' He came and sat next to me on the sofa with two cups of tea. 'Did you eat anything tonight?'

I thought about his question with a scrunched face. 'Nnnnn-nope.'

'Ahhh, well, that explains a lot. I'll make you some toast.'

'I want hot chips.' I did. Real bad.

'I don't have any,' he laughed. 'Toast will help soak up some of the booze, though . . .'

Fridge doors opened and closed and toasters were pressed down. I decided to lie down and wait. Just for a minute. One little minute.

'. . . Han, honey, do you want to get into my bed? I'll sleep in the spare room, but it's silly you sleeping here.'

Someone sounding a lot like Jesse was talk-whispering at me. I looked around me. Everything was dark, save for a fish tank. What the hell?

'What happened?' I was very confused. Why was Jesse here? Why was *I* here?

'You passed out, Han. You're at my place because I found you very drunk outside The Royal. You've been asleep for an hour. Everything's okay.'

I liked his soothing voice. It made me feel nice. I snuggled into my blanket and attempted, for about two nanoseconds, to get a bit of clarity before closing my eyes again. They were so *heavy.*

'I should go,' I said, with no intention of doing anything as arduous as changing positions, let alone suburbs.

'Stay here, Han. I'll take you home first thing in the morning. You need to sleep it off.' I felt his hand on my arm, rubbing it in a soothing, loving way. I melted just a little bit. He felt nice. He smelled nice, too. I wanted him to just lie down next to me like he used to. Just for five minutes. That was all. Five teeny minutes.

'Lie with me,' I said with my eyes closed.

'Are you sure, Han?'

'Lie,' I repeated.

He carefully pulled out the back supports of the sofa and lay down behind me, leaving me all the pillow and blanket.

'I love this pillow,' I muttered.

'I love that you're here,' he said almost inaudibly.

I reached behind me and grabbed his arm, pulling it roughly across me. He took this as a cue to face the same way I was, and he delicately moulded my body with his. I could feel his breath on my neck. It was quick but regular.

I became intensely aware of his body behind mine, and every time he moved a bit, I wondered if he would be game enough to try anything. After a few minutes, he shifted his body, getting closer to me as if by accident. I played too, by pulling out the blanket from underneath me, and placing it over both of us. When we resettled, he had both arms on my body, and his face was so close to my neck, it sent a shiver down my back. I realised, very suddenly, and very surprisingly, that I could Go There.

I made one small move to face him. I could see his eyes were wide open. I looked into them, and then he moved his lips to mine. We kissed, lightly, softly at first, then more hungrily as we reshuffled our bodies to accommodate our mouths. He moved his hands up behind my head and softly grabbed handfuls of hair as he kissed me. I started shifting my body more and more towards being on top of his, and with each kiss he nonchalantly pulled me further onto him. I took my hands down behind his back and pulled the bottom of his T-shirt up. He helped me lift it over his head, kissing me the moment it was off, before slowly doing the same with the T-shirt that was half-covering me. It felt disturbingly familiar, and yet entirely alien. After all, we hadn't carried on like this since we first dated, years ago. I felt a brief surge of panic, but his soft hands and soft kisses clouded any possibility of withdrawing now.

His hands moved around to my back to unclip my bra; I took a sharp breath in as his hands faltered at finding two clasps. God, *why* had I worn two bras? He said nothing; I slowly exhaled. Won't be doing that again. Bras dealt with, Jesse's hands gently massaged and cupped my breasts. He made soft circles with his thumbs, and stroked my chest with his fingers. He was doing everything so slowly and was being so delicate, almost to the point of irritation. I wanted him to get on with it. I was nervous and scared and excited; I needed things to begin. I kissed him deeper. As we kissed, I realised that the intensity in my kisses actually stemmed from anger: stupid boy, stupid Jesse; look what you lost.

Finally, his cautious hands, with the help of my impatient ones, slid down and skilfully removed my special lacy knickers, which, I internally applauded as a very salient choice. I reached down and wrestled off his shorts, and then abruptly it was flesh on flesh. It surprised me to feel his naked body on mine, even though I had just hastily created the situation. He felt good: warm, firm, like someone I wanted to have sex with. A flash of Dan danced through my mind; I shook my head to dislodge it. He was probably screwing Blondie this very minute. Jesse's hands were everywhere, grabbing at my skin, pulling me closer, and finally wandering down between my thighs. I pushed myself into his body, and pulled his hand away, signalling that I wanted all of him.

The moment he entered me, tears sprang to my eyes. Everything suddenly felt so wrong. What was I doing? Why was I doing this? He didn't deserve this; he didn't deserve me like this! Sensing my unease, Jesse immediately slowed down, right down.

'Han, honey, are you okay? Do you want to stop?'

I lay still. After a few seconds, he gently embraced me in a big bear-hug. He kissed my face and, feeling the wetness of my tears, stopped and looked at me in the darkness. He stopped moving altogether.

'Han, what's the matter?' Receiving no answer, he simply held me tighter and rearranged himself so that he was half on top of me, half on the sofa. He kissed me tenderly again and again on the forehead and arms and neck until my tears stopped, and then I fell into a heavy, uncomfortable sleep.

35.

Snake in the grass

Stuck at his place the morning after with none of your stuff? Leave him sleeping and clean up those panda-bear eyes, using some olive oil (seriously) from his kitchen, and make that party hair as 'daytime' as you can by finger-combing it and dabbing some flour into the roots. Now get home as fast possible. Go! Now!

My headache woke up well before I did, pounding me into a state of alertness I really did not wish to have anything to do with. I lifted my tongue a few times: cigarettes and what I imagined filthy socks might taste like flooded my taste sensors. Delightful. I slowly opened my eyes. I knew that ceiling. I knew that window. I felt a body to my right. Its bum was pressed against me and its feet were intertwined with mine. I looked. I knew that hair. That back. I recognised the way that person slept with their hands above their head. I put my hand on my tummy, which was gurgling, and noticed I was entirely nude.

Today was not going to be a good day.

I gently extracted myself from Jesse and the blankets and found my knickers. I popped on the less padded of my two bras and a T-shirt I vaguely recalled wearing last night at some point.

Where was my phone? I needed a taxi. Now. Ten hours ago would have been even better. I tiptoed to the kitchen and saw my clutch sitting on the bench. When I found my phone, I had six missed calls: three from Iz, three from Dec. Oh shit. I was in so much trouble with that family. My inbox told its own story, too:

Where r u? Dec. 11.15 p.m.

Have u gone? Iz. 11.30 p.m.

Dec said u left w jesse!!! evrythng ok??? Iz. 12.30 a.m.

Worried about u?? Call me call me call me! Iz. 3.32 a.m.

I quickly wrote back, punching in the letters quietly, lest Jesse wake to the tap-tapping.

Darling Iz, am safe but at the WRONG MAN'S house! Lord knows how this happened. I feel sick. I feel stupid. Breakfast please? So sorry to leave so early last night . . . Love, Friend of the Year

I checked the time. 8.14 a.m. Time to go; time to go. I dialled a cab and snuck up the hall to Jesse's bedroom to deliver the directions. The last thing I needed was for him to wake up.

Cab booked, I crept back out to the lounge room to put last night's ensemble back on. It wasn't slutty last night, just slutty now it was broad daylight and my hair and makeup made me look like a nasty old streetwalker called Candy.

I looked at Jesse sleeping on the lounge. He was all tanned and fit-looking. Damn him. If it wasn't for him, I'd never have left Iz's. And had sex with a man I didn't even want to *speak* to in real life. I needed to leave.

I yanked my dress down over my head. My phone vibrated; the taxi was here. I grabbed my shoes and tiptoe-ran to the front door, pausing to quickly rearrange my pile of shoes, clutch and phone before dropping it all and ruining my stealthy exit. Bending down to pick up all my stuff, I noticed a note on the small table where Jesse kept his change bowl and keys.

Sexy,
Next time I'M cooking! And dessert's on me . . . Literally.
Already can't wait for Sunday.
B xxx

My heartbeat quickened and the hairs on the back of my neck stood up. I picked up the note, trying to make sense of what was happening. I finally concluded that what was happening was that Jesse had a girlfriend, or at least the makings of one, but had slept with me anyway. Unbelievable. I shook my head in utter incredulity. He was fucking disgusting.

Bizarrely, my heart went out to *her* before it remembered it was meant to stay with me at all times, especially in situations like this. The poor bitch thought Jesse was into her when he was actually busy kidnapping and seducing his drunken ex-girlfriend under the guise of looking after her. I wondered who she was, what she looked like, if they'd 'done it' on the very lounge we had . . . I shuddered. The idea of that made me feel even sicker than I already was. I felt sorry for the girl, though, knowing that if she stuck with Jesse, she would no doubt go through what I had; I wouldn't wish that on any woman.

I put the note back, still shaking my head. I was meant to see that note, I thought. I was meant to see it so I'd know not to go back to him. I mouthed a silent thank you to Lady Fate for stepping in and saving me from all manner of headfucking. I considered leaving the note on the floor, so he'd know I'd seen it, but that would be too easy. No. I'd let him lose his mind trying to figure out why I never, ever, EVER spoke to him again.

I opened the door, taking care not to make any noise as I unlocked it. Gently closing it behind me, I exhaled deeply. *Jesuuuuus*. It was not even 9 a.m. and already it had been a huge day.

Perfect – the cab had come right into his driveway – I wouldn't even need to be seen on the street. As I got in and gave directions for home, panic suddenly gripped me: we hadn't used protection last night. Even though it was barely deserving of the label 'sex', it was still enough to transmit an STI. Oh God, I was a loser. Who knows what he could've picked up from any one of those filthy tramps he had on the go?

My phone started vibrating madly. It was Don't Answer. I was so angry I'd let him take me home last night. I would've been fine, but *no*, he had to play hero and whisk me away to his fishy lair, where 'B' had been only days, or maybe even hours before me. A mixture of fury, disgust, relief and regret engulfed me. I had a feeling it would stay for a little while yet.

Once I was back home, I let the scalding-hot shower beat down on me. It smelled so nice . . . I didn't want to get out. I had covered the drain with a face cloth and dripped in some essential oils, creating a 'mini day-spa'.

I knew I should get out, my hands were completely wrinkled, but I couldn't leave the cocoon of hot water and calming aromas. I leaned my head against the tiles and closed my eyes. Part of me felt like I wanted to rewind and start last night all over, and part of me wanted to still be at Jesse's, laying into him in the most violent manner I could muster. *Who did he think he was*, switching women like he was some kind of bloody movie star. Drying off, I wondered what Jesse would be thinking right now. A twisted smile crossed my face at the idea of him realising I had gone and wasn't answering his calls.

Knowing he was a certified cheat gave me a strange feeling of comfort. The decision had been made for me: he was gone from my life now. I didn't need to waste another nanosecond thinking about him.

With that thought, I went to the bathroom and luxuriously applied a hydrating cloth mask to my pale, dry face. It said 'leave on for ten minutes'. I would leave it for twenty.

For what felt like the first time in several millennia, I was in possession of crystal-clear insights. There would be no more Jesse. I had gone backwards, I had fallen, and I wasn't interested in nursing bruises and cuts for this man a moment longer. He was *gone*.

36.

Don't bother; it's domestic

> Cold sore on your lip, huh? Unlucky. Here's a magic trick: take a cotton tip with nail-polish remover and hold it on the sore for ten seconds. It'll kill, but it'll kill it, too. Repeat every couple of hours. If you need to cover it up, apply some foundation with a new cotton tip. No gloss, no lipstick. Just smoke up those eyes and leave the lips nude.

Monday morning I woke up with a cold sore.

I immediately began my war against the little mother. Most people will tell you to apply ice until you can get your hands on some Zovirax and then to start chomping on Lysine tablets before every meal. But I had a secret weapon that a makeup artist had told me about. Nail-polish remover. The strong gear full of acetone. None of that girly stuff. I poured some on a cotton pad and held it directly on the beast. It stung. Man, it stung. But according to the makeup artist, who'd had to heal and cover up many a model's cold sore, it would completely dry out the blister within a day. I could handle a much worse sting for a result like that.

My hair behaved – since being straightened it *always* behaved – but my makeup and outfit suffered because of the cold sore. I couldn't think; I was distracted and cranky. Vain and stupid? Guilty, your honour. After all, there were little boys in India with no legs, wheeling themselves around on skateboards and begging for coins by banging on pans with sticks, and here I was all worked up over a blister on my lip.

The global-guilt trick worked for about a minute, then I was back to doom and gloom.

I furiously huffed and puffed my way to a breakfast meeting at the Sheraton, where I (consciously) watched each of the five PR and marketing girls (subconsciously) rest their eyes on my angry-looking bottom lip.

Back in the office, the girls looked at me with pity/smugness/surprise. This seemed crystal-clear to me in my paranoid state. Because, while they didn't *say* anything, I knew they were thinking, 'Sucked in, beauty girl. Not even *you* can escape imperfection.'

I had a morning-tea function with a stack of beauty eds. As we waited in the sunshine, Fi brushed her newly cut hair and said, 'What's wrong with your lip?' She had never apologised for her form on the boat, and I had never made a big deal out of it. We'd both just pretended it'd never occurred. Confrontation was far too inconvenient in this industry.

'Nothing, just got a bit of a blister.'

Yasmin's ears pricked up.

'You mean a cold sore?'

'Well, yeah.'

'Looks pretty disgusting; you should use that stuff that gets rid of it,' said Yasmin helpfully.

'Really? I thought about that, but then I figured it looked so delightful I'd just let it get as big and visually offensive as possible.' I *was* in a bad mood.

'You know they're a type of herpes, right?' Fi's turn to be helpful.

'Yes, I do, Fiona.'

'Okay, okay. Jesus, just trying to hel—'

'Taxi!' I yelled out, and jumped into the road to hail it, thankful for the diversion.

In the taxi I applied a thick layer of gloss. It was against the 'dry-out' rules, and acted as a thin and inefficient mask for the lip monster, but it was a mask nonetheless.

The girls chatted about a lunch we'd had last week, and I redid my makeup several hundred times. I figured the more full-on the rest of my makeup, the less people would stare at my lip. I was irritated by how much time and energy I was wasting on this goddamn cold sore. Bet it was all Jesse's fault. He'd either given it to me, or stressed me out so much it had come on by itself.

At the function, I was wholly consumed with disguising the beast: holding my hand over my mouth as I talked, strategically placing drinking straws in front of my lip, and adding another layer of thick, opaque pink gloss.

'What's the champagne like?' Yasmin asked Fi.

'Don't bother; it's domestic,' she said, placing her flute down and snatching a mineral water from a passing waiter.

'Hey, Hannah, great gloss, which is it?' Ruby, the beauty editor from a gossip weekly, was staring at my vibrant pink lips. Great. I'd used so much gloss that now people were enquiring about the brand. I listlessly told her it was a Givenchy one and then excused myself.

It was a disturbing moment of vanity. I had become so self-obsessed that a blemish was controlling my day. I guess when you're scrutinised daily you are acutely aware when a wheel falls off.

When I got back to the office at midday, I made the unpleasant observation that I had six pages to write before I could leave the office. At 5.45 p.m. I was still two pages off being done. And really, really over it. I applied some more nail-polish remover – which had already dried out the bubble – and checked my phone. Iz and Jesse had both called, hours ago, but neither had called back.

My phone vibrated noisily on my desk again. It was Jesse. I didn't have time to think about him. I had the New Bob to write about.

I looked at Ron. It was a fiercely busy week, launch-wise. I was exhausted just thinking of all the outfits I'd have to figure out, and the late nights that would inevitably follow.

Wednesday night looked as if it'd be a nice one, though. The new spokesmodel for Tender skincare, Ashley Calton, the Oscar winner, was in town. An 'intimate tasting-plates event' had been organised for selected beauty editors. Neither Fi nor Yasmin had got a start, so I was particularly stoked to have been invited.

Of course, the fact I was pretty tight with the PR, Lloyd, a spry gay boy who dressed in Lacoste and Pringle head-to-toe, and who just happened to be one of Gabe's closest friends, might've had something to do with it.

Gabe! God, I missed him. He was acting as editor in his boss's absence and we hadn't caught up for ages. Maybe I would just call him to see if he was free for a late supper tonight . . .

'Hello!' he shouted into the phone.

'Whoa, Gabriella, is that any way to answer the phone?'

'Oh, honey, it's you. I'm so sorry; your number didn't come up. I'm having a prick of a day. 'Bout ready to knife someone, actually.'

'Me too! Hey, do you want to get a late supper? Maybe at the soup house? In, say, an hour?'

'Oooh, beauty, I don't know if I'll be done by then, we go to print the day after tomorrow and —'

'I slept with Jesse.'

'You what?' (Sigh.) 'All right. I suppose the mule has to be fed at some stage. An hour, did you say?'

'Yes, please!' I was so excited. 'Love *youuuu*.'

'Flattery will get you everywhere, darling. Oooh, one favour – do you have any Clarins Beauty Flash Balm lying around? My face is more hobo than homo, and I meant to call some in but I forgot . . .'

'I do, as a matter of fact. I shall bring it as thanks for making time for me.'

'Love you. You're the best friend a gay man with dry, dull skin could hope for.' He hung up.

Shit, now I really had to focus on getting this story done. Because if it wasn't on Eliza's desk tonight, like I'd told her it would be, my arse was grass.

I knew Gabe would rip into me for the weekend's slip up, but he'd be proud about my decision to completely renounce Jesse, following my fateful viewing of The Note.

'Isn't she astonishing? *Look at those pores!* That's right – *there are none*. None at all. And fine lines, *no fine lines*. She's *incredible*.'

Lloyd whispered loudly into my ear, staring at the goddess sitting at the end of the table. I nodded. I was right to be excited about this launch. Ashley delivered: she was funny, articulate, excellent at telling stories, terrific at impersonations of other famous people, and stunning to watch. Her ebony curls framed her face just-so, and her eye makeup hadn't moved all night, unlike mine, which had crept down underneath my eyes. Her face glowed. Her eyes sparkled. No jet lag to be seen.

Her outfit made the dress I'd borrowed from Marley look like something a first-year fashion apprentice had knocked up for her little sister.

Ashley wore a brocade A-line smock dress with Balenciaga ankle boots that Yasmin had been dreaming of owning for weeks. If only she were here to witness this spectacular outfit.

'Amazing. Look at her skin. I mean, could you have picked a better spokesmodel for a skincare brand?' Lloyd was still in awe. Three hours after having first laid eyes on her.

I was beyond happy I didn't have my cold sore any more. Seeing this vision in front of me would have been the best possible way to compound any feelings I had of looking fug.

Dinner had finished and, full of Mediterranean food and a delicious array of wines, we all sat around chatting loudly. Lloyd was still in panic mode, making sure the Tender brand manager was happy with how it was going, and that Ashley moved around the table so that all of us could have our turn staring at her like gobsmacked teens, and making conversational blunders when she asked us tough questions like, 'So, which magazine are you from?'

She was so normal. So unaffected. I wanted to be her. I figured she was roughly ten years older than me, so I still had time to stumble across some grace and elegance. I could start by not spilling food on my clothes every time I ate, I thought, as I scraped sauce off Marley's dress.

Within ten minutes of coffee and tea being served, the brand manager had Ashley's jacket, and Ashley was walking around the table farewelling us all individually. This from an A-list star, with a rock-star boyfriend and dinner company that usually included Kate Moss, Gwyneth Paltrow, Sting and Trudie.

'*Arrivederci*!' she cried as she walked out of the private dining room, waving regally. And then she was gone.

After spending a good half-hour discussing how gorgeous Ashley was, I decided to make a move. I was full, and fat, and very pleased with the evening's activity. I couldn't wait to text Iz about it; she'd been even more excited than me about the dinner. Jay wanted to know what Ashley was like, too. Everyone did. I was delighted I had nothing but praise for her, as there is nothing more boring than meeting someone Totally Famous who is completely underwhelming.

It was a beautiful night outside, so I decided to stroll for a few blocks to walk off my dessert. I was in the trendy district, in which super-hip wine bars were brimming with super-hip people whose conversations revolved entirely around jaunts to Morocco and organic breakfast cereal.

One bar in particular, Curt and Boyds, was overflowing, and a red carpet indicated a press event was in progress. I saw the logo of Doll lingerie, and made the connection that it was their summer-collection launch party. I recalled Fi and Yasmin and a few others saying they would be there. Should I go in? There was no door person. Well, I *was* invited, and it was only ten-thirty, and I looked good in my borrowed clothes . . . Stuff it. One drink with the girls would be fun. I could tell them all about Ashley.

I walked in: the room was packed. I saw a few reality-TV stars, some actors and models, and a lot of the usual magazine crowd. The room temperature was set to 'pottery kiln'; people were visibly sweating. The fans were on, but they were doing nothing but pushing hot air back onto the crowd. There was thumping salsa music coming from a DJ-band hybrid in the corner, to which people were dancing. This was very rare at a function. I saw a tray of dangerous-looking cocktails glide past and did the math: *everyone was completely smashed.*

I saw Yasmin all over a very hot guy near the bar. I made a beeline for her.

'Hey, Yasmin!'

She looked at me with glazed eyes.

'Baby! You came!' She gave me a big hug and stumbled as she pulled away. 'How was the dinner? What was she like?' She turned to Hot Guy and explained, 'Hannah was special enough to get to meet Ashley Calton tonight. I wasn't, but she was.'

I laughed. 'She was stunning, Yasmin. Funny and beautiful and just amazing. I've got a crush.'

'A girl crush,' said Hot Guy. 'That's *niiiice*.' He nodded salaciously and winked at Yasmin.

Yasmin winked back, and then they kissed messily. I looked around. In the context of the other people at the party, they were being quite tame. The place was bordering on an orgy.

'Is Fiona here?' I yelled.

'What?' Yasmin yelled back and cupped her ear.

'FIONA! IS SHE HERE?'

'Yeah, yeah. Went off with some dude. But she's definitely here. I've got her bag.' She kicked Fi's new Burberry handbag with her foot. I was sure Fi would appreciate that.

I decided to look around for her; it wasn't like I was going to get much from Yasmin. If I didn't see her within one lap, I'd go.

Fi wasn't down on the ground floor anywhere, but there was an upstairs bar and balcony.

I walked through a packed bar – no Fi – and looked for the exit to the balcony. I spotted Dave, Dan's friend. That was weird. Why would he be here? Guess there *was* a lingerie parade . . .

When I finally got to the door, I pushed past an oblivious couple into a haze of smoke camouflaging the balcony. I looked to the left – models were perched on chairs and each other's laps smoking, with full makeup and emo hair, skinny jeans, thongs and oversized Eighties-style T-shirts. As they do. No Fi.

To my right was a dense crowd of tall people. I saw a mass of blonde hair through them and a hand flying around. That was Fi. I navigated my way through, not looking up until I got to her corner.

And when I did, I saw who her hand gestures were for. And who had his arms around her. And who was leaning down and fake-nuzzling her boobs as she screamed with laughter. And who kissed her when he stopped nuzzling.

It was Dan.

I thought I was going to be sick.

I hadn't even known he was in the country.

The whole party blurred around me. I felt dizzy. I grabbed a guy next to me for support; he didn't even notice. I let go and steadied myself. I couldn't quite make sense of what I was seeing.

I watched as she fell forward onto him, and he fell back onto the table, and they nearly knocked the whole thing over. They laughed and laughed.

His eyes were red, glassy and he could barely stand up straight.

She was smoking, meaning she was really drunk.

He kept licking his lips, which is what he did when he was really drunk.

She kept flicking her hair, which is what she did when she was playing sexy.

He was grabbing her arse, which is what he did when he wanted sex.

I felt the anger rising, building, gaining momentum. Everything went silent around me as I tried to understand. I knew instantly, despite my failure to react or move, that this was a Defining Moment. I was being pushed by people trying to get past me, but my feet remained rooted to the ground. My breathing quickened and was so loud I thought everyone must have been able to hear it. For the first time in my life, I felt like I could cause real pain to another human. I wanted to hurt one of them, both of them. At once. With a large automobile, possibly. My fists clenched and unclenched.

As if sensing my wrath, Dan looked in my direction. He didn't drop his hands; he didn't let go of Fiona. He just blinked as if trying to figure out if I were an apparition. Can you spell b-u-s-t-e-d, Dan?

Fiona was trying to get an answer from him about something and play-slapped him to get his attention. Then she followed his gaze. She immediately pulled away from Dan, who staggered backwards and grabbed the table to steady himself. Her eyes were wide with the realisation of what she'd done. Or, rather, what she'd been caught doing it. She knew who Dan was; she had met him on two separate occasions. Both times he'd been with me; he'd been my lover.

She made a movement to come over to me, but I turned on my heel and pushed through the crowd with a strength and speed I didn't know I possessed. I was inside. I was on the steps. I was downstairs. I was ducking, weaving; I was racing through the bar, knocking drinks, getting stains on Marley's beautiful dress, pushing through, past the doors, and outside.

I ran towards the next block, across the street.

I hated them! God, oh God, I hated them. I wanted to scream with how much anger I felt for them, but I couldn't here, not here, people would stare and think I was crazy, which I felt I absolutely was.

Dan was a liar and I was a fool, he'd fooled me twice. I mean, I knew he was a rat – he had already confirmed that for me with his Blondie text, but he had travelled halfway across the world and failed to even mention it to me? I was worth that little to him. I hated that he didn't even want to tell me he was here, so that he could go and find another stupid girl to fall for his playboy trickery, and he didn't even *care* that I might see it!

And Fiona, why would she *do* something like that? What had I possibly done that had hurt her so much she would pull such a malicious, sinister move? I was lost. I had no explanation. I wondered how long they had been together. Had they screwed? Was this the first night they'd been on? If I hadn't seen them, would they have gone home and had sex, and then would she have talked to me tomorrow like nothing had ever happened?

I sat on a park bench. A young woman walking in exercise clothes looked at me, and I thought she might ask if I was okay, so I feigned a smile. She kept walking. I knew the words to this song:

always maintain a demeanour of being fine, even if you're not. Keep your tears and fears behind closed doors.

I reflected momentarily that I had just experienced a real-life *Sliding Doors* moment. What if I hadn't gone to the party? What if I'd never seen that and kept thinking of Fiona as a friend? Or if Dan had texted me tomorrow saying he'd just arrived, and I'd forgiven him for Blondiegate and got back on with him? I managed to mumble a weak thank you to the universe. I followed that up with a quiet fuck you for the number of men thrown my way who fell for other women when they were supposed to be into me.

As I sat hunched over, I tried to forecast what this situation would mean. Work would certainly be awkward, but I could cope with that. Screw Fiona. I didn't care. I would live my life as though she didn't exist. And if people asked, I would tell them she was a man-thief. Or ex-man-thief. Or potential-man-thief. Whatever – they'd get it.

My phone was going mad. It had rung around ten times since I'd left the party. I turned it off and hailed a cab. I was going straight to Iz's.

37.

Come to New York!

Keep your boyfriend from looking at anyone else with a shade of eye shadow that makes your iris colour scream. Green eyes? Go for lilacs or purples. Blue? Coppers and browns. Brown eyes? Baby-blue or turquoise. Make it sheer or bold or even just use a liner – just do it, already.

'Who is it?'

'Iz, it's me.'

I heard the door unlocking and it opened to reveal Iz in her undies and a T-shirt. She took one look at me and grabbed my arms.

'Han, Han, what's happened, what's wrong? Shit, come in, come in . . .'

I moved inside the door but wouldn't let go of her. I think part of me was crying because if this had happened the same time next week, I wouldn't have had an Iz to collapse onto. That realisation made me sob even harder.

After we'd hugged for a few minutes, and I'd calmed down enough to be able to speak, I took a deep breath and wiped my eyes.

'I went to a party and I saw, hic, Fiona and Dan kissing, and all over, hic, each other . . .'

I started crying again.

Iz's eyes were wide open, complementing her dropped jaw.

'Shut UP!' She was incredulous. 'Fi? Was with Dan? When did

Dan get into town? You didn't tell me he was here!'

I wiped my nose with the side of my hand. 'That's just it; I didn't even know he was here!'

'Is everything okay?' Dec's voice came from the hallway. He was walking towards us, peering to see who he was looking at. He was wearing only boxers. He looked like something from the Man Perve pages of *Gloss*.

'Han, what's happened? Are you okay?'

As we all know, the most dangerous sentence a human can hear in the moments after they've been crying involves the words 'is', 'everything' and 'okay'. It's like you've been carefully nursing a precariously placed bucket of emotion and they've just waltzed up and kicked it over.

I looked at him as I gulped back tears; his face was full of alarm and he walked quickly toward us. I wanted to have him tell me everything was going to be okay. He would never be capable of these acts of brutality; he'd be a perfect, caring boyfriend. That Elle didn't know how lucky she was. Cow.

'Dec, it's okay. Maybe leave this one to me?' Iz spoke firmly but softly, and nodded towards the hall.

He didn't move. 'Han, would you prefer that? Can I at least . . . Is there anything I can do?'

I shook my head and smiled weakly. 'Just boy stuff, Dec. But thank you. And for trying to help on Saturday night, too . . .'

I felt like such a loser. First fuckface Jesse had given him a serve when he had tried to look after me, and now Dan had completely screwed me over, and he was still here being all lovely.

'Okay . . . well, if you need me . . .' He made some intense eye-conversation with Iz, and then slowly walked back to his room.

Iz looked at me and shook her head. 'That fucking Dan. I will cut his fucking balls off if I see him before I go . . . Argh! And as for that slut Fiona – who *are* these people, Han? They're seriously chemically disbalanced, that's for sure.'

I didn't bother to correct 'disbalanced'. I just sat there, stone-faced.

'Come sit down, darling, I'll make you a cup of tea. Do you want to stay here tonight?'

I nodded. 'Do you mind?'

'Don't be ridiculous.' She busied herself making the tea.

I looked around her stark lounge room and tears sprang to my eyes again. 'Iz, I can't believe you're going.'

'Oh my Hanschki . . .' She came over and hugged me. 'I know. I can't believe you're not coming with me. And, and I'm scared, to tell you the truth. Like, really scared. What if I hate it? What if Kyle and I don't get on? What if he meets some gorgeous model on the show? What if he pulls a Jesse?'

'Oh, Iz. No. Kyle worships the ground you walk on. He's not going near any of those stick figures. He only wants you. And anyway, you're going for you, not him, remember?'

She pulled back suddenly, her eyes wide. 'Is this whole thing tonight not a sign you should come?' Her eyes searched mine for a flicker of agreement, but I could offer none.

'Oh, Iz . . . I'd love to, but right now . . . it's not for me right now.' I looked down as I finished my sentence. Truth was, I had thought about it a lot, but it just didn't sit right. I couldn't leave *Gloss* and my life here, even if it did suck. I had to stick out the beauty gig a bit longer. Otherwise, what was the point of all my hard work? I'd rack off and come back and no one would even know my name. They'd be all, 'Oh hey, Holly, how was London?'

'I'm always just a call away, you know that, don't you? And Dec's always here for a chat. He'll be there for you in a flash. Quicker.'

I smiled with my mouth closed. 'He's such a sweetheart.'

Iz walked back to the kitchen and returned with a mug of tea.

'See, the thing about Dec . . .' She stopped and stared at me as if she were about to say something else, but after a few seconds seemed to change her mind. 'Nevermind. Hey, aren't your mum and dad back this weekend?'

'Yep, *finally*. I'm going to drive up there to see them when you've gone . . . Mum'll look after me in my melancholic, best-friendless state.'

'Good. I'm glad to hear you'll be in your mum and dad's care. I couldn't bear the idea of you being all alone this weekend . . . Now, my love, I've got to get up at five-thirty, so you have a shower and I'll see you in bed. You sure you're okay?'

'Yep, I'll go shower.'

Iz gave me a kiss on the forehead and I watched her walk out of the room. I hoped Kyle knew how lucky he was.

38.

Salty plops and eye drops

Cleverest trick you'll learn today: put black kohl on your inner *upper* eyelid rim. Just lift your eyelid up, tilt back your head and gently run a very soft gel or kohl liner along. Watch your lashes pop and eyes look fresher immediately.

I awoke confused. I knew where I was, but Iz had already left, leaving me in a bare bedroom and in yesterday's clothes. I should be used to the walk of shame by now, I thought.

I frowned and tried to put my finger on why I felt so heavy . . . Something bad had happened . . . Oh, yes. The dry-humping on the balcony. Today would be filled with salty plops and eye drops.

When I got home and turned my phone on, six texts and fourteen missed calls came through. Most of the calls were from Fi, and a few were from a number I didn't recognise. Probably Dan. I looked at the first message. From Fi at 10.46 p.m.:

Han, pls call me??

The third, from Fi at 11.15 p.m.:

I am so so so sorry, Han. I didn't know what I was doing. We were both so drunk. I didn't know u were seeing him again . . . i need to speak 2 u

And the eighth, from Dan, sent this morning at 4.32 a.m.:

Han, you're full of fury and I know why, but let a man say his piece?

That was all I needed to read. Their pitiful text messages cemented my anger about how weak they both were. They deserved each other.

Work was a two-way street, for not only could I not handle it but, seemingly, work couldn't handle me either. For all the stories they'd written or designed or sub-edited on 'How to Cope When She's Hurting', each Glossette's initial reaction to my melancholy was to suddenly remember page 45 in the unspoken workplace rulebook: *Don't bring your personal life to the workplace.* Everyone ignored me.

Jay was not in, thankfully. Well, kind of thankfully: some part of me wanted someone else to disseminate the message about Fiona's treachery, and I knew Jay would have been good for it.

In a job where you're supposed to be constantly happy, social and pretty, an It's All Gone to Shit Day isn't very productive. I cancelled two launches and spent most of the morning in my beauty cupboard.

An email notification chimed. God, it was from Eliza. Not now, not now . . .

To: Hannah@gloss.com
From: Eliza@gloss.com
Subject: Kate says you're upset. If you need to go home, you can?

I was stunned. That had to be as good as it got from Eliza.

Ding.

To: Hannah@gloss.com
From: Marley@gloss.com
Cc: Karen@gloss.com
Subject: Emporium

Did you know they've taken all their advertising from *Gloss* to *21*??

Han, have you not been giving them editorial?!

Kidding. Kind of.

Is there anything we can do for Sep issue to win them over? Wasn't there talk of a party makeup special? Can you come up with some beauty sponsorship ideas??

Cc-ing Karen?
Really? Bitch!
Ding.

From: Karen@gloss.com
To: Marley@gloss.com; Hannah@gloss.com
Subject: Re: Emporium

We're meeting with them this afternoon, Hannah. I thought I'd discussed needing some pitches with you, but obviously haven't. Am going mad. Anything you can come up with by then most apprec. The more gob-smackingly amazing the better.

K

I closed my eyes and took a deep breath. There was no need to stress out. I could handle this; it would be fine. I didn't write back; I would simply present them with the idea. Once I'd thought of one.

What had I learned in this job that would help me in times like this? I thought about my time at *Gloss*, and wondered exactly what I had been up to for the last year. I'd enjoyed myself, that's for sure: every day was fun, and I never knew what would land on my desk, or where I'd be off to, or what feature I'd be working on for the next issue. It was a wonderful job, and one that I'd covet insanely if it weren't mine. As for what I had learned . . . I'd learnt that each cosmetic company liked to think they were the only cosmetic brand. They wanted to believe we 'got' them, just as we wanted to believe the reader would 'get' us.

I wondered what I'd like to see in the mag, as a makeup-obsessed woman. Really extraordinary makeup was definitely always good to see, but with a how-to component by someone who was actually good at explaining it, which wasn't necessarily me or any of the other beauty editors. It was a unique skill, one best left to makeup artists who spoke on Madonna mics at department stores.

I started rifling through my references for good makeup features from other magazines. They were all utterly uninspiring – 'Sexy in Seconds', 'Put Your Best Face Forward' . . . Was this really what my job was? How depressing. There were people out there saving lives, and I was writing about liquid eyeliner. I guess I did help women feel better about themselves by encouraging them to look their best, but still, it was hardly rescuing orang-utans in Borneo.

I sat down and just stopped and thought about the brand. Emporium were pretty cool customers; they didn't use celebrities to advertise their wares, and wouldn't be interested in the usual red-carpet sponsorship we rolled out to clients. We needed to do something innovative, something that *21* would never devise. It would have to be something that reflected what they did with their own brand, so that they couldn't deny the synergy. God, listen to me, I was starting to sound like Marley. How revolting.

We could do the party makeup story . . . no, that was so done. We could do a fashion and beauty merger, showing models wearing new-season trends, and then get one of their makeup artists to tell us how to get a look to suit each trend . . . or, or . . . shit.

Then it came. The Idea. *A makeup-artist off!*

We could get four makeup artists to do a shoot using Emporium makeup – ooh, I could get that alien-esque model Kelsie, an unnaturally beautiful Russian model who was in town, and Jeff Arber would shoot it, he was here too – and we'd give each makeup artist free rein on a bare-faced Kelsie, and then readers would go online to vote for their favourite look for the chance to win a stupid amount of makeup and a session with the winning makeup artist, as well as a trip somewhere, maybe, a shoot in *Gloss* and, oh, I don't know, a gold-plated helicopter or something.

Where that had come from was a mystery, but the tingle down my spine told me it was a cracker, and I needed to write it down immediately. I wanted to give it to Karen and Marley, and then I wanted to go home 'sick'.

'And at the end of it all, Emporium finishes up with an even stronger marketplace position, because the country's best makeup artists have used their product, and then the readers will have voted on their favourite products, which, you know, fuses both the clout of the consumers and the power of the *Gloss* name and gives them that industry edge, too . . .'

I looked at Karen and Marley for a reaction.

'And you say you're not feeling well today, Hannah?' Karen said, her eyebrows raised. Shit, could she tell I wasn't really sick? How do bosses and mothers always know that?

'Um, yes, I'm feeling a little off.'

'Well, if that's what you're capable of when you're unwell, you must be amazing when you're in form.' She broke into a huge smile.

'Hannah, why the hell are you in editorial? Karen, she's wasted down here, we need her upstairs – she could bring us in millions! They are going to wet their pants when they see this. God, I've got to get Belinda onto making a mock-up – we've got to meet them in three hours, and you know how slow she is; a blind chimpanzee using MS-DOS would be faster, for God's sake.'

'Thanks, guys. I'm glad you like it.'

'We don't like it, we love it. We're amazed by it. We're thrilled with it. You've done an incredible job, Hannah. And we put you under the pump, which makes it even more impressive. Thank you.'

'Why don't you come present it with us, Han? Come on, it's your pitch, you know it better than any—'

'Marley, she's not feeling well, plus, she's done more than enough. Hannah, why don't you go home?'

'You're too soft on your girls, Karen,' Marley said as she walked out, winking at me on the way.

'Are you sure?' Not that what Karen said next would influence me leaving anyway – I'd just potentially earned them two-hundred thousand dollars; I was out of there.

'Okay. Less a question; more a statement. Go home. Watch some bad movies and drink some tea. We'll see you tomorrow.'

'Really?'

'Go. You did good today. In fact, you've done good ever since you arrived. It's a pleasure and a privilege to have you on *Gloss*. Take tomorrow off too, actually. So we'll see you Monday.'

'Thank you, Karen.' God, I loved her. As I walked back to my desk, I felt relieved but utterly deflated. I was thrilled to get Friday off legitimately as it saved me having to chuck a sickie to say goodbye to Iz at the airport in the morning. Plus, it meant I could go straight up to Mum and Dad's from the airport.

Just as I was about to walk out, Jay screamed into the office and came straight over to my desk. She had her hands on her heart, her eyes were wide open and she was panting from walking so quickly.

'Honey! Shit! Is it true about Fiona?!'

News travels fast around here.

39.

Now boarding

> Dark circles? Dip cotton pads in cold milk and place them over your eyes. Bag lady? Use moist, cool tea bags over eyes. (Don't bother with herbal; it's the caffeine that constricts blood vessels and reduces swelling.) Puff Daddy? Place chilled cucumber slices over the entire eye area. Or just buy an eye cream that does all of this and leave your kitchen the hell alone.

I looked in the mirror. I was hidden somewhere in a mesh of wild patterns and primary colours that could be loosely described as a dress. I'd picked it up at a market ages ago but had never worn it.

I had opted for it this morning because I needed something to distract me from how extraordinarily flat I was feeling. I'd slept atrociously. In the end I'd taken a sleeping pill from my flight kit. It had knocked me out hard, and now I had a drugover.

I tried on a belt with the dress. Nope. Belt off. Still, I now knew why I'd never worn it. I looked silly. Even for me. Plus, it was probably slightly inappropriate; it was like I cared that Iz was leaving but might slip off to start a conga line any minute.

Time was of the essence; it would have to do. I threw on some Roman sandals. Hair back. I squinted and squeezed in eye drops; I painted on and furiously dabbed in under-eye illuminator; I used a baby-blue pearly eye-shadow to make my eyes look awake, but applied absolutely no mascara due to the inevitable tears that would follow. I put concealer on a red nose and juiced up red, cracked lips with a balm, followed by a ridiculous shimmering pink gloss to draw attention away from my tear-guilty peepers. I plastered on a fake smile that Miss Universe herself would envy, and I was off.

As I drove to the airport in Yasmin's car, which she had kindly donated for my trip, the Red Hot Chilli Peppers' song 'Scar Tissue' came on. I sung along, sifting, sitcom-style, through my memories of Iz. I realised that a lot of them were to do with one of us being upset by a boy, with the non-heartbroken one comforting the crushed one. That or being wild and drunk and wearing inappropriate attire while out dancing. And then there was her food, her amazing food; she was half-friend, half-mum the way she cooked for me, and then gave me leftovers to take home for lunch. And then there were her made-up words, and her adorable way of texting any random thought that happened to flutter through her mind, whether it was 3 p.m. or 2 a.m. I couldn't believe that was all about to be taken away.

I parked the car, feeling heavy, and schlepped into the departures hall. I felt alone already.

I found Iz's flight number and went to her departure lounge. I scanned the area – no Iz or Dec. I sat down and waited. Five minutes passed. Where were they? Iz's phone had been disconnected and I didn't want to call Dec just yet. In the drama of Iz's departure, my nerves about seeing him didn't even register a hum in the background of my mind.

I decided to wait in the newsagent's. I picked up a few slanderous weeklies detailing the rocky romances of reality-TV types I'd never heard of nor would ever care about. I checked my phone. Nothing. Where were they?

I was too on edge for this. I called Dec.

'We're just checking in.'

'Oh, thank God. I was starting to think I'd got the flight wrong!'

Iz jumped on the phone. 'Han, darling, I'm so sorry. I had a shocker of a morning – Kyle needed a bunch of documents from his mum's, and then I couldn't find my bloody visa, and, oh, never mind. I've worn mascara so I won't cry. What do you reckon my chances are of staying dry?'

'Slim to none.'

'Me too.'

'Bye.' I choked up. Taking deep breaths and fast strides, I walked back to the lounge.

I looked around. A speaker announced the plane was boarding. Shit! They were *so* late. By the time the announcement had finished, several teary farewells were in progress.

I looked up. Iz was scurrying across the smooth tiles of the airport with her wheelie bag swerving and tipping behind her, and her short dress creeping up her thighs as she ran.

Dec walked behind her, smiling as he watched her small hand-luggage case dance. He was wearing a simple grey T-shirt and jeans, and carrying a stack of magazines for Iz's trip.

'Oh, Han!'

We hugged tight.

'Can you believe it?' Her eyes were wide open, and brimming with tears.

'No, I can't.'

Dec came up behind Iz and kissed me on the cheek. 'Hi, Han, how's it going?' He looked right into my eyes, the way people do when they're not going to believe you if you say 'fine'.

'Um, I'll leave you two for a minute.' He took Iz's bag and sat down where I had been.

I looked at the screen behind her. 'Your plane is already boarding, Iz.'

Her eyes looked as sad and hopeless as I felt.

'I love you so much, Iz. You're going to have an amazing time in New York. Amazing. Plus, you've got a gorgeous man who loves you to bits waiting for you at the other end of this flight. And if it all turns to shit, you know you can always come home and live under my bed.'

She started crying, and I hugged her tight.

Through her tears, Iz managed to say, 'Oh, I know it's all good, Han, I know . . . But what will I do without you? And I feel so bad for leaving just as some stupid boy hurts you again . . .'

'I can deal with him. Have before, haven't I? I'll be fine, you know I will.'

'I know that, but still . . .'

'Shhh. None of that matters; this is all a good thing. And I'm sure in a few months I'll believe my own words.'

We laughed softly and then just looked at each other in silence.

'Love your guts, girl.'

'Love you more.'

'Have an excellent flight, get drunk and fall asleep and call me when you arrive. After you and Kyle have, y'know, reunited and stuff.'

She grinned.

She turned and grabbed her bag from Dec. He stood up and gave her a huge bear-hug. His eyes were wet, but there were no tears. He was blinking furiously, and they were talking to each other softly. Iz laughed and wiped her eyes, pulling away. Dec and I walked her to the gate, where, after one more hug, I stood back and folded my arms and cried gently. Dec kissed Iz on both cheeks and squeezed her hand. We watched her walk through the gate, she turned and blew us a kiss, and then she was gone.

Before I realised what was happening, Dec softly placed his arms around me. He held me close as I cried – his body smelling of apples and cinnamon and wood – and as he stroked my back gently,

I turned my head and leaned against his chest. It was as though all these months of being awkward around each other had never even existed. His touch was so comforting and masculine that I didn't want him to break it.

After another minute or so, I slowly pulled back, smoothing my hair and wiping my eyes.

'This blows, doesn't it?' I straightened my dress and took a few deep breaths.

'I know, Han. I know. Shall we get a coffee? You know, normalise a little?' he asked.

I looked at Dec. His eyebrows were raised, and his tone was kind of shy. My nerves tiptoed back in, happy to be roaming around me freely once again.

'Sure, Dec.' What, I couldn't go for a coffee with my best friend's brother?

He smiled. 'Wouldn't be much fun for you to walk out of here all sad. Even if your parking is going to cost you a couple of hundred.'

I took a deep breath and shook my body as I exhaled. Iz was gone, and I had to deal with it.

'You obviously don't know how rich I am, Dec. Us beauty editors are kind of a big deal. In fact, I will even shout you your coffee.'

As I finished my sentence, I noticed a Cindy Crawford double walking towards us. She was wearing heels, skinny-leg jeans and the kind of tight singlet that allowed people to determine what cup size she was from several hundred metres away. It was halfway through the alphabet.

I stared at her; I couldn't help it. I was waiting for Dec to notice her, like every other person in the airport – and, I'm sure, the universe – had.

Next thing, she'd stopped and was smiling at Dec. Really? I was invisible in *this* dress?

'Pardon me, but can you tell me where the nearest newsagency is?' She spoke with an upper-class British accent and beamed a smile that could light up London.

Dec looked over his shoulder, and hoicked his thumb behind him. 'Up there on the right.' He finished with a tight smile before turning back to me. 'Now, Han, are we talking coffee-coffee, or that revolting Starbucks stuff?'

As I laughed and he made a move to keep walking, Cindy's face dropped. I felt very smug indeed.

After ordering our coffee-coffees from a small Italian café outside the airport, we sat and talked. And talked. It was like the wake after the funeral; the sadness of Iz leaving was replaced with a kind of hyper-frenzy of bad jokes. It was so refreshing to just be myself with a guy. Not to have to be cute, or sharp, or pretty; just me. No rules, no being hardcore; just me.

'So, um, everything cool after the other night?' He sipped his latte as he asked, in an attempt to make his probing appear blasé.

'Oh, you know,' I replied, 'just some old flame completely screwing me over.'

'You mean the nice chap I met last Saturday night?'

'Uh, no, actually.' I covered my head with my hands in shame. 'Mr Hawaii. I know how to pick them, huh? About Saturday night, I'm so . . . so sorry and embarrassed about that whole thing.'

'Are you thinking you'll go back to him?' Dec looked me straight in the eye as he said this. I felt a shiver creep down my back.

'No, I'm not. He had a second chance, one that admittedly he didn't deserve, and it didn't work. No more now.'

Dec took his time answering. 'You speak with conviction, Han, but sadly it's that kind of bravado that usually gives away true feelings.'

I took a deep breath. 'I guess. But I'm not a galloping romantic any more, Dec. I'm adamant about cutting him off. I was fine for a year without him; one week of backtracking isn't going to set me back for long. I'd much rather be single.'

'You're pretty amazing, Han.' He had cocked his head and was leaning his chin on one hand. His eyes were smiling, and locked on mine.

I blushed. Of course.

'You don't give yourself nearly enough credit. You're a remarkable girl. Any guy would be incredibly lucky to have a girl even one-hundredth as good as you. And for you to go through that, and Iz leaving, all at once, and to still be in good form is pretty special.'

'Dec, I've been in rotten form, trust me.' I laughed feebly.

'Han, you gotta stop deflecting like that. You're a fantastic girl and you don't even seem to know it. When I broke up with Pia, the first thing I had to learn was to appreciate myself again. But I guess we're always way too hard on ourselves, especially after someone leaves us.'

My head jerked up. 'She left you? But I thought . . .'

'It was mutual inasmuch as we agreed she was better off alone. But I loved her, Han. And it's taken me a while to feel like that agai—' He stopped mid-sentence and focused on fidgeting with his coffee cup.

The hairs on the back of my neck stood up. I was suddenly very aware of my every move. I coughed nervously to break the silence.

'Han, I should go. We both should . . .' He pushed his chair back and stood up.

Had I said something wrong for him to want to leave so abruptly? I tried to think of what offensive thing I'd said.

As we walked out of the café and into the parking lot, we both remained silent.

'Where are you parked?' He was so formal and weird now.

'Um . . . red level. I think. I hope!' I laughed at my own lame comment to try to diffuse the tension.

'I'll walk you there.' He looked straight ahead as he spoke. Now he was just freaking me out. We found Yasmin's little red racer, and as I fished the keys out of my bag, I had to ask.

'Um, is everything okay, Dec? You seem to have gone a bit strange.' He stopped and turned to face me.

'No, no, I'm cool . . .' He took a deep breath and shook his head. When he looked back at me, the words came tumbling out of his mouth. 'Han, you've had a big day, and a huge week, so I'm not going to dump a whole lot of emotional stuff on you. But, well, actually, maybe I am.' He laughed nervously and ran his fingers through his hair.

'Ohhh, this is hard.' He cleared his throat. 'Okay, maybe this is the wrong time to say this, but I'm a huge believer in going with your gut, so I hope our guts are in tune. That sounds bad. Ignore that. But, well . . . I . . . I want you to know that . . . that I'm here for you.'

Was that it? 'Oh, Dec, I know that. Thank you. Iz told me I could call you if I needed a friend. Or just wanted to mooch around in Iz's old home.'

He looked into my eyes and held his hands in a prayer position, tapping them against his chest in a fidgety way.

'Han, when do you get home from your mum and dad's?'

'Sunday night.'

'Can we maybe hang out? Next week sometime? Just, you know, whenever you're free?'

'Um . . . sure . . . How come?' My heart was pumping now. I wasn't sure what was happening, but my body seemed to think something was going on. It was a similar feeling to the one I'd had the night Dec had kissed me, but with more of a nervy edge. It seemed that just being this close to him set it off. God! Would I always be like this around him? Even when I was old and married and had no teeth? Crushes were so energy-consuming!

Until suddenly it all dawned on me.

'Ahh, I see. I'm replacement therapy.' I smiled and winked.

'Well, no.' He stopped and moved closer towards me. 'It's because, um . . .' He looked to his right and tapped his foot. 'Well, I guess it's because I'm, maybe, kind of . . . a little bit into you. Okay, a *lot* into you.'

I blinked furiously as if clearing my vision would help me understand what had just been said.

He wiped his chin with his hand and then took his fingers back through his hair. 'And I'm sorry to freak you out, Han, I really am, but I've felt this way for months, well, ever since that kiss, to be honest, before even, and Iz made me promise, *promise*, that I wouldn't wait another day to tell you. I told her it was completely the wrong time, but she said it was the best time, the only time, and, well, you know what she's like. Bossy. But her final words were literally "tell her".' He grinned sheepishly.

I was frozen, staring at Dec but blinking like mad. I had no idea what to say.

'Han, I'm so sorry to spring this on you. Maybe just forget I said anything, and have an excellent weekend with your mum and dad. Okay. I'm going to let you drive away from the madman now. And again, I'm sorry to confuse you. Iz's fault.' He had quashed his smile, but his eyes still sparkled.

He leaned in and kissed me delicately on the cheek. 'Drive safe.' I took in a deep breath of him, and found myself wanting to pull him close, but he moved away and started walking.

And then, just like Iz, he was gone.

I got into the car and sat there, my hand holding the key against the ignition, leaning forward with my head on the steering wheel, trying to make sense of what had just occurred.

Sweet cheeses, as Iz would say.

Dec. *Dec!*

My mind went back to our kiss. So it hadn't been just a drunken thing! I thought back to all the times Iz had implied that Dec liked me. I'd always been flattered, but never actually thought anything would come of it. He was Dec! My lifelong crush! I shook my head as to how blind I had been . . . The flirting and the gentlemanly gestures . . . And all the while I'd been too focused on Jesse or Dan or my stupid rules to even see it. Turns out I didn't need my bloody rules to land a man.

I started the car and began winding my way up the car park's concrete mountain.

As I came into the daylight, the sun shone directly onto me, filling the car and warming my skin. Dec liked me. *Dec liked me!* A warm, happy glow enveloped me.

I paid the cashier seventy-five dollars without flinching. Who cared how much it cost? What had just happened within these walls was priceless.

My phone beeped several times. I pulled over to read my text messages before hitting the highway.

The first was from Don't Answer. Unbelievable timing, as always.

Han, please, can we talk? You never return my calls or texts. Just a coffee?

Not likely, champ.

Pressing delete was tremendously cathartic. I resolved to delete him permanently from not only my phone, but my life. It felt wonderful to be so resolute.

Another beep. Gabe.

Beauty, I miss you, you lovely thing. Hope a special man has swept you off your designer rip-off shoes since I've seen u last. Catch up soon, please. Gxx

I had to reread it. This? Coming from Gabe who knew nothing about what had just happened? Spooky. He would be thrilled to his frills to hear my Dec tale.

The third and most recent was from Dec.

I can't stop smiling. Take off the spell . . .

I threw back my head and laughed with pure joy. I hardly recognised the laugh as it vibrated from within me. I felt extraordinarily good. No more dirty secrets. No more lies. No more bullshit. Life felt new, crisp, like things were changing, and finally for the good.

I placed my phone – the vessel of so much torture and elation – on the passenger seat, and then eased my way out onto the highway. As soon as I hit a decent speed, I turned on the radio. 'Take It Easy', my favourite song *ever*, came on.

I turned it up as loud as the speakers could handle. And as I sung along as loud as I could, I couldn't wipe the smile off my face.

Apparently the spell was mutual.

Acknowledgements

Thank you, Kirsten Abbott, for seeing potential in my story, and for being the coolest, cleverest and most considerate publisher and editor a writer could hope for. Thank you to *all* of the Penguins for being so dizzyingly enthusiastic and supportive – I feel incredibly lucky, proud and privileged to call myself a Penguin.

Thank you, Mia, for suggesting I do this, for your support, props and help, and for introducing me to Tara. Tara, thank you for keeping a sister grounded, for explaining things like 'contracts' and 'rights', and for being the best possible agent I could ask for.

Thank you, Mum, for being such an extraordinary woman, mother, healer, supporter and teacher, and for having such a generous, thoughtful, radiant spirit. Thank you, Dad, for the top-shelf 'wordy' genetics, and for being unwavering in your support of my writing: how lucky I am to be able to learn from you and how much I cherish being able to discuss my work with you. I love you both more than these sentences permit me to show.

Thank you, Donk, for providing me with such an adorable

character reference (remember, 'it's *fiction*!'), and for always reminding me where exactly it is that eagles fly. Thank you and muchos love to Figgy, Levi, Honky, Pede, Marie, Panth, Barb, Foxy, Juz, Hamish, Rina, Danny and Tali for being so excited for (and with) me throughout this adventure. Youse are worf your weight in gold, ay.

Thank you to the shiny, happy beauty industry for being so generous and supportive of my silliness; it's the finest industry in the world, and I feel lucky to work within its glossy confines. Lastly, thank you, Meowbert, for your 24-7 company, your ridiculous face and for lovingly gnawing on the corner of my laptop as I type. You make my insides smile.

ALSO BY ZOË FOSTER BLAKE

Sometimes you don't know what you want until someone else has it.

'Maybe this was finally Lily's time. Maybe this was the year she became a grown-up. She would have a proper, impressive job, and she could maybe even move out on her own. She flinched a bit when she realised that the missing element to this glorious new life was love, which seemed to be further away than it ever had been. Was it too much to ask for a guy to present himself who wasn't a nob or an alcoholic or a loser?'

From the bestselling author of *Air Kisses*, *Playing the Field* and *The Younger Man* comes a funny, heartfelt novel about what happens when life, love, work and friendships collide.

'The Wrong Girl *is funny, charming and lots of fun. Zoë's writing is always fresh and full of heart.'*
JESSICA MARAIS

In the glossy world of footballers' wives, love is the toughest game of all.

'I turned from the bar and prepared to navigate my way through the mass of heaving, loud, beautiful people to our seats in the courtyard. I was doing a brilliant job, nursing the drinks to my chest and caving my shoulders to protect them, until I was knocked from behind. Half of each drink went flying onto the back of the guy unlucky enough to be standing in front of me. He turned slowly around. With my hands full and covered in vodka, I was unable to do anything but offer what I hoped was a sincere apology via my eyes. His mouth was open and his fingers were pulling his shirt out from his substantially wet back. And somewhere high above, God was high-fiving someone on his incredible handiwork.'

'Zoë Foster tells an engaging and fun contemporary tale with her fabulously wry wit.' NEW IDEA

'This glam and "fictional" exposé of the lives of WAGS is a rollicking read.' NW

THE *Younger* MAN

He was only supposed to be a bit of fun . . .

When Abby enjoys a memorable night with a delicious 22-year-old, she easily waves him out of her life the next morning. She doesn't have time for these sorts of distractions. And he's only 22, after all! A child. But the charming young Marcus isn't going to let her get away that easily. He knows what he wants and takes it upon himself to prove that age is irrelevant where the heart is concerned. Abby, though, isn't convinced. She feels certain she should be with someone her own age, someone more impressive, someone more . . . settled. Surely nothing can ever come of this relationship?

'Charming, witty and oh-so addictive . . .
A great read that will have you yelling, "I know exactly what she means!" over and over.'
WOMAN'S DAY

Amazinger Face

Fully revised and updated! Over 60 new pages! New longer title!

Sometimes a lady just needs to know the most flattering lipstick for her skin tone, or how to correctly use sunscreen, or a very quick hairstyle to conceal her unwashed hair. And there's no reason she shouldn't know which foundation or mascara is best for her, either.

All the answers are here, in this top-to-toe beauty extravaganza. Former *Cosmopolitan* and *Harper's BAZAAR* beauty director, and the founder of Go-To skin care, Zoë Foster Blake suggests makeup colours and brands for every occasion; useful, practical skincare routines and products for every age; and step-by-step instructions for winged eyeliner, arresting red lips, foolproof tanning, simple updos, sexy-second-day hair, and much, much more . . .

'A beautifully written book with thoughtful explanations, helpful step-by-step instructions and even a healthy dose of humor.'

FASHION JOURNAL